PROMISES

BOOKS BY BELVA PLAIN

PROMISES

BELVA PLAIN

Delacorte Press

Published by
Delacorte Press
Bantam Doubleday Dell Publishing Group, Inc.
1540 Broadway
New York, New York 10036

ISBN 0-385-31110-9

Designed by Rhea Braunstein/RB Design

Manufactured in the United States of America

PROMISES

PROMISES

PART ONE
1973

ONE

"**T**urn," said Isabella, with pins between her lips.

In the pier glass, looking down, Margaret could watch careful fingers working over a cascade of white silk. Looking up, she saw her own disheveled, curly red head and her shoulders rising in unfamiliar nakedness over an intricately tucked and pleated frill.

Margaret's mother sighed. "I don't know how you do it, Isabella."

"Sewing is recreation for me, Jean. And to make a wedding dress for my own daughter-in-law, whom I knew before she was born—how many people can have a pleasure like that?"

Affection shone from Isabella's eyes. They were opalescent and wide set, like her son's. Like Adam she was erect and dignified. But where she was talkative, he was silent. His intelligent face with its even, symmetrical features was somber, a somber, romantic face. Mysterious. Heroic. Margaret had fallen in love with it when she was fifteen years old.

If Adam ever leaves me, she thought suddenly, I shall die.

He had last telephoned on Monday, just after she had come home for spring break. Before that he had not called since the previous Thursday. But they had always talked to each other every evening after eight. They would talk just under three minutes, yet it seemed, although two states lay between his university and her college, as if he had his arms around her.

When had it begun to change? Or had it really changed? After all, he was on the final stretch of the hard road toward his degree. So perhaps she was only imagining things. A word unspoken, a glance evaded, a telephone call missed—if you were looking for signs, you could find them, couldn't you? You could always force something out of nothing, merely because you were too sensitive. Yes, that was it. She was too sensitive.

And she looked around at the familiar room as if its very familiarity might reassure her. An extraordinary warmth was here. It came from the house itself, this solid Victorian, built by her great-grandfather and meant to last, complete with front porch and wooden gingerbread, on this broad midwestern street. It came from the two women, both plain, kind, and unexceptional, who had known widowhood since the Korean War, had each worked and reared a child alone. It came from the cheerful shrills of children playing in the yard below.

From where she was standing, Margaret could see the group playing some ancient circle-game, with Nina in the center, taking charge. At six she was the neighborhood leader. Such a delightful, demanding person she was, Jean's little orphaned niece!

Adam used to joke: "After we're married, people who don't know us well will think that she's really ours, that we'd had her hidden away."

"Are they all right down there?" Jean asked. "I always worry when she's out of my sight."

"You worry too much, Mom. Nina's going to make her way in the world. With that pert little face and all that energy, she's going to be a charmer and a winner. Anyway, you know very well that when she's in my charge, I keep her safe." And Margaret had to laugh. "I don't let her get away with too much, you can be sure."

"You'll be a fine mother," Isabella said as she got up from her knees.

" 'Fine mother'!" Jean laughed. "Oh, yes, of course, but she's got quite a few things to do first. Graduate from college in May, then Adam will graduate, and then the wedding June twentieth—you know, I've forgotten to give the date to the photographer! Good Lord, I'll go phone right now!"

"Wait," said Margaret. "I—we're not exactly sure about the date."

Two startled, high-pitched voices chimed. "What do you mean?"

Struggling out of the confining silk, Margaret felt suddenly exposed and very vulnerable.

"We thought—Adam said—he thought maybe we have too many things all crowded together. All these dates. Maybe he should have a little time to buy stuff for himself—"

Isabella interrupted. "Buy stuff! All he needs to get ready is a new suit. And knowing how little he cares about clothes, I'll have to argue him into buying that."

As thoughts that had been forced down now rose to the surface, all the good warmth ebbed from the room.

"Well, it's not only that. Maybe, when you think about it, maybe he really should have some more time, a couple of weeks to get used to the new job. A little time."

"And you had to wait until April to think about all that?" Jean said, with some exasperation.

The two older women were properly alarmed. Without looking Margaret knew they were questioning, glancing toward each other. How they *wanted* this marriage! It was safe. Each was to get a dependable in-law. There were no dangerous unknown quantities. She understood.

"Why, he never said anything like that to me!" exclaimed Isabella.

"Well, we weren't sure. It just crossed our minds. Just a thought. Anyway, we'll have to decide this week one way or the other." They were examining her. It felt as though cold air were blowing on her body. She slid into her jeans and buttoned her shirt, saying lightly, hurriedly, "Goodness, it's no problem! There's no big difference between June and July, is there? But we'll let you know. Definitely. This week. Positively."

Isabella, the more easily appeased, hung the wedding dress into a plastic bag. "Okay, as long as you do. It won't take long for me to finish this skirt," she said cheerfully. "I'll have to come back once more to get the hem right, that's all."

As soon as they were alone, Jean asked the expected question. "What is it, Margaret? Is there any trouble?"

"No. What could there be?"

"Because if there is, I can't go off and leave you."

"Because of this little business of changing the date?"

"If that's all it is."

"That's all it is."

A pair of her familiar vertical worry lines appeared between Jean's eyes. "I sometimes think I shouldn't be going, anyway. India. It's crazy."

"Since that's where the consular service is sending Henry, it's where you have to go. What's the fuss?"

"Maybe it's crazy for me to think of marriage anyway, after all this time being a widow."

"All the more reason, Mom."

Jean looked weary. It was as if her years of work in the library had worn her as it wore books, graying the once-bright surface. She had had so little time to love her husband and be loved. Day after day there had been only the routine of work and the care of a child. Sadness and pity touched Margaret. Sometimes it almost seemed to her that their positions were reversed, that Jean was the daughter and she the mother.

"You know, Mom," she said firmly, "Henry's a good man, and you're very lucky. I'm glad for you. Stop thinking about me. I'll be fine. I can manage things."

"Yes, yes, I know you're strong. But I'm leaving you with the responsibility of Nina. Starting a marriage with a six-year-old child to care for simply doesn't seem right."

"It's quite right. I love her, and Adam doesn't mind having her at all."

"Yes, he's a prince, he really is. But you're a princess, Margaret, beautiful and good. Sometimes I think you're too good."

"Spoken like a mother! Now, do you mind? I've still got reading to do and finals coming up around the corner."

The late-afternoon sun was watery, and the old scraggly lilac was still winter bare. In her chair at the window Margaret looked out at the well-known landscape, letting her troubled and restless mind wander.

She thought how amazing it was that she had been born into this house and that now, Mom having given it to her, she might possibly even die here. It would not be in this room, though, but in the large one across the hall, the one with the massive dark bed and the wardrobe that, when she was a child, had seemed to loom above her like some dark giant.

She thought about her early dreams, the allure of medicine, her vision of herself in an operating theater, or maybe on a hospital ship bringing modern miracles to remote places.

"You can be anything you want to be," her advisors told her. "You have an aptitude for many things."

But as she grew older during these last years at college, it became clear that choices would have to be made. Adam was the elder, the one who was now prepared to move from the study hall into the real world. And he had made a truly giant step. A Phi Beta Kappa student in college and now certain to receive his graduate degree with honors, he had already been engaged to work right here in Elmsford at Advanced Data Systems, one of the busiest computer companies in the state. It promised a glowing future. Now, since the state university was more than two hundred miles away, medical school for Margaret became an impossibility.

There could be no question as to this decision—their decision. They were everything to each other. Everything.

A sudden and frantic agitation possessed her, so that she started up, dropping her book to the floor, and, seizing a sweater, ran clattering down the stairs.

In the yard Jean was pushing Nina on the swing. "I thought you had to study," she said, surprised.

"I guess I've finished everything."

Jean smiled. She had a way of making up for her anxieties with a smile.

"I always tell people you will read the phone book if there's nothing else around."

It was true. Her imagination ran and ran everywhere, up mountains, back in time, down dead ends. Just this morning there had been a funny name in the phone book. Socrates O'Brien. Had an O'Brien perhaps been a sailor with the Mediterranean fleet and met a Greek girl to bring back to America? And was this Socrates their son? Or perhaps these O'Briens were classics scholars and all their children had names like Psyche or Cassandra. . . .

The swing creaked, back and forth, up and down. It was hypnotic, the creak repeating itself at the same spot on the return. Hypnotic. *Psyche, Cassandra,* it creaked.

On the rise the child's legs were tilted higher than her head, and her laughter rang, while on the downswing she squealed in mock terror. Brought from Chicago when Jean's sister died, she had become Jean and Margaret's child, more accurately, Margaret's—a rescued child, innocent product of careless sex and an anonymous father.

Nina, Nina, the ropes creaked.

"What's the matter, Margaret? You're a thousand miles away."

She came to, blinking. "I need some air and exercise. I've been in all day."

"It's tension. I remember how I was before my wedding. Go on, dear, take a walk."

The street was pleasant, the old, well-tended houses far apart. Most people had some fruit trees and an ample vegetable garden out back. Almost everybody had a dog who roamed the neighborhood as if it belonged to him. Margaret and Jean had the vegetable garden, a quite splendid one that they worked themselves, but no dog.

I suppose we'll get one now that Nina's older. It will be good for her, Margaret thought.

Her mind flitted, fighting reality. She walked with her head down and her cold hands in the sweater's pockets.

Past the streets with the small-town, nineteenth-century air she came downhill into the city that Elmsford had become. Here was the main library, Gothic and ivied, where Mom had been head librarian. Here was the high school, where Margaret Keller, freshman, had so miraculously caught the attention of Adam Crane, senior. True, they had been aware of each other's existence long before that, but "being aware" and "catching attention" were very different. And holding their attention until it grew into a wedding dress and a pair of white satin slippers in a box on the top shelf of the closet was different still.

Nostalgia drew her onto the playing field. Here from a small plateau one looked downward toward the river, edged on this side with a clutter of industry, and turbulent from the long spring rains. Across it lay fields of corn and wheat, stretching for a hundred miles or more and sprinkled sparsely with small groves of trees, like islands on the calm sea.

Elmsford was a comfortable place. It was good to have grown up here, and it would be good to rear one's children here. Margaret was not a roamer, but a home person, as was Adam, although his mind roamed far. And she stood now, cold in the rising wind, thinking. . . .

Her high school advisor, Mrs. Hummel, had said last summer, "I hope you aren't rushing into anything, Margaret. You've been preparing for medical school all along, and now you're giving it up! Do you have to?"

"I'll compromise. I can teach biology and chemistry here if they'll have me."

"Is that really a compromise?"

"I think so. I'll be teaching future doctors."

"Well," said Mrs. Hummel. "Well."

No doubt she had thought that because she was Mom's friend, advice from her would be acceptable. But she had been wrong. Margaret's expression had told her so, and she had added quickly, "I only mean—you have so much promise, Margaret. And you really are so young."

Young! She felt old right now, very old. And she longed for Adam with such a yearning, such an ache! If she could only talk to him, not over the telephone, but while she could look into his quiet face! Unlike her he was not given to explosions of emotion, but once he understood her bewilderment, he would reassure her.

Yet he had not reassured her. . . . When, after he had rather vaguely suggested delay, she had asked him whether there was anything that he had not told her, he had merely, with equal vagueness, denied it.

"Nothing except that the exams are tough, and I'm tired out. Anyway, what's a couple of weeks' postponement?"

She had felt an *atmosphere,* as when the lights go out during a storm and the familiar house, with its corners and closed doors, becomes abruptly dangerous and strange.

Was he tired of *her?* Could he have found somebody else? It happened. But to them? To Adam and Margaret?

She had to ask him. And she began to walk, almost run, toward home and the telephone. Her heart was sick in her chest, now hammering, now fluttering, as she sped back up the slope. She had to stop for breath, to lean against an old stone wall.

But she knew she could not possibly ask him. She would simply have to wait for whatever might come next. It was a question of pride: a woman did not beg. At least, this woman didn't. No doubt hers was an old-fashioned concept, quite outmoded since men and women were now supposed to be the same. Yet they were not the same. *Equal,* yes, but not *alike.*

Now another thought came: He had remembered her birthday last week. He had sent flowers, the *Collected Poems* of Auden and a box of chocolates. She was always lamenting that she was a "chocoholic," and he was always telling her that with a figure like hers, she could afford to be.

You're looking for trouble, Margaret. You're seeing things that are not there.

Almost at her feet a chipmunk, emerging from hibernation, went racing beside the wall. And watching his erratic, zigzag flight, she wondered about the tiny brain, what its motivation to reverse direction might have been, and what the tiny eye might have noticed that she, standing right there, had not seen.

Zig. Zag. Things seen by some, not seen by others.

Slowly now, she turned into the street. Her mother, who was religious, liked to say, "God doesn't give anybody more trouble than he can bear." Perhaps so, but from the little that Margaret had yet seen of living, she doubted it.

If Adam ever leaves me, she thought again, I shall die, no matter what Mom thinks. Or no, I shan't die, but I shall want to. I shall go on living and wanting to be dead, which is worse than being dead.

TWO

Whenever he saw Randi, or thought for an instant that he was seeing her, on the campus or on the street in town, everything in him, heart and breath, responded. She was never out of his mind; sitting in the lecture hall or studying in his room, he was aware without looking at a clock of the hour when she would telephone or come to his door. Sometimes he would catch strangers smiling at him tentatively, as if they were trying to place him, and then he would realize that he himself had been walking along with a smile on his face.

Adam had not ever imagined that a man could be possessed as he was now. There was no way that this possession could be compared with anything he had ever felt for Margaret.

Randi was small, with the curves of a plump little woman, although she was not plump at all; the curves were simply her structure. And soft: her clothes had ruffled touches, flowered scarves and lace; her voice was soft. All the enticements and allures that you found in the books and the manuals were hers. She had, too, a quality that could be called "demure"—if that were not an absurd adjective to apply to a person whose laughter and chatter were so beguiling—a something secretive in her public manner that *was* demure. Still, men knew otherwise. Often he had caught them looking at her and had read their thoughts, had seen their envy of him when he walked away with her arm in his.

She worked at an office in town and lived in a small, neat apartment near the campus. She was somebody's cousin—he hardly remembered whose—and was usually seen at the best parties with the best men at the schools of medicine, law, and engineering. Still, no one had ever claimed her as his own; she had kept herself quite free until she had met Adam.

He had first taken real notice of her in the front row at the Drama Society's musical in which he played a small part. When the group took its bows at the conclusion, he was aware of her eyes upon him. He did not even know her name; he had had in the past only a hurried impression of her, but he had not forgotten it. When, at a repeat performance a few nights following, he saw her again, and their eyes met again, he sought her out.

She said she had enjoyed the music. "I grew up in my grandfather's house. He played in a band, and he knew music. That's how I learned the little I know. But I have no talent at all and probably not even a good ear."

Adam, who knew rather a good deal about music, thought her modesty appealing.

"Would you like to walk over to my place and listen to some records?"

"I'd like to walk over and talk to you," he said.

The infatuation had been immediate and intense for both. When it had been going on for well over half a year, she said suddenly one day, "They tell me you have a girl back home."

With a sense of approaching disaster he replied, "Who tells you?"

"People. Somebody always knows somebody who knows something."

They were having a Sunday-morning breakfast in her kitchenette. He would remember the moment exactly, her pink robe and the sunlight turning her hair into a black satin cap. There was a little twist on her lips, caused either by anger or by a precursor of tears.

"What is her name?"

"Margaret," he answered, very low.

"Is it true that you're supposed to be married in the summer?"

"I was," he murmured.

"So you've broken it off?"

"Not yet."

"What are you waiting for?"

In his agitation he rose from the chair, so that she had to look up at him with her question; her eyes were filled with accusation. He felt chastened, and rightly so.

"It's—it's very difficult." And he knew that his words were awkward and foolish.

Difficult! Margaret's broad forehead framed by the short, carved curls of a stone cherub. Curve of her white-lidded round, gray eyes. A calmness. Astonishment, disbelief, and suffering—such suffering!— when he should begin: "Margaret, I have to tell you—"

"Why did you hide it from me?" Randi demanded.

"I shouldn't have. I guess it was, well, that there wasn't any real need to talk about it, since I planned—plan—to end it."

"What is she like?"

He went numb. How could he have let things reach this pass? For months now he had fooled himself with promises that tomorrow or next week at the latest he would straighten out affairs, would make all clear to Margaret. And to his mother, and her mother, and everyone at home in that close community where the union of Margaret and Adam had been as certain as the sunrise, God help us. But in his new enchantment here, he had kept putting it off.

"I asked you, Adam, what is she like?"

He said hopelessly, "Smart. She wants—wanted to be a doctor."

"And what else?"

"She's friendly. Yes. She has a lot of friends."

"What does she look like?"

"Randi, please. Please."

"Just say whether she is as pretty or prettier than I am."

"She's—different."

"How different?"

He fumbled and stumbled. "She's not fashionable. Doesn't care much about things like that."

"Oh, why won't you talk?" Tearful and exasperated, Randi cried out. "Can't you see how you've hurt me? And all you do is stand there like a dummy not telling me anything real. Talk!"

"Randi, darling, darling," he pleaded, as with a sudden access of fright it occurred to him that he might lose her. "The last thing I'd ever want is to give you one minute's grief. Don't cry. Please. It's true that I should have broken off with Margaret last September. I should have told you about her at the start. The thing is, I just dreaded the mess and the pain. I admit I've been a rotten coward. I'm ashamed of myself."

"You should be."

"I swear to you that I'll take care of everything this week. I swear."

"You really don't want to marry her? I heard you'd been engaged for years."

"Oh, not years, exactly. But a while. Listen, Randi; whatever I felt before is over."

"I hope so."

"It is. Look at me. Look into my eyes. What do you see?"

"I don't know. I'm not sure."

"This is real, Randi. You and I are real."

And he had kissed her. And after another half hour of tears and protestations, they had gone back to bed.

This encounter had occurred three months ago. And now, walking through the cold spring night toward Randi's apartment, he had still not "straightened things out," had merely taken a few hesitant steps, and those few had already caused enough of a stir.

Only yesterday his mother had telephoned for the third time. She was an easygoing woman, so that her agitation, her scolding, were especially impressive.

"Your reasons for postponing the wedding are ridiculous, Adam. If I didn't know how much you love Margaret, I would be suspicious. As it is, you sound merely careless or lazy or irresponsible, and I know you're none of those things. Are you getting cold feet about the job, afraid you won't do well or something?"

The hand that held the receiver was sweating. "Mom," he said with excessive patience, "it's only what I told Margaret."

Over the weekend he would fly home and lay the truth out plainly on Margaret's table. Just do it. But certainly he wasn't going to tell his mother first.

"Mother, I have class in ten minutes. I've got to hang up."

"You're worrying that lovely girl! What's she supposed to tell people? It looks bad. Everybody thinks it's to be in June, and—"

"Mother, I've got to go."

That lovely girl. Yes, she was completely honest, without wiles. But then, I also am completely honest, he protested. He knew he was, or had been until now.

Before he had gone to the war in Korea, his father had left a letter for Adam, to be opened when he should be old enough to understand it. Among the admonitions had been one about candor, about doing nothing underhanded. In his mind's eye he could even see his father's vertical script, and he felt like a traitor.

Margaret loved him, and he had loved her, too, and counting himself so fortunate, had been contented. Their path had stretched ahead, straight, smooth, and gleaming, until Randi had crossed it and turned him about face. Was he really so wicked, though? God knows, he wasn't hardhearted; it was anguish to think of doing any harm or hurt to Margaret. It was simply that he couldn't help himself. And God knows, too, that he was neither the first nor the last man who couldn't help himself. Was not the world's most moving poetry and music all about what was happening between himself and Randi?

Yet, regardless of all that poetry and music, when it comes down to specific cases, words fail, he thought now, and, raising his collar against the wind, made another circuit of the walk, as if through using energy he might somehow clear his mind.

Margaret had possibilities, he argued. Might she not eventually marry Fred Davis, who had never made any secret of his feeling for her? A positive person, cheerful, kind, but rigidly judgmental, Fred would condemn Adam Crane in disgust, and yet rejoice that Adam's loss could well turn out to be his gain. Or Margaret might go on to study medicine, if that was still her interest; he didn't really know, because her whole interest during these past few years had been in himself. So now he was back where he had started.

"What's wrong?" Margaret had asked when, during spring break, he had suggested weakly that perhaps they had better wait a little. He had meant to prolong the conversation, drawing gradually nearer to the truth, until after an hour or two, the truth would have emerged into full daylight. But her puzzled alarm had defeated his courage, and he had ended—how could he have?—by trying to relieve her. His effort had been halfhearted, to be sure, and he knew that it had not put her at ease. And he knew he should not have done it.

He rang Randi's bell. Music floated from within, an airy show tune from the thirties made for dance and song. When she came to the door, she wrapped her arms around him and pulled him inside. The table in the alcove was set with a bowl of jonquils and a bottle of wine, while from the kitchenette behind the screen there came a rich aroma.

"What's this, a celebration?" he asked. "Is it some special day?"

"Why not? Every day is special, isn't it? You look tired."

"I guess I am tired. I had that paper to finish and got about two hours' sleep last night." He sat down on the sofa. "They tell me that's the real world, though, so I'd better get used to it."

"Do you think you will? Are you really going to like that life?"

"Randi, I'm going to love it, regardless. It's what I always wanted to do."

"Then I'm glad for you. Sit for a minute while I bring out the food. Everything's ready."

The little space was crowded with homely objects: a bicycle leaning against the wall in the vestibule, the desk with the day's mail scattered. Beyond the open door he could see the bed, which took up most of the room. In the light of a bedside lamp he could see that the sheets were pink. Sometimes they were baby blue. He smiled, feeling the comfort in all this domesticity and the coming thrill of the bed. This comfort is what he would have every day once they were married.

But first, he had to climb a high hill and descend on the other side. And he thought again, with a sickening thud of his heart, that Margaret's wedding dress was already made, and he thought of all the questions he would answer at home, and of the condemnation that would descend upon his head.

"Here's a good California red. Come on, it will lift your spirits," Randi said.

Between them they finished the bottle and finished a very nice little supper, for she was a competent cook. After a short evening they went to bed and, after a most marvelously exotic hour, fell asleep.

When he woke in the morning, she was lying wide awake on her back beside him, staring at the ceiling. It seemed to him that she looked strangely solemn, and he inquired tenderly, "What are you thinking?"

"Of how sweet you are."

He laughed. " 'Sweet'? That's a word to describe you, hardly me."

When, drowsily, he reached to draw her to himself, she slid away, put on her pink robe, and sat down on the edge of the bed.

"Wake up, Adam. I've something to tell you."

Her tone aroused him. "What is it?"

"I'm pregnant."

"My God," he said.

She was watching him. For a few moments neither spoke, and he knew she was taking his measure. Possibly she was fearful that he would not receive the news kindly. If so, she was mistaken. For just a second he had indeed been stunned, but reaction followed almost at once: there was nothing to fear, he was to have an excellent beginning salary, there was nothing to fear. . . .

A smile began to spread up his cheeks. "Well. That's not bad, not bad at all."

There were tears in her eyes. He sprang out of bed and took her in his arms. "Be happy!" he said. "I know it's an unexpected shock, but we'll manage. We'll get married, even before commencement if you want. There's a new building on the bluff side of the river, high, with a view. Oh, be happy," he murmured against her cheek. "We'll be young parents."

"I want to have an abortion," Randi said.

He let her go. "Oh, no. No, no."

"Oh, yes. Don't look so distraught." For he had jumped up in astonishment and stood staring at her.

"No," he repeated.

"Is it a matter of principle with you, or what?"

"You haven't been raped! To destroy it—I feel as if a part of myself would be destroyed. It *is* a part of myself. Of us."

She did not answer. Her eyes were still wet, with a great tear poised in one, ready to drop, and he put his hand on her shoulder, saying gently, "There's no reason, Randi. Think. It's wrong. Wrong."

"There is a reason," she answered with equal gentleness, "but it's so hard for me to tell it. Oh, Adam, it's so hard!"

"Tell it."

"I'm not going to marry you. I can't. I don't want a baby without a father."

"What do you mean you can't?" An awful, aberrant possibility flashed to him. "You're not already married or something?"

"No, but I'm going to be. To somebody else."

First he thought he had not heard correctly. Then, as if she had struck him with her fist, he felt a blow on his chest, and he knew that he had heard. There came a wave of the most hideous shame, and remembering that he was naked, he seized the nearest piece of clothing, his overcoat, and covered himself.

"Adam, it's not so absolutely appalling as I know it sounds. At least I don't think it is. You see, it's for your good too."

"My good." Fire burned in his throat, but his voice came out cold and cracking. "Go on. Perhaps you can explain for me."

"I feel I've led you, and have let you lead me, into a predicament. You haven't worked out your relationship with that girl. You've had months to do it in, and I know you haven't done it."

"How the hell does that connect with 'somebody else'? Unless you've lost your goddamned mind."

"I've never thought as long and clearly about anything in all my life."

"What the hell are you talking about?" he cried. "Who's the guy? Where is he? When did this happen?"

He could not bear to look at her, huddled there with the robe drawn tight, as if to protect herself against assault. Yet he could not look away either. A killing rage swelled in him.

"If you'll listen quietly, I'll tell you. I started to say you haven't even broken up with Margaret."

"You don't know that at all."

"You would have told me if you had."

"And would that have made any difference? Is that why you've found another man for yourself and slept with me last night too? Hey? Hey? Answer me!"

"I can't say what came first. It's all sort of twisted together."

When she gazed up at him, he watched the tear that had been caught in the rim of her eye slide slowly down her cheek. In the cramped space he got up and walked, striking his fist into his palm. He sat down on the single chair and waited with his head in his hands.

"Maybe if you hadn't been so tied up . . . I was at your place one night and your mother called, and you went to your friend's room to use his extension, and shut the door. But I could hear anyway, could tell how disturbed you were, and I thought what a pack of trouble all this was. And this man Chuck, that's all the name I'm going to give because I don't want another pack of trouble, with you being furious, Chuck had business in the office where I work. And he saw me and asked me out to dinner . . ."

Adam thought grimly, I'll bet he did.

"And after a few times he asked me to marry him. He's divorced, he lives in California, and he showed me a picture of his house, just beautiful, with palm trees around a pool, so sunny, so peaceful—"

"Just beautiful. 'Palm trees and a pool.' Do you know you're disgusting?" And he wondered how he could survive this horror.

"I know I must seem so. But it isn't only the glamour, Adam, believe me. He happens to be a very nice, kind man. And no old sugar daddy either. He's not even forty." Randi wiped her cheeks with her sleeve. "You can't imagine how many nights I couldn't sleep and cried. Because I care about you so much, Adam. I understand why you can't believe me, and I can't blame you, but it's true. I swear it's true, that I've been torn into pieces."

"I would like very much to tear you into pieces myself. Don't you understand that any fool can see through the whole sham? We had wonderful times in bed, but that's all it was to you, and nothing more. Somebody with money came along, so now you're off and away. That's the story. And you're a bitch. That's the rest of the story."

"No, I'm not. I'm a practical person. Do you think my life has been a bed of roses?"

"Most people's lives aren't."

"True, but this is my life. I need to get what I can out of it. I need to understand myself."

"You're not hard to understand. Glitter and gold, the fleshpots."

"Well, some of that, I'm not denying it. Doesn't everybody like money? I've often told you I want to get away and see things. I've never seen anything but this town. People come here to the university and talk about where they've come from and where they're going. And I listen to them, thinking, When am I ever going to go anywhere? California, New York, anywhere?"

"And you just found it out now when this nice, kind man from California appeared."

"I've never made a secret of my longing."

Maybe—probably—she had mentioned something, some of her longings, but they had seemed trivial, nothing to which you would pay attention.

"Perhaps there's a part of me that knows I wouldn't be happy forever in a small midwestern city like yours. I imagine it's not too different from here, only larger. And if I were to be discontented, I wouldn't be doing justice to you."

"How selfless, how noble!"

"I'm sorry, Adam. I'm so sorry to end this way. But I've had to make a quick decision."

So soft she was! The black hair, the milky skin, the silk robe, the little velvet slippers—all soft. He wanted to seize hold of that softness and crush it, just stamp on it; he understood how, in one swift second, a dreadful crime can be committed.

"I beg you to understand," she pleaded. "I beg you to try."

All their nights and days—what had they meant?

"We made love last night. . . . What was it to you? Why did you do it?"

"I wanted us to finish with something beautiful to remember."

She was sobbing. When she held out her hand to him, he pushed it roughly away and went to the bathroom to change into his clothes.

"In the long run you wouldn't be happy with me, Adam," she said when he came out.

His heart was thumping and his hands trembling as he buttoned his overcoat. She followed him to the outer door. The wine bottle was still on the table.

"Quite a celebration," he said as he passed it.

"A farewell dinner, Adam. I hope I've done the right thing, and I believe I have. It will work out better for you this way. You'll see. You'll get over it faster than you think."

"God damn you," he said. "Drop dead." And he slammed the door.

His heart, in its killing rage, still shuddered so dreadfully that for a moment he had to lean against the railing before he set off toward his room. He made a detour through the park. The thought of his room, the books and the Sunday silence, was unbearably depressing. The morning was overcast and gray, with wind sharp as a knife and the world gone insane, without logic, without reason.

It's not, he thought, as if she were merely another tempting body without heart or brains. She had charm, refinement, feeling—why, her feel for music alone must show that! And yet she had played with his love so lightly and, aware of his enchantment as she must have been— had he not told her and shown her often enough?—had kept on playing with it until she was ready to toss it away. What did her tears mean? Leaving him, taking a part of himself with her, to be flushed down a sewer. And she said she loved him!

On the black, still water of the pond lay islands of white melting ice. Three ducks floated round and round among them, going nowhere. Like me, he thought, and halted to watch. Where now? Then it came to him that Margaret could have said the same if he had struck her down as Randi had just now struck him. . . . And for a long time he kept standing there in the cold, watching the ducks.

I wouldn't be happy in a small city like yours. In the long run you wouldn't be happy with me.

It was true that now, when he considered it, he could not see Randi raking leaves in an Elmsford yard. Margaret raked leaves. . . . But he had lost his first love for Margaret. More's the pity, a great, sad pity.

How long he stood there, he did not know. His hands, thickly gloved and thrust into his pockets, were frozen, and there was no place to go but back to his room.

Long past midnight he was still awake, turning and turning his thoughts in a great circle.

"Do you have to have 'love'?" he asked himself after a while. Cannot trust and friendship, respect and admiration, be enough? Or even more than enough? For look what "love" had brought him!

Of course, there was no reason why he should commit himself to anyone or anything. Surely there was no need for him, at twenty-five, to marry. Or to marry at all, ever. No reason, except that he already *had* committed himself. And he had a vision of a pathetic dress drooping unworn in a closet. He had a vision of Margaret, crushed and humiliated as he himself was now.

He was a rationalist who believed that for the most part, you were the determinant of your own fate, yet it seemed to him now that all this—this affair—with Randi had obviously not been meant to be. It had been a diversion from his ordained path.

With a shiver of revulsion he suddenly recalled the "beautiful house, the palm trees, and the pool." Great wealth did not interest him. To make a decent living was enough. He would settle with his work, and for love of it he would do his best. It would not be the thrilling world he had pictured with Randi, but it would be worthy, and he would try to make it happy in a different way.

An enviable position, a fine girl, these had been given him, and he should be grateful.

PART TWO
1988 to 1994

PART TWO
1988 to 1994

THREE

In the long June evening on the longest day of the year, the sun drew swooping curves of lemon-colored light upon the grass. In the shadow of the elms, where the little group sat, the grass was darkly blue. The fire had died in the barbecue pit, and near the picnic table a pair of squirrels foraged for crumbs from the anniversary cake, while under the table the dogs lay sleeping off their dinner. From the farthest edge of the yard, past the garden where tomato plants throve and peas had climbed halfway up the poles, came the cheerful click of croquet balls. Nina, home for vacation, was having a game with Adam and the children.

Margaret, surveying this intimate little world, searching as usual for just the right word to describe it, could find nothing more apt than *cozy*.

"Adam looks well," remarked Cousin Louise, "not a minute older than on your wedding day."

It was true. His sandy hair was as thick as it had been, his slight stoop was no more pronounced than it had been fifteen years ago, and in Margaret's mind the word for him was still *elegant*.

"How about Margaret?" asked Cousin Gilbert. "Margaret will never grow old."

He and Louise bore out the rather silly saying that long-married couples begin to resemble each other; they were both comfortably padded, with florid cheeks and friendly temperaments, talkative, and kindly.

"Margaret will have her beauty when she is eighty," observed Fred Davis, with his pale blue eyes going grave and thoughtful.

"Oh, I shall be covered with freckles by then," said Margaret, regarding the sprinkle on her white arms. "So far, thank goodness and thanks to big hats, my face has been spared."

She was feeling a pure, light calmness. This was one of those blessed moments in which all the strands of life seem to come properly together, to fit and weave. Fifteen years! Now, looking up at the old roof that sheltered them all, herself and Adam with Megan, Julie, and Danny, she made the impossible wish: that life might always be as it was this minute.

"Do you by any chance want to part with this puppy?" asked Fred, who had taken the mongrel pup on his lap and was stroking its head.

"I think I have some people who'll give it a home. Why? You don't want a dog, do you?"

"You know, I think I do. The house has developed echoes since I lost Denise last year. At first I was glad that she hadn't left children to grow up without a mother, but now I wish she had." And as if to himself he repeated, "The house has echoes. My own footsteps are too loud."

There were sounds of sympathy from Louise. And Margaret said, "I'll find a dog for you. Ever since I made that contact with the pound the time I found the sick collie abandoned on the road, they've kept calling me, two or three times a month, to find homes. So far I've been lucky. I'm sure a nice, man-sized dog will be turning up."

"No, this one suits me fine, if I may have it. He's small enough to ride along wherever I go and to sit in the office with me."

The little animal and the tall, powerful man were incongruous, although Fred's hands and his mild eyes were very gentle. There was something touching about him since he had become a widower. He was only five years older than Adam, but he looked older than that. His firm, square face could take on a wistful look. He had always been something of a neighborhood older brother to the boy Adam, and was now one of the few people whose informal visits were at all welcome to Adam.

"He's lonesome," she had remarked more than once. "He really needs to be married again."

And Adam in joking mood replied, "He's waiting for you." And she in joking mood answered, "Why? Are you planning to divorce me, or to kill yourself? Which is it?"

"He's yours," she said now. "His name is Jimmy, unless you want to change it."

"Jimmy will do." And again the pale eyes regarded Margaret with that thoughtful, grave expression.

"I must ask Adam how he marinates the meat," Louise said briskly, changing the mood. "I was looking at your spice shelf before. You have things that I never heard of."

Margaret smiled. "Whenever we travel, we go exploring markets. Last year, I think we saw every Chinese food store in San Francisco. Adam knows fruits and vegetables that I never knew existed either. His computer and his exotic recipes are his two loves."

"What's this about two loves? I have three," asked Adam as the troop came carrying balls and mallets.

"Megan, Danny, and me. Mostly me!" cried Julie.

She was ten and, like her older sister, was almost a copy of Adam even to her thin, straight nose.

"But our team won the game," Danny said. "Me and Nina. We beat them, didn't we, Nina?"

"Yes, and we'll do it again," said Nina, ruffling the curly red hair that Danny naturally hated.

The children adored Nina, and not merely because she adored them; she possessed a charm that could not help but attract anyone. The headstrong child had become a confident young woman, filled with a vivid enthusiasm. And to some extent Margaret had to credit herself, because she was the one who had argued against Adam that Nina must be allowed to make her own choices, to go her own way.

"I hear," said Louise, "that you're a big success in New York."

" 'A big success'? No, but with a little luck I hope to be. Anyway, I'm feeling better about myself than I would be feeling now if I hadn't left college after the first year. I'd have graduated last month with a B.A., a smattering of history and English literature, and nowhere to go, nothing to do with myself."

"You make it sound awfully bleak," Adam said. "A B.A. from a good college has no value in your estimation?"

"For most people I'm sure it has. I was never a student. You know that. You're not comparing me with Margaret, I hope." Nina turned suddenly to Margaret. "Sometimes I think I must have been a disappointment to you. All those nights when you pulled me through chemistry and math! Right up there," she said, pointing to the window above, "at my desk next to that window. And you were never impatient, you never made me feel ashamed."

"There was never any reason to be ashamed. Not then, and surely not now. You were you, and I'm glad you're doing what you wanted to do."

With a particular tenderness different from that which she felt for

her children—who had a mother and father of their own—she met
Nina's clear gaze. Such a sprightly young thing she was in her short
yellow dress!

"I just wish New York wasn't so far away," murmured Margaret.
She had not meant to say it; the thought had simply escaped into
speech.

"I know. But it's wonderful! Every day you can choose from a
hundred things to see or hear. I guess I'm just not a small-town person," Nina said, adding quickly, "not that Elmsford is exactly a small
town."

Louise urged, "Tell us what's been happening to you."

"Well, after I finished that course in design, I had to look for a job,
of course—"

"But tell what happened before that, at the school," Margaret
prompted.

"Yes, at the school we had a contest, to plan a room. I was assigned
a boy's room, a boy about eight, so of course I thought of you, Danny,
and since I know what you like, I had a head start." Nina concluded
modestly, "And so, I won."

"Don't be modest," said Gilbert. "We're only family. Go on."

"Well, somebody wrote an article about the winners, so when I
went job hunting, I brought the clipping with me, and after the third try
I got a job. That's about it."

"You started at the top," Margaret reminded her. "Crozier and
Dexter. Whenever I pick up a decoration and art magazine at the hair-
dresser's, I see their name."

"Oh, they're the top, all right," Nina admitted. "I guess I have to
say it was a coup, a lucky coup for me. I'm learning so much from them!
They even let me help a bit, green as I am, with the room they're doing
in the Farnsworth Settlement's model house benefit. That's the most
important annual showhouse in the city. It was great fun, and I think I
learned a lot."

"Crozier and Dexter," said Louise. "I must look for the name. Are
they men or women?"

"Two guys, Willie and Ernie."

"Aha," cried Gilbert. "Which one has his eye on you?"

Nina laughed. "Neither, you can be sure. Willie and Ernie are—
married, so to speak."

"Oh, dear," said Louise with a little sniff.

Adam laughed. "It's safer for Nina that way, don't you see?"

And Nina retorted, "Not at all. I can find plenty without Willie and Ernie."

"I'm sure of that," said Fred, who still had the puppy on his lap. He made a mock face of sorrow so that everyone laughed. "Oh, if I were younger, Miss Nina! I remember you sitting in your stroller."

It was growing dark. A narrowing line of hazy pink wavered in the western sky. Then a slight wind stirred, and the birds went silent.

Adam stood up, saying, "Let's go inside. Who wants popcorn?"

He always knows what the children want, thought Margaret. And Louise, expressing the same thought, remarked, "Do you realize that Adam's been entertaining those children all afternoon? Between softball, croquet, Japanese origami, you name it, those are three lucky kids."

"Yes, and I think they know it too," Margaret said comfortably.

Indoors, after the popcorn had been made in the kitchen, the men, followed by children, dogs, and a trail of popcorn on the floor, went to the computer room to see Adam's latest miraculous acquisition. The three women went to the parlor. Before the evening ended, Julie would be asked to play something on the piano. This was a routine in the Crane house; family and close friends expected it and found it pleasant.

Nina looked around at the familiar room, the banjo clock, the old sepia photographs, and the rolltop desk heaped with chemistry and biology final exams to be graded. "It seems ages since I lived here," she said. "Do you think you'll ever move?"

Margaret shook her head. "Why should we? It's home."

"Don't you get tired of it? It's typical gingerbread."

"My great-grandfather built it."

"That's sentimental."

"Maybe so, but I don't care," Margaret said with a smile. Nina had always been blunt. But that was good. It was good to know what people were really thinking.

"Then let me fix it up. There's plenty of space here, tall windows and high ceilings. I could do things with it."

"So? What would you do?"

"Get rid of all this heavy furniture, to begin with."

"Why? It's good stuff, well kept and polished, nothing wrong with it. And it's old."

"But not the right kind of old. If it were eighteenth century or French Empire or something, that would be different."

" 'Empire'? Which empire?" Margaret teased.

"Napoleon, of course."

"The first or the third?"

"Oh, you know I don't know any history. I only know there's one with the eagle and the bee and a lot of ancient-Rome business. One handsome piece, a desk for instance, could change this whole room. That alone, and perhaps a touch of gilt here and there around the room, would do wonders for it." Nina got up and walked around. "Also, a small fruitwood table next to this chair," she mused. "A pair of lusters on the mantel, reupholster everything pale blue and dark red, a pair of plain modern pull-up chairs here—I love an eclectic room. I'm positively itching to try."

"Itch away, darling. We can't afford it."

"Really?"

"Yes, really. We haven't got thousands to spend on fruitwood or gilding. Adam doesn't own the computer company! And you know what teachers earn. Also, what it costs to educate three children. Anyway, I really don't care tremendously about having *stuff.* Never have."

"I'm so different from you, but I love you so much." And Nina kissed Margaret on both cheeks.

"Gil and I are going to Europe in the fall," Louise said. "I was thinking we might stop off in New York for a couple of days and see you at your place, Nina. Our house hasn't been touched since Bobby and Tim moved out, and I'd love to do over the downstairs, at least."

"Oh, fabulous! I'd love to bring in some business of my own. I'll give you my card."

Gilbert owned a heating and air-conditioning business; the Ferrises were prosperous. They took an almost childish pleasure in what Adam called their "adult toys": Louise's fur coats and Gil's Jaguar. *Overstuffed* was the adjective that he applied to them, and Margaret knew that he only tolerated them for her sake. It was too bad, yet she understood that they were intellectually no match for Adam. Yet they were such good people, so generous and loving! Gil, although not old enough to be her father, had been the nearest to a father that she had ever known. . . .

"You men are very rude to leave us alone in here," Nina called. "Come on out. You've had enough time with that electronic stuff."

Fred came in chuckling. "If Adam were speaking Chinese, I'd understand him about as well. Semiconductors, disk drivers—all I know are bricks, cement, and two-by-fours. I guess I'd better stick to the building business. Although seriously, I've got to educate myself. We're in a new age, the age of Adam."

Adam, visibly pleased, now turned his attention toward Julie. "Do we get our after-dinner music tonight, Mrs. Chopin?"

The name, which was a family joke, caused Julie to blush with a touch of embarrassment and a deal of pride. Margaret thought of all the theories about the difficulties of the middle child; as far as anyone could see, Julie had no particular difficulties. Perhaps it was because she had her talent.

"What shall it be?" Adam urged. "The new Erik Satie?"

Julie nodded. "I haven't got it perfectly yet. My teacher only gave it to me two weeks ago. But I'll try it. It's a waltz," she explained to the assembled group as if she were instructing them. "It's called 'Choco-late-Covered Almonds.' "

"A show tune?" asked Louise. "I never heard of it."

"It's a very old piece," Julie said solemnly. "He's a French com-poser."

It was tranquil music, evening music, summer sounds for lamplight and leaves rustling at the open window. From where she sat, Margaret could see her daughter's profile as she swayed in harmony with the mood of the waltz.

Her gaze traveled around the circle, where no one moved. Even Danny sat quite still, probably not because he was enjoying himself—at eight he vastly preferred baseball—but out of respect for his father, for whom music was a serious part of life. Those two were as connected as a hand to the arm, she thought, as she studied the boy's round cheeks, short nose, and jaunty curls, all so like her own. Her gaze then rested upon Megan, who at twelve was already browsing through popular medical books at the library. Maybe she would be the one to do it. . . .

Nina was smiling. She had rested her head against the back of her chair and closed her eyes, yet even in such repose she seemed to spar-kle. Her heavy chestnut hair was piled high above her small, piquant face; her rather large, sensuous mouth was glossed with the same red-brown lipstick that she had been wearing since, at fifteen, she had used up her allowance to get a professional makeup.

"What a handful!" Mom used to sigh. And Mom had not even lived to see Nina as a grown girl. She had known her only as the mis-chievous child who liked to scare them by pretending to run away and then, an hour later, popping out of the neighbor's garage to laugh at them. It had taken more than a little patience to rear Nina!

But it had been worth the effort to watch the unfolding of her imagination, with its recklessness and generosity. There was the time she had given her little savings to a poor girl in her class. There was the time she had bought a reproduction, expensively framed, of Manet's "Luncheon on the Grass." "Isn't she nervy?" Nina had said of the naked woman sitting with the gentlemen in their dark, formal suits. And "It makes my room, doesn't it, with all that color splashing on the wall?"

Remembering all this now, Margaret felt inner laughter along with a few inner tears. Over time she had taught hundreds of teenagers and thought she understood them fairly well. Yet Nina remained unique. Clearly, the circumstances of her birth must have had their effect; again and again she had asked questions about her father, questions that had been answered simply with "I don't know." The truth was that no one knew. It was possible—ugly thought—that even Nina's mother had not known. Jean had believed it best to tell Nina that her father was dead, and it was too late now to say otherwise. Perhaps the man really was dead, anyway.

And with a surge of gratitude Margaret thought again about her own three sitting there, who had no such uncertainties, no unanswered questions, nothing hidden. Father and mother were here together and always would be.

Fifteen years! In the course of history that was not even the wink of an eye, yet for this little handful of people, much had occurred in that wink of time. Adam's cheerful mother, who had lived with them long, too long, past the inception of Alzheimer's disease, was now in an institution. Jean and her new husband had been run over by a taxi in Hong Kong; he had been killed, and Jean had lain in the hospital there for three months before Margaret had been able to bring her home, where she had later died. When travelers returning from Hong Kong rhapsodized over that fabled city, Margaret shuddered. That fabled city was, in her memory, only a hospital and a cheap hotel. After that, there had been a miscarriage, and after that, Danny. . . . You wondered, looking back, how you had managed to weather it all.

Perhaps, though, when two people loved each other, problems even strengthened a marriage. Together you overcame. Of course you did. For here they were, held close in prosperity and health. Adam had his good job, and she was assistant to the head of the science department. Their children flourished. Nina was on her way. What more could one ask of life?

Presently, the music came to an end. Fred Davis departed with Jimmy and a temporary supply of puppy food. The cousins left with praise: *Delicious food, a lovely family, a lovely day.* And Nina prepared her good-byes, for she was to leave in the morning.

"Remember, you two, that you promised to come to New York in the fall."

"We'll be there," Adam promised. "It's four years now since we've been at the opera, and we owe ourselves a treat. Besides seeing you," he added.

The house was closing up, with lights out and doors locked. Margaret was the last at the back door, waiting for the dogs to come in after their final run. The sky was misted, a few drops pattered, and the air was cool on her face.

"A lovely day," Louise had said, and so it had been. Blessed, she thought. We are blessed.

The only way you could tell that it was fall outside was to note that brittle leaves were dropping from the meager trees on Nina's street. Adam, standing at the window, was ready to depart, but the women were still chattering over tea and cookies. It was good, though, to see them so happy with each other, so eager to hear about each other's school and children, boyfriends and job. Furthermore, he was himself in a mood of well-being. They had tickets for *Der Rosenkavalier* at the Metropolitan tomorrow night, and just before leaving home, reports had been circulating through the company about a possible move into European markets. If so, it should certainly mean a step upward for him. Ramsey, vice-president for programming, would probably go to Europe and then . . . So reflecting, he was interrupted in these pleasant thoughts by catching Margaret's words.

"Adam deserves to be head of engineering. And it's not just a loyal wife talking either." She was so earnest, with that little righteous frown of hers! "Wives tell tales, you know, and I've heard some of them talking about how people who work with him respect his knowledge. They know what he's worth. I just hope the big bosses know it too."

"When you get rich," Nina said, "you'll let me do your house for you. Wait till you see the things Louise and Gil have ordered. They really gave me a free hand. It was great fun."

"I shall never be that rich," Adam said. "People who actually make things, or invent things, rarely make as much money as people do who merely *sell* things."

The words were bitter. He knew it, and was at once displeased with himself because he did not want to sound like an envious or bitter man. And he said quickly, "It's remarkable what you've accomplished here with just one room."

"Do you really like it? Willie and Ernie let me have the furniture at cost. They're the sweetest guys. And they gave me a bonus for Gil's big order too. I was going to buy some handsome cabinets to fit that wall, but then I thought that I surely am not going to live in a studio apartment forever, so I bought this ring instead."

Nina held up her hand, flashing a pretty round stone of a shade between green and blue.

"Nice," Adam said. "An aquamarine, isn't it?"

"Cool, like the sea," Margaret said. "I can see how it might make you feel good to look at something like that every day."

The remark was slightly surprising to Adam, since she had never asked for jewelry, and he had never given her any. All she owned was a pearl necklace and a narrow bracelet, perhaps not even real gold, that her mother had left her. In any case, they had too many expenses to think of jewelry. Pity the man who gets Nina, he thought; they are undoubtedly flocking around her already, but the one who gets her had better think twice unless he is rich enough to provide rings and antique tables.

"I've been working on the most wonderful library," Nina said, "paneled from floor to ceiling in dark blond wood, honey colored. And moss-green silk curtains on the windows, very tall windows with a view of Central Park. Can you imagine? But the funny thing is the books! They're all matched sets, Dickens, Balzac, and whatnot, bound in leather to match the curtains. You could die laughing."

"Books that have never been read and will never be," said Adam.

"True, yet they're not stupid people by any means. You'd be surprised. He's somebody on Wall Street, and she's very interesting, very quick witted."

"It's the fast lane," said Adam.

Nina shrugged. It must be a new habit, he thought, not having seen it before.

"I'm meeting people I never knew existed. I hear them talk about restaurants and theater and resorts and business deals. So very amusing." She laughed. "Educational."

"Oh, I miss you," Margaret said. "We all do, especially Megan. She's getting so grown up for a twelve-year-old."

"Don't you think I miss all of you? Here you are, going away again, and I haven't said half the things I want to say."

"There's always the telephone," Margaret reminded her as they stood up to leave. "Sundays and after eight. Remember us, Adam, when I was in college and you at engineering school? What phone bills we had!"

"Yes," Adam said when they were out on the street, "she's in the fast lane, all right."

"Fast? You have to be more precise than that."

"I can't be precise when I'm feeling vague about it myself. It's just something—the kind of people, the grabbing for goodies and sensations, cravings for every kind of sex, always something new—oh, you know the weaknesses I'm trying to describe. You heard her. You know the type."

Margaret laughed. "And you think Nina's about to drown in a sea of wickedness?"

"Not on purpose. But look at her, twenty-one, beautiful, and all alone here. She's a prime candidate for trouble."

"She's twenty-two, adorable, and smart. She'll take care of herself." And Margaret laughed again. "You old puritan! Wait till our girls are turned loose into the world. I'm afraid that nice dirty-blond hair of yours will turn gray. But if it does, never mind. You'll still be the handsomest man in the world."

Adam had looked forward to his trip with as much pleasure as if they had been going abroad. Packing the suitcase and boarding the plane with the list in his pocket—*Philharmonic on Friday. Impressionist exhibit Saturday*—he had felt a glow. Margaret was physically glowing; her very white skin could turn pink with emotion of any kind. Now, as they walked downtown and he caught in plate-glass windows the reflection of her healthy stride and happy face, he could not help but think how pretty she was and how well they looked together.

The cold was severe, and coming out of a shop on Fifth Avenue near their hotel, he lowered his head against a sudden blast of autumn wind. When he raised it, there stood Randi.

Afterward, when he went over what happened, and he was to go over it hundreds of times, he could think only of the word *materialized* to describe it. There had been no sense of approach, no moment or two during which he felt uncertain of recognition, no time to take a second or third look, to prepare his mind or arrange the expression on his face. It was simply that, out of the moving colors on the street, the kaleidoscope of anonymous faces, the flash of light on metal and plate glass, in the middle of all the moving glitter, she was there. Just there, in front of him. Randi.

Her cry was a trickle of musical notes. "Why, Adam! It is you, isn't it?"

Adam's glance flicked over her, barely touching, as it might have flicked over a lamppost, and went northward above her head, where a gray sky floated and a green awning flapped.

"Yes," he said. "How are you? This is my wife, Margaret. This is—"

"Randi Bunting, that's my name now. Adam, I can't believe it's been fifteen years, can you?"

"No," he said.

"You haven't changed," she said.

Now he had to look at her, to pay the same banal, anticipated compliment. "Nor have you."

But she had. She looked fashionable. He had learned enough over the years, although not from Margaret, more probably from young Nina, to recognize the alteration, even to recognize a detail like the expensive handbag with its straps and brass buckles. Someone had taught her, and someone was paying. All this went through his mind in an instant, along with a streak of anger that he would, a minute ago, have sworn was impossible to him.

"I'm just in from California, looking around the city. Where are you staying?"

"Over there," Adam said. "Across the street."

"Why, so am I. Listen, let's get out of this wind and have a cup of tea together. The light's green. Let's go."

How stupid of him! He should have thought quickly, should have said that they had an appointment. But he had not done so, and in two minutes they were across the street in the hotel. She had always known how to get her way. And silently, his anger entrenched itself as, in his sudden awkwardness, he was led to the tea table.

Margaret made polite remarks. "Were you in school with Adam?"

"I? Heavens, no. I was lucky to get through high school." Randi's laugh, at least, had not changed; it chuckled up from the throat. "Seriously, I worked in town and lived near the university, close to the school of engineering. I went to all the parties and had a wonderful time."

Discreetly, the two women were examining each other as women did. It pleased Adam that Margaret was so impressive in her simplicity. Her refinement was unmistakable, and Randi would not mistake it. But, good God, why should he care whether Randi did or did not know how well his life had turned out without her? Had he been so humiliated that her opinion should still matter to him?

"Yes," she was saying, "once you're past your twenties, the fun is never the same. The things I remember! Do you hear of Smithy? Or

Tommy Barnes? He was a nice guy when he was sober, which wasn't often."

"I don't see or hear of anybody," Adam said. Then, because there seemed to be a need to add something that would soften this curt reply, or perhaps only because he was so ill at ease, he added, "We live pretty much to ourselves. We're both busy. Margaret teaches biology and chemistry in the Elmsford high school."

"Oh, that's wonderful. In another life I would have liked to do something important too. I always loved the atmosphere of learning." Randi laughed again. "I guess that's why I kept having crushes on students, including you, Adam. Oh, I had such a big crush on your husband," she told Margaret.

Margaret smiled appropriately, and Adam read her scornful thought: *Stupid. Crude.*

But Randi was neither stupid, nor often crude. She was simply blunt and apt to say without forethought whatever might come into her head. Inwardly, he squirmed and tried to avoid Margaret's eyes, which he thought were seeking his.

Seeming not to notice that Margaret and Adam were so quiet, Randi prattled sociably about last night's play, and California. Her silvery voice was agreeable, and her remarks were amusing. Yet it would be unbearable for him, he thought, after ten minutes had passed, to live with such a flow of words.

"I'm in a rather unsettled state of mind just now," she confided. "Certain circumstances—but no need to go into them. Anyway, I'm trying to make up my mind whether I want to stay in California or pull up stakes. So I've been touring the country to find a place that talks to me, that says, 'Stay here.' I have an idea it may be New York."

What had she meant by "certain circumstances"? Then she must have left the man. And what about the child? The most astounding thing was, Adam thought as, in acute discomfort, he shifted in the chair, that he had been able to bury the fact of its existence. No matter that it had been merely an embryo, and been aborted, it had been alive and it had been his. Yet for him it had ceased, even in memory and until this moment, to exist.

The women talked about unimportant things, another fifteen minutes passed, and the end came as Randi said brightly, "Well, this certainly was an unexpected meeting, wasn't it? Who would imagine it, right in the center of New York?" It was agreed that no one could have imagined it. "If you people ever get to L.A., look me up. I'm still living there, I'll be in the phone book."

And does she really think we would? Adam wondered.

Margaret said politely, "Thank you. Perhaps someday."

"Well, I guess I'll run along. I've had a long day. Do you happen to know whether there's a bookstore around here? I need a couple of paperbacks."

The question had been directed to Margaret, who answered that there was one a few blocks distant and that it was open all evening.

"Good. That's what I'll do, then. It was good seeing you. Enjoy the rest of your stay."

"Randi," Margaret said. "And she had a crush on you."

"The way Fred had on you." He thought he understood that Randi's mention of a crush was an absurdity in Margaret's eyes. Her tone had had a faintly scornful ring, as if it were inconceivable to match him with someone so different from himself. And in fact, from the distance of fifteen years, it did seem inconceivable.

"She's striking, in a way, isn't she?"

"I don't know. I suppose so. It's probably the clothes."

"I thought you never noticed women's clothes."

Irritated, he cried, "For Pete's sake, Margaret, what is this?"

"I'm only curious to know why she is upsetting you so much."

"Upsetting me? What are you talking about? Upsetting me!"

"You were acting so stiff and uncomfortable, shifting around in your chair. It was noticeable."

"I was shifting because it was a damned uncomfortable chair, and I wanted to go have some dinner."

After dinner they strolled. The wind had died, the city flashed its lights, and there were chrysanthemums in shop windows.

"A nice evening, cold or not," Margaret said, "but I'm suddenly sleepy. Shall we go in?"

"It's too early for me, but you go. I'll just walk up as far as the park and come right back."

He walked slowly, missing nothing as he went. Here was probably the liveliest bazaar in the world; all the glittering arts were concentrated in this city. He wouldn't want to live here, for he was comfortable in Elmsford. Nevertheless, he was enjoying the change of scene. It had been a good day, up to a point, up to the shock of seeing Randi. Out of all the millions in New York, he'd had to encounter her!

He walked on toward the bookshop. It was brightly lit and fairly crowded. In the window there was a display of a new biography that he had planned to read, so he decided to go in and buy it to read tonight.

There was something homelike about having your own book with you when you were staying in a hotel.

Then he remembered that Randi might be in the shop, although there was little likelihood that they would each have chosen the same few minutes out of a long evening. Yet it was possible. Undecided, he stood in front of the window staring at the biography. It had a red jacket with embossed gold lettering and the author's name in a running script. A man came out of the shop lighting a cigarette. He was wearing a camel-hair coat and weighed close to three hundred pounds. A taxi stopped with squealing brakes. Shall I or shall I not go in? he asked himself. It might be interesting to know what has been happening to her in all these years. Not that it's any business of mine. I'm only curious. It's natural to be curious in the circumstances, isn't it? Anyway, she isn't there.

He went in. Randi was standing at the first counter facing the door.

"I had an idea you'd come," she said. "I've been here almost an hour, waiting."

"You actually thought I wanted to see *you*?" he retorted.

"Well, didn't you? Don't tell me you aren't the least bit curious."

"For your information I came here to buy that book"—and he pointed to the pile on the counter.

"Buy it, then."

While he handed his credit card to the clerk, Randi waited. When he started toward the door, she went with him.

"I'll walk back with you," she said. "I waited in there so long that they must have thought I was planning to shoplift."

"I don't know why you did. We have nothing special to say to each other."

She was almost running, her heels clacking on the sidewalk, to keep up with his purposely long, rapid strides.

"You could slow up a little," she said nicely, "even if you do hate me."

He looked down at her. She was such a little thing! He was used to walking with Margaret, whose face was almost on a level with his own. It occurred to him that he was behaving badly, and so he said, "I don't hate you. I'm long past all that. I just don't want to talk about anything."

"About what happened, you mean?"

"Yes," he said, and would have sprinted the remaining few yards to the hotel if it had been seemly.

"All right, we won't. You won't mind if I tell you that I hear how well you're doing? One of those people you said you never hear from or see told me about you."

Adam said shortly, "Very kind of him, whoever he was."

"It was Tommy Barnes."

"I met him in an airport about five years ago. He doesn't know the first thing about me."

Three thousand miles across and two hundred sixty million population in this country, he thought, and still a person can't keep himself to himself.

"He said you have a pretty wife, and so she is."

"Thank you."

By now they were in the hotel lobby, approaching the elevator.

"Well," he said, "good night. I'm going up."

She caught his arm. "Can you wait a minute?"

"What for?"

"I need to talk to you. I won't take long"—and she looked at him appealingly.

"Randi, you don't need to talk to me." He spoke not unkindly. "I don't understand what you're doing, waiting for me in that shop, and now—what do you expect?"

"I don't expect anything. I only want to tell you something."

"Then tell me." They were in the way, and people had to brush past them impatiently. "Then tell me."

"Not here. We have to sit down. I'll be quick." And again she appealed, "We can go where we had tea this afternoon. Please."

He followed her, and they ordered coffee. Since she was across from him with only a very small table between, they had nowhere else to look but at each other. Warm air enveloped them in a velvet, perfumed atmosphere. The room might have been scented or else the fragrance was hers. He remembered—what tens of millions of trivial, seemingly forgotten things can resurrect themselves from our stored memories—that she used to put perfume behind her ears. He found himself glancing at her ears, on each of which there sparkled a tiny spray of diamonds.

For a minute nothing happened. And he was angry at himself for being there, for having let himself be led.

She was staring straight into his eyes, "fixing" him, he thought, with a deep, penetrating look. He felt a shiver.

"Don't you even want to know what happened—afterward?"

"You said—" he stammered, "you said you were going to have an abortion and get married."

"I didn't get married to him, and I didn't have the abortion."

"What?"

He became aware that he had been holding the coffee cup; when he put it down, the liquid sloshed onto the saucer and soaked his cuff.

"I got as far as the front door of the clinic and then wasn't able to go through the door. The idea shocked me through and through. I think it was because it had been so shocking to you. 'It's wrong, it's wrong,' you said. I remember how you looked when you said it."

He was too numb to say anything but "And then?"

"I left for California. I told him I was pregnant, but he didn't mind. He liked kids. But then I had a miscarriage. It was just as well, because we only lived together for two years, and the kid wouldn't have had a father after all. He wasn't the marrying kind. He wasn't even the staying kind. So when he left I went to work for my brother, who had come out to L.A. and became a big-time real estate broker. After a while I met a man, much older, who wanted to marry me. That's how I got the name Bunting. We lived in an enormous house with pink marble bathrooms, statues on the lawn, two tennis courts—never saw anything like it."

Adam, recovering speech, made a sharp comment: "It sounds like a racketeer's house."

"Maybe he was one. But he was nice. Then he died. He left me a little money, not much at all; he had nine grandchildren. So I went back to work with my brother, and then his son joined the business, things didn't go as smoothly as they should, and here I am."

"Why are you telling me all this? It's no business of mine!"

"I thought you might have been wondering all this time whether there was a kid of yours running around anywhere. I guess it was just an impulse. The same as I had that day when I said good-bye to you."

"Impulse!" he cried, loudly enough to cause people to turn and stare. "A casual impulse! Just like that!"

"It wasn't casual. It was painful."

"Bitch," he muttered. "You bitch."

"If I hadn't met you, I would be able to sleep tonight. Now I know I won't sleep."

"What do you mean? What do you want? Come out with it, Randi, and don't try playing cat and mouse with me."

"I don't want anything from you, and I never will. You've nothing to fear from me. I'm just so terribly sorry that I hurt you, that's all. I've been thinking about it all these years, and wishing I could tell you."

Cat and mouse. She is too complicated for me, he was thinking as he watched her now. Fundamentally, I am a simple man. Or am I? Am I just not as clever as I think I am?

When she put out her hands to touch his, he drew his own away, demanding, "What's your game? Whatever it is, I don't want to play it. You're the past, the dead, forgotten past."

"Not entirely forgotten. Don't you ever have moments when you wonder what it would be like if we had—"

He ejaculated: "No!"

"Ah, but you must have," she insisted gently. "I do. It's only natural. And it's only speculation, after all, because I'm quite happy as I am. I hope you are too."

"Very," he said now.

First she says she won't be able to sleep, and now she tells me how happy she is.

One hand, with its shell-pink nails, was playing with her pearls. She knows how pretty that gesture is, he thought with scorn. And raising his cup, he encountered her eyes: soft, dark, and glittering, they were, sloe eyes like the plumfruit.

"It would never have worked, you know. Even though I had been willing to live where you do, or you had been willing to go somewhere else, it wouldn't. Even in spite of all our love, it wouldn't. We're too different, you and I."

He flared up. "So why talk about it? What's your point?"

"None, really, I guess. It was just seeing you again that's brought things back."

He didn't want to be reminded of that gray morning, of his despair, of himself walking through that park alone.

There had been melting ice and ducks on the pond. He hadn't thought about it all in years. Years. He didn't want to think about it now.

"Well," he said, "well, here we are. There's enough material here to fill a book. But since I've no intention of writing one, I'd best go."

Randi stood up. "Yes. Good-bye, Adam. Good luck."

For a moment they stood looking at each other. Flower face, he thought. Then they shook hands and parted.

For about ten minutes he stayed outside in front of the hotel, just stayed there in the cold night air.

After a while a phrase from Shakespeare popped into his head, that business about life being a stage and all men players. So, briefly, he had played a part with Randi; then the show had closed, the actors dispersed, and everyone had gone home, where each belonged.

"Where have you been?" Margaret cried when he opened the door. "I was beginning to worry. All these muggings in New York—"

"I browsed through the bookstore. I would have bought half a dozen more if we had room enough in the luggage. Hey, what's this?"

A tray with biscuits and a bottle of champagne in a bucket stood on the table.

"It's a celebration," she said.

"Of our holiday. What a nice idea!"

"No, of more than that. It's the anniversary of the day you proposed."

Women, he thought. They remember everything.

"It was the next-to-most wonderful day of my life. Next to our wedding day."

Her face was illumined. Intensely moved, he took her into his arms and kissed her.

"Oh, Margaret," he said.

Then he opened the bottle with a triumphant pop, poured two bubbling glasses full, and made a toast.

"To love!" he cried, raising his glass. "Bless it, and bless us always."

FOUR

One morning in the middle of January, Adam, raising his eyes from a stack of charts on his desk to answer the telephone, heard an unexpected voice.

"Hello! This is Randi. Are you shocked?"

Actually he was, but he replied calmly, "Not shocked, but surprised. Are you calling from New York or California?"

"Neither. I'm here in Elmsford. I've taken a six-month sublet on a garden apartment in Randolph Crossing, and I'm in Elmsford for the day on business."

He felt a stirring, an unwelcome sense of nuisance. He wished it were possible simply and crudely to tell her not to bother him.

"I've so much to tell you, Adam. I'm sure you're busy right now—"

"Yes, I am," he said.

"So I thought maybe we might have a sandwich together. Whenever that's good for you. I'll be in town all day."

"I have an appointment, a business lunch."

"Then how about a quick drink, twenty minutes of your time around five? Just for old friendship's sake?"

"Randi, we were never 'friends.' "

"But we can be friends now, or I hope we can. Nothing more than that, Adam, I assure you. I told you when we met in New York that I have no designs on you. You seem to be afraid that I have."

She had perhaps not intended to provoke him with the remark, but to his ears she seemed to be making a fool of him, as though he were some sort of male spinster.

"I assure you that never entered my mind," he retorted.

"Good. I was about to wish you well and hang up. So then, will the coffee bar at the Hotel Bradley be all right? It occurs to me that you might not want to go home with liquor on your breath."

"I'm free to go home in any condition I please, Randi. What do you think I am?"

"Five-thirty, then?"

"Five-thirty."

Before he went back to his charts, Adam passed a few minutes to contemplate a brief fall of thick, wet snowflakes, settling and melting on the windowsill. The slow drift and the gray air were suddenly dispiriting; the energy that had pressed him to work so briskly only minutes ago had left him. What the devil had made him acquiesce to a pointless meeting this afternoon? There was no reason in the world why he should meet her, and there were several reasons why he should not. If there were any way of reaching her, he would call her now and cancel. And he stood there with his back to the room, staring into the snow.

Still, she did not seem to have had much luck with her life. You could certainly argue, he reflected, that it was her own fault, and you would be right, but where would that leave common compassion? When you thought about it, a total rejection would really be too harsh, wouldn't it? And he wondered curiously what she might possibly be planning for herself. An apartment in Randolph Crossing was very out of the way. And what was she doing here in the first place? She had been talking about a choice between California and New York. Perhaps she was about to be married?

Then he thought, I really was rough with her. And he remembered how agreeably she had spoken to him that time in New York, how she had admired Margaret and asked about their children. No, there could be nothing wrong in giving her a few harmless minutes of his time this afternoon.

"The last time I saw you, I'm afraid I bored you with my dreary troubles," Randi said. "Now I can tell you that things are looking better."

"I'm glad to hear it."

She seemed more familiar to him than she had seemed when they met in New York. She looked midwestern, dressed as small-town women are in the middle of a snowy winter with a thick woolen cap and a heavy windbreaker. But when these came off, he saw a coral choker and a silk scarf printed with cabbage roses.

"I don't remember whether I mentioned that I once worked in real estate in California."

"You told me."

"Well, I've applied for a license here, and as soon as it comes through, I have a job waiting. It's in a small agency run by half a dozen women, but the area's being developed, and it's a good opportunity for me, I think."

"What brought you back to this area?" he asked.

"One of the women who run the agency knew my brother, and so the contact was made. Anyway, the Midwest is home, and I decided I wanted to come home. That's all there is to it. There are two main areas opening up," she continued with enthusiasm. "One has huge houses that remind me of California. But it's the other that I would love to live in. Wonderful little houses in a wooded area with enormous yards."

Adam was asking himself while she talked what she might want of him. He had in his field no contacts that could be of any use to a real estate broker. Actually, he was tired of the subject, having been too often bored by Fred Davis's talk of malls and mortgages. Nevertheless, he listened and watched her. Randi's voice had a mesmerizing effect, as did the way her fingers played with things. Not nervously, as high-strung women played with them, but lightly, touching the coral at her throat or pushing a strand of hair away from her cheek.

"Randolph is really growing. I guess people are attracted because it's one of the few places in the state that has some hills. And being only fifteen miles from Elmsford, it's convenient. So I expect to do well. I'm a good broker. I guess it's because I enjoy meeting people, all different kinds, and trying to match them up with the right house. It's funny how I can generally tell after ten minutes or so what their tastes are." She smiled. "Now you, you don't care where you live as long as there are bookshelves and a workable kitchen. Do you still make your special chili?"

"Good Lord, you remember that?"

"I remember everything, Adam."

He looked away from her, glancing obliquely at a pair of Japanese men across the aisle, and wondering what they might be doing in a place like Elmsford. Abruptly, he had become uncomfortable.

"Now tell me something about yourself, will you? Here I've been doing all the talking and haven't let you get a word in edgewise."

"That's all right. I don't have that much to tell."

"Don't be silly. Of course you have. Everybody does."

"I suppose I have if you're interested in computer engineering, microchips, and stuff."

He was aware that in an awkward way he was trying to put her off and to keep his privacy. But she persisted.

"Oh, I'll listen if you want to talk about them, but I'd always rather hear about people. Your children must be pretty grown up by now, aren't they? I forgot how old they are."

"Thirteen, eleven, and nine."

"Do you have a picture with you?"

"I don't think so."

"You mean you don't carry a picture in your wallet? I don't believe you."

Suddenly, he reversed himself. Suddenly, he felt an urge to display his handsome children, the happy proofs of what, in spite of her rejection, he had achieved without her. And handing Randi the snapshot of his family with himself included, the one that had adorned their Christmas cards, he felt a small thrill of pride along with a touch, a mere touch, of revenge.

"Beautiful," she said wistfully. "How lucky you are."

"I think so."

"You know what I'm thinking, don't you?"

Indeed he did, but he was not going to be inveigled into any poignant reminiscences.

"Things will work out for you, too," he said. "You'll find someone."

"It had better happen soon. I'm thirty-seven."

"People are starting families later these days. Maybe it's even better," he told her, not meaning it.

Placing her elbows on the table and her face in her hands, she leaned forward. A gap forming between the buttons on her blouse gave him a glimpse of cleavage; then into his memory there leapt a picture of her breasts; he recalled them exactly, the size and the feel.

And again, he looked toward the Japanese, who had risen to depart. One of them had two cameras slung around his neck.

"Why do you look away?" asked Randi.

"Did I? I wasn't aware of it."

"You do keep looking away. You think I'm going to bite you or something."

"You're talking foolishly," he said, feeling the heat mount into his cheeks.

"You're right. I am, and I'm sorry. I shouldn't tease you."

He frowned. "No, you shouldn't. I'm too old for that sort of thing, and so are you."

"You win. I sometimes get into a silly mood, that's all it is. Shall we have a refill?"

"No. I have to get home."

"Of course."

There was, then, nothing to say, which made for a difficult moment. He certainly was not going to make any of the usual remarks, such as *I'll call you,* or *call me when you can.* It's too bad, he thought ironically, that my mother taught me to be gracious. Otherwise I could just grab my coat and get away.

With grace, therefore, he helped her on with her jacket, saying, "Good luck, Randi. I'm sure you'll have it."

She gave him a rosy smile. Flower face, he remembered. Damn her.

"Wait. Take my card. It won't be official till my license comes next month, but here's my home address and phone in case you come across anybody who's house hunting. I'd appreciate the business."

"Glad to," he said, and they parted.

On the way home he felt confusion. Should he mention this encounter to Margaret or not? Mulling it over, he decided not; to do so would give the matter an importance that it definitely did not have.

It angered him that his mind, which had for so long been wiped clean of any thoughts about Randi, was now wasting itself on absurd conjectures. It was ridiculous for him to be considering even for the space of an instant what course his life would have run if he had married Randi. And yet, in spite of his will, his mind persisted. He would probably not have taken the job in Elmsford, he would have wanted to flee from here, from all the embarrassment. . . . Then Megan and Julie and Danny would not exist. And he recalled those miserable days when he had fought with himself, had so desperately sought a decent way to tell Margaret that he no longer wanted her. . . . He wondered whether she might possibly have felt a lack in him then, or worried that something was wrong. If she had, and he hoped she had not, he had certainly made up for it all these years. He was certain that all men must speculate about their old love affairs, but he had never asked anyone. There was a basic privacy in him. . . .

He made a loose fist and pounded the steering wheel. Idiotic thoughts!

The car turned the corner and moved down the street toward home. In the warm old kitchen Margaret would be preparing their dinner, the girls helping. Sometimes when she had a huge pile of papers to correct, the girls made dinner by themselves, and it was always a good one; their mother brought them up well to be competent. On the white lawn he saw Danny, with his great sheepdog Rufus, waiting for his father. And the lighted house, the boy, the snow-hushed evening, the first stars, all filled him with a thankfulness for which he had no words. He was close to tears.

FIVE

Danny needed a new desk. He was nine and a half, and very tall, almost tall enough to use Nina's desk, which still stood in her room between the windows. But Margaret had objected, "I don't want anything disturbed in Nina's room."

Nothing had been changed there. The striking plaid carpet that Nina had chosen for her birthday present when she was fourteen—a carpet that had horrified Margaret until she had seen how right it was—looked new. The Monet prints still hung on the wall, and the stuffed kangaroo still sat on the white bed.

"I'm sure she wouldn't mind if Danny were to take the desk," said Adam.

"That's not the point. This is still Nina's room until she marries and has one of her own."

She knew she was being unduly sentimental, that Nina would never be coming back to this room and no longer considered this house to be home. Yet there was something in her own heart that could not let go all the way, even though it had been she herself who had urged the girl to take her independent path into the world. And she knew that the "something" was her own indelible picture of the child in the dirty dress, the tiny waif whose mother was dead and whose father was unknown.

"Louise told me about a man who makes wonderful pine furniture," she said. "It's sturdy and not at all expensive. He's upriver on this side in Santee. How about riding out there Saturday morning? We could take a picnic lunch and visit the Indian museum. There's a new exhibit, I heard."

It turned out to be a day that pleased them all, with something for everyone. Danny chose a table desk, large enough to accommodate his many paste-and-cardboard projects. In the museum shop the girls bought white leather moccasins with Indian beading. At the side of a country road they all ate roast beef sandwiches, oranges, and Margaret's chocolate brownies. The midday sun was filtered through new leafage, a tender apple-green. Not very high above them came Canada geese in a great V-formation, speeding with their long necks thrust forward toward their summer home. Their deep honk cut the noon quiet.

How sweet my children are, thought Margaret, watching them as they craned their heads up toward the sky. So clean, so decent, so miraculously untouched by evil or pain, considering the world of the 1990s. They are my work of art, she thought. I grew them. And that, too, is a miracle.

"It's nice to see hills," Megan remarked after a time.

"These are nothing," Adam said. "They're only little slopes, only a beginning. If you want to see real hills, you have to keep going north. North or west. A long way."

"Hear the wind," said Julie, who was the more sensitive sister.

"There's no wind," Danny said scornfully. "Look at the trees. They aren't even moving."

"Yes, they are. Look up yourself."

"One inch. That's just a breeze. It wouldn't make a sound."

"Who knows what kind of trees these are?" asked Adam, interrupting.

"Pines, of course," said Megan.

"Yes, but what kind?"

No one knew, so naturally Adam was left to explain. He has such a skillful way of deflecting arguments, Margaret thought. He could have been a marvelous teacher. Indeed, within the family he *was* the teacher. And she thought as always how curious it was that he who was usually so reserved, so unwilling, in social situations, was totally expansive with children, any children, not just his own. It was as if he felt completely secure with them. Yet why should a man of Adam's quality be insecure anywhere?

"These are red pines, and fairly young. They grow much taller than this, up to eighty feet."

"I guess they'll be very old by that time," said Megan, who was factual and exact.

"Not very old. About two hundred years or a little more."

"Two hundred years!"

"That's not old for a tree. Why, hemlocks can live more than five hundred years. And," Adam continued, obviously enjoying himself, "sequoias in California can live—who knows anything about them?"

"Two thousand years or maybe more," Megan said.

"Why don't we go see them?" Danny demanded.

"California's a long way from here," his father answered.

Danny argued, "But Cousin Gil and Cousin Louise went there."

"Cousin Gil is a rich man. He has his own business."

Margaret wished Adam wouldn't say things like that. He sounded bitter, although he could not have wanted to sound that way, and there was no reason why he should be bitter. It was not as if he or she had any craving for luxury that they were unable to fulfill. Did he not even disparage what he took to be Nina's "materialism"?

"We don't have to be rich to take the Jeep across country," she said. "There are lots of cabins and motels that don't cost a fortune. I think it would be great fun, important, too, to see our country."

"Maybe next summer," Adam answered. "We'll see."

"Why not this summer, Adam?" she suggested gently. "Start at the Badlands, then Utah—Mom and I were in Salt Lake City once, and it was fascinating—then Yosemite, and maybe San Francisco if there's time."

"I don't know. You forget, I'm not my own boss."

"I don't forget," she said quietly. "Come, people, let's gather up the papers and soda cans. Leave the place the way we found it and start home."

Danny wanted to know when he was to have his desk.

"Dad will bring it home next week, when it's ready."

On the way the children suddenly demanded Cokes.

"We can stop off in Randolph Corners," Margaret said. "We came through it, didn't we? I didn't pay attention."

"It's Randolph Crossing," said Adam, who had certainly paid attention.

And remembering now as he drove along, he began to feel ashamed of this unaccustomed rudeness. Furthermore, it was a stupid way to behave; it was as if he were afraid of the woman.

Yet, what did she want? On the one hand, he thought perhaps he knew very well what she wanted. On the other hand, though, he might be all wrong, merely a conceited fool who thought he was irresistible. He probably was all wrong.

"This is a pretty little town," Margaret remarked when they arrived at the soda fountain. "Look across the street. There's a florist, a dress shop, and an attractive bookstore. There didn't used to be much here, as I remember."

"There isn't much now," Adam said. "There haven't been more than a dozen cars passing through in the last five minutes. Something tells me that they've picked a bad time to gentrify the place."

"Oh, 'gentrify,' " said the waitress, joining the conversation. "It'll be great when it happens, we can sure use the business. I know we sure can, but there's no sign of it yet, that's for sure." A large woman, poised between middle age and old age, she spoke with authority. "Up there in The Grove, that's what they call those new houses on the hill, mighty nice houses, too, I wouldn't mind having one, ha-ha. Me! Fat chance. Up there, half of them aren't sold. They can't move them. Well, it'll take time, I guess. Things'll pick up. Want a refill on those Cokes, kids?"

"I think they've had—" Margaret began, when Adam interrupted.

"Things'll pick up. They always do. But it must be hard on the real estate people, waiting around for the pickup."

"I guess so. Those women next door, they come in here every day for lunch, and I hear them talk. Mind, they're not starving, but it's slow, that's all. Well, you want the check."

"Talked your head off, didn't she?" Adam said when they were in the car.

"She was lonesome."

Margaret was always quick to catch impressions. She really noticed people. I do not, he thought.

"I had the feeling that she's a widow. I imagine she has children who've moved away and whom she never sees. She lives alone and doesn't get much chance to talk. A sad, abandoned woman."

"All that in two minutes' worth of conversation? You ought to write novels. Sad novels."

Of course, he was teasing her. And yet there was truth behind the teasing: Margaret had *heart*.

Everyone else in the family being occupied on the following Saturday, Adam went alone to fetch the desk. On the way back he took the route that led through Randolph Crossing. The other way was more direct, but the day was brilliant, and the road on this side of the river went past pleasant scenery through diminishing hills down toward home.

After a while, as he neared Randolph Crossing, he turned the radio off to examine his motive without distraction. The scenic route was certainly the more enjoyable, and it was quite possible he might have taken it even without any other consideration. Still, he had to admit to an element of—should he say "curiosity"?—in his choice. It would be interesting to learn what she was doing with that helter-skelter life of hers; that is, it would be interesting if by any chance he should encounter her. That, however, was most unlikely. In that case, no harm done. And if he should not encounter her, why, no harm done either. He was really making much ado about nothing.

It was almost noon when he entered the main street. He was hungry and the thought of a sandwich was agreeable; he would buy a paper and read while he ate. The street was very quiet, so he parked a few doors down and waited for some signs of activity, although there really was no reason why he should not go in at once. Nevertheless, he waited long enough to feel drowsy in the sunshine that was pouring into the car, long enough to see the shop's door swing open and a group of men go inside. Then he, too, went in, took a table facing the door, was greeted like an old friend by the waitress, and gave his order.

When the door opened to admit some chattering women, he pretended to be absorbed in the newspaper. Conscious of a queer tension in his muscles, as if he were expecting something, he hoped it would happen while at the same time hoping it would not happen.

"Adam!" she cried. "What on earth are you doing here?"

Immediately he recalled the encounter in the Fifth Avenue bookshop. And he hoped that his face was not red, but knowing it must be, he consequently heard himself replying, very awkwardly, "I had errands, some furniture, having a little lunch. And you?"

"I work here, right in the office next door. This is Adam Crane, everybody, an old friend. You won't mind, will you, if I desert you today and sit with him?"

No one minded, and after the introductions Randi took her seat with Adam. Planting her elbows on the table in her usual fashion, she held her mischievous face between her hands. The word *twinkle* shot into his mind; her bright eyes and her shining mouth were twinkling at him.

"Now tell me, if you can, why you've been snubbing me."

"Snubbing you? That's ridiculous."

To avoid her eyes he kept his eyes fixed on her mouth. The lower lip was fuller than he remembered, not that he had given much thought to it in all these years. The rosy upper lip was scalloped. Between the parted lips an even line of teeth was barely visible. Now suddenly he remembered that her teeth were perfect.

"What are you looking at? Is my lipstick smeared?"

He faltered. "Nothing. No, it's not smeared."

"You haven't answered my question."

"Oh. You mean those phone calls?"

"Yes. I mean those phone calls. I'm sure your mother taught you better manners."

"I'm sorry. I should have called back that time. We've been awfully busy, overworked really, and I simply forgot. I'm sorry."

" 'That time!' I called five times. You didn't 'forget' all those times. You've been avoiding me."

"I'm sorry," he repeated, thinking, *Fool. I'm being an ass, a tongue-tied idiot.*

Randi laughed. "Oh, Adam, grow up! I called because I thought you might give me some helpful professional advice about this area, this part of the state. You grew up here, after all."

"I'm really sorry," he said then, and was aware that this was the fourth time he had said it.

"You should be. But it doesn't matter. I've found other people to advise me. Is that pizza any good?"

"What? Oh, the one I'm eating?"

"No. The one that man over there is eating. What's wrong with you, anyway?"

"Sorry. I wasn't thinking. I had asked for a sandwich, and they got the orders mixed up and brought this instead. It looked good, so I kept it."

"Give me a bite. If I like it, I'll get one too. And stop saying you're sorry, will you?"

Before he could get up to take a fork from the next table, she had seized his.

"I've used it," he protested.

"So what? Have you got AIDS or something? No, with a nice, steady, faithful, married man like you there's no danger, is there? I'm not worried."

It seemed to him that she was taunting him. There was mockery in those glinting eyes and that hint of laughter.

And he, who had truly never strayed from his wife, had to protest, to answer with scorn. "What do you think you are? A palm-reader or a crystal-gazer? You don't know the first thing about me, Randi. So don't make a fool of yourself."

She looked at him thoughtfully for a moment before saying, "You're right. Seriously, I do need some advice again. I'm going to have a small pizza and tell you my problem—unless you're in a hurry. Are you?"

Adam pushed his sleeve up from his watch. It was half past twelve. He had been planning to get home quickly, having promised Danny to help give shaggy Rufus a badly needed bath; he was also supposed to bring Julie home from a friend's house while Margaret and Megan took the other car to go shopping.

When he hesitated, she said, "It'll take ten minutes. Here it is. I think I mentioned that my apartment's a sublet. It's a nice apartment, just around the corner at the next intersection with this street, very convenient, but my lease is up and there are no more apartments for rent."

She paused to take a bite of the pizza. He liked the fact that she waited until the food was wholly swallowed before resuming speech, for he was critical, and it disgusted him to see half-eaten food in someone's mouth. Randi was fastidious, from her polished toenails to her pink fingernails. But Margaret's hands were pretty, too, though in a different way. Her hands were more useful. And he pictured her strong hands that cooked, worked in a chemistry laboratory, and planted vegetables. They were so unlike, these two women. They even ate differently. Margaret ate moderately, while Randi ate hungrily; she did everything hungrily. . . . So, haphazardly, his thoughts raced.

Randi came to a conclusion. "The minute I heard about this house going to foreclosure, I realized that it would be a great buy. It's not too far away, and yet it's like being in the woods."

"Woods? Where?"

"Weren't you listening? I've just been describing that little group of houses in what we call The Grove. We're the agents for it, and I'm wondering whether a woman alone should make an investment and take on the responsibility of a house. I need some practical advice from a practical man."

"If you like it that much and can afford it, do it. You won't always be alone, anyway."

"You don't know that."

"Yes, I do. You're a good-looking woman. Don't be coy about it."

"My mailbox hasn't been exactly stuffed with marriage proposals lately. I remind you again, I'm thirty-seven."

Margaret was thirty-eight. Why did his brain keep signaling these comparisons? It was as if a line had been drawn down the middle of a piece of paper with a name on either side. It's—it's *sick,* he thought, now furious with himself.

"Be that as it may," she said briskly now, "I really need an impartial opinion about the house. My firm naturally wants the commission, and I understand that, but it does mean that I can't rely on their opinion. I was wondering—I mean, now that you happen to be here—whether you would take a look at the house for me."

Again he consulted his watch. It was undoubtedly very foolish of him to involve himself with her, even so far as to go look at a house. Innocent as that was, it would probably entail future conversations over the telephone, and he didn't need that, didn't want that.

"It's only a stone's throw away," she urged, and, when he still hesitated, burst out laughing. "I swear you think I'm going to seduce you! How dumb can you be, Adam? That business is ancient history. It hasn't got the slightest connection with your doing me a friendly favor."

"Okay, okay, let's go. My car's outside."

They rode back in the direction from which he had come earlier and branched off the highway. He kept glancing uneasily at the clock on the dashboard, calculating the time it would take to reach home. He should not have let her talk him into this business! He should not!

Randi inquired, "Is that an antique you have back there?"

"No, a good copy. A man makes them up near Santee. It's for my son."

"I remember the snapshot you showed me. He's the one with curly red hair. He's cute."

"He hates his hair."

"It's like his mother's, isn't it? That time we met in New York I thought she was so pretty. Different looking. Ladylike."

He wished she wouldn't bring Margaret into the conversation. It made him feel guilty. Then the fact that he could feel guilty when he was doing absolutely nothing wrong made him indignant. No one said that a man, because he married, had to account for every minute of his time or every person he ever spoke to. Not at all.

"I'm so glad you're happy, Adam. You deserve to be." There was a pause. "You are happy, aren't you?"

"Yes, very. Very happy."

"I'm glad. I really am."

The conversation was becoming too personal, and again that feeling of unease swept over him. Nevertheless, a certain curiosity piqued him too. And almost without his willing it a question popped out of his mouth.

"Why did you do it?"

"Do what?"

"You know."

"Leave you?" And when he did not answer, she said, "Because I was a fool. A stupid, inexperienced young fool with a lot of foolish daydreams about having a glamorous life somewhere over the rainbow in California. Besides, I was jealous. You didn't move fast enough."

Again he said nothing. He should never have asked the question, should never have brought the dead past into life or any semblance of life.

"However," she said gaily, "that, as I said just now, is ancient history. Turn off here onto the dirt road. I told you it wouldn't take long."

Not long, he thought, worrying about the time, only an extra three quarters of an hour.

Running through pine woods up the side of a modest slope, the narrow road passed half a dozen picturesque low houses, each settled into and separated from the rest by old trees and heavy shrubbery. At the dead end they turned into a driveway.

The house was, he supposed, what one would probably describe as "modern," and yet, although it was not built of logs, it had an indefinable feel, a reminder of some historical American log cabin. When they got out of the car, he followed her through knee-high grass toward a gap in the line of trees.

"Come over here," she said. "You can almost see the river way down there. With binoculars I'm sure you could see it clearly."

A small wind whistled in the pines. The springtime air was soft and fragrant. He felt a sudden lassitude. He could have lain down in the warm grass and watched her standing in that shaft of sunlight with the wind billowing her skirt. Instead, he turned to the house, saying brusquely, "I haven't much time. Let's go in."

The house had the peculiar smell of vacancy and desertion. The paint was faded on the walls. The shades were torn. The compact little kitchen had been neglected; handles had broken off the stove, and the linoleum was damaged.

"Of course, it needs a new kitchen," Randi said.

"That's expensive."

"There's a man in town who redoes kitchens on Saturdays and Sundays. He's very reasonable. I love this great room, don't you? I'd put a round table in the bay, a pair of love seats at the fireplace—but

I'm boring you. I always forget, men aren't interested in placing furniture."

"Unless they happen to be decorators. My young cousin Nina works for a pair in New York."

"Nina? Was she the other girl in the snapshot?"

Then he must have shown her his whole folder of pictures. Sharp, she was, missing nothing, remembering everything.

"She's unusual looking, I thought. Not pretty like Margaret, but striking. So she's a New Yorker?"

"No, she used to live here." He was irritated, thinking, This is too intimate, she wants to know too much. Why should she care where Nina lives? But also: Why had he mentioned Nina in the first place? Because he was making clumsy conversation, that was why. Because he didn't know what to do with himself.

"Come see the bedrooms. There are two, but this is the one I would use. The bed would go here, opposite the clerestory windows. I love these windows. You have total privacy, and still, as you lie here, you can see the treetops and the stars or the moon."

He looked away from the place where the bed would stand. It would be a fluffy bed, no doubt, with a pink quilt and down pillows. He went into the bathroom, gave a cursory inspection, and reported that the tile was in good condition with no need for grouting. Suddenly he was in a rush, almost a panic, as if some danger, something unknown and threatening, were about to loom before him in this house.

"Can we hurry?" he said impatiently. "I'm late."

On the way back an uncomfortable silence settled, so uncomfortable that he needed to break it.

"You really should hire a contractor or building inspector to check the roof and the plumbing, the whole place. I'm not qualified to give you an opinion."

Moreover, he thought, she knew I wasn't qualified when she asked me to go here with her, and I knew it too.

"You can drop me at my apartment, please," Randi said.

When they drew up at the curb, she gave formal thanks, adding, "I'd ask you in if you weren't in a hurry. It was really kind of you to do this, and I appreciate it, Adam. I'll take your advice and let you know what the man says. But did you like the house?" Her pink face was turned up to his in appeal.

"Yes," he said, putting the car in gear. "It's lovely. It suits you."

Flower face. A flower-faced witch.

He reached home late, annoyed with himself and more annoyed to

see Fred Davis's car parked in front of the house. He hoped Margaret
had not invited him to dinner. Fred could be too full of cheer and good
humor; at the moment Adam was not in the mood to respond in kind.

"Where's everybody?" he demanded, rushing into the kitchen
where Margaret was unpacking groceries. "Sorry I'm late. What's Fred
doing here? If you'll help me take the desk out of the Jeep—it's not
heavy, just awkward—I'll rush over and get Julie."

"Whoa, whoa. You're all out of breath. Julie's home. Fred went for
her. He's in the yard putting up the croquet set. Danny couldn't wait till
tomorrow."

"Don't tell me you phoned Fred on purpose to go for Julie."

"Of course not. He just happened to come by with something to
tell us, something nice, and he offered to pick her up, since you were
late. What happened?"

"I had a flat."

"Oh, dear. New tires too."

"It wasn't much. It happened near a service station, and they fixed
it."

Now, why the devil hadn't he told the truth? *I met Randi Bunting—
remember her?—and went to look at a house.* All innocent, clean, and
aboveboard. He felt contempt for a liar as for a thief. So why had he
lied?

"What's the nice thing Fred has to tell us?"

"Here he is. He'll tell you himself."

Fred's amiable face wore a happy grin. He sat down at the kitchen
table, took a crumpled map from his pocket, and spread it out.

"See here, a hundred miles east of Banff? Remember Denise's
brother-in-law? You met him once when they were visiting from Canada. Well, you remember, we told you about their summer camp?
Camp! It's a little too splendid to be called a camp. It's on a lake with
beautiful cabins. The main house is large and, well, the good news is,
I've been invited up for three weeks this summer and they want me to
bring friends. I can bring five or six, whomever I want, especially if there
are children, because their own grandkids are coming too. So, I'm inviting you. All of you. What do you say?"

Everyone looked toward Adam. Every face was animated. Recalling last week's conversation about a summer trip, he felt a sinking in his
chest: He did not want to go. And they were expecting his enthusiasm.

He said warily, "It certainly is good of you, Fred, but I don't know
what to say."

All three of his children had imploring eyes. "Oh, say yes, Dad!"

"It's not so simple. I work, you know."

"Of course. But you're entitled to a vacation. It'll be a great time," Fred assured him. "Water-skiing, canoe trips, a sailboat, even an island for picnics. The lake is huge. There's a tennis court too. There's everything."

A millionaire's paradise, Adam thought, having heard something long ago about Denise's sister having married into a Canadian mining fortune. They will be sitting around after dinner talking about where they're going next winter, whether to Morocco or Tahiti.

Margaret, who knew his predilections, caught his eye. "They're very lovely people," she said. "I remember very well when they visited Denise and Fred. Very simple people. Friendly."

She wanted to go. Perhaps if he hadn't had things on his mind, he would go in spite of his reluctance, just to please her. But there were things on his mind. The rumor now was that Ramsey would not be going to the European market after all, which meant that he, Adam, would not be moving up the ladder. And there were no good lateral moves in the offing either. If you weren't a glad-hander, if you didn't have what they call "personality," with a big, flattering grin on your face, you got nowhere. . . .

They were waiting for him to answer, and he said, "It hurts me to disappoint you, but I can't go. I can't take the time off. The vacation schedule was made up months ago."

"Why don't you ask? Try," Margaret urged.

"It can't be changed."

This was not true. The schedule was fairly flexible, and Ramsey was a decent sort who would, if Adam were to ask, quite probably say yes.

There was a silence, a heavy, poignant silence that pained him. And with an attempt at gladness he cried out, "Listen. There's no reason why you all can't go without me. I won't mind at all. I've a lot to do here, and—"

"Oh," Margaret said, looking mournful, "what kind of vacation would it be without you? We've never done anything like this before, and I don't want to begin now."

"Mom!" the three wailed. "Mom!"

"Two years ago I went alone to that conference in Washington and was gone for a week. What was so bad about that?"

"It was entirely different. It was business, and you had to go."

It seemed to Adam that what he felt now was fear, a vague fear of multiple uncertainties that he could not and would not put into words.

What it came down to was simply that he did not want to leave home, did not want to be a charity guest among strangers, did not want to leave the office where, during his absence, he argued, anything might happen. Besides, the house had no burglar alarm. They were too expensive. And supposing vandals were to break in and destroy his magnificent new computer, the piano, and all the books? Then there were the dogs. Rufus had never been put in kennels. . . .

Some of these reasons that were churning around in his brain, maybe all of them, were idiotic. Or maybe they were not. Nevertheless, *he did not want to go.*

Danny said stoutly, "It's not fair, Dad, you know it isn't."

Typically, Fred was tactful. "I'll run along now and leave you all to think it over. I don't need an answer this minute."

"You won't stay for supper?" asked Margaret.

"No, thanks. I'll take a rain check. Let me know."

The evening meal began, quite naturally, with a discussion of the invitation, a subdued discussion, since reasonableness was the style of the house. At the end it was decided Adam's way.

"I spoke to Nina while you were gone today," Margaret told him when later they were alone. "She's invited, too, and she's thrilled. She's going to fly up for ten days. Business is quiet in the summer, so there was no problem about getting time off. It's really wonderful of Fred, isn't it? He could have asked anybody he wanted."

"Apparently, he wanted you. That's nothing new, is it? I suppose I ought to be jealous of him."

The subject of Fred's early love had long since been exhausted. It was a tired joke. On this occasion, however, it was just something to say.

"Maybe I'm a fool for giving him such an easy opportunity."

"How silly can you be?"

Near the window, she was brushing her hair. Gilded by evening light, loose curls circled her pearl-white face, with its deep gray eyes and its delicate high cheekbones, like a wreath. He saw anew how happy she was about going away with the children. Also, he knew that she was puzzled, or more accurately, troubled about his refusal to go. But she would never argue the point. She sensed that he was worried again by the uncertainties at the firm and that he did not want to talk about them. How well she knew him! And how well he knew her! She was as familiar to him as the palm of his own hand. After sixteen married years, not to mention the years that had gone before, there could be no surprises for either one of them.

"You'll have a good time with Nina there. She always livens things up," he assured her.

"I would rather have you," she said. Then, coming to put her arms around him, pressing against him, "Sometimes I think you don't know how much I love you, Adam."

He kissed her. "I do know. You're a lovely woman. Lovely."

This was not what she wanted. She wanted him to take her, roughly and hastily, to the bed. Then, tenderly, to make love to her. But a man couldn't simply turn himself on as one turns a faucet. Well, people were different, and she was always more passionate than he. Maybe he was simply growing old.

"You're tired," she said, releasing him. "Go on to sleep, and I will too."

SIX

A fter sending his family off on the plane, after he had stood
watching it rush down the runway and lift off, Adam drove home
to a list of chores. The roses had to be sprayed for black spot,
the vegetable patch needed weeding, the bird-feeder had to be filled,
and the dogs had to be fed. When he had dutifully accomplished all
these routine things, he went into the house with a sense of content-
ment, satisfied to acknowledge himself as a homebody.

Margaret had filled the freezer with good things, soups, lasagna,
baked chicken, and even an apple pie, enough for three men. He sat
down at the kitchen table, propped a book against the coffeepot, and
read while he ate. When he was finished, he washed his dishes and,
taking the two dogs, walked down the street to the schoolyard to watch
the fifth graders play ball, then followed his usual circular route for half
an hour's brisk walk.

"A fine night, hey, guys?" he said, addressing Rufus and Zack,
who, wagging agreement, apparently shared his sense of well-being.

Back in the house he went to the desk, spread out his work without
danger of any interruption, and resumed his study of a new software
code. It had already been licensed by some nine companies; the question was now whether Advanced Data Systems should be using it too.
His report, giving pros and cons, would be carefully evaluated. And his
future direction in the company might well depend on it. So he spent a
diligent few hours, almost hearing the click of his own brain, itself as
quick and accurate as a computer. After that he listened for a few
minutes to the news, was satisfied, and went to bed.

The next day was Sunday. It was early when Margaret telephoned to say that they had arrived safely after a wonderful ride through the mountains, that the place was gorgeous, the children were thrilled, Nina sent love, and Danny wanted him to remember Rufus's evening treat.

"You sound sleepy. I woke you up," she said.

"No, no. I'm almost dressed. On the way downstairs to make bacon and eggs for myself. The hell with cholesterol this morning."

"I miss you so much already, and I feel guilty being here in all this luxury while you're home eating your breakfast all alone."

"Margaret, honey, I'm fine. Just enjoy yourself. Give the kids my love."

Actually he had been still in bed, lying there in the midway state between sleep and active wakefulness. It was strange not to feel Margaret in bed next to him. And it occurred to him that it was also strange that he felt absolutely no qualms about her spending three weeks in the company of a man who so obviously admired her. He would have told anyone who might ask him that Margaret was the last woman in the world, etcetera, etcetera. Still, most husbands would be jealous. Even with a wife as trustworthy as Margaret, they would be wary. So why wasn't he?

After a while he roused himself from these aimless musings and went downstairs, ate his breakfast, and took the Sunday paper outdoors. The heat was rising. By ten o'clock the birds were silent and no leaf moved. Back indoors where it was cooler, he returned to the computer. But by midafternoon he was sweating. He lay down and turned on the radio to learn that a heat wave had begun; it was to be a thorough Midwest wave, predicted to last all week or longer. He thought how nice it must be to have a pool. Two or three of their friends had pools. He wished one of them would invite him over right now. But the fact was that these friendly contacts were really the result of Margaret's associations with the wives; the husbands were not his friends. It wasn't that they disliked him and therefore had deliberately withheld any invitations. It was simply that they had not given him any thought.

Then he remembered that he had eaten no lunch. It was now four-thirty, too late for lunch and too early for dinner. But what difference? He'd eat because he was hungry. After that he'd watch television, then go up to the bedroom, where there was air-conditioning, and read for a while.

The day dragged to its end. He looked forward to Monday.

Randi said, "I told you I'd phone you when I had news about the house. I hope I'm not interrupting you at work."

As it happened, he did have a very important appointment for lunch, but still it wouldn't hurt to be a few minutes late.

"No, go ahead. What's your news?"

"The inspector said the house is okay, so I've bought it! I'm terribly excited and a little scared, because of course I had to take out a pretty big mortgage. But, oh, hell, you only live once, right?"

"Right," Adam said.

"I ran up there just this morning before work. I can't believe it's mine! It was so cool! I guess it's all those trees or being on a hillside. It was as cool as my air-conditioned apartment. How is it down in Elmsford?"

He had a flash of her standing in the wind that day with her skirt billowed out like a sail. He seemed to remember the skirt was yellow.

"Fine in the office, but an oven on the street. And in my house," he added, for no reason at all.

"No air-conditioning at home?" she asked.

"The house is a hundred years old, and it's big. You'd practically have to tear it apart to put ducts in the walls. Not worth it," he said.

"It must be hard on the children in this weather. Kids run around and get so overheated."

"Fortunately, they're all away. In Canada, on a lake."

Now, why was he having a conversation like this one? Randi didn't give a hoot about his house or his children.

"You must be lonesome," she said.

"Not really. I've a ton of work to bring home from the office. That fills the evenings." A silence followed until he thought to say, "Congratulations! It's a big step for you to take, but I'm sure you'll be glad you've taken it."

"Oh, I will. Maybe sometime you—and the family—if you get up this way, maybe you'll stop in and see the place after I've fixed it up."

"Well, thanks."

"I do hope you wouldn't feel awkward about doing it, Adam. Because all that old business is past. I've told you so, and I'm telling you again. You do understand, don't you?"

"Sure. Yes."

"So I would love to see you, Adam. Anytime."

Bill Jenks poked his head in at the door and, pointing to his watch, mouthed, "Lunch."

Adam nodded, speaking into the telephone at the same time. "Someone's here for me. I'm late. I have to go. I'll talk to you."

I won't talk to her, he said to himself. It's trouble. I don't need trouble. I don't want it.

I would love to see you, Adam. Anytime.

Pleading a headache, he left the office early. He was tense all through; the cords in his neck were taut.

At the lunch meeting Jenks, who had taken a quick look at Adam's report, had expressed some doubt that Ramsey would be satisfied with it. "I think he expects something more extensive," Jenks had said. When pressed for a suggestion he had been elusive, and Adam had a fleeting impression that Jenks was enjoying his discomfiture, that he actually wanted Ramsey to be displeased. On the other hand, this impression might be a total mistake; it worried him that he was often too suspicious; Margaret told him he was. But then, Margaret was not competing in this hard world, where a man's reputation could be destroyed in a few minutes by a Saturday-morning cabal on a golf course.

In this gloomy mood he arrived home, let the dogs out, took a shower, and changed into shorts. Then he went outside and filled the birdbath, which had gone dry under the blazing sun. Hoping to relieve his tension through exercise, he got out the hand mower and cleared a few swaths on the front lawn. But the heat was intolerable, and he had to go back into the house. The dogs lay down on the bare floor in the dark rear hall, and Adam took another shower. For a few minutes he thought about getting a dinner out of the freezer and putting it into the microwave, but he was not hungry enough. So he made a sandwich instead and ate it in the living room in front of the television. The five o'clock news was on. There was nothing of any interest to him.

I would love to see you, Adam. Anytime.

He sat with his head in his hands. When he looked up, he found in the direct line of his vision the photograph made last year of Margaret and the children. He got up and went to the window, walked back, and stared at the piano keys. Running his fingers down the keyboard, he startled the silence. He lay down on the sofa, hoping to doze, but was unable to.

It's all in the head, they said. Without a doubt it began there, he thought, as long-forgotten pictures flashed their colors. But then it traveled, running and beating through the veins and arteries so that he could barely contain the crazy explosion inside him. His heart seemed to plunge. He thought there must be something terribly wrong with him, that he was losing control of his decent common sense.

And suddenly a surge of the wildest sexual desire shook him through and through. . . .

It was twenty minutes past five. Traffic going north on the river road was never very heavy. He could be there in minutes. . . .

If she should not be home, he would have lost nothing by going and might even have gained something, might have found out that he did not, after all, want her.

At six o'clock he stopped in front of the apartment. A wave of fear swept over him: He should not have come. He should listen to reason, turn the car about, and go back. Yet he knew he would not. . . . And getting out of the car, he walked up the brick path between petunia beds and rang the bell.

"Who is it?" Randi called.

"Adam. You said I might come anytime."

"I'm in my robe, but if you don't mind, come on in."

Suddenly and inexplicably embarrassed, he looked not at her but at the room. A banal comment was the first remark to come to mind.

"Believe it or not, I still remember that picture."

A landscape in oil hung over the sofa; garish flowers surrounded a white Italianate villa lying under an impossibly blue sky.

"Yes, I love it. I took it with me to California and I brought it back. That and some dishes that belonged to my mother, along with my bed, are things I'll never part with."

The door into the bedroom was half open. He seemed to recall that it always used to be so. In the small apartment where he had grown up with his mother, the bedrooms had never been exposed in that way. Margaret, too, would certainly keep the doors closed if the bedrooms were in the line of vision. But Randi—Randi just *lived.* He wasn't sure whether he approved or not.

She sat down in the corner of the sofa close to his chair. Her white robe, of some heavy, shining silk, fell open on one side, revealing a firm thigh. He stared at it, wondering what had happened to the fierce desire that had brought him to this place. And he was suddenly engulfed by a wave of fear.

She stretched and sighed. "It's good to be home. I had a long day, but I think I made a sale. And you? How've you been since I talked to you at noon?"

He surprised himself with his own reply. "Restless."

She gave him a long, thoughtful look, starting at his feet and rising up to where the look made contact with his eyes.

"You're all buttoned up," she said. "You're so tight, you're ready to burst. You need to get loose."

"That's easier said than done."

"Let me massage your neck and shoulders. Bend over."

Her fingers were strong and hard. As they pressed and prodded, they soothed. Her murmuring voice soothed along with them.

"Here we go, here we go. You're all in knots."

She began to hum. The sound was tuneless, monotonous, and curiously sweet. He closed his eyes, letting a soft relief pour through his blood. After a while he said, "You must be tired."

"No, it's good exercise for me."

She was pushing so hard, leaning so close, that he could feel the warmth of her breath on the back of his neck.

"How did you learn to do this?"

"It came naturally. Like this." And she kissed the back of his neck.

He jumped up, turned around, and stared at her, at the dare in her eyes and the crooked smile at the corners of her lips.

"Well," she said, "you do remember what you came for, don't you?"

He could barely speak. "Yes. Yes."

"Well?" she said.

"Come here. Take that thing—"

But the white silk had already slithered to the floor and lay in a heap around her feet. Still curved and light, unmarked and white as the silk, she was unchanged. It might have been yesterday, he thought, as he lifted and carried her to the bed. Yesterday.

It was not yet six o'clock when he awoke. She lay with her back against him. They were as close as nested spoons. For an instant he felt a startling sense of unreality; the window was in the wrong place, the wallpaper, Margaret's butterflies and birds, was missing. Then reality took hold, and his heart pounded. He was in panic. Before any words could be spoken, he must escape from there. . . .

Carefully, he slid out of the bed, threw on his clothes, and tiptoed out of the house. At seven he reached home. People were already about, attaching lawn sprinklers and taking in the paper from the front steps. A neighbor waved. The man would be wondering why Adam was arriving home at that hour rather than departing from it.

He went into the house, let the dogs out, made a cup of instant coffee, and went upstairs to shower and dress. As he stood in the bedroom taking a suit from the closet next to Margaret's, as he looked at the pillow on her side of the bed, he felt as if he were sinking into deep water.

How the hell did this happen?

Last night had been an aberration, or to put it less elegantly, a one-night stand. Quite simply, he would refuse to see her again, not even in a public place. There would be no lunches, no drinks after work, nothing.

With that determination he went back downstairs again and was in the car when he remembered the bird-feeder and got out. He had promised to keep it filled. It meant a lot to Margaret. She always said that "Once you start feeding birds, it is cruel to stop because they depend on you."

At the office he told his secretary to screen his calls carefully. "I especially do not want to talk to a Mrs. Bunting," he explained. "She sells real estate, and she's been a pest."

At the end of the day, after learning that Mrs. Bunting had called three times, he started home. And catching a glimpse of himself in the rearview mirror, he saw that he was frowning. Clearly, Randi had no intention of forgetting him. It didn't make sense to think that any woman would, after a night like the last one; that she would just let it pass as if it had never occurred. A hot flush of shame crept over him; he had sneaked away as if he were afraid to face the light of day.

Yet he knew that he was very afraid. He knew that what had happened might well happen again, knew that he would argue against it and that he would lose the argument.

He was also aware that he must keep his head. And with this resolution he arrived home and set about his usual routines as if they were some sort of therapy: finished mowing the grass, ate a good dinner of Margaret's curried chicken, fed the dogs, and read the mail.

There were the usual advertisements and bills. From the children there were picture postcards of dramatic mountain scenery, and from Margaret, a moving letter.

I should have made you go with us. It is so beautiful, and you would love it. I think of you, with all you know about nature and trees, missing this. I worry because you work too hard. You never complain. I'm going to make you take better care of yourself. Oh, Adam, do you have any idea how much I love you?

The telephone rang. "So you're hiding from me," Randi said gaily.

He had not thought she would dare to call him at home. "Where did you get this number?" he demanded.

"From the phone book, stupid," she replied, still gaily.

"You shouldn't call me here at home," he said.

"Why not? You're alone. And you wouldn't talk to me at your office."

"I was busy. I'm sorry. It was a hectic day."

"Adam, stop it. You poor soul, I really believe you're filled with guilt. I was awake this morning. I heard you creeping away."

"I didn't want to disturb you. I was being considerate."

Randi laughed. "You amuse me, you really do. But never mind that. What I want to know is, did you have fun?"

"Oh, for God's sake," he said.

"I know I did. It was exactly like old times. I'm not too proud to admit that I haven't had anything as good in all the years since. How about you? Never mind. I know you won't answer. Of course you won't. You're a married man, a married gentleman, although, of course, not all married men are gentlemen. But you are."

"Oh, for God's sake," he repeated.

"Can't you say anything else? Listen, I'm phoning only to tell you not to worry. I'm not going to complicate your life, because that's the last thing I want to do to my own life. I've had complications enough to last me a long time. What I'm looking for is a nice single man with no strings attached. I'll marry him and settle down in my house and we'll watch the stars together from the bed. We can lie there naked in the moonlight, and no one will be able to see unless he climbs a tree."

He was quite aware that she was taunting him, yet he could not refrain from asking, "Why? Have you got any special single man in mind?"

"There are a few around. I haven't really made up my mind."

"You said you never had anything as good since—"

She interrupted. "Sometimes, darling boy, one has to settle for second best in life."

He was confused, angry at her and at himself for having a conversation like this one, here in the heart of his home. It was as if he were defiling it. At the same time he felt a strange exhilaration, the vivid thrill of illicit risk.

"So, good night, Adam. You've had a long day, and so have I. No more talk. Sleep well."

Now what was he to make of that? Did she mean no more talk just at present, or no more ever? In the gathering dark he stood uncertainly for a time, then sat outdoors in the full darkness, watching fireflies dart across the lawn. Without doubt, if that is what she really wanted, she would find someone to marry, and he would be rid of her for good. But the image of her, that heat and that pneumatic flesh, giving to another man what she had given him last night, roused within Adam a furious jealousy and a recall of desire that were almost unbearable.

All the next day that image kept recurring. At lunch, alone with Jenks, he broached in gingerly fashion the subject of marital infidelity. It was a delicate subject; you never knew whether another man would frown in distaste, as if you were prying into his head, or would perhaps laugh at what he might take as your naïveté. Having no reason to do so, he had never discussed it before.

Jenk's evasion was adroit. "Depends on a couple of thousand factors, wouldn't you say?"

Adam moved to another topic. "Nothing about Ramsey lately? Is anybody going to Europe in place of him?"

If anything important were going on, Jenks would know it. Curious and gregarious, he had found his place with the popular "in" group.

"Ramsey, for all we know, may lose his job," Jenks said, relishing his ability to inform. "Or else, he may be moved in glory to the main office. It can go either way if we link up with CBW. But nobody knows anything for sure about that, and may not know for months."

"So we're all really hanging by a thread."

"Pretty much. If the merger goes through, some of us will go higher, some will go lower, and some will go out. That's the way it is for us wage slaves."

Jenks shrugged. He could afford to be casual. If anyone were to stay on, he would. Intellectually, he's notches below me, and he knows it, Adam thought, yet I'm ten times more likely to be "out."

This awful possibility was chilling. What if he were dismissed and unable to find another job? Thousands of competent men were being displaced as corporations restructured themselves. And they couldn't possibly get along on Margaret's salary.

That evening, as he turned the key in the front door, he was both terrified and angry. What was it about men like Jenks or Fred Davis or Margaret's dull cousin Gilbert that enabled them to be, at least relatively, secure in their places? Davis, to be sure, had inherited a choice piece of land in the heart of Elmsford, but Gilbert had had nothing except a hale-fellow-well-met personality. As to his probable IQ, the less said, the better.

The dogs, who had been alone all day, rushed to greet Adam, but having no heart for them, he let them out without a word or touch. With the shades drawn against the heat the house was dim and dreary.

Every move he made, when he pulled a drawer open to get a fork, when he closed the door of the freezer and set a plate down on the table, resounded through the emptiness. He ate quickly without appetite, washed the dish, and after that did not know what to do with himself. The long night loomed.

He thought then of the previous night. She had not telephoned him today. Perhaps she had meant it literally when she said, "No more talk." But after all, had he not wanted her to mean it? Yes, certainly he had. And why? Because the weight of guilt on his shoulders was just too heavy, so heavy that it had been visible even to her. Had she not told him so?

But how weak he must look to her, like a man afraid to take the pleasure he wanted, a man tied down, regulated, and controlled as if he were a child! What he had done last night—had it harmed anyone? According to the articles that filled the newspapers, more than half the married men in the country took their secret joys on the side. Half of them also got divorced.

But that was something else again, something too utterly unreal to fathom. To leave Margaret, his good wife, and their three children! Unthinkable.

In the front hall there was a mirror over a small chest that held a lamp. Passing through, he stopped for a moment to examine himself. Not much more than forty, he was trim and youthful with a fair complexion and all his hair. He did not even need glasses.

"Don't we make a handsome pair?" Randi had said as they were standing before her full-length mirror.

Male and female, unclothed and ready, they had been perfect together. And he stood now, quite still, remembering. . . .

It was seven o'clock. He locked up the house, got in his car, and drove. Speed, dispelling the heat, filled the car with a joyful breeze. A part of his mind still recognized how absurd it was that the mere anticipation of sexual ecstasy could so swiftly smother all his very valid fears. Nevertheless, it was so. He felt free and younger than he had felt in years.

When he rang the bell and gave his name, she opened the door. She was totally naked and laughing.

"Ah, I knew you would come!" she cried, as he fell upon her.

SEVEN

It was a new experience for Adam to join with Randi in her spontaneous way of life. It was nothing for her to jump out of bed right after making love and go to broil hamburgers in the kitchen. Hamburgers at midnight were certainly not something to which he was accustomed. And he had to smile inwardly at the spectacle of himself with Margaret, both in their nightclothes, pouring ketchup on their French fries. After love they always went to sleep.

At home, even on weekends, they lived by the clock. Saturday was the day for all the errands and appointments that Margaret, occupied with school, was unable to fit into the week: the library, the dentist, Julie's piano lesson, new shoes or shoe repair, Megan's haircut, or Danny's Cub Scout meeting. They were always going somewhere, meeting some obligation hour by half hour. Sometimes it seemed to him that if all the clocks were to break down, the family might free itself from these demands.

Of course, this was sheer wishful fantasy and quite ridiculous. Fantasy, nevertheless, had its place.

In the office he found himself one day staring at Margaret's photograph on his desk. And studying her face with its calm, candid forehead, he felt such shame that he had to turn away. Yet he knew that as soon as the day's work was over, he was going to go back to Randolph Crossing.

On the second Saturday he arrived there with the dogs, explaining that since he was to stay until Sunday night, he couldn't leave them alone.

"They've been abandoned this whole week, poor things. I didn't think you'd mind."

"No, but it's a good thing they can't talk."

She had prepared an outing at the new house. Sleeping bags and a portable icebox were piled by the door, ready to go.

"The electricity's on, so we can cook, even though the stove's a mess. Or we can make a campfire. I thought it might be fun to stay overnight there and see how it feels."

For their first meal they made a campfire, roasted potatoes, and toasted marshmallows.

"This makes you feel young, like a kid," Adam said, watching the marshmallows turn brown.

"How many years is it since you felt like a kid?"

He did not want to think. He only wanted to lie back on the grass with his head in her lap. As the day cooled and the wind came up, the sunshine of late afternoon was friendly. A pungent pine scent blew on the breeze. From somewhere out of sight he heard the distinctive notes of a cardinal. How long it had been since he had stretched out on the grass, empty of thought, just drifting and feeling and drifting!

"Poor boy," Randi murmured. "Your scalp is so tight. You worry too much." She stroked his head from temple to crown, smoothing his hair with a gesture almost maternal.

His worries were nothing he cared to reveal: responsibilities for his children's future, expenses, promotions, and, like a shrouded ghost, the threat of unemployment.

"Poor boy. Relax. Randi just wants you to be happy. Do whatever you like. Why, you don't even need to make love to me tonight if you're tired. Just go to sleep now."

He slept. When he woke, she had still not moved. He turned on his elbows and looked up at her, asking, "What have you been thinking of all this time?"

She was gazing out through the gap in the trees toward the river. "Do you really want to know?"

"Tell me."

She looked down at him. "I've been thinking how sad it is that we've wasted all these years."

He understood that she must be expecting him to say, "Yes, I know," but how could he call a waste the years during which he had lived peaceably with his wife, rearing two fine daughters, Nina, and his Danny?

Yet, remembering how once she had been everything to him, remembering his anguish when she abandoned him, he was overcome with a sense of life's cruelty. And raising her hand to his lips, he kissed it.

"The one year you and I had was worth more than all the rest put together," she said. "I think of it all the time, of little funny things, like arriving at that surprise party on the wrong day, and the switched raincoats with the secret address book in the pocket. We had fun, didn't we? Oh," she cried, "I know you're remembering that it ended so horribly! I know. I guess I've deserved what I got. Chuck was wrong, all wrong. And losing the baby was such a queer, mixed-up experience, sad and still a relief because, poor baby, it wouldn't have had much stability in its life, would it? Bunting was nice, but there wasn't any *love* with him, just peace for a time, and then he died. I wonder what would have happened if he hadn't died. . . ."

Randi's voice trailed away. He was trying to find something encouraging, something conclusive, to say when abruptly, she jumped up and pointed to the house, where the dogs were lying on the doorstep.

"Why, look how they've made themselves at home! I want you to do the same, Adam. I want you to consider this your house, where you can come and go as you please."

"I won't be able to come very often, Randi."

"I know. But you can invent a conference out of town now and then to allow for a day, or even a week. You'll keep clothes here, and we'll hide out together in comfort. Someday I want to build a pool in back of the house. With my first sizable commission, after the place is completely furnished, I'll do it."

He smiled. "It sounds luxurious."

"Not really. I've saved a few dollars, and I never spend what I haven't got."

Through the high windows late that night, they lay watching the stars. "Just as I promised," Randi said. "Before you fall asleep, let me tell you what I thought of. You know that strip of motels on the highway south of Elmsford? Well, I can easily drive in sometimes and spend the night there. You can leave home early in the mornings, say that you have a load of work at the office, and come to my room. That way, we can have a couple of hours together."

Not quite two weeks more, he was thinking. I won't be able to end this then. . . . Yet he would have to. . . . The thought of all the lies, of going home to Margaret's bed, of her not knowing, was appalling.

"I hate to lie," he said very low.

"Well, it isn't the best thing in the world. But it isn't the worst, either, and sometimes you have to lie a little. The fact is, this is our private affair, and we aren't hurting a soul by having it."

No, he had to admit they were not hurting anyone.

"All right, then, my darling worrywart, enough. We've had a great day, and tomorrow will be another one."

On Monday, Margaret telephoned the office. "I'm beside myself," she cried. "I was almost going to call the police, but everyone here talked me out of it. Where were you last night?"

"Why, home. Where else would I be?"

"I don't understand. I kept calling you again and again, from eight o'clock on. Didn't you hear the phone?"

"At eight I was outdoors. I did some weeding, took the dogs for a walk, and stayed out as long as I could. The house was hot as hell, except for the bedroom, and I didn't feel like sitting there."

"I called at eleven. Then I gave up."

"At eleven I was asleep. The air conditioner hums, and I sleep like a log, anyway. You should know that."

"Well, as long as you're all right. I was so worried. I didn't sleep all night."

"Gosh, I'm sorry, Marg. Were you calling for anything special?"

"Only because I was lonesome and wanted to hear your voice. I had mailed a letter to you, but that wasn't enough for me. You'll probably get it today."

"Well, you'll soon be home."

"Ten days. It seems too long."

His mind raced as she spoke. A double life! He, Adam Crane. He wasn't the kind of man who lived that way. But what kind of man did live that way? Was such a man in some fashion marked so that you could recognize him? When he hung the receiver up, he was sweating.

At home that evening, Margaret's letter was in the mailbox. She had enclosed a snapshot of Danny grinning over a huge trout which, presumably, he had caught himself. For a long minute Adam held the picture as though he were memorizing it: the grin, the torn sneaker, and the red hair so obviously slicked flat because he hated curls. It seemed to him that his Danny had grown taller in this short time away.

Then he sat down and read the letter, which was a long one.

A rainy day, a real storm and a long afternoon indoors. Downstairs they are playing board games, and upstairs I have a hunch most are napping. I don't feel like doing either, or even like reading. I want to "communicate"—isn't that the "in" word today—

with you. If the trip to the airport weren't horrendously long, I think I'd go right home. This absence has been too long, and we're not going to do it again. My room has an enormous bed, wider than our own old double bed, and I feel so *bereft* in it without you. Do you know what I mean? Yes, I'm sure you must, after all our years of being so close every night. Oh, my darling Adam.

But I shouldn't complain. In other words it's been delightful here. Fred's relatives are so hospitable, with no airs at all, in spite of owning all this splendor. The children are having a marvelous time. Julie plays the piano cheerfully when asked to; Megan has a boyfriend, a handsome old man of seventeen, and she's all puffed up about it; Julie, naturally, is envious. You would laugh to see it all beginning, romance, sex, whatever you want to call this thing that is so marvelous. But don't worry, he left yesterday, and he lives in Vancouver. As for Danny—he's everybody's favorite, as always.

Nina just came in for a second and, seeing me writing to you, sends love. She has a boyfriend, or I really should say a man, because he is twelve years older than she. Anyway, his name is Keith Anderson, and he is apparently mad about her. She met him semiaccidentally, through her job. I don't know how serious it will turn out to be. Anyway, I told her not to rush into anything. She's only just turned twenty-three. She reminded me that I was twenty-one when we were married. So I said, sounding like a really old biddy, that that was different because you were an unusual, responsible man. And she said that Keith is too. In fact, he reminds her of you. She says that's the highest compliment she can pay him.

She gave me some Polaroids of her new apartment, three rooms in a renovated mansion. The building is filled with young people on their way up. I think Nina must be the youngest, though. It's really extraordinary how she has climbed. Her bosses have given her another splendid raise, because she's been able to bring a whole new kind of customer to the firm, young, sophisticated New Yorkers with limited budgets and expensive tastes. Apparently, they save and buy one fine piece at a time. Like Nina they have an eye and a taste for art. I'm so happy for her, and proud of her. Fred says she's adorable. He teases her, and pretends to sigh, "If only I were younger!" Well, I wish he were younger. She'd be a lucky woman. He's the "salt of the earth," as Mom used to say. Now, don't go making cracks again about Fred, Mr. Adam Crane.

Shocked to the core by the reality of these written words, he dropped the letter. The words had moved him into a state of terror, as when you are trapped in a nightmare, locked in a dark place with blank walls and no windows.

"They're coming home late Sunday," he said on Friday evening.

"That gives us two days."

"No. I've neglected the garden, coming out here every night. It'll take me most of Saturday to work on it. The corn's up to my knees and choked with weeds."

During the days since the letter had arrived, he had spoken twice to Margaret. The sound of her living voice, unlike her letter, had filled him with pity and shame, shame for himself and pity for the situation to which he had brought them both. Uppermost in his mind was the determination that she must never know. Never! He would go through fire first.

And he said now, "Randi, she—my family—can't ever, ever know."

She gave him a small reproachful smile. "Have you any idea how often you've told me that? Of course they mustn't. If they ever do find out, Adam, it won't be from me."

"My children," he said. "And she—I can't do that to her."

"I understand. Darling, I really do."

They were in the apartment. On the windowsill sparrows hopped, pecking at crumbs, causing him to remember that he had not fed the birds at home as he had promised to do. Randi, too, was staring out of the window into space.

She said suddenly, "You won't let this mean the end for us, will you? You'll just take each day as it comes, as long as we stay together?"

He nodded.

"You remember my plan? Here, and then the house as soon as it's ready? And trips now and then. You remember?"

He nodded again.

"It won't be so bad, Adam. Anyway, we have no choice, have we?"

No. No choice.

"I don't understand what's happened to me," he cried. "I was contented. I thought I was happy."

"You were in a rut, darling, and didn't know it."

How was that possible? If one was content in the rut, was it really a rut? But no answer came. Filled with tumultuous confusion, he knew only that he could not do without what these few weeks had given to him.

"Oh," he said, for perhaps the hundredth time, "what harm can come of this? We're not hurting anybody."

When she stood up from her chair, he, rising, too, took her into his arms. She was so soft, with her eyes cast down, her lashes brushing her round cheeks, her magic flesh, so soft.

And a thrill of peril shook through him, as if he were guiding a ship through a storm or standing on a cliff in the wind with rocks and ocean below. Yes, he would guide this ship through the storm and keep his balance on the cliff. Yes.

Quite simply, he needed this woman.

EIGHT

Nina stepped back to study the effect and decided that it was good. In fact, it was so well composed that it was charming and could have been photographed for any illustrious magazine. Over the mantel hung a bull's-eye mirror, its convex surface reflecting in miniature the room's lovely mélange of pinks and dusty greens. The round table set for two was impeccably dressed with old Coalport plates, remnants of a broken-up set found at a secondhand shop, and an age-mellowed Irish lace cloth found in the same place. At the center in a crystal bowl, a rather extravagant Christmas present to herself, she had made a frothy arrangement of freesias and ferns.

All these possessions, now at home in the new apartment, were precious to her. They soothed the senses, as did the very nature of her daily work: the tactile sense, when fingers touched silks and polished woods; the visual, of course, as experience improved her judgment of color and proportion. Nina lived, and was aware of living, in a sensuous world.

All her friends, several of whom had apartments in this building, were in some way involved with the production and appreciation of taste. Among them there were a model, a student of architecture, and an aspiring actor living with a ballet dancer. Here were the women who bought old dresses from the forties, who knew how to tie a scarf or choose the bag that would make a difference. They loved the city's fashions, its museums, its concert halls and art films; occasionally, when flush with cash, they sampled its famous restaurants.

At this reminder of food Nina glanced behind the bamboo screen into the minute kitchen and, for what must have been the tenth time this evening, counted on her fingers for reassurance: the wine—she needed to buy a book and learn something about wines—a white, to accompany the blackened fish, Portobello mushrooms, a platter of broiled vegetables, salad with sun-dried tomatoes and goat cheese, and for dessert, a *tarte tatin*, with cappuccino or espresso, whichever Keith might prefer. She looked at her watch. In ten minutes it would be time to heat things. She mustn't forget the French bread. Thank heaven for New York's delicious takeout caterers. The little dinner would be perfect.

The clock moved too slowly. And she took a book from the shelf, thinking it might fill the minutes before the doorbell should ring. He was always punctual; it was a trait that Margaret would definitely appreciate, she thought, smiling to herself. And she imagined Keith's first meeting with the people at home. The way things looked, that meeting seemed inevitable, for they had come very, very far in the half year since they had met.

Not having read a complete sentence, she put the book away and went to the mirror in the bedroom for further reassurance. What she saw there pleased her: black velvet pants and white sweater on a body that never bore a pound too many; eyes wide with expectation, and shining hair still piled high in the style that she had worn for years and would never change, for it was her signature.

"I know this is a cliché," Keith said, "such an awful cliché as to be embarrassing when you tell a woman that she's 'different.' In your case, though, it happens simply to be a fact, and I can't help but say it."

They had been having a drink in a snug downtown bistro, and he had been entertaining her by inventing a background for people at surrounding tables.

"The proper study of mankind—" he had begun, and stopped then, with his head tilted first to one side and then the other, studying Nina from all angles as if she were a statue. "In New York there are three or four general types of women: the Upper East Side fashionables, very expensive, half-starved, dressed in next year's fashions from shoes to hair; the Village woman, just barely but not quite counterculture, sometimes natural and pretty but sometimes unkempt in jeans and sloppy sweaters. Then there's the theater crowd, and so on, and so on. You don't fall into any of the categories."

"Maybe that's because I came from the Midwest."

"No. You would be unusual anywhere, Nina. Do you know what I first noticed about you? Your voice. I was talking to one of the men at your place, when I—"

"You were talking to Ernie about your mother's antique Chinese lamp that somebody broke."

"You remember that?"

"I remember. I thought you were the handsomest man I'd ever seen, and I wondered who you were."

She was not coy about the admission. He had come into the shop to replace the lamp in time for his mother's birthday. And she had indeed wondered very much about this quiet young man whose air of authority and polished manner were those of a much older person. There had seemed to be something oddly aphrodisiac about the combination of youth and age.

Ernie had never seen him before. "He appeals to you, eh? An aristocratic type. Even has the arched nose, the rich voice, and the natural-shoulder suit. Very attractive. He's straight too. I guarantee it."

"Ernie! How silly can you be?"

They had long gone past the first formal distance between employer and employee. Among the three of them, Ernie, Willie, and Nina, serious discussion, arguments, and banter passed equally and freely.

"Not silly. I saw you watching while I was talking to him. He saw you too."

"And what in heaven's name does that amount to?"

"Probably nothing. But the lamp still has to be electrified, so unless he wants us to deliver it, he may be back next week to get it. And if you're in the shop when he comes, you'll have a chance at him."

"Foolisher and foolisher, Ernie."

But it had not been foolish. The most farfetched fantasies can sometimes come true, she reflected now. For when an order for delivery arrived, the boy who usually fetched and carried for the firm was doing something else. And so it was Nina who delivered the fragile lamp by taxi.

The great apartments that filled the fifteen-story limestone buildings on Fifth Avenue near the museum had no mystery for Nina. She had been in countless numbers of them, in the beginning as Crozier and Dexter's humble trainee and more recently with real authority. That authority, too, was a fantasy come to life. So with poise she had passed beneath the green awning, given her name, and taken the elevator up to the door that had been opened to her by Keith himself.

For several seconds they stood as if startled; she had an impression of white collar, soft olive complexion, and vivid recognition. In the background lay a vista of mahogany and well-bred portraits in gilded frames.

"Come in, come in. Let me take that from you. Mother will be so pleased. Her luncheon's tomorrow, and she's been so worried that the lamp wouldn't be here."

Carefully, he placed it on a table beside the fireplace, adjusted the shade, and plugged the cord in.

"As you can see, the room would be positively naked without this thing." And he twinkled at Nina. "Well, it does look nice, though."

A frail woman with silver-gray hair and a dress that matched it came into the room.

"Oh, it's lovely!" she cried, clasping her hands in a gesture that might be thought charming or else affected, depending on one's point of view. "Do you know, I think it's even prettier than the old one? But you've always had good taste."

"Not mine, Mother. The compliment must go to Miss—"

"Keller," she said quickly. "It's not mine either. It was Mr. Dexter who helped you."

"No matter. The thing is, my mother is happy."

"Yes, it was very nice of you to bring it here, Miss Keller."

"It was my pleasure," replied Nina with equivalent formality. "Well, have a lovely party and a happy birthday."

"Wait," Keith said quickly as she moved toward the door. "I'll go down and make sure the doorman can get a taxi for you."

"Thank you, I'm sure I can manage."

"No, I insist."

They rode down in silence. There were no cabs in sight.

"Perhaps," Keith said, "if you don't mind a walk, we might have a drink before dinner? There's a little place on Third. It's not far."

"I know. I live just west of Third."

"So I take it that the answer is yes?" And again he seemed to twinkle with some private amusement that lighted his eyes and drew amiable crinkles at their corners.

"You may take it that way." And she laughed.

"Why are you laughing?"

"It occurred to me, in a very nice way, how like you are to your mother."

"So they always tell me. Rather formal, they say. I'm not aware of it."

"I think you do more laughing than she does, though."

"That's true. It comes from my father. He could find humor in everything, even in his own final illness. I'm not quite that funny, sorry to say."

They had halted for a red light, when he looked down at her, half a head below him, and demanded why they were talking about him.

"I want to know about *you*. Where are you from? Surely not from New York."

"No. I'm a midwesterner. A small town—a small city—woman. How did you guess?"

"Something indefinable. I just felt an awareness of you. You felt one, too, that day in the shop."

Looking straight into a face that had abruptly turned solemn, she answered frankly, "Yes. Yes, I did."

"Good. Now each of us knows where he stands."

An unfamiliar thrill went through Nina then, a sense of some vague, looming happiness. Let come what may, she thought, as she kept pace with his steps.

At the "little place on Third," Keith was evidently well known. The proprietor gave cheerful greeting and provided a table in an ell that was almost private. Keith drank scotch. Nina had an aperitif, and they talked. After a while he ordered dinner. "This isn't fancy. The cooking is Italian home style. You'll like it. I come here often."

"What about dinner at home? Or don't you live with your mother?"

"She's invited out tonight. She's been very ill, just over quadruple bypass surgery and a broken hip two years before that. It's one reason why I was so eager to get that lamp on time. It was important for her, although it probably might seem ridiculous to other people."

"Not to me. When you're part of a close family, you're tolerant of people's little quirks, including your own. At home the big things aren't lamps and things, but dogs and birds. Heaven help you if you're late with their feed and water." She smiled, remembering.

"Tell me about your home, please, Nina."

So, at his behest, she talked about herself. Then he talked about himself. By the second cup of after-dinner espresso she had learned that he was an investment banker, had lived in France, knew rather a good deal about art, was an active sponsor of cancer research, and was twelve years older than she.

When they parted at her front door, he asked to see her again and gave her a gentle kiss. The fact that he did not fumble or grab intensified the gravity of what was happening. Back in her room she examined herself in the mirror; it seemed to her that she was seeing something different and new in her face, an *alteration*, and a kind of wonder. This surely had to be what is meant to "fall in love." And she knew she was too sophisticated to scoff at "love at first sight"; undoubtedly, it could happen. It did happen.

The second time they met he took her far downtown to a Chinese movie. He had been in China, and afterward at dinner in a Chinese restaurant, she was full of questions. His answers were clear and unpretentious. She had met too many men who, with their comparably slight experience, were yet too satisfied with themselves; Keith's simplicity was therefore all the more impressive.

Other men were boys compared with him. Not only the teenagers she had once known at home, but the much older people she was meeting here and now, were boys. Keith was a man. She was filled with respect. And that night, they went to bed.

A gardenia plant in full, creamy bloom arrived the next day. It came with explicit instructions and a warning: *This plant requires tender, loving care.* It seemed to her as she watered it and wiped its glossy leaves that the admonition was also apt for the care and guarding of human love. It was true that her sexual experience had been limited— by prudent choice, to be sure—yet it had been broad enough for her to recognize differences. The night with Keith had been a revelation of skill and tenderness. She was enchanted; she was overwhelmed with gratitude for the incredible, haphazard accident that had brought them together. All this had evolved out of a broken porcelain lamp! Imagine!

So began the lovely, mellow weeks of early summer. Together, they wandered through the city's far-flung places, from art galleries and dance recitals in renovated downtown factories to Thai or Russian restaurants and Irish pubs.

"I like to get off the beaten path," Keith said. "It takes no imagination to keep going back to famous places. We've all seen them often enough."

Nina's neighbor in the apartment across the hall, noticing that he left at ten o'clock one night, remarked, "Your friend doesn't stay very late."

"He lives near here on Fifth Avenue with his mother."

"Not really with his mother?"

"Yes. She's been ill, and so he's moved back with her for a while. He's that sort, very kind."

"And very rich, I should think."

The woman was too curious, but there was no malice in her, and Nina was merely amused.

"What makes you say that?"

"Well, Fifth Avenue, after all."

"Probably he is. I suppose so."

"Is it serious?"

"I hope so."

"Not bad for you, if it is. Not bad, living on Fifth Avenue."

Now Nina spoke brusquely. "I don't care at all. Not at all."

This was true. Any inference that her emotions could be influenced by money made her wince. She had her independence. She cherished it and was proud of it. Everything she possessed had come to her through her own efforts.

In the second month after meeting Keith she had moved from the studio apartment to the present one.

"Nice as this is," he had said, "in my opinion you deserve better. I'd like to see you in a building with an elevator and a doorman."

"I can't afford it," she had told him.

"Let me help you."

"No, Keith. Thank you, but absolutely no."

"Just in part, then. A joint venture."

"I couldn't possibly."

Then, curiously, he asked why not. She knew why not. Because it would be quite simply, and for lack of a better word, *cheap*. Love should never be mixed up with money. She knew quite well what Margaret and Adam would say about that.

She did not, however, tell him anything more than "I'm a very independent person. I see you haven't learned that about me yet."

"I think I have. You wouldn't even let me give you that little silver bracelet in the craft shop window."

"Flowers and chocolates will be graciously received," she told him, laughing.

"That sounds like something out of an ancient book of etiquette."

"As a matter of fact, it is. I used to read my grandmother's mother's Emily Post."

"A proper lady, you are. Except in bed. Then you're hardly proper at all," he said with his by-now-familiar twinkle.

"That's different."

"Tell me, are books acceptable to a lady?"

"Ah, yes, I forgot about books."

As a result of that little conversation Nina's bookshelves were rapidly filling. It was interesting that, once away from formal education and required reading, she had become a reader. The great books that Margaret had loved, the novelists and poets, now lay about her rooms. Before her on the coffee table Balzac's *Père Goriot* was open at the page where, in her impatience, she had put it down.

When the telephone rang, she jumped to it, praying that it wasn't Keith to say he couldn't come. It was Margaret.

"I thought maybe I'd catch you at home with your feet up after a long, hard day."

"It was a long day, but not hard, since I love what I do. And my feet aren't up. They're in new shoes. I'm expecting Keith to dinner any minute."

"Then I won't keep you. I had nothing special to say, anyhow, nothing more than a chat. What have you made for dinner? Steak and potatoes, or is he watching cholesterol and fats like practically everybody else?"

"What have I made for dinner? Nobody cooks anymore, not around here at least. The takeout places are fabulous. I've got blackened fish, vegetables, and a stunning lace tablecloth. You should see my new place. I've two big rooms and a kitchen. It's really lovely. Can you come soon for a weekend?"

"You know I'd pick up and travel at the drop of a hat. And Adam would, too, just for a chance at a couple of operas. But he can't possibly get away right now." Margaret's clear soprano dropped to an anxious tone. "Things aren't going well at the office, Adam says. Everybody's worried about what may lie ahead. Meanwhile, they're working people to death. He keeps slave hours. Really. Some nights he doesn't get home till eleven-thirty or after, and then he's up in the morning before six to get to his desk. It's inhuman. We hardly ever have dinner together anymore, which is especially hard on Danny."

No matter how far you went from home or how long you were away, you were connected, especially if there was any kind of worry. Feeling a sudden sinking around the heart and knowing what the reply would be, Nina asked, nevertheless, whether there was anything she might do.

"Nothing, dear. Nothing. I'm sure it'll come out all right in the end. We've been through crises before. Remember Hong Kong? That was the absolute worst."

Margaret was tenacious. Left to her it *would* come out all right in the end. Thinking so, at the same instant another thought flashed: Instinctively, one conceived of *Margaret* as the source of confidence, not Adam. Perhaps it was because he was more sensitive than she. . . .

"Danny's birthday's coming up soon. What shall I give him?"

"I'll find out and let you know. But don't go spending a fortune."

"Only what I can afford."

"You're too generous sometimes, Nina. I want you to save for yourself."

"Darling, don't worry about me. Oh, there's the bell. It's Keith. Talk to you tomorrow, maybe. Or Saturday. Bye."

"Who was that on the phone?" asked Keith. "I heard you say 'darling.' Do I have a rival?"

"Idiot. I was talking to Margaret."

He kissed her; cold lips and cold cheek pressed hers.

"Ouch! You're freezing."

"It's freezing out, starting to snow a few flakes."

"Don't worry. I'll warm you. How was your day?"

"Not bad except that I'm starved. What's for dinner? We should have gone out, but you insisted. I like your velvet pants. Can I do anything?"

"No. I'm all ready. You can uncork the wine. Is it okay? I'm only just learning about wines, although I should know more. Adam always had good wines."

"Nothing wrong with a Sancerre. I'd say you've already learned very well."

It was cozy there, with the lavish little table between them, the cat asleep under the window, and the old clock's tinny bong as it struck seven. Man and woman together at the end of the day, she thought. Husband and wife, she thought, embarrassing herself for being so hasty, and then rebuked herself, mocking: *Hold on. A little feminine modesty, please, and wait till you're invited.*

"Are you going back west over Christmas?" Keith asked.

Not knowing what to say without knowing his plans, she hesitated.

"I'll be in Florida. My brother has a place there. He lives there all year round."

She said promptly, "Yes, I'll take a few days. I miss them all, especially the kids."

"They always sound like such special people when you talk about them."

"Well, they are. And our relationship's rather special. Margaret's fifteen years older than I am, sort of halfway between being a mother and a sister. Maybe more of a mother," Nina reflected. "She's a completely giving person. She gave up medical school out of love. Took care of her mother and her mother-in-law, teaches school, reared three good kids, plus me, for heaven's sake."

"She sounds almost too good to be true."

"She's true, all right. But Margaret's no martyr type, believe me. She's too strong for that. The whole thing is, she adores Adam. She'd go through fire for Adam."

"And he adores her too?"

"Oh, absolutely. I guess that's what's made such a good home for all of us. It's been the foundation. People always say the Cranes are ideal together."

Keith reached across the table and took her hand. "You're the sweetest girl, Nina."

"Not that I mind, but you are supposed to say 'woman' nowadays, you know."

"The hell with it. Sometimes I think you are still almost a child, naive and trusting. And yet at other times I think of you as ambitious, smart, and sexy. A young woman of the nineties. You confuse me."

"Well, you should have seen me today. Pardon me for boasting, but I've got to tell somebody, meaning you, that this morning I signed up a ninety-five-thousand-dollar order for a penthouse redecoration. The whole place is to be done in Art Deco. Even the woman's jewelry is Art Deco. Can you imagine all that platinum filigree? Anyway, I thought Ernie and Willie would jump out of their skins, because she's a tough-minded customer, and they had been sure she was just shopping around, wasting time."

"You'll be a partner someday if you keep this up."

Nina sighed. "I hope so. They like me and I like them. They're critical, touchy, funny, and very kind. When I had the flu—that was before I knew you—they sent dinner in for me every night. You ought to see where they live. The whole building belongs to them, you know. They have a duplex apartment above the shop with a marble staircase between the floors. White marble. It's all quite dramatic, quite eclectic, with French antiques, old portraits, modern sculpture, flowering shrubs, the works. They give great parties. Maybe I'll take you next time they invite me. If you want to go," she added quickly.

"Right now I want to go in there with you," Keith answered, pointing to the bedroom.

For a while they lay together in the profound peace that follows the joining. Keith had sent a second gardenia plant, which she had placed near the window, close to the bed, and the air was sweet with its fragrance. The lamp's light was reflected in the window, from which there sounded a faint intermittent rattle.

"Sleet. I'd better get up. I hate to leave you," Keith said reluctantly. "I wish I could stay all night like this."

"Can't you?"

"Clothes. I have to get back. It's nine-thirty, and this may turn out to be a real storm."

"Luckily, you've only a few blocks to go."

"Five more minutes." He looked at the glowing figures on the bedside clock. "Then I'll jump up at once." He paused. "I was thinking . . . Nina, after Christmas do you suppose they'd let you take a few extra days?"

"I'd just be getting back from a holiday. Why?"

"I have business in Prague. I thought maybe you'd like to go with me."

She sat straight up. "Like to! Like to! Europe? Would I ever!"

"Well, ask them. I'll bet that your Willie and Ernie would say yes."

She considered for a moment, then, shining with delight, said slowly, "You know, I really do believe they will. I'll make them say yes."

"Darling Nina."

At thirty-seven thousand feet they had left winter far below.

"I read the international weather report this morning," Nina said. "It's even colder in Prague than it is here."

"Don't worry. I think you're well prepared for either one of the poles."

"Ernie told me to buy a shearling coat. I always wanted one, anyway, and never got around to it."

"I can't imagine why anybody would choose to go to Europe in January unless for the skiing," Ernie had said. "But do buy a shearling while you're at it. I always think black is appropriate, with an adorable hat to match."

The coat and the adorable hat now hung in the closet and a new leather carry-on was tucked under the seat. The flight attendant had brought cocktails, the last announcement had come from the cockpit, and over all there was an agreeable atmosphere of safe adventure.

"I can't believe it," murmured Nina.

"Can't believe what, darling?"

"That we're really on our way. Let's see, we've been out for half an hour. Didn't he say we fly seven hundred miles an hour? Or was it more? So we're at least three hundred fifty miles out over the ocean."

Keith smiled. "I get such pleasure just from watching your expressions, the way they go from wonderment, so serious and wide eyed, to that smile of delight. It's like taking a child to a toy store."

No, she thought, it's far, far more than you know or than I'm going to admit to you.

The truth was that, as they streamed through the lonely black darkness, here in the miraculous warm comfort of the first-class cabin with his arm touching hers, she was feeling *married*. This must be what it meant to be *one*. It must be what Margaret felt when sometimes, in the evening, she looked over at Adam as with eyes shut he lay back in his reclining chair, listening to music; then Margaret, watching him, would smile her small, contented smile.

She reached over now and placed her hand on Keith's. The flight attendant, catching the gesture, would think that perhaps they were on their honeymoon.

"I'm very happy," she whispered.

"And so am I, little Nina. So am I."

When, hours later, they touched down in Prague, the ground wore a deep, white snow cover, and a few late desultory flakes were drifting.

Keith had ordered a car. Driving slowly to avoid slippery patches, he was able to give a brief guided tour.

"There's Hradčany, that huge structure on the hill. It's a compound, almost a town in itself, with the palaces, the cathedral, a town hall, a museum, a monastery—well, you'll see it. We'll spend almost a whole day there. There's the river, the Moldau. Lord, it's cold! Look at those floating ice chunks. You should see the crowds on the Charles Bridge in the summer, artists doing portraits for the tourists, musicians, happy kids dancing—it's a spectacle. You'll want to come back here, I guarantee. This is my third time."

Nothing was ever wasted on Keith. He savored, remembered, analyzed, and enjoyed. His curiosity was catching.

"Do you realize," he said, "that we've been awake since yesterday morning? I propose that we go upstairs and have a good sleep."

"Upstairs" was a suite of two rooms filled with an enormous bed, with chairs and sofas all overstuffed, very comfortable, and incredibly dowdy.

Keith laughed. "Typically middle European. It would hardly do for Crozier and Dexter, would it?"

She burst out laughing at the thought of Ernie and Willie confronting the bulge of that armoire. But the feather bed, after thirty hours without sleep, looked wonderful. And this was to be their first time to spend an entire night together.

It was the first time, too, that they made love in the morning before breakfast. "It's different in the morning," observed Nina.

"How different can it be?"

"Just—I don't know."

But upon reflection she found that she did know very well. It was the feel of permanence that made the difference, as if they belonged together and could do whatever they wanted, whenever they wanted.

"Today's the day for Hradčany. The whole day. We can take a bus, or we can climb. I warn you that the hill is like a stepladder."

"We'll climb," said Nina, filled as she was with energy and joy. "I want to see everything." And she flung her arms out. Everything. The world.

The view from the top was glorious. The cathedral was dressed in stone lace. The gardens around the royal summer palace, though covered in snow, were beautiful. In the museum Keith led her on a little tour of his own, stopping before a portrait of a woman who held in one hand a streamer of her own long, gleaming hair.

"It's a famous Titian," he explained. "She lived a few centuries ago, but she could be you today."

"I don't see that at all."

"Look again. Even the arc of the eyebrow is yours."

And he stood there, in the dimming light of the old museum, looking back and forth with satisfaction from the portrait to the living woman.

There were flowers in the hotel room when they returned to it that night.

"They should have been here on the first night," Keith said, frowning. "But somebody forgot. There's no excuse for that."

He was meticulous, never late himself, never forgetful of even a casual promise. Nina had already learned that he had little tolerance for people who were late or forgetful. And this awareness of a small human failing gave her a secret pleasure, because it made him real instead of a romantic girl's dreamy, impossible creation.

So ended their first day.

And their few days raced by. They saw the old Town Hall, went to a concert and ate goulash and strudel in smoky little restaurants. In a gallery Keith bought a watercolor, a sketch of the Moldau under soft spring rain, for her to take home.

"Whoever did it is an artist, no amateur," he said. "With a really good frame you'll cherish it. You'll remember our days here."

"Do you really think I could forget them?" she asked. And she looked at him, feeling the truth in the cliché about "having one's heart in one's eyes."

"Sweet Nina," he said. "Wonderful Nina. I'd like to go around the world with you."

"Well, invite me," she answered gaily.

"How about Outer Mongolia for a start?"

With mock correctness she considered the offer, and then, truly in earnest, responded, "I'd rather take Paris for a start."

"Fine. That's easy enough."

A daring possibility occurring to her, she asked whether they had seen everything they should see here.

" 'Everything'? Of course not. But we have had more than a good bird's-eye view, that's sure."

"I was thinking that maybe—can we maybe leave here a little sooner and have one day in Paris? If I could just see it for one day I'd be so thrilled! I'd have that much to remember of it and look forward to seeing again. Can we, Keith?"

They were at dinner in the hotel, almost finished, and Keith was taking a credit card out of his wallet. For a moment he stared at it, replaced it, took out a traveler's check, replaced that, and took out the credit card. Nina's question, her little appeal, went unanswered. It was as if he had suddenly become confused, suddenly somber.

"We can't talk about it here," he said then. "Let's go upstairs. There's something I've been wanting to say to you anyway."

She felt her breath quicken, not with alarm, but rather with expectation, as if some surprise was coming: the Question, perhaps?

When he took his seat in one of the fat, overstuffed chairs, she sat down across from him in its twin and waited. After a silent moment or two he got up to stand at the window, looking into the night. For what seemed a long time she waited.

He turned around, looking intensely troubled. "We'll have to postpone Paris for another time. That's one place where we can't be seen together."

She was astonished. "I don't understand! Not be seen? That sounds crazy."

"I know it does, but if you listen, you will understand."

"I'm listening, Keith. Go ahead."

He walked the length of the room and, returning, began. "Have you ever done anything absolutely stupid and absolutely unforgivable? And knowing that it was, postponed the confession of it because you were so ashamed and afraid of not being forgiven?"

"No," she said truthfully. Her heart had begun to pound and she trembled. Instinctively, she crossed her arms, as if for protection, on her chest.

Very slowly, very low, he said, "I'm married, Nina."

She went numb. *Married.* If he had said, *I just robbed a bank,* or *I just shot a man,* the words could have been no more stunning.

"I should have told you that first night when we went out for a drink, the time you brought the lamp. But I knew I had to see you again, and I was afraid you'd refuse me. A lot of women these days, at least the ones I've met, wouldn't care one way or the other, but I had the feeling that you would." Keith's voice pleaded. "And I didn't want to lose you. I don't want to lose you now."

How dared he! How could he?

"I'm getting a divorce, Nina. So my deception really isn't as bad as it must sound. The trouble is that the damn business takes so damn long. If you'll just bear with me . . ." And he wrung his hands.

She stared at him, thinking: After all, you're a stranger. What do I know about you?

Keith was saying, "That's the reason, you see, why we can't be together in Paris. You almost always meet someone there who knows you. There's much less risk here, especially in the winter. Someday I'll take you to Paris, but—"

"Risk?" she cried. "Do you think I give a damn about *Paris* after what you've just told me? And anyway, what risk is there, since as you say, you're getting a divorce?"

"It's more complicated than that. We haven't made it public yet. We're still seen as an intact family."

" 'Intact family'! You bastard! You lied, you tricked me, you put me in this position where you have to hide me as if—as if I were a whore that you're ashamed to be seen with!"

She burst out crying and covered her face with her hands. Pain, such pain! She had been pierced through. She was bleeding.

Kneeling on the footstool before her, he tried to take her hands away, to wipe her tears.

"Nina, please, darling, don't cry. Be patient with me, please. Please. I know you're furious, and you have a right to be. But I know you love me too. I know you do. When you think about it, you'll forgive me."

Married. A rage of jealousy raced through Nina's body. All the time, as he had lain with her, as she slept beside him feeling the thud of his heart against hers, inhaling the warm, clean scent of his skin, so he lay with another woman, one who bore his name, wore his ring, and had the legal, honorable certificate tucked away in some drawer, some vault. . . . Married. She turned cold, unable to speak, with a silent scream stuck in her throat.

"Nina, for God's sake, say something."

People passed in the corridor; a man's voice said, "You haven't met my wife yet, have you? Annie, this is—"

Through her fingers Nina whispered, "What is her name?"

"Cynthia."

"And are there any children?"

"Nina, sweetheart, we needn't go into all this. It's too hard on you. I'm getting a divorce. That's all you need to know. Nothing else matters."

She had a need to reach and touch the uttermost bounds of anguish. "No," she said. "I must hear everything. There are children, aren't there? And you don't want to tell me." She wiped her face. "How many children?"

He got up from his knees, saying wearily, "Two. A boy and a girl."

Children. A wife. A house. She saw him so differently now. All of a sudden he was not the same desirable young man beside whom, only a few hours ago, she had walked so confidently with a light and hopeful heart. As if a spring, stretched to the snapping point, had indeed snapped, she jumped out of the chair, snatched her coat, and ran to the door.

"Wait, Nina. What are you doing? Nina—"

The door slammed in his face. Almost opposite, the elevator door had opened; before he was able to reach it, she was in the elevator going down, then out on the street and running. She was wild and well aware of it, aware that it made no sense to be running at night through the streets of a foreign city or of any city. She had no idea where she was going. Behind her lay disaster, smashed pride, and, far worse, smashed trust. How could he? Oh, God, how I hate him!

People were looking at her, thinking, no doubt, that she was being pursued or was demented. Her breath came hard, as if blood had risen to her throat, and she had to stop, pretending to look into a shop window. Ahead at the top of the street lay a wide open space, quite surely the great square where they had watched the old clock and gone into the church behind the square; that was where she must go now, to the church.

Someone had been rehearsing or practicing at the organ that afternoon, sending majestic waves of sound to the pinnacle of the ancient building. Bach, Keith had said. "When music moves you with such grandeur, it almost always turns out to be Bach." The church was almost vacant now. Only a few old people sat facing the altar, and an old woman knelt in prayer. The cold was damp. And as she drew her coat more tightly around herself, the pretty coat, bought with such anticipation of joy, she was overcome with a conviction of irreparable loss.

She needed to be home. If she could only make a wish and be instantly at home in her own place, burying her head in her own pillow and sleeping! Just sleeping! But she had no money, no tickets, nothing. She was helpless, dependent upon him. And she sat there, gazing at the votive candles and the old woman kneeling in prayer. God knew what her troubles might be, poor soul!

After a long, long while when one by one the church emptied, she was left alone in a dark blue immensity. How many thousands of men and women, betrayed and deceived like herself, must, through all the centuries, have sat beneath this roof and pondered what to do! And ultimately made resolve, gotten up, and walked out to face what had to be faced. She could hardly sit there all night grieving and raging. . . .

To be led by emotion instead of mind was to walk panicked through strange woods. You could only end at the point in the circle where you had started. She had no choice but to return to the hotel.

From the distance of half a block she saw Keith standing in the doorway, looking up and down the freezing street. When he recognized her, he came running.

"Nina! I've been hunting for you since eight o'clock. I was frantic. I thought something awful might have happened to you, that you might have—"

"Have what? Committed suicide?"

He had loosed his tie and was without his overcoat. In one way these proofs of his distress were satisfying to her; yet in another way they aroused a grudging pity.

"You'd better go inside," she said harshly. "Or you'll get pneumonia."

When, in the room, he tried to help her remove her coat, she rebuffed him.

"Don't touch me, Keith."

"All right. I won't touch you. But you have to listen. You have to hear the whole story."

"The story of your 'intact family'?"

"It's not intact. I said, we're *thought of* that way."

"So you're still living together."

"Yes. In the same house. We aren't sleeping together, I assure you." He paused, and then said with difficulty, "My little boy is sick. Or not exactly sick, but recovering from surgery. He was born with a club foot, and the first operation didn't work. There were complications, and he has to have another one, but not till next year. I can't—can't upset things now. He's only eight years old. It's not the time. You can see that, can't you?" he pleaded.

"I suppose so."

"Please take your coat off and sit down. Hear me out. Then judge."

She was silent.

"In another year, as soon as Eric is on his way, things will be different. There'll be no money problems and no child problems. Cynthia can take care of the children. She's a good mother."

Should she believe him? Nina asked herself.

He had remembered his tie and, standing there before her in all his anxiety, was fastening a proper knot. It was so typical of him, this almost unconscious propriety, this weakness, if you wanted to call it such, that she was inexplicably touched.

"I hardly know what else to tell you except that I'm terribly sorry," he said, "and I'm asking you to forgive me."

Should she forgive him? she asked herself.

"Am I being unreasonable, Nina?"

"No, probably not." Anger still lay like a hard knot in her chest, but it would not take much more to soften it. For pride's sake, though, and to be certain, she had to press him further.

"That's your side of the story. What does—she—think about it?"

"We've agreed not to discuss the divorce right now, to keep the quiet and peace for the children's sake, especially for Eric. But it'll be all right, I promise." Keith smiled, his forehead wrinkling with the piteous smile. "So what if you and I go on as we are for a while? We'll be seeing each other as we have been doing. We'll even manage a trip now and then in a discreet way. Fortunately, my work takes me out of town and keeps me late in town."

"Then you don't live in the city."

"No. I'm an hour's train ride away, maybe a little more."

"I thought you lived with your mother."

"Lord, no. I never told you I did."

That was true. She had merely surmised that he did.

"Does your mother have any idea—"

"Lord, no, again. She'll be told when it's over, not before. My mother still thinks divorce is a horror."

"I don't think that, but I do think I would hate to have it happen to me."

"Naturally. But if you were miserable, you would think differently."

"And are you miserable?"

"Not since I met you."

There was a pause, during which Nina asked herself whether she really wanted to know certain things or might be better off not knowing them. But the question forced itself.

"What is she like?"

"Well, it's hard to explain—"

"It's not hard. Describe her for me."

"Nina, must we? It's very distasteful."

"A question of loyalty?"

He shook his head. "No. Well. All right. I'll make it short and sweet. She's bright. She has a degree in psychology. She's cranky."

"Go on."

"We don't get along. There's—it's like nothing. You understand? I don't even want to think about it. What else is there to say? Isn't that enough?"

"But you live together."

"What do you mean? Sex? I told you we don't sleep together, since that's what you obviously mean. We haven't since Susan was born, and Susan is six."

So the woman, the wife, in spite of the name, the children, and the house, in spite of the ring and the license, really didn't have him after all. *The woman really didn't have him.* She gave a long, exhausted sigh, as when pain suddenly ceases. Yet there was one thing more important that she needed to hear.

"Tell me what she looks like."

"Looks like? Nothing much. Nothing any man would turn to stare at. About as old as God."

She could not help the little smile that quivered on her lips. Seeing it, Keith broke out into a grin.

"Truce, Nina? Can we go on from here?"

And when, with a little catch in her throat, she replied, "I guess so," he took her into his arms. And swept by enormous relief, she wept on his shoulder.

NINE

"That was Nina on the phone," Margaret said, returning to the dining room. "She's coming next weekend for our anniversary. Isn't that darling of her? It's such an expensive flight, and it's not as if we were doing anything unusual. She just wants to be with us."

"And Gil and Louise and Fred," said Megan, "especially Fred. They'd make a nice couple, wouldn't they?"

"No, they wouldn't. He's much too old for her."

Megan objected, "Her boyfriend's twelve years older than she is. She should marry Fred. Then she could live near us. Fred could build a house for them, and she'd have fun furnishing it. She could buy anything she wants. Fred could afford it."

"Money," said Adam. "I'm tired of people's talking about Fred's money all the time, and I'm surprised to hear you doing it too."

Much offended, Megan cried, "That's not fair, Dad! I didn't mean anything so terribly bad. I only said—and besides, I don't remember hearing anyone in this family talking about Fred's money 'all the time.' "

"Well, maybe Fred talks so much about it that nobody else ever gets a chance to."

Margaret gave Adam a look of severe disapproval. He really was too critical, too *touchy*, these days. To be sure, it wasn't that often, just sporadically, when the mood came over him, but it was such an unreasonable mood, set off by a totally innocuous remark such as this one of Megan's now. Of course, Fred, innocent Fred, had long been a target for Adam's cranky arrows. . . .

Megan was glowering at her father; at fifteen she was quite naturally going through her own sensitive stage.

Deciding to gloss over the incident with humor, Margaret said,
"Well, if you all plan to do any matchmaking, next weekend is your
chance. One of you girls talk to Fred, and one of you talk to Nina."

"Aw, Mom," Danny said in disgust. "Women make me sick, talking
about weddings."

"When is Nina's wedding going to be?" asked Julie.

"I have a hunch," Margaret said, "that the real reason she's coming home is to discuss it."

It occurred to her that Nina might even be bringing Keith along to
surprise them. For the past year and a half he had been brought into
every telephone conversation and mentioned in every letter. If the man
was as wonderful as Nina said he was, what were they waiting for?
Margaret was no believer in delaying the march of life. Goodness knew,
she had not delayed it long! And she looked around the table, as she
often found herself doing whenever her children were assembled there:
at Megan's serious expression, with eyes alert and mouth a bit too
determined; at Julie, the dreamer, so quick to laugh and equally quick
to cry: at Danny, already three quarters a man and still one quarter
baby boy.

"If she has a real wedding," Julie mused, "I suppose Megan and I
will be bridesmaids. I'd love a long dress. Pink. A long pink dress and a
bouquet of red roses."

"She might not even want a big wedding," Megan said with a hint
of scorn in her emphasis. "Nina's practical, and a wedding can be an
awful waste. Over in a few minutes, and it costs a fortune."

Margaret disagreed. "I never thought so. It's really never over. You
remember it for the rest of your life. We had such a lovely wedding.
And I had the most wonderful dress, all handmade. Your mother sewed
love into that dress, Adam."

"Yes," he said.

He was annoyed. Perhaps, or even probably, she thought, it's because I've invited Fred and my cousins to our anniversary barbecue.
They annoy him. . . . I'm sure they have no idea that they do, especially since he and Fred were so close when they were young. But it's a
tradition by now, and they would think it strange if they weren't asked.
Besides, they're very dear to me, and I want them here. They don't
come that often. And she felt a rise of righteous indignation.

Adam was holding the coffee cup between both hands. Above the
rim his eyes looked out, unfocused, toward the opposite wall. On her

own forehead as she watched him, she felt the gathering of a troubled little frown, but he did not seem to see it, nor turn to look at her. And again, as she had several times before, she had an impression of *absence,* as though he wasn't *there.* Sometimes, even when they were talking together, whether about what was happening in Washington or Bosnia, or else, as now, about something insignificant, he simply wasn't *there.*

Driving the car she had rented at the airport, Nina arrived at noon. With an overnight case in one hand and a broad, square box in the other, she came rushing up the walk. Exclamations came rushing too.

"What glorious weather! You always manage to have such perfect weather on your day. It's so wonderful to be here. It feels like years since I saw you. How long is it? Since you had that blizzard? Danny, you're going to be seven feet tall if you don't stop growing. Here, take this before my arm breaks. It's your present. Married eighteen years! Does it seem possible?"

She comes in like a fresh wind, Margaret thought. They are all truly happy to see her; you can tell in their faces that there is nothing perfunctory in this welcome. Nina is loved.

"Wait till you see what's in this box. I hope you'll really like it. Keith says you will. It was his idea. He says he's heard so much about you that he almost knows you. Here, be careful with those scissors, Danny. It's fragile."

The fragile object was a large Japanese garden in a moss-green container half the size of a card table. Luxuriant bonsai trees surrounded a traditional house and a smooth stretch of raked ground with a low, red-painted shrine in one corner; a delicate arched bridge covered a make-believe pond. The effect was of an exquisite calm.

"Take that vase off the table between the windows," Nina commanded. "It has no meaning. It's dinky. Now, let's put this in its place." She stepped back. "So how's that instead?"

"Your taste, Nina!" Louise cried. "Why, it changes the whole room."

"But this time it was really Keith's taste."

"He sounds like an interesting man," Gilbert said. "When are we going to meet him?"

"Oh, one of these days."

Margaret was thinking: When she smiles, a light, all pink and pearl, goes on inside her. It glows right through her skin.

And then the whole day glowed. All was as it had been year after

year: the croquet contest, Louise's harmless local gossip, the girls and
Nina hovering together, Gilbert's old jokes, Fred's private recipe for the
punch, Adam's secret barbecue sauce, and, naturally, the anniversary
cake. After the croquet contest, as the afternoon grew late, Megan's
boyfriend, who had just gotten his driver's license, came proudly by to
take her to a party. Danny departed for the ball field, and the cousins
went home. Adam, inviting Fred to stay awhile, told Margaret with this
gesture that he wished to make amends. She smiled her thanks.

The two women went upstairs, where Nina stretched out in the big
chair with her feet on the ottoman.

"My eyes still see you there doing your homework," Margaret said.
"It almost seems as if you've never left at all."

"I know. I felt that way the moment I turned the corner and saw
the house." Nina yawned, apologizing. "Excuse me. I'm just feeling
relaxed. In New York, somehow, I never do. I'm always running someplace. But I love it all the same."

As she stretched, she kicked off her shoes, beige leather strips that
matched her short linen dress, and heels three inches high.

"How on earth do you walk in those?" asked Margaret.

"I don't. If I plan to walk, I wear sneakers until I get where I'm
going. Everybody does."

Margaret, regarding this smart young woman whom she had
reared, could never decide whether their relationship was mother to
daughter or sister to sister. Depending upon the circumstances, however, not the least of which was Nina's passing mood, the relationship
always managed to make its own choice. At the moment it had apparently chosen the mother-daughter way.

"That's a lovely dress," she remarked. "But linen wrinkles so. I'll
press it for you. As I recall," she teased, "you were never very good at
ironing, were you? Unless you've learned."

"Lord, no. I send things out. Don't bother about this, though.
Linen is supposed to wrinkle. Nobody minds. Keith likes the look of
linen, so I wear it a lot, especially if it's black and sleeveless."

"So you dress to please him. That's nice. Nice that he takes such an
interest too."

Nina smiled. And Margaret, with some tenderness, recognized that
certain little smile that women have when they are remembering some
secret intimacy.

"He loves black. I had a beautiful new black coat to wear to Europe last winter."

Margaret, having been a daughter and being now the mother of daughters, knew not to be inquisitive. Still, she was unable to suppress a remark, half an observation and half a casual question: "I thought when you went to Europe that he must be pretty serious."

"He's very serious."

"Then you're engaged?"

Her glance, going automatically to Nina's hand, saw the gold bangle bracelets on her wrist but no ring.

Nina missed nothing. "No, I haven't got a ring," she said.

"It doesn't matter. I didn't have one either. Adam couldn't afford it then, and I've never thought about it since."

"Oh, Keith can afford one. That's not the problem." It was as if Margaret was waiting to hear what the problem was, and Nina was waiting to be asked.

Nina spoke first. "Well?"

"Well what?"

"Don't you want to know the rest?"

Margaret felt a strange disquiet, a harbinger of alarm. "If you want to tell me."

"He's married."

"Oh?"

Questioning this noncommittal reaction, Nina raised her eyebrows. And Margaret, shaking her head, said quietly, "I'm sorry, but I'm not happy about that."

"Why? He's getting a divorce."

Now alarm had settled itself on Margaret's chest; drawing breath, she felt the weight of it. Nevertheless, she spoke evenly.

"Are you the cause of the divorce?"

Nina laughed. "Heavens, no. They've been planning it for ages."

"Planning it? I don't understand. Why the delay?"

"Their son has had medical problems. They don't want to upset him until he gets through some surgery."

"So they're still living in the same house?"

"Unfortunately for Keith, yes."

"I don't like that, Nina. Really not."

"Why? It has nothing to do with me."

"You're into your second year with him."

"Don't you think I know that, Margaret?"

Since Nina was becoming defensive, Margaret must be very reasonable, very mild.

"Divorce, when both parties want it, doesn't take that long, I think."

"I know that too. By this time next year we'll be married."

"Then why not wait until he's free before you commit—"

At that Nina sat up straight to interrupt. "I should stop seeing him? Give him up? Is that what you're telling me?"

"No. I didn't say you should give him up. I only meant for a while, until he's free. When a man still has a wife—how many children are there?"

"Two."

"Ah, no, Nina. It's wrong. You can do better than that. Traveling around with a man who has a wife and children at home—it's not worthy of you."

Nina stared. "I positively don't believe this! I didn't think you'd be such a killjoy. I really expected that you'd rejoice with me, that you'd be glad I'm loved and I'm happy."

"I am glad you're loved, and I want you to be happy. Can you doubt that about me. *Me?*"

"Well, you're not showing much gladness."

Margaret's eyes met Nina's and were held so long that she, reminded of the children's game of "staring down," had to turn away from that pair of angry eyes. It had not occurred to her that this was so serious a game.

And she said gently, "I don't like to think of you in a clandestine life, that's all. You must have to go hiding about the city, careful not to be seen together. That's ugly, Nina. If you really love each other, you can wait until you don't need to hide, until there's no harm in what you're doing."

"Harm! What *are* you talking about?"

"I'm talking about adultery."

"Margaret, this is 1992! That sort of stuff is a hundred years old."

"No, it's more than two thousand years old."

With a mocking groan and a jangle of bracelets, Nina clapped her forehead. "I never knew you to be so saintly."

"You don't have to be saintly to know right from wrong."

"I didn't come home to hear a lecture," Nina said.

Aware now of the need to patch what was rapidly tearing apart, Margaret apologized. "Don't be angry with me. I don't mean to lecture. Be fair. You have to grant me the right to have an opinion, don't you?"

"All right, all right, I'm not angry. And you won't be, either, once you meet Keith. He's your type of man, for heaven's sake! Intellectual, thoughtful, charming—and you'll be charmed, I promise."

Giving Margaret a bright, forgiving smile, Nina got up and went to the mirror. There, leaning close to it, she examined herself, brushed her eyelashes, smoothed her hair, which did not need smoothing, and then, stepping back for a full-length view, frowned and adjusted the roll of her collar, which did not need adjusting. It seemed to Margaret that all these abrupt and finicky motions were nervous. . . .

Quite suddenly, she was seeing something in Nina that she had not ever seen before. Nina was *different.* The change was subtle, hard to put into words, but it was there, and that man was the cause. She was sure of it, and she heard herself now accusing him: *What have you done to our Nina, our girl?* Maybe Adam had not been so stuffy after all, when he talked about the "fast track."

"Yes," Nina repeated, "you'll be charmed."

No, she would not be charmed. Whoever this man Keith might be, he was at this moment piling a dreadful worry on Margaret's head. *Whoever you are, I don't like you,* said Margaret's inner voice.

"I'll tell you what. Some weekend this summer whenever Keith can get away, I'll bring him here so you can meet him."

When he can "get away," thought Margaret. From what? A wife and two kids? And she said it aloud.

"Get away from a wife and two kids?"

Nina gave a loud, incredulous laugh. "I see I've made a little bit of a mistake by confiding in you, haven't I?"

"If you want to look at it that way, although I don't think so. Incidentally, do your bosses know?"

"They are the only other people who do know, and they couldn't care less."

"Of course. They don't love you as I do. Why should they?"

"They care. But they're not as narrow minded as you. Not many people are."

"Nina dear, please listen to me. You have to be careful where you give your trust. A man must earn your trust first. You never know whether—"

"Good God, I never knew you to be so rigid, so—so unfeeling!"

"And I never knew you to be dishonest."

" 'Dishonest' you call me?"

"Yes. I assume that Keith's wife knows nothing about you. Isn't that true?"

"Well, really. What purpose would it serve to complicate matters? He wants to keep things as clean as possible. And incidentally, Margaret, I don't like being told I'm dishonest."

"I don't like having to say it, but it does seem to me that this whole affair is thievery."

"Thievery! We love each other, Keith and I. Don't you remember anything about love? That one woman should talk to another the way you're talking to me is horrible. It's unbelievable."

"Is it? Listen to me. You call yourself a feminist. You talk about 'sisterhood,' about women helping each other to face the dominant male 'enemy.' God knows, I've heard enough of such talk from plenty of others besides you."

Margaret's heart was hammering. She had risen to face Nina. They were confronting each other.

"Where's your loyalty to this 'sister'? You don't know the first thing about her, whether she even wants a divorce, or how she may be suffering, or her concerns about her children or—or anything. Sisterhood! What garbage! Taking each other's husbands with no conscience at all. Tearing the roof down on a 'sister' and her children."

"That's not true!" Nina shouted. "Keith's miserable. He was miserable long before he met me. It's her fault if she can't hold her husband and make him happy. Her fault!"

"Do lower your voice, please. They can hear you downstairs."

"You really, really make me sick," Nina said, and she bent down to put on her shoes.

"I can't get over it. You, who went to New York and cut your way through that jungle, you, who were independent from the time you could walk and talk, allowing yourself to be so weak as to let a man lead you downhill by the nose, cajoling you."

"Maybe, maybe you never were in love. It sounds as if you don't know the first thing about it."

"How can you say such a thing about Adam and me? You grew up in this house and this family. All you ever saw here was love. And everything I'm saying here is being said out of love. Adam would say the same if he were in this room now. We only want you not to make a mistake. This man—"

"This man is the love of my life. He's not a mistake."

"Women make mistakes for love, Nina. Believe me. They do. As of now you have no certainty. This could all come to nothing, and your heart break."

"I'm the judge of that, Margaret. Let me tell you, you've taken all the joy out of my day. What am I saying? Out of what's been the happiest year of my life." Nina refastened the clasp of her overnight case and thumped it down to the floor at her feet. "It's going to take a long, long time for me to forget the things you've just said. If ever, Margaret. If ever."

"Don't be ridiculous, Nina. We've expressed ourselves frankly, and that's healthy. This anger will pass."

"Oh, do you think so? Well, I don't."

"You can't be serious."

"Can't I? I'll tell you: As long as you feel this way about Keith, I'm not going to bring him here where he's unwelcome. He's worthy of more than that. And I feel unwelcome here myself. I'm getting out right now. There's a late plane, but if I miss it, I'll sit up all night at the airport till the first one leaves in the morning."

Margaret put out her hand, but Nina, defying her, brushed past it and went to the door.

"I will leave quietly," she said. "You needn't worry about a scene."

It was possible from the top of the stairs to hear the sounds of departure: Nina's bright-voiced explanation that she had really intended to stay only for the day and that she was needed back at work; Julie's protest, Fred's surprise, and Adam's regrets. Then came the car sounds, the slammed door, the starter, and the motor dying away down the street.

Trembling and sick, Margaret stood in the center of the bedroom. It was as if a storm had struck and left the house in devastation. On the news you saw pictures of people picking through ruins, searching and putting broken pieces together. . . . So it had been with the broken pieces of Nina's mother's poor life, the child Nina's questions, the steady plausible answers designed to give no hurt or burden, and finally the grown-up Nina's acceptance of these reasonable explanations. . . . But inevitably, somewhere in Jean's mind then, and now in Margaret's mind, there lingered, ever so faintly, the dread that Nina might go her mother's way. And so this man, this Keith, loomed very darkly, like a warning. . . .

"Do you mean to say that you really believed her story about having planned to come just for the day?"

Adam was already in bed, reading, or rather trying to read, in the face of Margaret's agitation. She was walking around the room, brushing her hair as she went.

"I assumed that she was probably bored and wanted to get back to her boyfriend, guy, lover, whatever you want to call him."

"Well, now you know. Adam, it was awful. I'm sick over it, sick, as much as I would be if Megan or Julie had lashed out at me like that."

He shrugged. "Megan and Julie have time yet. Nina's old enough to do what she wants."

"But you're the one who talked about the careless life in the fast track and all that stuff. I was the one who said we should let her alone, that she would take care of herself. And now you don't even seem to be particularly interested."

"I'm interested. I'm listening. Also, I'm seeing that there's nothing that we can do about it."

An emotional storm was rolling within Margaret: frustration, sorrow, and exasperation were a whirlpool of contending winds. And repeating, "Nothing we can do about it?" she wailed, "Nothing?"

Laying the book aside, Adam said patiently, "Times change, and we have to change with them whether we like it or not. Or—"

"Or what?"

"Get lost," he said.

It was a strange thing to say. Lost? How? And studying him as she stood beside the bed, she saw that he was truly weary.

He had closed his eyes, and propped against the pillow, he seemed suddenly—she searched for a word—remote. Absent, as when he had stared over the rim of the coffee cup. There were things he was keeping from her. Good husband that he was, he did not want to pile unnecessary burdens upon her.

They were working him to death, she thought now, as she often thought. His hours were disgraceful. An organization, if it were properly run, ought not to need conferences three or four nights every week. They were working him to death. And in her righteous indignation, her fear and love, she put Nina aside.

"There are things on your mind that you're keeping from me," she said softly. "You mustn't do that. Talk to me, darling. Let me help you."

"Well. Okay. Jenks got a raise and I didn't. I wasn't supposed to know about it, but it leaked out."

"Ah, that hurts!" she cried. And sitting down on the edge of the bed, she laid her hand on his forehead, stroking and soothing. "Yes, yes. It's bitter, not fair, when you deserve it so much more. I understand."

Adam looked up at her. "You're so kind," he said.

"Kind? That's an odd thing to say. I'm your wife. I love you."

He pressed her hand.

"So be it, Adam. The dickens with Jenks or anybody else. We have enough. We have so much. We have each other."

Smiling in gratitude, he closed his eyes.

TEN

"**P**retty, isn't it?" said Randi.

After the last guest had departed, they stood among the cheerful litter of an outdoor lunch, looking at the new pool, which was the reason for the day's entertainment. Under the slanting sun of the windless afternoon, its still surface lay like a gilded coin that someone had carelessly dropped upon the grass.

"For a few dollars more we could have had a bigger one, practically Olympic size, the man told me."

"Not a few dollars, Randi. Another three thousand."

"Adam, you're so tight!"

"You forget, I have to be."

He supposed that it was natural for her to forget. What, after all, could she know about orthodontists' bills and college funds? Actually, there had been no need for him to pay for half the cost of this pool. On the other hand, he spent so much time here at Randi's house that he had felt an obligation to contribute to it.

Anyway, it was accomplished now. The terrace had been newly bricked, there were new yellow awnings, chairs, tables, and a circle of potted September flowers: chrysanthemums and asters.

"End of summer," Randi said wistfully. "The year's growing late."

Adam looked at his watch. "The day is too. I'll just help clear this stuff away and get going."

"What's the rush? You said they all went to the dog show."

"I know, but I'm worried that somebody might decide to stop at the office and surprise me."

"When will you stop worrying yourself to death? But you were always like that, worried that you wouldn't get your term paper in on time and worried that you wouldn't graduate with honors. Yet everything you worried about didn't happen."

"This is different," Adam said.

It needed several trips back and forth to bring everything back to the kitchen. While Randi took her usual unhurried steps, Adam rushed. He was feeling the strain of the double life. The day had been wonderful; it was always wonderful here until it came time to leave, when the pressure upon him to reach home grew intense.

He had a terrible fear, then, of walking into the unsuspecting family circle and making some careless slip that would betray him, as well as a terrible fear that during his absence some betrayal might already have occurred. Today he was supposed to be looking up records for the income tax. . . .

"The kitchen turned out well, don't you think?" Randi said. "The last of Bunting's money. It wasn't all that much, though, and it's better here than lying in the bank."

She had bought the best. Supposedly, this was a European kitchen. Adam knew nothing about such things, about center islands and state-of-the-art ovens; the kitchen at home was what it had always been, he suspected, though during his marriage they had replaced things whenever it became cheaper to replace than to repair them.

But this bright new shine was so important to Randi. He found appealing the almost childish pleasure that she was taking in this house of hers, in fluffy lace curtains, fringed lampshades, and the new monster-sized television. It was all so tasteless, so innocent. And so touching.

"I need to shower and get into my suit," he said as he took off his shorts.

"The dog show lasts till five. I looked it up in the paper."

"You miss nothing, do you? But all the same I have to go."

She gave a little pout. "You're always leaving. I never get to see you."

"Darling, that's not quite true."

"Okay, I know it isn't. And I know you do your best. Wouldn't it be wonderful, though, if you simply lived here?"

He did not answer. Since their situation was hardly an easy one, but rather an almost impossible one, quite obviously the easy reply was that what she wanted was equally impossible. There were people back in Elmsford, four people. . . .

As if she were reading every thought that lay behind Adam's silence, she said briskly, "Okay, enough of that. You know what we'll do? Instead of a shower you can take a dip in the pool. I'll go too. Skinny-dip. Last of the season. It's almost too cold already." While she was speaking, her shorts and halter top came off. "Race you," she cried. "Race you to the pool!"

One tremendous splash followed the other. The sun burned their shoulders, and the water froze their legs.

"I feel like a baked Alaska!" Randi laughed. "Come warm me if you can. Make believe we're in bed. Haven't you ever done this? It's fun. It's crazy. Come on, I'll show you."

The fact is, he thought as he drove through Randolph Crossing toward Elmsford, that all the common sayings are true: *We're mad about each other,* and *Can't keep away from each other.* They were all true.

Good God, she must have learned every sexual variation known to man! She must have read every manual in English and a couple in Hindi besides.

Still, that was hardly the whole story. He felt *good* when he was with her. There was something in the atmosphere of her house that relieved him of care. He forgot about the office, about Ramsey and Jenks, and about Jenks getting the raise that should have been his, Adam's. It was the *atmosphere* that made the difference. In these two years that he and Randi had been together, he had entered another atmosphere.

He felt at home with her friends; he really liked her friends. Considering the fact that she was a newcomer, Randi had gathered about her a good number of nice people: the women at the office and their group, the druggist and his family, and the nursery man who had planted the grounds. They were all so relaxed, so uncompetitive, compared with the people among whom he lived in the other part of his life, the men at the office, the neighbors, and even Margaret's foolish cousins, Louise and Gil. . . .

And he reflected now: Every society has classes; it's not democratic and it shouldn't be, but that's the way it is. The professor of Latin does not spend his free time with the cabdriver. So it was refreshing, it made him feel *decent,* to be among people whom he did not ordinarily meet. He smiled to himself. It was ridiculous, but some of them were really in awe of him and what they spoke of as his "big job."

He wondered what they knew or thought about his personal life. Randi had assured him that they knew very little and wouldn't give a damn if they did. Besides, it didn't matter, because none of them would be likely to encounter the people who were acquainted with him back home.

No, it wasn't likely. Yet one could never be absolutely sure of anything. This game that he was playing was a dangerous one. And he thought of the morning he had gotten up early to have breakfast with Randi, when he had recklessly overstayed his time and arrived late at the office for an important meeting. Indeed, this was a very dangerous game. . . . And yet, in a curious way, it was enlivening.

"We had a good time," Margaret said. "It wasn't anything like the Westminster Show that we saw in New York—how many years ago, Adam?—but I'll tell you, I liked it better. We got to talk to people, especially the sheepdog people, so we could compare theirs with Rufus, and—you must be starved! Dinner will be on the table in five minutes. I've got your favorite corn soup."

"I'm not very hungry."

"You will be once you sit down. It's no wonder you're feeling logy after spending a beautiful Saturday in that airtight office." Margaret's hands were busy with cups and plates as she talked. "Danny's dying to tell you something."

"Dad, I was thinking, Zack is getting old, you know. And I was thinking," Danny said, looking very earnest, "that when he dies, Rufus will be so lonesome."

"Well, don't bury Zack yet. Poor Zack."

"Dad, I didn't mean that. I hope he'll live for years and years. But the fact is, he probably won't."

"That's true."

"So what I mean is, can we get another dog pretty soon?"

"What do you mean by 'soon'? While Zack is with us or not? You have to be specific."

The boy looks more like his mother every day, Adam thought, meaning not the obvious red hair but, far more profoundly, the thoughtful forehead, the candid eyes presaging the man he would be. And thinking so, his heart seemed to move inside him, while shame crawled up his back.

Danny admitted that he would like to have a puppy now, to which Adam replied that he would have to ask his mother.

Margaret said, "Oh, I don't mind. An extra dog only means buying another bed and bowl."

"Gee, Mom, you mean it? Gee, Mom, thanks."

"But I'll tell you. The time to bring a puppy home is the summer. I'm home then when school's out, and I can do the housebreaking. If we were to get him now, there'd be nobody home all day to train him."

"Okay. Next summer. Is it a deal?"

"A deal," Margaret promised solemnly.

That was another trait that Danny and she had in common: easy acceptance of reality. Neither of them was ever apt to coax or argue. And it occurred to Adam that he was feeling lately a sharpened new awareness of his children, as if he were examining them as a stranger might, at a distance.

This sense of *removal* persisted at the dinner table, as he observed them and listened to their chatter: Megan, who appeared to be so much older than fifteen; Julie's tender little face with its fluid changes of expression, fleeting from anxiety to mirth and eagerness; then Danny, the ultra boy, who he himself had never been.

He looked at the tablecloth that his mother had embroidered in red and blue cross-stitch and over to Margaret as she served the salad. Old Zack slept in the corner, while Rufus looked back at Adam and thumped his tail, no doubt in expectation of his evening walk. Everyone and every object here belonged to Adam. All was as familiar as his own body. Yet he had such a terrible sensation of intrusion! It was as if he did not belong here or had been caught in some strange place, unclothed and ashamed of his nakedness.

Margaret reproved him. "You're not eating a thing."

"I guess I'm too tired to eat."

"All right. Don't force yourself. Why don't you go in and lie back in your chair while Julie practices? Maybe you'll be hungry later."

He never wearied of hearing Julie at the piano, even when, correcting herself, she repeated the same passage twenty times. This evening she practiced a Liszt "Mephisto Waltz," whose glide and sway were so well fitted to her young, sentimental temperament. From where he sat, Adam could watch her body move with the rhythm. She was smiling. May nothing ever hurt you, he thought. Nothing. And resting back in the chair, he let himself be soothed by the music's charm and its secret sorrow.

When he awoke from a doze, Megan was speaking.

"Don't you like Nina to send us presents?"

Margaret said vehemently, "Of course I do. I'm glad she's staying close to all of you."

"How can we be close if we're never going to see her again? Is she ever going to come here?"

"That, as I have said many times, is up to her," Margaret answered.

Adam had no wish to be involved in this painful subject. For the past three months, ever since Nina's precipitate departure, he had tried to slough it off. It had been almost impossible to do. There had been first an exchange of letters, Nina accusing Margaret of having said "unforgivable" things, and Margaret responding that *"unforgivable* is a strong word. All I wanted to do was to advise you, because I felt, and I still feel, that you are making a grave mistake." The subject had already consumed too many hours. Yet how else could it have been, in a family as close as this one, after such a sundering?

And Margaret, patiently, had explained to the children why Nina was staying away.

"My heart aches for her, and for all of us who miss her," she said.

One day when they were alone, she had asked Adam why she herself sometimes had the impression that he did not agree with her.

"I don't know. I guess I never talk that much about accomplished facts," he had replied, quite aware that the reply was an inadequate one.

A moment later he had brought forth another thought. "Anyway, we shouldn't talk so much about it in front of the children."

To that Margaret had answered, "Why not, as long as they bring it up? We have never hidden the truth from them. I don't want to sound like a tub-thumper, but I believe children of their age should know what is happening to our country."

Now, lying back as though he were still asleep, he thought: I may not talk about Nina, but I am aware of her all the time. The thought was wry: It can surely be no mystery why I am. "Double life" is the expression, but it is more accurate to say it is an "inside out" life. Or maybe it is even better to call it "no life at all," since it has been so mangled and cut in half. And I am the one who has cut it. When I am with Randi, I can never, in spite of all my longing to be there, forget that I have no right to be there. When I am here at home, I long to be back there. . . .

"Ah, you woke up. You needed that nap," Margaret said. "Do you feel ready to eat something now? I can reheat the soup, or do you want the salad or some eggs? You tell me."

She was so good to him. Even though, after a day spent eating and drinking, the idea of food repelled him, he was unable to resist that gentle, worried plea.

"I'll have the soup," he said.

"Good. I'll keep you company."

At the kitchen table he ate the thick, good soup under Margaret's loving gaze, and he felt like the dirt beneath her feet.

Later, upstairs, she came out of the bathroom wearing a new chiffon nightgown, fire-engine red with a bare back and a ruffled flounce at the hem. She stood in the doorway waiting for his comment.

"Going dancing tonight?" he said.

"Do you like it?"

"Very, very pretty."

It was, and she was, with her milk-white skin and her bright hair.

"I felt extravagant. It was on sale at Danforth's, so that helped."

She began her nightly ritual with the hairbrush, picking things up with her free hand and putting them away in drawers and closets.

"I hardly ever wear red. People always say that redheads shouldn't because it clashes, they say. But I think that's nonsense, don't you?"

Wondering why she was making such a fuss over the nightgown, he agreed that it was nonsense.

"I don't think this clashes with my hair, do you?"

"Not at all," he said, beginning to feel a strange apprehension of— of what?

"Well," she said, laying the hairbrush on the dresser, "you've had a long day, and so have I. So let's put the light out and turn in, shall we?" And to his astonishment she pushed down the shoulder straps and slid out of the gown.

Then it occurred to him that he should have shown more admiration for the picture she made as she stood there in her red silk draperies. He should have removed the gown himself and taken her into his arms. But to his sorrow he had not done so and, lovely as she was, had no impulse to do so now.

Yet impulse or not, he knew he must try. For the message in her eyes was unmistakable. So when she lay down, he opened his arms to draw her to him. And murmuring softly into his neck with eager response, she moved against him, curving her body into his.

Nothing happened.

For a long time, as their unions had become fewer, less intense, and farther apart, he had feared a day when he might be impotent with Margaret. And he knew perfectly well, when that day should arrive, what the cost would be. He was already having as much sex every week as the average man was having. There was not much desire for more.

A sickening, shaming weakness drained through him, and he whispered, "I can't. I'm sorry. I'm sorry."

She tried to kiss him. She tried. . . .

A few hours ago in that pool and afterward on the floor in front of the fireplace, he had done such things—and he whispered again, "I'm sorry. I'm just too tired."

She drew away to lie on her back and, taking his hand, said quietly, "It's all right. I understand."

Oh, God, he said soundlessly, hear her. She wants to comfort me.

Neither one of them moved. They were both rigid in the bed. The room was absolutely still.

Margaret said then, "I think you should find out why you're always so tired."

"I'm not that tired. I'll be all right."

"No," she insisted, "I want you to have a checkup. You haven't had one for a long time."

"I'm fine. It's just been hell at the office. Everyone's complaining. I'm not the only one."

"Still, I want you to see Dr. Farley. Will you promise?"

"Okay. Okay, I will."

"When?"

"Soon."

"I want you to go this week. You'll put it off. I know you."

No, he thought, you do not know me. Oh, Margaret, you don't know me anymore.

"Please, Adam. Promise me."

"All right. I promise."

And now I do not even know myself, he thought.

ELEVEN

A t night for a week or more, Margaret lay with her head on Adam's shoulder. Believing that she understood how he feared the loss of his potency, for he made no attempt to make love to her, she wanted to give him all the warmth of her loving reassurance. Glorious joy that it was, sex was, after all, not the entire purpose of everything. To be loved and trusted and not to be alone, these were what mattered most. Surely if these were nurtured, young as they both were, the rest would be returned to them. Just let Adam be well. He was simply worried and overworked. And he had never been a demonstrative man at best. She had known it almost from the beginning, even on their honeymoon. She had accepted it. People differed in their appetites; that was elementary. Adam was a brilliant, sensitive man, more complicated than most people are. She had always known that too. Just let him be well.

On the tenth day when she asked him what Dr. Farley had reported, he told her that the doctor had found nothing wrong.

"Nothing physical?"

"Nothing physical."

"Then it must be psychological. Didn't he tell you so?"

"No."

"Didn't he say anything, for heaven's sake?"

"Not really."

This puzzled Margaret, for Farley was an especially keen and thorough man, even a rather talkative, unhurried man.

"Didn't he say that something should be done? What are you supposed to do, just go on this way?"

It seemed to her that Adam was looking especially uncomfortable. The thought came to her that the doctor had recommended a psychiatrist; wasn't that the expected recommendation in these cases, as long as there were no discernible physical causes? Knowing Adam, she was suddenly sure that that must be what had happened and that he was having a typical resistance to the idea.

"I'll bet he suggested a psychiatrist," she said. "Tell me the truth."

Wiggling like a caught fish, he admitted it. And then there followed another series of questions, urgings, and objections, until finally a promise was made.

"I'll go! I'll go!" Adam cried, "although I don't know where I'll find the time, let alone the money."

"You'll make the time and we have money enough."

"All right. Just let me alone. I'll go."

Two weeks passed. Still nothing happened in bed and nothing was said on the subject. So one afternoon Margaret went to see Dr. Farley herself. She was afraid when she took her seat on the other side of his desk. Possessing vigorous health, she had had little occasion to visit a doctor. And so she associated her presence there with bad news.

"I've come because I'm so worried about Adam," she began. "There's such a change in him—but of course, you know all about it."

"I don't believe I do," the doctor replied, looking puzzled.

"You mean he hasn't told you?"

"Why, no. I haven't seen him."

"You haven't seen him? He told me he saw you two weeks ago. He admitted to me that you said his trouble was psychological and that's why I'm here, to ask you to refer him—"

"I haven't seen your husband in at least two years, Mrs. Crane."

Dumbfounded, she stammered, "I don't know what's going on. I just don't know."

"Suppose you tell me what you do know."

So she told him as sensibly as she could, while blinking away the tears that persistently gathered in her smarting eyes.

"What shall I do now?" she concluded. "It's not that I mind so much—I mean, it's not the loss of—of natural pleasures so much as what they symbolize. I think Adam must be very unhappy, and I can't imagine why. We've always been such a contented family. Oh, I don't want to sound boastful, that would be stupid, but we're often told that people point us out in the community; we've such wonderful children, we're so lucky, and I've always been so grateful, but—there's something wrong with Adam, Doctor. What shall I do?"

"From what you tell me, I'd say the first thing is to quiet your fears. There can't be anything so drastically wrong that it can't be fixed. Next I'd say go home and tell him the truth about having been here seeing me. Tell him to lay all his cards on the table. You know how to do it. And then maybe it would be a good thing if you were both to come back here together."

Dr. Farley was a kind man, and this advice was certainly reasonable, but even as she sat there hearing it, even as she thanked him and departed, Margaret knew that the situation with which she had to deal was not subject to such an easy solution.

And as she made her way down the bustling street, past shop windows filled with fall plaids, she went hot with a turmoil of many emotions, all fighting one another, humiliation, pity, and anger. Much, much anger.

Not more than half a mile away Adam, on his way back to the office after lunch, met Fred Davis on the street. Fred had been climbing into his van when he saw Adam and hailed him. Adam had been hoping that Fred wouldn't see him because whenever he was into his stride and had a definite destination, he hated having to stop for a chat, however short.

"Adam. How're you doing? It's good to see you. I don't get to see you much now that you work on Saturdays."

Adam said quickly, "Not every Saturday."

"Well, sometimes anyway. Going back to the office? Want a lift?"

"Yes to the first, and no, thanks, to the second." Adam smiled broadly because Fred was doing so. Fred was always smiling. He was so damn amiable. "I need the fresh air."

"Oh, fresh air. In my business I sometimes get too much of it, especially when it goes below freezing. However, no use complaining."

No, hardly any use, with his new van, tweed jacket, expensive boots, the whole bit, the rugged country look, out inspecting his properties on a fine fall morning. *No use complaining!*

Inside the van the dog barked. The tips of his small brown paws pressed the window glass.

"That Jimmy," Fred said. "He loves the car. I took him along this morning up north of Randolph Crossing. Very pretty country. They're starting to develop out among the hills. In fact, some fellow did build a community a few years back, but he was a little too far ahead of the market and didn't do too well. The Grove, it's called."

Adam wouldn't have believed how quickly sweat can start, if someone had told him so. Within the space of seconds he was so wet, he might have been wearing a rubber suit. And he grunted something, words without meaning, merely for the sake of a response.

"You ever been up that way?" Fred asked.

The pale eyes and the placid face were innocent. The question was careless. And Adam answered in the same vein.

"I've passed through. It's nice country."

Fred nodded. "Funny thing, I thought I saw you a couple of weeks ago coming out of that place I just mentioned, The Grove."

Adam shook his head. "Me? No, I'm afraid not."

"Funny. Fellow looked like you. Had sandy hair like yours. The car was a green Ford like yours too." And suddenly, from behind the innocent eyes, there shot a gleam.

Cold now in his damp rubber suit, Adam shook his head again. "Coincidence! They say everybody in the world has a double, and it makes sense when you think about it." He was talking too much. Voluble denials were suspicious. Yet he kept on. "Undoubtedly, we all have more than a double. There are probably a couple of hundred people in the world who look like you. Or me."

"You're right," Fred agreed. "Of course, there was the car. You don't see many that shade of green. But after I saw the lady in the car, I knew it couldn't be you."

"No, not me."

He knows. The nice cheerful bastard knows and wants to warn me. For my sake? Hell, no. For her sake.

The dog whined, drawing attention away from Adam. Good dog, he thought. "Good dog," he said. "Patient little guy. And my Margaret rescued him. Sometimes I think her heart is big enough to take in the world."

"Yes. Yes, it is."

For a moment Fred's vision and Adam's collided. Margaret said Fred's eyes were always "thoughtful." You didn't have to wonder too much about what Fred's thoughts were right now. . . .

"Well," Adam said, "I'd better move along. Nice seeing you, Fred. And you, too, Jimmy."

Damn, he thought, hurrying away. I hope to God my face didn't show anything. What the hell was he doing poking around up there? Randolph Crossing. The Grove. Nobody goes up there except real estate bastards. Christ Almighty. Fred. Of course, he'll never tell Margaret, he'd never hurt her. But I have to tell Randi. We'll have to hole up in the house like bank robbers on the run. God damn! All you want is a little peace and freedom in your life. Am I harming anybody? No! I'm taking care of the home, and it's a peaceful, good home, no fighting, hardly ever an argument, the best environment a child can have and I intend to keep it that way. If only the world would let Randi and me have each other now and then in peace! God damn.

Back at his desk he tried to piece things together. Perhaps he should have acknowledged that it had been he in the car, that he had been—well, for instance, driving one of the employees home; she had been taken sick at work, maybe. Given time, you could embroider a believable story. The trouble was that there never was enough time when you were handed a shock like that. Anyway, it was too late now. . . .

He made a halfhearted attempt to get through an afternoon's work, did it poorly, knew he had done it poorly, and arrived at home in a state of frustrated rage.

Margaret was alone in the kitchen when Adam came home. As she stood at the window watching him walk from the garage with his tie loosened and his jacket flung over his arm, she had an immediate sense of impending trouble. Whatever it is, she thought grimly, I am in just the right mood for it.

She went straight to the offensive, inquiring with saccharine sweetness, "So you saw Dr. Farley, did you?"

"What do you mean?" he questioned back.

"Oh, stop it, Adam! Don't hedge. Don't fence. You didn't see him. You lied to me. Why?"

"I don't have to explain anything I don't want to explain."

"Adam, I'm your wife. I want an answer."

"You're not talking to one of your sophomore students, so don't you tell me what you want or don't want."

"My sophomore students would be amused to see a grown man acting like a damn fool. If you didn't want to see the doctor, you could have said so. You didn't have to lie."

"I lied to stop you from pestering me. It's that simple."

"Does it perhaps occur to you that I pester because I'm worried? What are you hiding? Have you got cancer or something that you're afraid to talk about, even to me?"

"No, I haven't got cancer or anything else," he retorted.

He was still standing with the jacket over his arm. Angry as she was, he seemed pathetic to her, like someone standing on a street in a strange city, looking around for help. And this flashing picture began to soften her anger.

"Sit down here for a minute," she said quietly now, "before the gang comes downstairs. I have to know what's wrong. It isn't fair to me this way."

His response then was equally quiet. "It's a phase, Margaret, one of life's phases, and I suppose it's unexplainable. I have pressures at work and they spill over at home. You know that."

Of course he meant the sex business. Poor man. It was a far greater blow to a man than to a woman when that business went out of order. And she thought she understood that he was afraid to talk about it, to *delve*, for fear that delving might make it worse. She thought she remembered having read something to that effect; the papers and magazines were so filled with pop psychology these days.

"All right," she said. "I do know. Let's drop it for now. Let's just relax, have dinner, and afterward some music. Let's put what's bothering you up on the top shelf of the closet. Okay? I won't be angry, and I hope you won't be."

"I won't be." And he gave her the weak, grateful-seeming smile that she had been noticing of late whenever she was especially soft toward him.

She was fearful, with a cold hollow in the pit of her stomach, although what it exactly was that she feared, she could not have told.

She bought some sex books, a pseudoscientific text as well as a popular illustrated guide, and concluded after she had read them that there was not much in either of them that she had not already known. The general effect of her reading was discouragement, not because the advice and admonitions were not valid, but because if a person was not *willing*, they certainly would not work. She had left the books on a night table where Adam could see them, but whether he had looked through them she did not know and did not ask, remembering again that the worst thing she could do was to make him self-conscious. Patience, then, must be her way.

When, she asked herself, did this all start? The immediate answer might be: on the night when Adam had so plainly rejected her. But as she considered, it became plain that it had begun some time before, in gradual, small accretions, isolated incidents that, if it were not for the present trouble, would have receded into the blur of daily living and forgotten trivia.

A few weeks ago there had been that totally untypical brush between Adam and Megan.

"Only a little more than a year till I'll be seventeen," Megan had said brightly. "What are my chances of getting a car, Dad?"

Adam, who had been relatively silent all evening, had looked up from the newspaper and given a cross reply.

"None. Absolutely none."

"Dad! Why not?"

"Because I'm not a millionaire, that's why."

"I only meant a secondhand car. You don't have to be a millionaire to have that," Megan pleaded. "And I'll help with my baby-sitting savings."

"I said no," Adam said sharply, "and that's what I meant. No. The neighborhood's too full of spoiled babies who think the world is one great big toy store," he added.

"If I'm spoiled, and I certainly don't think I am," Megan argued, "I wonder who spoiled me."

"That's enough," Adam said. "I don't want to hear any more. The subject is closed."

This was not the way of the household, and Megan, bewildered and hurt, turned toward her mother with a silent question.

At that point Margaret intervened. "You're not quite sixteen yet, Megan. So why not wait till the time is ripe, and then we'll talk about it. For my part, I do think it might be very convenient for you to have a little car."

Adam got up and left the room.

Margaret looked at the three puzzled, upturned faces. Certainly she was aware that a great many families bickered and snapped, and that a great many fathers habitually spoke to their children as Adam had just done. But we have never been such a family, she thought, nor has he been such a father. And suddenly, the room seemed hostile, a strange place, not like home.

"Dad's tired," she had apologized.

"He's always tired," Megan had said.

"Megan, that's not true."

And it was not true. Adam was not "always tired." Most of the time he was his recognizable self. But he was too often tired.

He was well aware of the change in himself. The awareness troubled his days and his nights. He knew that he was testy, absentminded, tense, and frightened.

Why had he snapped at Megan simply because, like most other

teenagers, she dreamed about having a car? True, he had later gone to her room in an attempt to explain himself and apologize. . . .

Why had he shouted at Danny last Saturday? He had gone to Randi's for lunch and forgotten his promise to take Danny and Rufus to the vet. The dog had a painful infected ear, and for a whole day afterward the boy had been unforgiving. That time, too, Adam had apologized. . . .

Mounting worries stabbed at him. And he recalled those medieval paintings that showed a flock of little devils poking pitchforks at a man ten times their size.

Fred was a worry. Each time they were together, when he and Margaret unexpectedly met him one evening at a restaurant, or when he dropped in on a Sunday afternoon, as he had been doing for years, Adam reassured himself that Fred would never say the wrong thing. What information, after all, did he possess? Nothing worth a red cent! And yet he was a worry. You never could be certain that someday something, whether deliberately or accidentally, might pop out of Fred's mouth. And he found himself watching Fred, wondering whether there was any slight, subtle change in his manner. He worried when Fred came to the house, and worried when he did not come; could this absence mean that he was staying away because for a second time he had seen the green car with Randi in it?

Disturbing events were taking place at the office too. The place was a spy's nest of rumors. In New York, at headquarters, they were negotiating a deal with Magnum to sell its latest software for a song, a giveaway, because the company was starved for cash. Some, on the other hand, were saying that the company had made a profit in every quarter this last year. But then, back to the other hand again, the Elmsford office had just let three men go, three bright young men. Of course, they were newcomers and lacked experience, so it was not as if they had dismissed anybody on Adam's level. . . .

But what if the rumors were true, and a real downsizing were beginning? And he, Adam, were called into the office one day and politely, regretfully, told— Imagining himself sitting there in front of the uncomfortable, smug, safe bearer of the news, he turned cold. The family's bills were enormous. Or so they seem, he thought bitterly, to a wage slave like me. I suppose I'll have to work and worry till I die.

It's not that we all want so much either. We're not extravagant, unless it's extravagant to want the best colleges for your children. My mother managed for me, but I was only one. Now I have three. And each one of them had to have his teeth straightened. If I were Fred

Davis, I'd put up another couple of houses and it would be no problem. Or if I were Dr. Farley, or Margaret's moron of a cousin, Gil. Now, up at Randi's, her friends are satisfied with less. They don't even think about the Ivy League. If the teeth are a little out of line, it's not the end of the world to them.

He had expenses on Randi's account too. Eating so many meals there, especially now that, ever since the encounter with Fred, they no longer went anywhere near Randolph Crossing to eat, he certainly had an obligation to contribute. There had been the occasional weekend in Chicago or Houston, when ostensibly he had gone to a business conference; delightful, gala days they were, but inevitably expensive. Sometimes it seemed, as he reckoned with his separate credit cards, almost as if he were supporting two households.

Certainly he was juggling two in his head. That morning, two years ago now, when he had spent the night with Randi, he had opened his eyes into confusion, missing the wallpaper in the room he shared with Margaret. Now it often happened that when he woke beside Margaret, he looked for the sky above the clerestory window. And then for a while he would lie still in an agony of self-blame and doubt.

He would look at Margaret's head on the other pillow, seeing there a slight frown on the forehead that had been always so serene; it was likely that her troubles had followed her into her dreams. She didn't deserve her troubles. She deserved to be desired. But he couldn't help that he was unable to desire her; ever since Randi had come back into his life, he had lost the ability to want Margaret. The shame and the pity had come when, for what he knew must be her final effort, she had tried to tempt him, and he had been unable to respond. He had felt her humiliation as if it were he who had been rebuffed.

What was to be done? Where were they heading?

One morning, lying a few minutes late in bed, he listened to the noises of the household; the back door opening and banging shut was somebody letting Zack and Rufus out; the front door was someone getting the newspaper from the lawn. The brief squabbling in the hall was the girls' inevitable disagreement over the ownership of a sweater or scarf. . . . In an access of terror he sprang out of bed. This thing that he was doing, this brinkmanship, must stop before it destroyed the life of his family. These were his people! What the hell was he doing to them?

"I think," he said to Randi after they had been talking for an hour, "I think we should stop."

"Stop talking?" She wiped her swollen red eyes. "Is that what you mean, or—"

"Both."

His voice caught in his throat. Women weep their tears, he thought, and men's throats ache from stifling them.

"You can't mean it, Adam. Can you really walk away after these two years? We've been—why, we've been married for two years here, Adam! This is your home!"

Home, he thought. But my children are home. If only I could have my children and Randi, too, all in the same house every day. . . . But the very concept was absurd. It was idiotic. It was sick.

She got up and walked to the fireplace to stare into the tumbling flames. She had prepared the fire against the gray fall day for him, he knew, because he loved a fire. She had made a hot toddy and put a bowl of autumn leaves on the table. These were things that wives do, wives who care about their home and their man. And he sat there watching her struggle, her head bent and her shoulders shaking.

When he could bear it no longer, he went to her, turning her toward him, and in his broken voice saying for the tenth time or more that day, "Listen to me. I don't want to mean it, but what can I do? We are all, or will be, torn in half if this goes on. What we are doing, this road we're traveling, leads nowhere."

"I don't care, Adam. I'll take this. It's better than nothing."

He wondered about that. Her hints, her faint, vague hints, had not gone unnoticed by him. She wanted permanence, marriage. Of course she did.

And he said very gently, "I have no future to offer you."

She cried out, "*You* are my future. You're all the future I want. Oh, Adam, I love you so. You can't leave me. I won't let you. And you don't want to leave me."

No, no, he did not want to. She was pressed against him, enfolding him, pounding heart to pounding heart and mouth to mouth, while she murmured against his lips.

"We'll manage. As long as we can have a little time together like this—like this—it will be all right. Oh, it's so sad to think of parting! It would be like dying. My darling, it will be all right."

Yes, like dying, he thought, and we're not ready to die.

And her eyes, her lovely, weeping eyes, implored him. "Tell me we'll live. Say so."

His grief was dispersing slowly, like smoke. "Darling, darling, we'll live," he said.

* * *

In the evening when Julie finished practicing, Adam often asked her to play something for him. His choice was Romantic music, Schubert's or Brahms's, music with a dying fall. When he closed his eyes and laid his head back on the chair, Margaret observed a little smile on his lips. It was an odd sort of smile, with a twist to it, as though he were keeping something to himself. Still, wasn't it rather stupid of her to be reading things into a mere smile? And she would go back to her tenth-grade papers.

Then after a while, she would look at Adam again. Had he always had such a slack, weak mouth? Her thoughts embarrassed her. And she tried to account for the nasty thought with self-analysis: I am hurt and scared by my helplessness. Therefore, I am angry and finding ridiculous fault with him, whereas I ought rather to comfort this overworked, possibly sick husband with all his responsibilities.

The trouble was that he did not respond to her comforting. He was away somewhere in a place of his own. Even when he was doing ordinary, pleasant things with them all, having dinner, taking a family walk, or helping with homework, there was a part of him that was absent. And she wished there were someone in whom she could confide to ease her stress. But there was no one. The subject was too intimate, too intimate even for Nina, if she had been there.

And that was another pain in Margaret's heart. That such a total breach could have happened between Nina and herself! And between Nina and the children! Poor children. How could they possibly understand it all?

Without a warning the weather had changed, as weather does; winds and currents were buffeting the family's little boat, and they had no chart. They drifted.

TWELVE

I t was one of those mild days that sometimes appear in December when, even though fall is hardly over, one can already imagine spring. A silvery sunshine streamed through the bare trees, and sparrows flitted across the still-green grass.

Adam, looking anxiously toward the window and Randi's back, appealed to her: "Let's take a walk. A little air and exercise will lift you out of the dumps."

Without turning she said dully, "I need more than that to lift me. I'm alone too much, that's my trouble. Yes, I'm with people all day at work, but when I come back here at night to these empty rooms and silence and all that space outdoors—it's so dismal. I can't describe it, I can't tell you how I feel."

He could say only, "I can imagine. I know. I'm sorry."

"At Thanksgiving I was a guest, a fifth wheel at somebody's family table. All I thought of was the dinner I could have made for you at our own table."

This was the first time that Randi had gone beyond hints or other oblique remarks, and it scared him. Looming ahead he saw a crisis; and now as she turned about, he faced a piteous kind of accusation.

"Of course, it will be the same at Christmas. Then there'll be New Year's Eve, all my friends kissing their boyfriends or their husbands at midnight, while I stand there trying to fake a happy smile. It's too depressing. The fact is, Adam, I'm going into a depression."

"No, no," he protested. "You're too strong, too sound, for that."

"I'm not made of iron," she said.

When he saw tears well into her eyes, his alarm mounted. Good natured as she was and easy to please, Randi was yet capable of making an emotional, explosive decision without regard to any hurtful consequences; had she not once before, and to her own sorrow, broken away from him?

"I know how hard it is for you," he said hurriedly. "I promise I'll manage a three-day business meeting someplace early in January. And we can go there together. But right now I'm hamstrung by these holidays. My kids, second cousins coming all the way from Denver, Christmas stuff at the office—you know how it is."

"Can't we manage a tiny little something for ourselves just once? You can knock off early one day, can't you? Say around four o'clock? Tell everybody you have some business to take care of and run up here for supper. I'll buy food, a feast for us two. And you can go home whenever you want. Can't you do that?"

"Well," he said, "I've been doing an awful lot of that stuff lately."

"Come on, Adam, let's do it. It'll be our own secret Christmas."

"You're irresistible," he said, shaking his head in wonderment at himself.

"I know it," she answered, laughing now.

Shortly after four, as Adam left the office, the snow began. By the time he was halfway to Randi's house, it was falling in sheets. He had an ominous feeling that he ought to turn around and go back while the going was possible. But he did not.

The house was filled with holiday cheer. He ate a fine dinner, drank a champagne toast, and made love to Randi, all the time aware that sleet was tinkling on the windowpane. When the clock began to strike, she turned up the background music to disguise the number of strokes.

"No use, darling," he said. "I've got to start."

They opened the front door onto a tumult of whirling snow, and Randi protested, "You can't possibly drive back to Elmsford through all this."

"I can't possibly stay here all night either," he said, buttoning his overcoat.

"What if you get stuck on the road? How will that look? You're supposed to be at a meeting in the office."

"I have to chance it."

"Talking of possibilities, I think it's pretty clear that this situation is impossible."

It was clear to him that she was not referring to the night's

weather. She was asking him once again about the future of their relationship. And they looked at each other, neither speaking, while the
question hung in the air between them: What is to be done?

Then he kissed her, raced to the car, and slid down the hill.

Fortunately, the route was either level or downhill all the way.
There was hardly a car on the road, and those that were took care to
crawl and keep away from the shoulders where, if anyone were to
founder, he had better be prepared to spend a long, cold night. It had
been totally foolhardy to venture up here, yet the need to see Randi
had been more powerful than caution or common sense. Even as he
cursed at the ice and struggled to hold the road, Adam had to smile at
the picture of her in her red velvet robe and golden slippers. Temptation, sweet temptation in a velvet robe.

He was on the very outskirts of Elmsford, almost two hours into
the journey, when his luck gave out. Making the final turn off the highway onto a narrow street, the car skated across the ice, turned a full
circle, and landed in a heap of snow more than two feet high.

The rest was agony. He got out and tried to shovel. He got back in
and tried to rock the car. The motor roared and the wheels spun; when
he smelled hot rubber, he gave up. For a minute he stood there in an
empty street of shut-up shops and warehouses, pondering the next
move. Thinking it an unnecessary expense, he had never bought a car
phone, but even if he had had one now, whom would he call at this
hour? He was about to leave the car and trudge the few miles to home
when two young fellows came walking around the corner and directed
him to a nearby bar where somebody might have a suggestion.

And so it happened that indeed the bar owner was willing to call
his brother, who had a tow truck and would, for a price, come to
Adam's rescue.

"It'll cost you, mister," he said.

"I don't care what it costs," replied Adam.

It was after half past one in the morning when he entered his own
driveway. Lights were on in the house, and Margaret would be waiting
for an explanation that he really did not have.

The moment he put the key in the lock, he heard her racing downstairs and calling.

"I was frantic! Where in heaven's name were you? I phoned the
office, thinking that perhaps you were all marooned there, but all I got
was an answering machine. Then Megan heard me and got up. We were
both imagining some horrible five-car pileup—but where *were* you?"

"The meeting lasted forever. Afterward, I'm embarrassed to say, a couple of us went over to the Hotel Bradley bar."

Margaret sighed. "Well, as long as you're home and safe. It just never occurred to me that you'd go anyplace afterward." She managed a little laugh. "You've never been the type to go 'out with the boys.' But, please, next time, take a minute to phone."

"I know. I should have. It was stupid of me. I didn't think."

"Well, all's well that ends well. You're soaked through. Better take a hot shower right away. Poor Megan, I sent her back to bed. She was so worried that she even called Fred."

"Called Fred?" he cried. "Why the hell did you let her do *that*?"

"I didn't. She went downstairs and did it, then told me. She wanted to ask Uncle Fred whether we should phone the police."

"Police! And what did he say?"

"Not to call them and not to worry. He said he was quite sure you were all right. I can't imagine what made him so sure. But then, you know Fred. He always looks at the bright side of things."

The bright side? Oh, very bright indeed, said Adam to himself. Even after the hot tea and the hot shower, he shivered.

The next night was the night of the company Christmas party. Most often held at the office, it was to be held this time in a private dining room at the Hotel Bradley.

"That looks like a good omen," Margaret said as they were getting dressed.

"Why so?"

"Well, things must be looking up for them to be spending that much extra money."

"Not necessarily. It could be just the reverse, that they're expecting bad news and want to soften the blow, especially at Christmas. It would be typical of those fat cats."

Margaret did not answer. There was something fundamental in their differing approach to life. She was an optimist, perhaps sometimes foolishly so, while he was the pessimist, perhaps sometimes more wisely realistic than she was. Recently, though, she had been observing in his remarks an overlay of cynicism that was saddening.

She was determined to use this social evening to raise her spirits, which had for so long now been sunken. To that end she had bought a new dress. It cost more than she had ever spent, but it was her favorite color, periwinkle, that odd, lovely shade hovering between violet and blue; she had been unable, and had not wanted, to resist it. Now, at the

mirror as she adjusted a new pair of imitation sapphire earrings, she
was pleased with herself.

Megan and Julie were enraptured. With upturned, expectant faces,
they were waiting at the foot of the stairs when Adam and Margaret
came down.

Laughing, Margaret said, "You look like bridesmaids waiting to
catch the bouquet."

"But, Mom! We never see you like this. You're gorgeous! Isn't she
gorgeous, Dad?"

Adam looked. "Yes, that's a very nice dress."

"You should be dressed up like this every day, Mom," Julie said.

Megan scoffed. "What, in school? You are such a dope."

And Adam said, "Let's go. We'll be late."

They drove the first few blocks in silence. If I knew anything about
psychology, Margaret thought, maybe I would analyze myself and understand whether this weight on what poets call the heart—and is more
likely the solar plexus—is the weight of grief, fear, pity, rage, or all of
them.

And quite abruptly, she blurted, "Do you really like this dress,
Adam? Somehow I have the idea that you don't."

"Why, yes," he replied. "Of course I do. Why do you ask? I said I
liked it. It's very pretty. Very."

He had turned his head toward her as he spoke. His voice had
warmed. But if he had only put his hand on her arm! If only he would
give her something! Something.

Eventually, she must speak out, laying everything flat upon the
table, saying: Here it is, it's your fault, I don't want to blame you because I love you, but I've been waiting long enough, I can't bear it any
longer, it's your fault that you won't tell me anything, won't do anything
about it, if you're ill I'll help you because I love you, don't you understand that in spite of everything, I love you—

Tears started. Stupid tears. Stupid thoughts sometimes that maybe
there was another woman. But that was absurd. In the darkness she
fumbled for a tissue, and through sheer force contained the thoughts.

Don't be an idiot, Margaret. Act your age.

Silence resumed.

Then, slowly, a kind of defiance began to rise in her. She smoothed
her mother's gold bracelet and stroked her silk skirt. It felt smooth and
rich. This was to be a festive night, and there were so few of them at
best in the routine of their lives. She was damned if she wasn't going to
have a good time!

Adam asked pleasantly, "Wasn't Megan saying something about taking AP European history next year?"

"Yes, her advisor thinks she should. She's not especially interested in the humanities, but she'll do well. She always does."

"It's hard to believe she's only going on seventeen next year, isn't it?"

"Megan was always five years ahead of herself."

And the rest of the ride was spent in the agreeable discussion of their children.

She had always been able to pick herself up quickly after a stumble. By the time she walked into the Bradley's rooms, her head was confidently high. She was even faintly amused at herself for being as pleased as a child with the very idea of "party." The sights and sounds of music and bright clothing, chandeliers and flowers, came toward her in a vivid wave, and she plunged right into it.

The Cranes had made no close friends among the people at ADS, Adam being of the belief, which Margaret did not share, that business life ought to be strictly separate from life at home. But she herself had contacts here, many of them originating in her school, since so many of ADS's families had children whom she had taught or was now teaching. So she had barely gone through the door when she was seen and greeted, caught up into the swirl around the bar, introduced to new people, and approached by others whom she had known for most of her life.

Adam stood quietly beside her, holding a drink. She was used to drawing him into social situations and did so now.

"Who is the new man from the main office?" she whispered.

"Who? The new man?"

"The one you mentioned awhile back. I think you said his name was Hudson."

"Oh, him. Over there. The gray-haired man with the woman in the black dress."

"It would make sense to be friendly with him, Adam. He's next in line after Ramsey, isn't he? One round above Jenks."

"I'm hardly unfriendly with him, Margaret."

"That's not the point. Take me over and introduce me."

"This whole business is a pain. All right, let's go."

Rudy Hudson was immediately cordial, as was his wife. They were an older couple, of the sort whose sense of position was unmistakable without being in the least offensive.

"I've heard a lot about you since we moved here," Ruth Hudson told Margaret.

"About me?"

"Yes. Two of our neighbors know you from school. From the way they praised your teaching, I somehow assumed you were a much, much older woman, an old-timer. And when I joined the Red Cross, I heard you work there too."

"Not as often as I'd like. There's never enough time for everything you would like to do, is there?"

The other agreed that that was true. Rudy Hudson, who, Margaret was aware, had been looking at her with interest, remarked to Adam, "You've never said a word about your beautiful wife. I suppose I can't blame you for keeping her a secret."

Embarrassed, Margaret observed that the door to the dining room was opening. As the couples moved apart, Adam murmured that the man was an idiot.

"Why?" she countered. "Because he said I was beautiful, which I'm not?"

"It was just bad taste," Adam said.

Suddenly, she wanted to needle him. "Yes, 'beautiful' really is an exaggeration. But how about 'pretty'? Would you argue with that, or not?"

"Now you're being an idiot," he said. "You know very well you are."

"It wouldn't hurt to hear it from you once in a while."

"All right. You're a very pretty woman."

Now she was angry. Crazy, how her moods shifted from moment to moment! And with valiant determination she concentrated her thoughts away from her injured, angry self.

At the table, where inevitably among the men a stream of business talk flowed back and forth, the women were forced into their own conversations. Margaret was seated near Madeline Jenks and Ruth Hudson.

"So we meet again," said Madeline. "Seems we never see each other between one Christmas party and the next, unless we happen to run into the supermarket at the same time."

Margaret nodded. "I know. But we're all so busy. I sometimes think we could use four or five more hours in our day."

"Well, we women could, anyway. The men have it so much easier. Home on the dot every night to eat and relax while we're hardly through before midnight."

"Some men, yes, but you don't mean the men at ADS, that's for sure."

"Why, what do you mean?" asked Ruth Hudson in surprise.

"The late hours! All the night meetings. I think the men here work very hard."

"There are not that many meetings," said Madeline Jenks.

Now Margaret was surprised. "Not many? Two or three every week. Of course," she said, mindful that she must not seem to be complaining, "the work has to be done. Goodness knows, they do marvelous work. Oh, but yesterday! Half past one in the morning! In all that storm. I thought Adam would never get home from the office. It was awful."

The other two women said nothing. Then the men's conversation took their attention; somebody rose to give a brief welcoming speech, and the orchestra struck up for dancing.

Adam, not liking to dance, moved stiffly around the floor with Margaret. After that she had three or four dances with assorted men, one nice old man whose wife was on crutches and a couple of young ones who had come without a companion. She danced well and was complimented for it.

When the time came to leave, she made a mental assessment of the evening: Like her life it had been satisfactory—except for its one bewildering, huge, miserable trouble.

Adam sat in his office unable to concentrate on the work that lay piled before him. The pounding in his head had begun to nauseate him. The pounding questions would not and could not possibly let him alone. They were crying for a solution. Should he end it with Randi? On the one hand: yes. He should never have begun with her. On the other hand: no. They loved each other. But Margaret was so visibly distraught; he thought, knowing her as he did, that her heart must be aching now, and surely it would break entirely if she should find out. As for the children—he could but shudder at what the news would do to them. And yet, how could they possibly go on as they were? The mood of the house was grim and dark; whenever light did flash through the gloom, it was artificial light and all of them must feel that it was. . . . Besides, how long would it be before his deception would become known? And he thought of Fred, hovering silently in the background, and of last night's narrow escape.

It was a mess, a dreadful mess. He got up to stare out of the window, as he tended to do whenever he needed to think hard, and as if there were some solution to be found in the air or on the street. But the air was empty and the street was banked with dirty snow.

One of the secretaries knocked and entered with a message. "Mr. Jenks wants to see you in his office."

Arrogant bastard! Before his promotion Jenks would have come to Adam's room to say whatever he wanted to say. Now because of it he had suddenly become superior to Adam.

Two men were apparently waiting for Jenks in his outer office. Jenks had a larger office now, one for himself, and the outer one for his secretary. The two rooms were separated by a glass partition.

Jenks began. "I hear you're not so happy at ADS."

In utter astonishment Adam stammered, "I don't know what you mean."

"You complain of overwork."

"I never—why, that's absurd. Who told you such a thing?"

Jenks looked him in the eye. "All those late-night meetings. After one o'clock in the morning in the storm, your wife said."

"My wife?" repeated Adam.

He cursed his blasted tendency to break out into a sweat. And just as he had that time on the street with Fred Davis, he went wet. And he stared back at Jenks.

"Don't be angry with your wife. She meant no harm, Crane. It was just idle talk. I understand that. Or should I say 'innocent' talk?"

"I don't know what Margaret could have meant. I never discuss the company or my work here, even at home." The words emerged in a mumble. "I like my work here, you should know that. I'm loyal."

"Be that as it may, any talk of long hours and late meetings makes us look inefficient or on the rocks, which we definitely are not. As *you* know, as you should well know, Crane." Jenks's voice rang loud enough to be heard beyond the office. "So I would advise you to see to it that neither you nor anyone in your household does it again."

"Of course not, of course not. It was an error, not seriously meant. A complete misunderstanding."

"As to your private life, that's your concern. As long as it doesn't interfere with your work here. Is that clear, Crane?"

He despises me, Adam thought. A C student, I'll wager, from a tenth-rate college in Squeedunk.

"It's clear," he said, still mumbling.

"Good," said Jenks.

The two men in the outer office looked at Adam and quickly looked away. They had heard the whole thing. He had been humiliated, like a schoolboy who has been sent to the principal's office. And as if naked he walked down the corridor to his room, where he sat with both hands pressed over his burning face.

He seethed with the outrage of it. What I should do, he thought, is march right back there and say, "You could have talked to me in private like a gentleman, or better still, you could have ignored the whole business instead of repeating all that silly women's gabble. And as to your allusions to my private life—" But of course, he could not march back there and say anything at all.

If he could only escape from his whole complicated life! Life pulling at him from every direction! Just go someplace with Randi, some quiet, simple place, sit in the sun and walk through pine woods in the shade without having to *think*. He was always *thinking*!

And he experienced now a bad sensation, a loss of equilibrium, as if he were falling, tumbling, with nothing to grab on to. If their mutual dislike had turned Jenks into an enemy, there was no telling what might happen. Among all the rumors that buzzed like bees around a hive was one about some young genius of twenty-four who had been researching software at the state university and was being wooed by a few companies, including ADS. A fellow like him could move in here with his team and turn the place inside out. . . .

The dinner was about to be served when he got home. He had driven three times around the block trying to slow his heartbeat and still his fury.

"I thought you were going to be late again," Margaret said. "We were just going to start without you. They all have so much homework tonight."

"Let them eat without me. I've no appetite. I want to see you upstairs now, anyway."

She followed him into their bedroom. Filled with alarm, she sank down on the dressing-table bench and waited.

Still wearing his outer coat, Adam stood frowning with his hands in his pockets, jingling coins and keys. He was obviously so disturbed about something that he was unable to begin.

"Listen," he said roughly. "Listen to me. Jenks called me in today. He treated me like dirt. You told his wife I wasn't happy in the company."

"What? Are you crazy? I never said that. Do you think I'm a lunatic that I would say such a thing?"

"You said something. They didn't make it up out of whole cloth."

What could she have said? Whatever it was, it must have been trivial indeed, for she had to strain to recall it. Adam was glaring at her, making it harder to pull her thoughts together.

"Well, I'm waiting, Margaret."

"All I remember is saying something about how hard the people work at ADS. It was really a compliment. Oh, yes, I mentioned all the meetings and how you got caught in the storm the other night. That was all."

"That's all? All?" Adam's cheeks and eyebrows, his whole face, seemed to rise toward his hairline. "You damn fool. You utter damn fool. You may do fine in the chem lab teaching a bunch of teenagers, but you haven't got the faintest notion of the real world, have you? Shooting your mouth off in front of those women—"

"I did not shoot my mouth off, Adam. I never do. I can't help it if they chose to exaggerate a passing, innocuous remark."

"You were talking to Jenks's wife, of all people! If I'm transferred out of here to some backwater or even fired, God forbid, I'll have you to thank for it. Do you realize that? Do you?"

She stood up. He had never in all their years spoken to her with such fury, such venom. He was breathing heavily and still glaring. She thought she saw hatred in his eyes. At that her adrenaline began to pour, and rising to her full height, she brought herself up almost to the level of that hatred.

"Now you listen to me," she cried, seizing hold of his coat lapels. "I've had just about enough from you. If you're sick, and I do believe you are, go get some help, as I've asked you twenty times to do. But sick or not, I won't take this from you anymore. I can't stand the way you treat me! What is this about? Who are you? You're not here, you're someplace else where I can't find you. Where are you hiding? I've been fighting clouds and shadows, and I'm tired of it. I've tried to be patient, to understand that there's something wrong with you, yet there's a limit—"

"Oh, you've got a lot to complain about, you have. Go ask other women, women whose husbands come home and raise hell over every little thing, while I go out quietly to work in the yard or stay in and teach the children at the computer. Do I fight? Do I ever raise my voice?"

"It would be better if you did once in a while. At least it would be more human. We would know you were here. What is the mystery about you? Why won't you talk about yourself, anyway? How long can I go on feeling as alone as I have been feeling? I try, I try. . . ." She began to cry. "Why do you treat me like this, blaming me for something I didn't do and would never do? Why do you hate me, Adam?—because I know you do. I see it in your cold eyes."

"I don't hate you. You're being ridiculous. It's laughable."

"I don't think so. Laughable? There's been mighty little laughter in this house for a long, long time. When I think of the way it used to be . . ." She stopped and wiped her cheeks.

A momentous change was taking shape, as something previously unthinkable, and therefore denied, insisted upon returning. And she looked around the room as if there, in the familiarity of the wallpaper with its yellow butterflies or the pictures of her parents in their double frame or the books on the night table, she might find either agreement with or final denial of this unthinkable thing.

There was no denial. And she said, speaking shrilly and loud, "There's somebody else."

Adam threw up his hands, addressing an invisible audience. "I come home to tell her that I may be in hot water at the office on account of her stupid remarks, and all she can do is accuse me of having 'another woman.' Does that make any sense? Does it?"

There was indeed no logic to it; the facts had no connection with each other, and yet the idea had taken hold, and she could only repeat it.

"It's true! Yes, it is. It happens to women every day, so why not to me?"

"Not true, Margaret," Adam said calmly. "Not."

"It's been eighteen years. Time for a change, a new woman, right? Who is she, Adam? Who? Who is the woman who's going to take my place?"

"You're hysterical. You're making a fool of yourself."

When she saw him looking beyond her, she turned and saw the group in the hall outside the door: the girls and Danny were standing there in numb astonishment. Now she was struck with horror: her children had caught their parents in a forbidden intimacy, almost as if they had come upon them in bed making love.

"Oh," she cried, "oh, what are you doing here? We—it's only a foolish argument, it's nothing. Go have your dinner."

And Adam echoed, "Yes. Go downstairs. Who told you to come up here? There's nothing to worry about. Go."

Obediently, they started to the stairs, but not before Margaret had seen Megan's stricken face.

"Well, now you've done it," Adam said. "Did you see Megan?

You've given your young daughter something nice to remember, haven't you?"

Margaret sobbed. Her nerves were going. She who had never had "nerves," who was known for being "steady," had just disgraced herself. She dropped her face into her hands and sat there shaking.

How long she sat, she did not know. When she looked up, Adam had removed his coat and was sitting on the bench watching her. He spoke to her quietly.

"We're making too much of all this. I'm sorry if I began it, coming home frazzled and taking it out on you. I'm sure Jenks exaggerated that business. It's like him to do. I'm sorry."

She wiped her cheeks and nodded.

"But as to that other, the thing you said—it's not true."

"I don't know why I thought—for a moment there, I was so sure," she murmured. "And then I saw the children, and I knew it couldn't possibly be true. You wouldn't do that to them. I know you wouldn't."

"If I could help it," Adam said gravely, "I would never hurt them."

Whenever he spoke like that, with his dignity, his gravity, and the wise touch of his consoling smile, he touched her heart, touched it as he had done when she was seventeen.

"I'll go down and straighten them out. They must be terrified. But they have to learn that sometimes people's emotions make them say outlandish things. They haven't heard much of that in this house."

"No," she said, "no, they haven't."

"Perhaps that wasn't all to the good. Perhaps they would be better off with a little toughening."

This talk is becoming ambiguous, she thought, and my head aches. Probably I've been holding too much in for too long. And so I went a bit crazy just now. That's all that happened.

"I'll bring up something for you to eat."

"Why? Do I look too frightful to go downstairs?"

"Not frightful. You just look as if you've been crying, that's all. Stay here and let me wait on you for a change."

"All right. And explain to them, will you?"

"Of course."

He left her sitting quietly, under control, thoughts streaming through her tired head. He had spoken so gently just now, so kindly, like the Adam she knew. And yet she was quite aware that he had still not touched her flesh. Even a cheek or a hand laid upon either of hers would have meant so much. It was strange, all so strange.

What was happening to them?

* * *

"So she really knows, you see. She doesn't want to know, but she does," Adam said wearily as he concluded the story.

Randi sighed. "I suppose this is your way of saying that we can't have that little trip you promised for January."

"How can I do it now? Besides all this business at home, things are uncertain at the office, as I've been telling you."

He had not, however, told Randi about Jenks's tongue-lashing. There was no reason to do so. A man had his pride too. And in addition he had lately been feeling compunction over the burdens he was laying upon Randi.

The effects were evident in more ways than one, in her sometimes plaintive voice, in her sighs which revealed perhaps more than she intended, and in her very posture. At the moment she made a drooping silhouette at the window, where the strong light washed against blue-gray shadow and made dark blurs of her downcast eyes. An Impressionist would emphasize her pallor, he thought irrelevantly, by dressing her in some sort of long, graceful robe: plum-purple, maybe, or wine-red? His mind was wandering.

When the clock struck the half hour, she looked up, exclaiming, "I'd like to throw that damn thing out! It's like a prison guard when you're here. 'Time,' it calls. 'You've ten minutes left. Five, four, countdown!' I hate the thing."

"It's only two-thirty. I can stay till four."

"Oh, Saturday night, of course. An invitation to a diplomatic dinner at the White House."

"Randi darling, try not to be bitter. Do you think I really want to have dinner at Gil's house along with his country-club show-offs? And best of all, oh, best of all, with Fred Davis?"

"The snoop. Your wife's lover."

"Don't say that. Don't talk about her."

"Why? Do you still love her enough to be jealous?"

"Randi, please. She has no lover. But I wouldn't mind if Fred were her lover."

He sat down on the floor beside Randi's chair and looked up at her face, pleading, "I wish I could do something to keep you from being so sad."

A vast sadness permeated everything. A blight lay over home, office, and suddenly now over this place, too, this source of joy. Mankind wants certainty, and there is none, he thought. Even the weather mocks you; outdoors now in the January thaw you can hear the drip of melting snow, but tomorrow the wind may howl again.

"I feel," he said, "as if I'm in a toboggan racing downhill toward a stone wall, and I must get off before it crashes."

"It won't crash if you steer it right. You have to go around the end of the wall." She stroked his head. "You're all knotted up again. You can't keep on like this." When he did not answer, she kept stroking and talking, gently stroking and gently talking. "You said you wished you could do something to relieve my sadness. Well, you can, and relieve your own at the same time." She paused. "It's not as hard as you probably think it is to get a divorce. That's your real answer, Adam. Bite the bullet."

Divorce. The word shocked him. "I haven't been thinking of divorce," he said.

"Why not? Don't you owe anything to yourself? Don't you have a right to be happy?"

Alarmed, he cried out, "Randi! You're not thinking of leaving me, are you?" And he sat up straight to seek her eyes.

She leaned forward, kissed his forehead, and whispered, "God knows, God knows I don't want to, but—"

"I've been saying stupid things," he said desperately. "It's a mood, that's all, and it will pass as it came. Believe me, we'll be ourselves again. In an hour from now we'll—"

"No. No, Adam. We can't stay the way we are. You can't go on dividing yourself."

"Why not? In Europe they used to accept—maybe they do yet— the fact that a man can maintain a family and still have a lover. Sometimes the wife even knows about it. And life goes on without wreckage, the children don't suffer, they have their father and no harm is done. I don't say it's the best way, but it's better than tearing everything apart."

"That was all right once, Adam. When there was no other way for a woman in my position, she had to accept back-door love. But I want to walk in at the front door. Women have rights today."

He saw that underneath this indignation lay a powerful anger that she was trying to curb.

"I love you. I want to have a home with you. I want to have a baby. Don't look surprised. Why shouldn't I want one? You talk about your children. . . . When am I going to have mine? When I'm fifty? I'm already thirty-eight years old."

With a small sob Randi paused, while Adam, dismayed by this outburst, waited for it to resume. He had naturally guessed what she wanted, for it was no more than what most women wanted. But he had also believed that she had accepted the impossibility of getting it.

"I'm sick of hiding, of all these narrow escapes, like yours in that snowstorm. Or being scared that some busybody will catch us out together in your car. Or needing eyes in the back of my head. Sick of it all. I feel as if I've been caught shoplifting or something."

He saw before him a great divide. It was as if he were standing on a hill observing below him the place in the road where it formed a junction, and he would have to choose which way to take.

There was, however, a fair distance still to go before he would reach that place, and he need make no choice yet. So he spoke very carefully, with his hand on hers, saying almost timidly, "Darling Randi, you knew how it was with me. You said you understood."

"That was more than two years ago. How could I have known how I would feel living this way? I feel married to you now, and you feel the same toward me. You've said it many, many times."

That was true.

"Must she be a drag on you for the rest of your life?"

Now Randi placed her hand on his so that his one hand was held between two of hers; it seemed to him that the currents of their blood were flowing into each other.

"I'm telling you now, Adam, go home and talk to her. Tell her things have changed between you, as she well knows, and that it makes no sense to stick out the rest of your lives together annoying each other. Tell her she'll be better off herself. She can make a new start. She's young enough—how old is she?"

Tell Margaret she'll be better off! Margaret, of all women, who lived for him and family before everything. Family. His mother. Her mother. Their children. Even the cousins. He was hardly able to get the word out.

"Thirty-nine."

"One year older than I am, but years ahead of me in living. Her children are almost grown! Of course, that's a good thing for you. It's not as if you were leaving her with babies on her hands, or with children too young to understand and accept the situation."

Accept! The day he would carry his things to the car, back out of the garage and down the driveway, would they be on the front porch watching him? Accept!

"Anyway, from all that I read, divorce is much better for children than the atmosphere of a failing marriage."

"I don't know," he mumbled.

"Of course it is. You've told me yourself that you've been snapping at them. And what about that scene they overheard while they were standing in the hall? Was that good for them?"

"Of course not."

"Well, then. And it's not as if you were going to move to Australia and abandon your children. You'll live right here, fifteen miles away, and see them all the time, anytime. It'll be much, much better for them in the long run."

Better for them!

Megan that night, turning away toward the staircase. Her stricken face, with a dreadful knowledge being born. Julie, that wisp of a shadow, following him on every errand, looking to him over the piano keys, asking for his admiration. And Danny, the best catcher in the Little League. . . .

"Don't you think your children can sense that you don't love their mother? You haven't loved her for a long time, Adam, if ever. If ever."

Yes, it was true that he did not love Margaret, not in any way that sends a rush to a man's heart or makes him count the days and hours before he will see her again. He cared very much for her, though; he wanted nothing to harm her ever. Ever—But that was something else.

He stood up and got his coat, saying dully, "I have to go. I don't want to go, darling, but I have to."

"I know." She straightened his collar and for a moment they clung together in the doorway. "I'm not pressuring you," she said. "I'm not saying you should go home and do it tonight."

Wanting to part on a light note, Adam smiled. "Hardly tonight. We're going to Louise and Gil's, remember?" And he gave a mock groan.

Randi laughed. "Well, have a good time. Maybe the food will be worth it." Then she grew serious. "Honey, think over what I've said. Get up your spirits and your courage. You can do it."

"Yes," he said.

On the way home, in the tumult of his thoughts, an image from some long-ago history class came suddenly to mind: a drawing of a medieval instrument of torture. It had shown a living man spread out and being pulled apart. What was its name? The rack? Yes, that was it. The rack.

During the evening meal there were unexpected lapses into silence. Suddenly the normal talk about schools, sports, local events, or news of the world would come to a halt. And Margaret felt a wave of consciousness pass over them all, a great, swelling wave, a mutual awareness of change that had occurred or was about to occur. The three youngest would look up at the two eldest, questioning, and as quickly look away. Then either Adam or Margaret would hurriedly take up the interrupted topic as before. Where had Adam's bright enthusiasm vanished? What had happened to his nature lectures, his Saturday-afternoon putterings with herbs and spices in the kitchen? Even his zeal for music, for Julie's evening piano practice, had faded; half the time when she played, he fell asleep in his chair.

Nothing had ever been said about the night of Margaret's outburst. Remembering it with shame, she worried over the impression that she had written with indelible ink on her children's minds, worried that, of all their myriad accumulated memories, this one would remain forever.

Yet she could argue with herself: I am human and I'm not supposed to be perfect; I was driven, he drove me beyond my endurance. Should I then, she asked herself, say as much to my children? At least to Megan, who studies me sometimes with such a deep, troubled, curious gaze? Perhaps it is wrong to let childish ignorance last too long—as if, she thought wryly, children ever really are ignorant! Perhaps I should relieve whatever troubles Megan has by telling her simply that her father and I are going through a hard time and that these things happen and that they pass.

Yet she said nothing. For surely it would pass. In many ways life was already resuming its usual course. On a day when Margaret had taken her class on a field trip, Julie developed a dangerously abscessed tooth, and Adam had to be summoned from work. By the time Margaret returned, Julie was home again, lying on the sofa, while he applied compresses and fed her with ice cream. When poor old Zack got sick, both Adam and Margaret took him to the vet, saw him out of this world, went home to break the news to Danny, and gave what comfort they could. When Julie got the second lead in the ninth-grade play, Margaret and Adam sat in the front row, and Adam brought a bouquet of pink rosebuds.

And so, in some ways, life seemed to be trying to get back on its usual course. . . .

Yet Adam did not sleep. In the wide bed where they lay apart, Margaret was painfully aware of his tension. Without raising her head to peer through the darkness, she believed that she saw him on his back with arms at his sides. She imagined that his fists were clenched. Waking sometimes in the middle of the night and sensing his absence, she would listen for his footsteps in the hall, creaking over the old floors.

Back and forth they went, fourteen steps to the turn and fourteen steps back. It was maddening. And now it was she who lay awake until eventually he returned to the bed.

One night she got up and confronted him. "What is it, Adam? Why can't you sleep?"

"What are you getting excited about? Have you never heard of insomnia?" Then, in the dim hall light, he must have seen her despair. "I disturb you," he said, "and you need your sleep. Perhaps I should use the downstairs bedroom for a while."

In another era, when people had household servants, a "hired girl" had slept in a little room at the back of the house. Later, when Margaret's mother had stayed with them after her accident, she had used it. Since then, no one had.

Hearts do sink, Margaret thought. There's a good reason for every cliché. And she replied very quietly, "Yes of course, if you want to."

Megan was the one who inquired why.

"He isn't feeling well," Margaret told her. "He doesn't want to keep me awake."

"I see," said Megan, stone faced.

And where do we go from here? Margaret asked herself. He has left our bed. There was no one, no one at all, no shoulder on which to lean. Besides, she had too much pride, whether stupid and false or not, to lean on anyone. If Nina had been home, perhaps—no, probably—she would have been the exception. But it would be a year this coming summer since she had spoken to Nina. I shall simply have to lean on myself, she thought. In the end that is what we all have to do.

THIRTEEN

From the enclosed terrace where they were placing the furniture, Nina could see the peacock-blue Atlantic and a line of snow-white beach umbrellas along its rim. From every window on the housefront this view expanded to the horizon. If you were to fly straight across the ocean from here, she reckoned that you would probably land in Morocco.

The house was marvelous, with airy spaces and flowers everywhere, on tiles, in great glass bowls, and on the walls. Not in the usual Florida style, it was more like a planter's house in Bermuda or on a Caribbean island. The exterior was the palest pink, and Nina had furnished it as the planters had furnished theirs when they brought their Chippendale treasures from England. Willie and Ernie had let her handle most of the work by herself; she had secretly been nervous about having so much responsibility, but now that everything had turned out well and everyone was so pleased, she was feeling much pride.

"It was a great idea of yours, Nina, telling the folks to enclose this terrace. Jerry and I only get to use the place during school vacations when Florida's too hot for outdoor sitting, so we're going to appreciate it, I can tell you that."

The speaker was one of the owners' daughters, and it was for the benefit of three generations that they had bought and refurbished this vacation house, complete to Mother Goose murals and a canopied crib.

Nina smiled. "It looks as if you'll be making good use of the nursery."

The other young woman smiled back. "Me first and next my brother's wife. This house intends to be used."

The table was set for lunch when Nina fastened the last tieback on the last curtain. Driving away, she saw the husband walking home from the beach with his little boy riding on his shoulders. Together they would all sit down at the table and plan the rest of the day. And although there was certainly not the least resemblance between this lavish house and the one in Elmsford, they both gave forth the same feeling of stability and calm, so that all the way back to her hotel she had a sense of happy recollection.

She had planned a swim on this last day before returning to New York, but had no sooner entered her room before the telephone rang.

"What's up?" asked Keith. "How's everything going?"

"Just perfectly. I'm in the most gorgeous hotel. Willie and Ernie treat me like a princess when I go on these business trips."

"Why not? You are a princess. How would you like some company?"

"What do you mean?"

"I've got a little business to do in Florida, and I can take an extra day if you want me to."

"If I want you to! I'm floating around in a wonderful room with a king-sized bed."

"No, no, I wouldn't dare come there. There's bound to be somebody on the east coast of Florida who knows me. Or the west coast too."

"Where, then?"

"My brother's horse farm. Or I should say his and my farm. I've some matters to attend to there. Can you fly up for an overnight? It's about twenty minutes by air from where you are."

"What about your brother? I mean, do you—"

"Trust him?" Keith laughed. "With my life. Anyway, he won't be there. A couple of maids will make us a nice dinner, and we'll have the place to ourselves except for them and the horses. Doesn't it sound good?"

"Very good," she said.

A long, low house lay within a grove of pin oaks at the end of a long, curving drive. Green level fields were intersected by rail fences and were dotted now, in the bright afternoon sun, by the dark shapes of grazing horses.

"It doesn't look at all like Florida!" exclaimed Nina.

"Not the Florida most people think of. I'll never forget the first day I saw it. The rain was teeming and it certainly didn't look its best, but I knew I wanted to have it. The funny thing is that I hardly ever get a chance to use the place. But my brother and his family get a lot of fun out of it."

They walked into a great central space with a fireplace at either end, a gleaming wall of windows, leather sofas, and stacks of books all around.

"If you can say that any space this huge can be cozy, I'll say so," Nina remarked.

In various nooks and corners stood clothes racks holding outdoor gear, tennis rackets, fishing rods, and boot trees.

"Most of that stuff belongs to Pete's kids. He's my older brother. He's got teenagers. Come on, I'll show you where you're going to sleep. Where we're going to sleep, I should say. Then we'll go out and look around the grounds. Do you know anything about horses?"

Nina laughed. "Only that they eat oats and that some people ride them."

Excited and enjoying himself, Keith raced her through the upstairs hall into a room with dark Spanish cupboards and a carved bed, hung with red silk, whose fat pillows reminded her of Prague; tonight would be their first entire night together since then. And, she knew, he must be having the same thought.

"It's a pity you don't ride," he said. "Maybe now's a good chance to give you a lesson."

"Oh, not now!"

"Why? Not scared, are you?"

"No, honestly not, only embarrassed about looking foolish. Besides, I have nothing to wear."

"Jeans will do. I'll send Camilla to find one of the girls' hats and some boots for you. The hat's for safety's sake and you'll need boots because sneakers don't fit right in the stirrups. If there's anything else you need, just ask Camilla," Keith called back over his shoulder. "She understands English pretty well."

The marble bathroom opened into another bedroom. Through the partly open door a wall of photographs and medals was visible to Nina, and entering farther, she saw that they belonged to a boy about Danny's age, as well as to a magnificent horse whose bridle he held.

"Nice picture, no?"

"You must be Camilla," Nina said, turning to the woman, hardly more than a girl, who presented an armful of boots and hats.

"You try on. Yes, nice boy. You have kids?"

"No," Nina spoke briefly, not wanting to be caught up into any intimacies about herself.

But Camilla was only a "kid," curious and talkative. "They have five. Big, big boys. Tall. Come here, ride horses all day. Nice family."

"Yes," said Nina. "I'll take these. And thank you, Camilla."

Keith was waiting at the front door, and they started off across the fields.

"I've a pocketful of sugar cubes for you. They'll help you get acquainted. Look there," he said, as they stood leaning over a fence. "Now, there's an example of a prime English Thoroughbred."

A stately stallion with a coat like black satin came at a trot to thrust his quivering nose across the rail.

"He knows we have something for him. Hold out your palm, Nina."

After a moment or two awareness spread across the field and four more handsome heads leaned over the fence.

"Pete knows almost all of them by name, even the ones he intends to sell. Oh, look there, Nina! Now, there's something interesting for you. See that gold-colored fellow? See anything different about him?"

She said carefully, "His face is especially thin, and his neck seems much longer."

"Right. He comes from Central Asia. It's an ancient breed, very rare. I forget the name. Pete learned about it and somehow managed to get hold of one. They're very strong, very elegant, but not as fast as our regular Thoroughbreds. Come on, let's go to the stables and put you onto a saddle."

A little wind came up, ruffling the trees, bending the grass, and perhaps delighting the horses, for many of them went running with it.

"What a wonderful day!" cried Nina.

The stables were cool and fragrant with the sugary scent of last fall's remaining hay. A mother was nursing her foal, born yesterday.

"She'll be a beauty, don't you think so, Mr. Keith?" asked one of the stable boys.

"Like her mother, a gentle lady. Have you got another gentle lady for my friend? This is her first time on a horse."

So a docile, rather elderly mare was led out for Nina; Keith explained how you mount on the left, keep your heels down, adjust the reins around the little finger, and straighten your back.

"Now, off we go, Nina. I'm right behind you."

She was not a bit nervous. They walked slowly around the paddock. After a while they went out onto the bridle path. After a while more they began a slow trot. The wind rose higher, beating softly on Nina's flushed, sun-warmed cheeks.

It was all marvelous, a golden day.

The candle flames swayed in a sudden gust from the open window. Music filtered out of the great room into the dining room. This beauty was contagious; invigorated by the afternoon's activity, and yet rested, Nina felt lovely. She felt the pearls resting on her throat. She felt the delicacy of the hand that held her glass of wine.

Keith was smiling at her. "You're having fun," he said.

"Oh, yes! Wouldn't you love to stay here forever?"

"I could never afford to. Actually, I have only a moderate interest in the land. My brother makes money with the horses, you see." Suddenly Keith grew serious. "He's a fairly rich man, I'm really not."

It seemed to Nina that, lately, he had been mentioning rather often that he had concerns about money. He must have been having some troubles about it at home.

And she reached across the table to touch his hand, saying gently, "I see that you're worried, aren't you? I suspect you're thinking about keeping up two homes and all that. Don't be afraid that I have any illusions about your wealth. I'm earning a fine income myself, and I'm very careful with it. I wasn't reared in luxury, just in a nice middle-American home. What's that old saying: 'Use it up, wear it out'? Something like that. Well, I know how."

When he did not respond she knew that her words had moved him; he had seen that they came from her heart.

Now into the silence the music broke with rising power. Keith stood and went to the player. "Landowska on the harpsichord. I'll turn it up."

The melody soared into the room; passionate and trembling, it mounted, broke, and descended in a sweet, flowing stream. Somewhere in its depths there recurred a phrase that Nina recognized: Julie had been practicing it the last time Nina had been home. And she was pierced by a sudden sad nostalgia.

Home! In the evening after dinner there was music, or talk, or the whisper of turned pages. . . . They were together. . . . At that pink house, lunching by the sea today, they had been together. . . . Here in this house now, where the tennis rackets and the boots stand in the corner and the boy smiles beside his horse in the photograph upstairs, and the rocking horse left over from somebody's childhood is still in the hall, they are together. . . . In New York, in the apartment, there is only waiting, waiting alone.

The candles' constant flicker was making her dizzy. Feeling faintly sickened, she pushed the dessert aside and took a long drink of water.

The music stopped and Keith asked, "Don't you like the cake?"

"Yes, but I've had enough."

"What is it, Nina? You're worried about something. Tell me."

"You know," she told him, hating even to mention the subject.

He sighed. "I guess I do. It's hard, very hard." Shaking his head, he blew a soft whistle. "A friend of mine was telling me the other day what his divorce was costing. Astronomical."

"Why? The legal fees?"

"That's part of it. Lawyers charge whatever the traffic will bear. But that's only the beginning."

"Her father's a lawyer, so that means he'll know how to put up a hard fight, if it comes to that. Will it come to that?"

"Nina, I don't know. I haven't gotten that far. I wasn't talking about myself, about specifics. I was talking in generalities." He sighed again. "It's been a hard year. A hard couple of years, what with Eric's operations and my mother being sick again."

His eyes appealed for understanding. And she did understand; she knew that he was the victim of a wife, an iron chain around his neck, a barrier to his peace and happiness.

"I feel so sorry for you," she murmured. "For us both."

He got up and raised her face toward his. "We don't need this sort of talk. It's not good for us. If you're just patient, everything works out. Don't you know that?"

She smiled then. "I suppose it does," she said.

"You know it does! Listen, we came here for fun together, and we're going to have it, little Nina." His eyes went bright with his familiar twinkle. "We have a long night for a change. A whole long night again!"

When he kissed her, she rose and clung to him. Treasure the moment, she told herself. Patience, patience! Things work out. You'll get what you're waiting for. It's stupid to waste one beautiful hour in worry. Just trust him and love him the way he trusts and loves you.

Yet patience wavered. Depending upon degrees of fatigue or the vagaries of the weather, it came and went. So one day Nina went to Ernie and asked whether she might borrow his car. "Tuesday, maybe?"

"Well, you've been working like a beaver, so I don't know why not. Where are you going?"

"Just up to Westchester. I won't be long and don't worry about your new car. I won't get a scratch on it."

She had looked up the address in the telephone book and had already consulted a township map. It was in the back country on Plum Tree Road. And as she drove up past the city limits into the newly green suburbs, she asked herself whether it was morbid curiosity or masochism that was urging her on toward Keith's house. Undoubtedly, whatever the reason, it was a foolish one because the very sight of that house was sure to hurt her to the quick. Nevertheless, she had to see it.

The area was beautiful. Large, tasteful houses, none of them ostentatious or too new, lay among fields, slight hills, and luxuriant shrubberies. Here was nature educated and well brought up, a setting absolutely right for Keith.

His house, too, was what she had imagined, a low white country house at the top of a long, sloping lawn. Here and there were specimen trees just beginning to leaf: an enormous beech that must be close to a century old, a cluster of cedars and English hollies. She parked the car not too close to the driveway—for in a neighborhood like this one they were wary of strangers—yet close enough to get the feel that she needed. There were three windows on either side of the central doorway. One of them on the second floor must be in Keith's room. Or perhaps he slept at the back of the house? And she thought of him going in and out at that door, up and down that driveway, walking across that grass.

Then the front door opened. Three shapes emerged, a woman followed by two small children. They were too far off to be seen with any clarity, but straining her eyes, she was able to discern their crouching, the gleam of a shovel, and a thin wand, a stick, that stood by itself when they drew away from it. They had planted a sapling.

A touching sight, one would think, a mother and children planting a tree. And yet Nina tasted acid on her tongue. Hanging on, sauntering out into the sunshine, taking her own good time as it suited her, this—this woman whom her husband no longer loved, if he ever had loved her. Just hanging on!

Why don't you grow up and face reality? she raged. When a mistake has been made, for God's sake acknowledge it and let go! He doesn't want you anymore, you fool, you.

She wanted to scream it aloud, wanted to walk up and shout it into the woman's face. Instead she put the car into gear and, vastly depressed, turned back to the city.

In the semiprivate ell where Nick always kept a table for them, Nina waited for Keith. By now the "little place near Third" had acquired a homelike ambiance, as if Nick were almost a member of the family.

"Mr. K. phoned with a message for you," he said. "He'll be about twenty minutes late. Shall I get you a drink now, or do you want to wait?"

"Not now, thanks."

The first day "Mr. K." dropped his disguise, the feel of shackles would drop off Nina's arms and legs. It couldn't be long now. It simply couldn't. She had seen Keith only three times since the lovely night in Florida and she could hardly wait to see him come through Nick's door. Their times were too few, too few. Always something intervened of late: business, his sick mother, always something. And yet people waited years for each other. So if it was going to be years, let it. . . . But she had to know. At least if you knew you could check off the days on a calendar; it would be more bearable. Or would it? She was feeling terribly unsure. . . .

"So," Keith said after he had kissed her. "I'm starved. No time for lunch." He sat down and unfolded his napkin. "How was your day?"

"Very good, to tell you the truth. The pink-house people in Florida paid me such compliments and Willie was so pleased that I'm almost embarrassed."

"You'll soon be a rich woman at that rate."

"I don't know about 'rich.' I like nice things, but I don't die when I don't have them. I can get along on very little."

"You always tell me that. I've heard it at least fifty times."

"Really? I wasn't aware of it."

"Anything new since last week? Your girls coming to visit?"

"No. Their mother won't let them. Adam would, but she says as long as I don't communicate—that's her word, 'communicate'—with her, she will not send Megan and Julie here over spring vacation. It's a pity because they've never seen New York."

"Too bad. You could give them a wonderful time."

"Adam says—we had a long talk, over his office phone, of course—that Margaret is really terribly sad about what's happened between us and wishes I would come home for a visit. But I won't go without you. It's absolutely degrading. It makes me furious. What's a man supposed to do, live on with a wife who won't even make love to him? What's he supposed to be, a human sacrifice?" Nina sighed. "I never knew Margaret to be narrow minded like that, quite the contrary. She was always more tolerant than Adam, although I do adore him. He's my brother and my best friend."

"I'm glad for you. It's a good thing even for an independent woman to have some strong male backing in her family, in case she should ever need it."

"Well, I hope I never will. And that's my news of the day. What's yours?"

"Nothing much."

She looked at him, questioning. "Nothing yet?"

"It's a slow business. Roadblocks," he said tersely.

She did not want to spoil the evening, did not want to bring up the painful subject at all. Yet she was driven to hear more.

And, very mildly, she observed, "It's so awfully slow. All those 'roadblocks'—what are they?"

"Oh, the usual. Need we discuss them now?"

"It's just that you never tell me much. . . . I was thinking, it's odd, isn't it, but I don't even know what your wife looks like, after all this time."

"I've told you. What else do you need to know?"

"You told me she 'looks older than God,' that's all."

"Isn't that enough?"

"Can't you tell me any more?"

"Please, Nina. There's no point in it. Let's enjoy our dinner."

He swirled his glass and took a sip of wine and made a face. "Nick ought to do better than this. I guess I'm spoiled, though. My brother's an oenophile and he's making one out of me. Didn't you notice the wine we had at his place?"

"It was good, but I'm no judge."

"Well, it was superb, one of the great Burgundies."

She did not want to talk about wine. *A slow business. . . . Roadblocks. . . .*

Suddenly she felt very tired. It was time, time right now, to speak out bluntly, to ask what the roadblocks were. She put the fork down, about to begin, when Keith spoke first.

"I was going to wait till after dinner, but I can't wait. Do you want to know what made me late? This."

With a triumphant smile he opened his jacket and took from an inner pocket a narrow velvet box.

"Open it, and don't dare say no, as you always do."

"But why, Keith? Why? You know I—"

"Open it," he commanded.

Feeling the most peculiar confusion of emotions, she opened the box and was overwhelmed. There, glittering against black velvet, lay a bracelet, a solid strip of large baguette diamonds, breathtaking in its bold simplicity: no gold, no pattern, just pure, virgin gems.

Keith was still smiling in expectation of her astonished joy. She was indeed astonished, but joy failed her. There was no reason for her to own this fabulous thing.

"Well?" he said.

She gasped appropriately. "It's magnificent! But you shouldn't have—I mean, it's so wonderful of you, but it's far too much. Really, truly, far too much. I can't accept it, Keith. I really can't."

"Don't be silly. That's for me to judge. Put it on. Nobody's looking. I want to see it."

Having no decent choice but to obey, she clasped it on her wrist. There it gleamed, and there it spoke to her, saying; I am far too costly for you, Nina. We are not meant for each other.

Keith nodded with satisfaction. "Yes. Not too narrow or too wide. It's elegant and classic."

She protested, "It doesn't suit my way of life, don't you see? I have no use for anything like this. It's not that I'm ungrateful, please understand, but—"

"It's not a formal piece! You can easily wear it to lunch with a certain type of client and in the proper place."

"Not the neighborhood sandwich bar."

If I were his wife, she was thinking, I would gladly accept whatever he might want to give. But not now. It's premature. There is something wrong here. And with what she believed to be great sensitivity, she pleaded, "Keith, it is the most beautiful thing imaginable, but, darling, I don't feel right about it. In spite of what you say, it doesn't fit my life or our lives now—yet. Please, will you take it back? Please?"

"No, I will not take it back. It fits you, it's as lovely as you are, and I insist that you have it. You've never accepted a decent present from me. Don't make me angry. Here, put it back in the box and in your bag. Have it insured tomorrow. Nina, listen to me." He gave her a long, serious look. "This is my way, perhaps a clumsy way, of saying thank-you for all you are, for the happiness you bring. And you have brought me very much, little Nina."

And now, at this, she felt the start of tears. He had caused her to lose her resolve, and she was ashamed.

Keith laughed. "Here, take my handkerchief. How funny women are, crying when they're happy! You are happy, aren't you?"

He was so pleased. He looked the way adults look when they have brought delight to a child. There was such a sweetness in his expression; how could she pressure him? And she thought, as always, of the pressures under which he must live, going back every night to a place where he did not want to be.

"And you really like the bracelet?"

"I do, and I still say you shouldn't have done it, but I will never forget this night and what you said when you gave it to me."

When she looked ahead at the mirrored wall in the distance, she could see herself smiling. For an instant it startled her to see this young woman, in leaf-green with sparkling earrings and shining hair, smile back. And a wonderful sensation of warmth and comfort poured through her.

So they finished a festive dinner. When they were on the street in the fresh spring night, she remarked, "It's so beautiful. Shall we walk back to my house?"

"Nina, I can't come tonight. I must get to the train to ride home with my partner and go over a report that's overdue." He kissed her. "The fact is I've got about a hundred things on my mind."

For a minute she watched the taxi recede into the traffic. To be loved was everything! How lucky she was! How could she have had even a moment's doubt? And all the way home, as she walked among hurrying strangers, she felt an amazing goodwill toward them, a wish that they might be as happy as she was.

FOURTEEN

"**Y**ou shouldn't have gone there," Adam said gently. "Suppose she had seen you?"

"Don't worry. I took care that she wouldn't."

He looked up from the telephone to the photograph on the desk, a family photograph with Nina standing in the front row. Poor young thing, to be so entangled! He surely was able to empathize with her, and with her man Keith, who, like himself and poor Randi, was apparently caught between the devil and the sea.

"Don't worry about me," Nina said. "I was a wreck for a few days after going there, but I'm fine again now. You know how I can be in the dumps one minute and out of them in the next. Naturally, I don't call Keith at his office, so I call you when I feel low, and you're an immense help as always. It's amazing to me how well you understand me now, given the kind of marriage you have."

"Yes, I do understand you," Adam said.

"I wish Margaret would relent. I don't see why, though, when you always work so perfectly together, you can't change her mind about Keith and me."

"I guess it's just one of those things, but I'll keep trying."

"Well, enough of that. I think it's great about Megan's essay. We always knew she was smart, but this is really astounding. I want to send her a present."

"That's not necessary. Just write and congratulate her."

"No, I want to send something, a little recognition. Winning first place in a statewide essay contest should be celebrated. You've never been one for celebration, Adam."

"I guess I haven't. Gil and Louise are the folks for that stuff. Louise is planning something for Megan, I heard."

"She's got a big heart. I like Louise."

"You like everybody."

"Well, mostly yes, I do. Anyway, I have to go, and I'm sure you do too. I'll call you soon. Bye, Adam."

"Keep your chin up. You're going to come out all right, honey. Love finds a way."

"Love finds a way," Randi said, "and it's pretty clear to me that you've almost found it yourself."

He did not answer at once. His inner conflict was so severe that often now when the subject—what other subject was there?—came up, he found it impossible to speak. No matter which argument he settled on, immediately he had his refutation of it ready.

His home was cold, cold as a tomb, and he wanted out of it. Yet conscience gave stern lectures. At night when he was unable to sleep, he heard his mother, almost in shock, admonishing him: "You would do this to Margaret? Remember how you brought your newborn babies home and fed them together? Remember how she cared for me, your mother, as few daughters-in-law would do? Remember?"

"Sometimes I feel as if I'll lose my mind," he said now.

"Darling, you won't. You'll wake up one morning soon and find that everything has been solved for you. But that's enough talk for today. Are you taking me out for a birthday lunch on Saturday?"

"Of course. I wish it could be dinner, but I have no excuses for Saturday nights."

"Your lively social Saturdays."

"Hardly. We're having our next door neighbors to dinner. It's our turn."

"You'll be back in plenty of time. I made an early reservation, twelve-thirty."

"Reservation? Where are we going?"

"Your head's so frazzled that you've forgotten? It's the Villandry, the French place that was written up last month. My boss went, and she says it's gorgeous, the only truly French food around here."

"It's not really around here," Adam objected, having recently developed a dislike of change, a nervous unwillingness to explore the new.

"Fifty miles down the highway. What's bad about that on a nice spring day? We'll be there and back in no time. And we don't dare be seen at any place nearer, damn it."

* * *

The Villandry, if not exactly "gorgeous," was a pleasant emulation of any French restaurant in any world-class city. Its walls were hung with paintings of chateaux, and its plentiful flowers, tulips, iris, and narcissi, were spectacular. The service was deft, and the food was excellent. Halfway through a dish of chicken and mushrooms in wine, Adam was glad he had come.

There were no familiar faces. The clientele, he guessed, came mostly from the state capital sixty miles away in the opposite direction. Anyway, he had settled on an introduction for Randi if the worst should happen. She was to be a customer's representative from out of state. Having made this decision, he was beginning to feel an unfamiliar, but very welcome, sense of relaxation.

Then suddenly he was struck down, shocked, quite literally stunned. Two people were being shown to a table near the door. One of them was Louise and the other was Megan.

"Oh, my God," Adam said, dropping his fork on the floor.

"What's the matter?" Randi cried.

"My daughter's here. Megan. The girl in the yellow suit down there."

"Don't panic. What are you going to do?"

"Drop dead, I suppose."

"Don't be an idiot. Who's the woman?"

"The famous Cousin Louise. This must be her surprise treat for Megan."

"Look, you'd better get hold of yourself before you do drop dead. Events are unfolding, my friend. You'll just have to accept them as they come."

"If there were some other way of getting out of here, I could pay now and leave before we're seen. But I don't see any way." In desperation Adam was searching for an exit.

"You could make a dashing escape through the kitchen, I suppose."

"Randi, don't be sarcastic. Oh, my God, Megan's getting up to go to the ladies' room. How am I going to explain—"

"You've made your plan, I'm a customer, consultant, whatever you want."

"Yes, yes, of course—why, Megan, what are you doing here? I didn't know you were going here."

"Neither did I. Cousin Louise took me shopping at home, and then we went here."

"Oh, that's great." He had risen to kiss his daughter and now sat down again. "Don't let me keep you. You're with Cousin Louise," he said, wishing that Megan would go quickly.

But well brought up as she was, Megan was waiting for an introduction. Or perhaps, more probably, she was curious. . . .

"My daughter, Megan," he said. "Miss—"

"Bunting, Randi Bunting," said Randi, very clearly.

Why the hell had she done that? And Adam, bringing his shoe sharply down upon her thin sandal, explained. "We're having a business talk here. Computer companies, you know. We have to keep on the ball. New ideas all the time." He was making an ass of himself.

"You look like your father," said Randi. "You and your sister look like him."

"So they tell me," replied Megan, who was examining Adam's hot face.

"She's prettier than I am," said Adam, being jovial.

Megan did not smile back. And in her very adult expression of thoughtful appraisal, Adam, recognizing himself, went from hot to cold.

"Well," she said, "it was nice meeting you. Enjoy your lunch." And she disappeared into the ladies' room.

"You hurt my foot," said Randi.

"I meant to. God damn it, why did you give your name?"

"Because the truth is the best policy."

"Go to hell. Look what you've done. I could wring your neck."

"Listen to me, Adam. It was bound to come out, so better sooner than later."

"What's better about it? It's easy for you to talk. You saw my daughter. And two more at home." There was a lump in his throat as big as an apple. Adam's apple, he thought with a laugh that came out like a sob.

"Yes, I saw your daughter. You think she'll be destroyed because of me? No, Adam. That's one strong, smart girl. She's a whole lot closer to twenty-seven, or maybe thirty-seven, than seventeen. That's my opinion. It'll take a lot more than this to destroy her."

"Thanks for your analysis." He pushed the plate away. "I want to get out of here. Can you hurry?"

"Yes, I'll hurry. My birthday lunch. Happy day."

"You're the one who ruined the day. If you'd kept your mouth shut, I would have gotten through it all right."

"Until the next time. I'll tell you what, Adam. You've got to give me a date. No more pussyfooting. Give me a date on which you will leave her, an early date. You've got to."

"What is this, an ultimatum?"

"You can call it that. I'm tired of this kind of thing, that's all. It's humiliating. And don't you dare scold me for giving my name. It'll bring things to a head and you'll be glad I did it. Now let's get out of here."

Crisscrossing through the tables, they managed to leave without having to meet Louise. Once in the car, Randi laid her head back and announced that she wanted to sleep. Adam drove in a silence so deep that it only accentuated the drumming in his ears, the sound of racing blood. Pressure must be at the top of the scale, he thought. A stroke might not be so bad, as long as it killed you outright. A quick way to go. Solves everything.

He looked over at Randi. Her eyelids were quivering. She was only pretending to be asleep. Then he saw, sliding down her cheek, a small, round, iridescent tear, and his anger at her began to dwindle. Possibly she was right when she said that the truth was always best. And yet it was so hard. . . . He thought of Nina. She had cried once over the telephone, and he had felt so sad that he was unable to help her. Was he also to be unable to help Randi? Her hands were held loosely in her lap, the curled fingers so delicate, so fragile.

"Watch the road," she said. "Don't keep looking at me."

"I can't help it."

"I thought you were angry."

"I was. I am. I don't want to be."

"You'll have to decide. Now I really want to sleep."

She woke when the car stopped at her house. "Are you coming in?" she asked.

"No. I'd better go home and face whatever I have to."

For a moment they stood before the door. Around in a wide arc rose a somber wall of spruce, dark except for the new growth at their tips, little round caps of yellow-green, chartreuse-bright. And he thought, as he stared upward, how many reasons there were to rejoice in this world. If only—

"I don't want you to come back until you can give me that date," Randi said softly. "I meant what I said."

She was crying again, and he could not bear to look at her.

"I'll try," he murmured. "Wait for me, Randi. I'll try." And he left.

* * *

Megan, still wearing her fashionable suit, was reading alone in the den when Adam came home. When she looked up from the book, not greeting, he again had the feeling that she was appraising him.

"Mom home?" he inquired.

"Upstairs. The Armstrongs aren't coming. She has a cold. Mom's changing her clothes."

"We'll have a company dinner all to ourselves." He paused to choose words, nice, normal, casual words. "That makes two rich meals today for you and me."

"So it does."

She talked like an old woman sometimes when she wanted to, while at other times she was just seventeen.

"Did you enjoy it? Cousin Louise really went all out for you, didn't she?"

"Yes."

"You said you'd been shopping with her."

"Yes."

Adam struggled on. "What did you get?"

"A sweater and some perfume. The perfume was from Uncle Fred. He gave me money so I could select what I want."

"Well, well. I'm proud of you, Megan. Your mother and I are proud of you."

"Thank you."

He cleared his throat, forced a cough, and said finally, "Megan, there's something I want to ask of you." It was wrong, all wrong, to conspire with one's child against the other parent. He had never done it, yet he felt now that, to avert a crisis, he must do it. "Please don't mention anything about today. There was nothing to it, an innocent business lunch, that was all. But I'm afraid your mother would misunderstand it, and I don't want to upset her."

Megan raised her eyes to give him a long, cool look. "Why should it upset her? Mom is never easily upset."

"It's hard to explain. The appearance of things can be very misleading, and—"

"Not telling Mom is like telling a lie to her," Megan began, "so—"

"Dad! I hit a home run!" When Danny entered a room, he plunged in, with Rufus plunging behind him, so that all other conversations were abruptly halted.

"A home run," Adam said, glad of the interruption. "That's great. Tell us about it."

Danny was still telling about it at the dinner table while Adam, pretending enthusiasm, glanced now and then toward Megan. Tonight she was in an adult mood. It had been stupid of him to make that proposition to her, not only wrong, but stupid. Danny and Julie would think it fun to have a little secret, and would probably keep it, but Megan is too wise and clever, he thought, not to be suspicious. Besides, Randi had not looked like a woman at a business lunch; Randi had looked frivolous and radiant. Still, he was probably making a mountain out of a molehill.

Julie said, "Mom, I heard somebody say Megan's lucky not to be in your bio class. Why isn't she?"

"They try never to put teachers' children in their parents' classes. But why do you think she's lucky?"

"Because you mark harder than Mrs. Duncan's section."

Margaret was amused. She had that funny little crooked smile that made her look winsome. There was also something vulnerable about that smile.

Oh, God, Adam thought.

"You're so silent, Megan," Margaret said. "You haven't told us anything about your fancy lunch."

"It was good. We had—"

"Mom, can I have more shrimp? Gee, we never have shrimp unless there's company."

"Yes, Danny, it's in the refrigerator. But you really must stop interrupting. Megan was speaking."

"It wasn't important," Megan said. "Only—" She opened her mouth and closed it.

"Only what?"

"Nothing important."

"Megan, that's so tantalizing. What is it? Say it."

"Only that we saw Dad in the restaurant. Didn't he tell you?"

"I just got home," Adam said. "I haven't had a chance. Yes, I was having lunch with a prospective customer. Incidentally, Mrs. Browning said you're very pretty, Megan. She's a nice person."

Megan regarded her father steadily. "Her name wasn't Browning. It was Bunting. Randi Bunting."

"Bunting?" Margaret exclaimed. "That's the woman we met in New York, the one you used to know at State U."

"Yes, Bunting. Did I say something else? I meant Bunting."

"I thought she lived in California," Margaret said.

"She did, but she moved back here a while ago, and I met her accidentally on business."

"You never told me."

Adam took a gamble. "I told you, Margaret. I told you what a coincidence it was when I ran into her."

"No, Adam, you didn't."

"Funny, I was sure I mentioned it. Well, no matter. It's not important."

Margaret straightened herself in the chair. When she looked over at him, her face had no particular expression. And it was this very absence of expression, this *flatness,* that told him more clearly than the most explicit words could do that she knew everything. *She knew.*

Megan was looking down at her plate. She knew too. Oh, Megan, he asked silently, why did you do this?

Danny and Julie, unaware that something was happening, were having another of their usual mild arguments. No one else spoke until Megan said, "I'll clear the table."

"Mom made ice cream," Danny shouted. "Strawberry."

The ice cream, served in individual dishes, was brought in. Adam was burning, and its frost was welcome. This dinner was taking too long. He needed to hasten it, for the suspense was unbearable. And he had no idea what he would say once he was alone with Margaret. Most probably it would depend upon what she would say first, and she would say plenty. There was a fluttering in his chest, a terrible foreboding. And he sat there silently, swallowing ice cream.

After Julie had practiced, Danny had gone upstairs to do his homework, and Megan had gone down the street to her best friend's house, Adam was left alone in the room that Margaret's mother had called the "back parlor." And it occurred to him as he sat there that these Victorian walls had never before heard what they would probably have to hear tonight.

It also occurred to him that he should be the one to go where Margaret was, instead of the one who waited for her. But his will had frozen. Whatever words might pass between them, whatever accusations, evasions, lies, or truths, still the ultimate question would have to be answered: What is to be done about all these? And he thought of the dialogues between himself and Randi that had ended—in his mind, never in hers, for she had her answer ready—with that same question: What is to be done?

Margaret was wearing a long white robe when she came in. It

surprised him that she had gone up to change, as if she had intended to go to bed without speaking to him and had then changed her mind.

"Do you want to begin?" she asked. "Or shall I?"

"Perhaps you should."

"I have a very simple question. Why have you been lying to me?"

The plan that had been gradually, tentatively, taking shape in his mind was entirely different from this one. In his plan he would have been the person to orchestrate the discussion, choosing the right time, probably after an argument, to approach the subject of divorce. He would not even have needed to mention the existence of another woman. Now, abruptly, he had become a defendant.

He said cautiously, "I wouldn't say that I have lied to you. I did omit, for instance, to tell you I was going to lunch with this woman, but it didn't seem so—"

Margaret interrupted him. "Please don't treat me like a child. Can you possibly have thought I was so insecure that I would object to your having lunch with a businesswoman? No, Adam. Let's get right to the heart of all those things that fit so neatly into the jigsaw puzzle. Let's get to ADS's late-night meetings that never were, to the Saturday pileups of office work that didn't exist, to the fact that you aren't even able to put your hand on me."

At these words her own hand, resting on the table beside which she stood, had clenched, and her voice shook.

"Not able to touch me! As if I were a poisonous thing. . . . Now I understand. Your desire was elsewhere, so I repelled you. I see it perfectly."

"No," he said. "You don't see. You don't repel me, Margaret, you—"

"I've been thinking about it for weeks, for months, actually, not wanting to, stifling my thoughts, telling myself that you were going through a crisis and that it would pass. You would go for help. Maybe in secret you were already doing so. I thought all that, but I didn't want to think you were, quite simply, having a cheap, underhanded affair. Stupid, stupid!" She struck her forehead with her palm. "It happens all the time, and yet I never thought of it. Even that night when I accused you and you denied it, I was so willing, I wanted to believe your denial. I *wanted* to, Adam!" She began to weep. "Maybe I did know the truth. Is that possible? That the knowledge was there, and I smothered it?"

He thought: This is what I dreaded. Now here it is, and what do I do?

He was not ready, he had no words with which to meet this torrent of emotion, so he could only evade, only parry and delay.

"Then explain yourself! Convince me, if you can, that I'm wrong. No, of course you can't. Look at your face in the mirror. The truth is written all over it. Oh, my God!" she cried, and sat down, huddled, clasping herself and rocking as if seized by some internal agony.

He felt a dreadful pity and was helpless. He seemed to be confronted with a catastrophe of nature. His strength ebbed and he, too, sat down, struggling to endure and somehow get through the horror. Once he leaned over to touch Margaret's shoulder and yet, as if paralyzed, did not do it.

Minutes passed on the clock, five, seven, ten, before she raised her suffering red face, and begged, "Can't you answer me? It's my life, my whole life! Don't you understand?"

He gave a deep, long sigh and answered, very low, "I don't know what to say."

"Just tell me why, why?"

"I don't know. . . . . It happens. It happens all the time."

"But to us? Weren't we happy, Adam?"

He was cornered. Unable to look into her piteous eyes, he let his gaze rest upon her white sash as he mumbled, "Infatuation. That's the answer, I guess."

When she sprang up he was shocked by the sudden violence of her move. Her arm swept out, sending a little porcelain vase to smash on the floor.

"No, leave it there. Let it smash. You're smashing the roof in with your 'infatuation,' aren't you? And for that awful woman we saw in New York telling me about her 'crush' on you—for her you will ruin everything. A long-lasting crush, isn't it, for her to follow you, after all these years."

"She didn't follow me. She just happened to move here. It just happened to work out that way."

Margaret swallowed hard and knocked her small fists together.

"Well, Adam, things will have to unhappen, that's all. Perhaps you've forgotten a few small facts, that we have three children. I'm not going to let this damn foolishness hurt them for one minute. You are not going to tear this family apart. You and I are going to go for some counseling and set things straight. But first, promise me that you're finished with her."

When she moved aside, Adam had a full view of the photographs that Nina had once so skillfully arrayed on the old piecrust table. Now suddenly he saw something new: They all looked alike, Margaret and her people, all, even the bearded great-grandfather, having the same expression, responsible and candid, yet slightly reserved, with kindly eyes and proud chins. And Megan, he thought, although they say she looks like me, is the same.

There was a quality in these faces that encouraged him to respond to them with their own pride and candor, or as much of these as in the circumstances he was able to muster.

"I'm sorry," he said. "God knows, I've never wanted to hurt you, and I still don't. But as people move through life, things change. Even when you don't want them to, they do. And I don't know what else to say."

Margaret walked to the window and stood there looking out just as the streetlamps came on. No one passed on the quiet, familiar street. And for a second Adam wondered what scenes were this moment being enacted in some other quiet, familiar houses on streets like this one.

When she turned back toward him, her eyes were filled again with tears. "The humiliation," she said softly. "The two of you tricking me, laughing together at my stupid ignorance, my foolish trust in you."

"No one ever laughed at you."

"Where does she live? What does she do? Since she certainly knows all about me, I have a right to know all about her."

For a moment he hesitated, and mistaking his hesitation for refusal, Margaret cried, "You might as well tell me. I can easily find out."

Thinking, If she goes there, and I don't believe she will, Randi can cope, he replied, "She sells real estate. She has a house not far from Randolph Crossing."

"And this has been going on how long?"

"A couple of years," he said.

Squirming under the cross examination, he suddenly felt the same helpless anger that Jenks had made him feel. Yet Margaret had every right to ask. What else would any woman do? As if she had read his thoughts, she cried out again.

"Do you know there are women who would throw you out of the house for this? Maybe throw a frying pan at your head too? Or file for divorce?"

Divorce. Bite the bullet, Randi said. It was inevitable. Nevertheless, there was a sinking in his stomach, a cold fear that brought back the sensation that students have when they enter the examination hall and the blue books are given out.

"Often," he said in that same low voice and not looking at Margaret, but rather at the suddenly threatening face of her great-grandfather, "divorce is the best solution."

She stared at him. "What? What did you say?"

"It isn't the worst thing in the world."

"For us?" she cried.

"It hasn't been working out for us," he said steadily. "Neither of us is happy anymore."

"What do you mean?" she gasped. "What are you saying?"

"That we will both be better off if we face the truth."

"The truth! Am I going crazy here? Am I really hearing this? You would leave me, just walk away from everything"—and Margaret waved her hand, indicating the house and, as he well knew, the children upstairs—"in exchange for that woman?"

"You make it too simple. Emotions are. . . ." He was faltering, yet there was no way to make plain a thing so complex, so contradictory, and yet so compelling.

"Oh, my God, what has she got that is missing in me?" And Margaret clasped her hands in the age-old gesture of despair.

He was pinned to the wall, and there was no escape. "It's not that there is anything missing in you. It's just that I love her. She is the love of my life."

"The love of your life! Then everything you ever said to me was a sham. All our years, almost nineteen of them, a sham."

"I didn't think it was. I didn't think they were. It's just that things happen."

"Things happen? Am I losing my reason? You really said that?"

He did not answer.

"And the children? The life we've built for them here?"

A look of disbelief came over her face such as you see on people who pass a hideous accident on the road and have to turn away. It seemed to him that he was actually witnessing the outflow of her strength and her vital fluids, as if she were about to die here in this room. He had cut her with a cruel knife, he had savaged her, and, knowing that he had done so, stood up to go to her.

She gave a shrill cry. "No, don't touch me! Don't come near me with your phony sorrow."

"It isn't phony. You can't know what grief I feel, doing this to you. I don't want to, but I can't help it."

She fell onto the sofa. And he said gently, "Margaret . . . I'll take care of you all. Don't think I will ever abandon you and the children. I could never do that. I will be a caring father, the same father I have

always been. And as for you, you don't think so now, but you're still
young and you deserve—"

"Get out," she said. "You have nothing more to tell me. You've
said it all. Get out."

So he left her lying there, went into the sterile little room where he
now slept, and sat down. Well, he had done it; the scene he had so
dreaded and so often postponed had been enacted. And yet his feelings
were ambivalent. Relieved of secrecy and deception, he certainly did
feel lighter and cleaner; he felt free; the way was finally open. Yet he
had killed Margaret's spirit. In spite of his mental reassurance about
her future possibilities, about Fred Davis or some unknown Prince
Charming, he had destroyed a part of her that would never be the same.
And feeling that to be true, he was deeply sad. Tomorrow, too, they
would have to inform the children. . . .

For a long time he sat quite still, thinking and weighing many
things. Probably it was a mistake to have been as blunt as he had been.
He should probably not have used that phrase *love of my life*. He could
hardly believe that he had really spoken it and had crossed the divide.
Yet it was the truth.

It must have been an hour or more before he walked with sound-
less steps into the kitchen, closed the door, and picked up the telephone.

"Well, Randi. It's done," he said. "I've done it."

FIFTEEN

W hen the sobs died away into exhaustion, Margaret began to feel the cold. The room was dark. Someone must have come in and turned off the light. She got up, lit a lamp, and, shivering, stood staring into the pink bulb. Turning her head slowly, she looked around the room. Nothing had changed. It seemed entirely possible that she had been hallucinating, that Adam had not been sitting in the green chair talking about a divorce. Yet there was the evening paper, and the tapestry pillow was on the floor where he always left it, although it belonged on the chair. The house was quiet in the stillness that comes after midnight. A few hours from now it would awaken, and its occupants would have to resume where they had left off.

How had this thing happened? What was going to happen to them all?

Upstairs, the bedroom doors were open. In the dim hall light she discerned Julie's huge stuffed panda on the rocking chair beside the bed. What was this going to do to Julie, tender Julie, who took life so hard?

Dear God, she murmured, clutching the banister. And Rufus, hearing the merest whisper of a voice, looked up from his bed. When she bent to stroke his head, he thumped his tail. And this small display of love from the dog—a dog!—was too much for her. If he had been able to understand language, she would have knelt beside him and asked him for comfort.

Then she thought of Nina, wondering what she would say if and when the rupture should come to pass, the total rupture of the five lives

beneath this roof. Given the direction Nina had taken, she would probably find an excuse for Adam, Margaret thought bitterly.

She lay down again in the dark with her mind going over and over
the unreality of this night, forming questions that had perhaps no answer. How is it possible after so many years that had been quite reasonably happy, that were contented, for an unknown woman to appear out
of nowhere and destroy our peace? Our trust? While I was living my
simple day, teaching, marketing, tending this home—or perhaps one
night while I was sleeping in his bed with my head on his shoulder—she
was already crossing the continent on her way here to rob and wreck.

And we have such beautiful children. Is that nothing to him?

There were more questions. At what point could she have stopped
this if she had known, for surely such things did not happen at first
glance, first contact? Or did they? That woman had come here looking
for Adam. And he. . . . Chemistry, they called it. In the laboratory,
chemistry followed the rules!

The first light was touching the butterflies on the wallpaper when
at last she fell asleep.

When Margaret awoke, full sunshine covered the carpet and the
feel of noon was in the room. There were voices and motion in the
house. It took a few seconds for her to orient herself, to grasp the facts
that this was Sunday, that she had a headache, and that Adam had
asked for a divorce. She sprang out of bed and ran to the mirror, there
to be appalled by the sight of her swollen, shining eyelids. Her impulse
was to go back to bed and hide this ugly proof of her devastation, but
when Megan knocked, she realized that hiding would be not only foolish, but impossible.

"I've been waiting outside your door for you to wake up," Megan
said.

Margaret could think of nothing better to answer than "I look
awful, don't I?"

"Yes. Cold water will help. And then you can wear sunglasses."

"I need to shower and get dressed."

"I shouldn't have told," Megan said.

"Yes, you should have."

"Is it going to be serious?"

"I hope not."

"I saw you on the sofa when I came back from Betsy's. I didn't
want to disturb you, so I just turned the light off."

"I'm sorry you had to see me like that."

"Do you want to tell me about it?"

"Not yet."

The two women studied each other, their visual contact accomplishing in moments what words would need minutes to do.

"I hear Dad talking on the porch. Who's with him?"

"Uncle Fred, making his Sunday visit. Do you want breakfast or lunch?"

"Neither, thanks. If I do, I'll help myself."

"It's almost as warm as summer out. I thought I'd play tennis with Betsy. Unless you need me?"

"No, darling. Go. I want you to have good times."

Standing under the shower, Margaret let tears mingle with the spray. How can he, how can he do this to a girl like Megan? Seventeen years old and already sickened with fear on such a bright spring day.

When she opened the window, which was directly above the porch, the two voices were distinctly audible, and Fred's voice made eavesdropping irresistible. "Try not to hurt her more than you already have."

And Adam: "I'm not deliberately hurting her. It's not what I *want* to do, for God's sake! It's something that simply happened. Neither of us has been happy for a long time. Why? It's hard to say."

Fred's voice rumbled: "Nothing hard about it. Actually, it's very simple on your part. You fell in love, didn't you? Head over heels in love!"

"I don't relish your sarcastic tone, Fred. Love exists, you know."

"That depends on what you mean by the word. Some people, if you'll pardon me, have been known to mistake an itch in the groin for love," replied Fred, who did not usually speak like that, at least not in Margaret's hearing.

"Look here, Fred. If you came here to make trouble, you'd better leave right now."

"If I wanted to make trouble, I could have made it long ago. Have you any idea how many times I've caught sight of you and that piece of yours going in and out of her street?"

There was a silence, during which, weak and shaking, Margaret waited for more.

"What the hell brought you over here this early?" Adam demanded. "Did Margaret phone you?"

"No, Megan did."

"Megan doesn't know anything about this."

"She knows more than you think, and what she doesn't know, she suspects."

"You may not believe you're making trouble, Fred, but you are. You're interfering, and I'm asking you to get out. You're standing on my porch without an invitation."

At this a sudden fury rose within Margaret, and she leaned out of the window, calling, "Don't you dare go, Fred! It's my porch too. I'm coming right down."

Throwing on an old sweater and skirt, she appeared on the porch below, in bedroom slippers with hair uncombed and without sunglasses.

"Perhaps we should go inside," Fred said when he saw her.

"Yes. I know I look like death warmed over. That's how I feel."

The disarranged pillows on the sofa were as she had left them last night. Still there on the floor was the newspaper that Adam had dropped when he pronounced the word *divorce*.

"Has he told you? He wants a divorce," she said.

Fred frowned. "He's told me, but I haven't been able to take it in."

Automatically, the two turned toward Adam, who, forced then to make some response, spoke to the air above the others' heads. "I admit it's shocking. It seems horrible to you, and I can see why it does. But you're not in my skin, you see."

"Skin or not," Fred said, "you can't do this."

"Margaret and I haven't been ha—"

"You told me. It's not only a question of you two being 'happy.' There are three others who didn't ask to be born, and certainly not into a broken family."

" 'Broken'! You make it sound as if nobody will ever see or talk to anybody else. I'll still be their father. I told Margaret that this will make no difference to them. I'm their father!"

"Yes, their father who has left their house and gone to live with his new woman," Fred said, putting his total contempt into the last two words.

Adam leapt from his chair and strode to the door. Fred was quicker and blocked the only exit.

"No, Adam, you can't get out of this so easily."

"Can't? Who gave you the authority to tell me what I can't do?"

"Margaret has no one to speak for her. I've known you both too long not to be part of this tragedy. Now let's sit down and talk. Nothing you say will ever leave this room. I don't think I need tell you that."

Fred Davis had simply assumed command. Margaret had never seen him taking the stance of authority, certainly not with regard to Adam, who would never have accepted it from him. Now, though, Adam, in spite of his bravado, was ashamed; suddenly she recognized the sullen, flushed expression that he wore after a disappointing session with Jenks or Ramsey.

"You've lived your life as an honorable man," Fred began.

Standing above them, he was the teacher addressing his class or the doctor directing his patient. And Margaret, as she raised her eyes to his eyes, now so uncharacteristically severe and keen, began to feel a gradual relaxation, thinking: I trust you to set Adam right. You will know how.

From the collection of photographs on the table Fred took the triple-framed heads of Megan, Julie, and Dan.

"Look at these," he said. "No matter how many hours a week you will spend with them after you leave their mother, how will you be able to look into their faces and explain *why* you left their mother? Because you 'fell in love'? Sounds pretty lame, doesn't it?"

Adam left Fred's unanswered question to float in a profound quiet. As to pictures speaking louder than words, Margaret was thinking, there are yet more to be listened to in this room. And at that exact moment Fred held up another.

"If I remember correctly, this is your mother, isn't she? She was very close to Margaret, that I remember well. What do you think she would have to say about this divorce business of yours?"

At that Adam raised his head, giving a short, ironic laugh. "My mother? She would kill me."

Fred said dryly, "I'll bet she would." For a moment he studied Isabella, the grave eyes, Adam's eyes, and the serene forehead under the slope of waving hair, before replacing her on the table.

"Maybe people were just different then," he said softly, as if to himself. After a moment he turned back to the others and was brisk again. "All right, let's talk. Let's begin at the beginning."

It was a long afternoon. Fred knew where he wanted to go, and he went straight toward his destination, driving Adam, however unwillingly, ahead of him. Years afterward Margaret would still remember the steady progress, the demolition, inch by inch, of every repetitious argument that Adam, growing weaker, was able to raise.

It was after five o'clock before Fred at last concluded. "When all is said and done," he said, "it comes down to the fact that you need counseling most desperately."

To this Adam objected. "I don't think we do. I'm a private person. I don't take kindly to the idea of exposing myself to a stranger. This has been very painful to me today. It's only the sight of Margaret's grief that has kept me sitting here."

"It would be easier for you to talk to a stranger than it has been to brook my interference," Fred argued, "and I'm well aware that it has been interference."

"No counseling," Adam repeated.

And quickly, Margaret, fearing an impasse, interjected, "I think if we try, we can manage without any outside help. This—this unhappiness—that Adam has felt began when that woman came here. I can place the time exactly. If she were removed, Adam, if you would promise never to see her again, we could go back to what we were before. I know we could." And thinking, I am not too proud to plead, for this is my life, our lives, she got up and stood before him, saying with all her heart, "I beg you to try again. I beg you not to leave me. I love you, Adam. No matter what you've done, I love you."

"Well," said Fred.

There were tears in Adam's eyes. "I'll stay. I'll stay. And I will not see her again. Take my word."

Make believe, Margaret said to herself, that you are a war wife as Mom was, and your husband has been overseas. You would surely know that he had not gone for three years without having a woman. You will accept the fact and, for your own peace, put it forever out of your mind.

Unfortunately, though, Randi was neither in Europe nor in Asia, but right here, just fifteen miles away. . . .

"I only had a glimpse," said Louise, "but I had the impression that she was dreadfully common. Madeup, overdressed. You know what I mean."

Pressed by the need to talk to someone and also because Louise was already involved, Margaret had made some very incomplete admissions to her.

"They used to know each other before we were married," she had explained. "The woman's a widow and desperate for another husband. Apparently, she thinks Adam has some connections for her, and she's made a pest of herself."

Whether Louise believed this tale was doubtful, but she was too primly polite and also much too kind to question it.

"Well, he needs to get rid of her," she said succinctly. "He needs to tell her flat out not to bother him. I wonder whether he can do it. Under that sometimes lofty way he has, I have always felt there's a lot of insecurity in Adam."

Louise, then, was not as naive as she appeared to be. The older you get, Margaret thought, the more often people astonish you with what's concealed in them. She would never have suspected that the cheery, rather depthless Louise, with her proper notions, had observed anyone that keenly.

Megan, as reticent as Adam himself, was obviously waiting for an explanation. With her arm around her daughter Margaret did her best to make it a plausible one.

"Woman to woman," she said with an appealing, wistful smile, "I'll admit I was an absolute fool to make such a fuss. The way I lay there crying that night—it was awful for you to see your mother in such a condition. The whole thing was all innocent, you see, just a business lunch, obligatory, you see. I concocted a whole story out of it, and I made an idiot of myself."

Whether Megan, like Louise, believed a word of what Margaret said was doubtful too. At any rate, she gave her mother a kiss and a look filled with—what?—thankfulness, pity, or disbelief?—that went to Margaret's heart.

And when abruptly on an April morning full spring arrived with cool south winds and birdsong, that, too, went to her heart as never before. On such a day in such green-gold splendor, surely a fresh start could be made!

So, almost as if nothing had intervened, the old life resumed. Suddenly there were no more late meetings; Adam took his place at the dinner table every night as he had always done. Saturday again was a home day. Seedlings were set out in the cold frame; together they all painted the rear fence one afternoon; one night Adam made a Mexican dinner with corn soup and guacamole. When Danny was given the part of Lincoln in the class play, Adam coached him as, dressed with beard and stovepipe hat, he gave the Gettysburg Address.

And Margaret, watching and listening for the slightest signs, became convinced that Adam was really trying. Feeling this, she felt that her own old, cold resentments of recent years were dropping away, as when one takes off a constricting garment and can stretch again. He, after all, was only another victim of the well-known "midlife crisis."

What really had brought him back from the brink, whether Fred's exhortations or the photographs of his children or the thought of his mother's condemnation, Margaret did not know. Perhaps Adam himself did not know. Once or twice she had come close to asking him now how he had ended the affair, but she did not do it. Once or twice he made a vague, brief reference to "weakness," admitting that a woman is often the stronger of a pair. So then, Mrs. Randi had been the stronger? And Margaret thought with scorn, no stronger than I am. . . .

Adam had returned to their bed. One night he had simply come and stood hesitating at the door. And she had been so glad! Yet, thinking it better not to make a drama out of what should be perfectly normal, she had just smiled and asked him whether he had had his ice cream yet. For years it had been his habit to have it in the kitchen before going to bed.

"Why not eat it up here in comfort in bed?" she suggested. And so now, in these new days of reconciliation, she began a new custom, bringing his ice cream to the bed. There, in amity, they sat together in the great old bed. He ate the ice cream, she read her book, they talked awhile, turned out the light, and went to sleep.

He had still not touched her.

And sometimes in that bed or in the car on the way home from school, or even at the table in the middle of the five Cranes' familiar conversation, she would feel again a wave of apprehension, a tension like that which precedes a thunderstorm and raises the hair on an animal's back.

SIXTEEN

"What are you doing to me? And you yourself? I can't go on like this!" Randi's voice was hoarse from crying.

In the telephone booth in the stuffy heat Adam shifted his leaning weight from one elbow to the other. These late-afternoon calls exhausted him. Also, the subject was exhausted.

"Randi," he said patiently, "we've got to stop this. I've tried to explain. . . . Maybe in a year or two. . . . But for now I can't, I simply can't. I promised I would give it a try. . . . It's too complicated. Darling, I can't cope anymore today."

"Cope!" she wailed. "But I have to. Every day, every night I have to. All alone. All alone."

"Darling, you gave me an ultimatum—"

"I didn't mean it! I thought I did. I never thought that this is the choice you'd make."

"I had to. The house. The children. You know I had to. Darling, let's hang up. It's been over half an hour."

"So I can't call you at the office?"

"Of course not. Not for these long conversations."

"Can I call you at home?"

"Oh, Randi. Please."

"When am I going to see you? It's going on three months."

"I'm trying. Randi, help me."

"No. I need you. I love you. Are you going to tell me you don't love me anymore? Are you?"

"No, darling Randi."

"Give me one hour on Saturday. Just one hour."

The pressure was enough to blow the top of a man's head off.

And he groaned. "We have to go to some relatives. They're giving a party. Not for us, but it happens to be our anniversary."

"Oh, happy, happy anniversary! What a celebration this must be! How many years?"

Adam sighed.

"You can't even answer. How many?"

"Nineteen."

"You poor thing. I pity you. Well, you just go on home and celebrate with Margaret. I hope she gives you a great time. She'd better, because there'll be no more of them with me. I'm through with you. This time I mean it. Through." The receiver slammed in Adam's ear.

"Yes, it really is nice for a change to be going to somebody else's party on our day, isn't it?" Margaret said.

She wanted him, of course, to acknowledge that it was nice. And he did so.

"It won't be a large crowd," Louise said. "I know how you hate mobs."

Margaret looked anxious. For the last few months she had been knocking herself out trying to please him, being vivacious when probably she would rather have read a book or taken a nap. Aware of all this, being sorry about it, he felt the pressure building up again in his head.

"Did I tell you that Fred sent some of his men over to build a gazebo in their yard? Louise always wanted one, a shady place to sit and read."

Read what, he scoffed silently, the comics?

"They've had some landscaping done. Their place is so lovely."

Of course. That's the reason for the party, Adam thought, so people can see the proof of Gil's prosperity.

At the center of the rear lawn stood the new gazebo, with roses climbing on its trellises. Splendid white rhododendrons, old and obviously transplanted, enclosed the lawn. Here and there were vivid pockets of perennials planted by a talented landscape architect. All was tasteful. All was expensive.

As if the hub of a slowly turning wheel, Adam stood and watched as people moved through the scenery, clustering, parting, and connecting with welcome cries and air kisses. Most of them he knew at least by sight or by name. When they had greeted him, they passed on; no one lingered with him. Perhaps they sensed that he would be just as pleased if they did not.

Margaret, as always, had become a part of the event. He found himself observing her, following her white linen dress and her copper head as they threaded through the crowd. And he thought with a pang that she lived with a man who did not touch her. He thought what a waste that was, an injustice to her. And yet there was no help for it!

"The buffet table is inside," said Louise. "I was afraid the food would melt out here. Come on in, Adam."

She was a foolish woman, but she meant well, he knew. Yet he also knew that she was keeping a worried eye on him. So was Gil, and so, damn him, was Fred Davis. They were all, these protectors of Margaret, so deliberately cordial, even familial, as if to make clear to him that everything was deliberately forgiven. And he followed Louise into the dining room.

There Margaret found him, standing with a full plate, eating by himself.

"Oh, here you are. Do you remember my telling you about the people who raise Old English sheepdogs? Well, they're here now, and she tells me they have some puppies. Do you think we might go out some evening this week and let Danny have a look?"

Her enthusiasm, the very thought of another acquisition, another obligation, wearied him, and he hesitated.

Margaret reminded him, "We promised Danny."

"Yes. Yes, of course."

"Then I'll go make an appointment."

Conversation floated past.

"—two in college this year. It's a fortune, but Harvard's worth it."

"Really quite charming, that Provençal print. They had a New York decorator, some cousin of Gil's or Louise's."

He had not talked to Nina in a while, and she knew nothing of their "trouble," which was just as well. It would be a good thing, though, if she were to be here for Margaret, he thought. In case I leave. In case. And he wondered what Nina would say about their "trouble"; it would be interesting to know, considering that this time the shoe was on the other foot.

When he was finished, he had to force his way through a blocked doorway and more conversation to get outside.

"—good for a million, at least, not counting stock options."

"—bound to be a huge upset at ADS—"

Everything these people talked about was a disturbance to him! Everybody was hurrying, racing, climbing! At Randi's place he could lie naked in the sun and not give a damn about anything. In Randi's room—

Then he recognized a voice, Fred Davis's, asking, "Is everything going all right at home?"

A tall woman blocked his vision and Margaret's reply. He could have punched Fred. Who did he think he was, a parole officer keeping in touch with some shady character?

"Oh," said Margaret as the tall woman moved away, "Fred is just telling me about his trip. He's going to Greece this fall."

"You two ought to plan something," Fred urged. "I always find a voyage is like medicine. Medicine with a good flavor. I'm sure you can find somebody to stay with the children." And he gave Adam a questioning look.

Tight lipped, Adam replied, "We'll see."

Who the devil did he think he was now, a guardian, a therapist, an advisor to the lovelorn?

Suddenly, he was sick of everything, sick of being monitored, lectured to, advised, and guarded. *Trapped* is what he was. Hemmed in among these people where he didn't belong and didn't want to be. Mentally he waved his arm at them all and scattered them.

"I have a couple of errands," he told Margaret the next day. "I may not get back in time for dinner."

It was not quite dark when he returned. He put the car in the garage and, walking back to the house, saw Margaret waiting by the kitchen door. Her expression told him that she knew where he had been. And for a moment he hated her for standing there like a jailer, awaiting the return of an escaped prisoner.

"Well?" she said.

Now, as if on moving film, she changed into the teacher that she was, reprimanding a pupil.

"Well what? You know where I've been."

"I knew when you left where you were going."

"It's no use, Margaret. I promised I'd try, and I have tried all these months, but it's no use."

"Nineteen years," she said.

"I can't help it."

"You dirty bastard."

"I don't want to quarrel with you. Let's do this decently."

"And she. A thief in the night. I have more respect for a prostitute. At least, poor women, they don't steal a man away from his family.

With them it's a business deal. They have something to sell and they name the price, which you can take or leave as you like. Honest value." And Margaret laughed.

"People will hear you! Be careful."

"What difference does it make? They're all going to know it, so why not now? Adam Crane, the exemplary citizen, the intellectual gentleman with the fine scholarly mind, has run away with a filthy slut."

"Margaret, the children. You're hurting the children."

"Much you care about them."

"You know better than that." He opened the door. "I don't want to fight with you. I'm going in."

For a long time, dry eyed and trembling, she sat on the step. In the first-floor bedroom the light went on, so he must have gone back there for the night. Over and over she repeated the evil words that had just passed between them. Yet it did not seem possible that those words could be final. She had been trying so hard, and things had seemed so promising! Adam had promised. . . . And he had not wanted to hurt the children. . . . And it would be different in the morning. . . . People were always more reasonable in the morning.

Shortly after eight o'clock she came downstairs to find him standing among boxes, suitcases, and bags in the hall. He must have been up all night packing. Speechless, not believing what she was seeing, she looked at him.

"I'm leaving," he said.

She began to cry, wiping her eyes with her knuckles.

"Margaret, stop," he said. "It won't do you any good."

"How can you do this?" she pleaded. "Don't, Adam. Please don't leave us. Please don't."

Without replying he picked up two boxes and went out the back door to where his car was parked in the driveway.

"I think you have lost your mind," she whispered when he returned.

"Perhaps." He picked up a suitcase and went out again.

One by one the children came down the stairs and looked at their mother. Afterward, Megan was to tell Margaret, who had no recollection, what she had said to them.

"Don't be afraid. I'm here, and I will never leave you."

"I'm not leaving you either," Adam told them. "There is someone else, but that's between your mother and me. It has nothing to do with you. I'm still your father, and you can count on me."

No one spoke. When he had assembled all his belongings, he climbed into his car. From the front porch they watched him drive down the street and turn the corner. A tableau, thought Margaret. We are a tableau: two girls and a boy in silent, staring shock, a weeping woman, and a shaggy dog.

SEVENTEEN

On the eastern seaboard at that moment it was just after ten o'clock, hot and raining. At the airport near the departure gates Nina searched for Keith through the bustle of business travelers in their wet tan raincoats. On sudden impulse she had decided to surprise him by seeing him off to Phoenix, and she was feeling a happy, childish excitement over the surprise.

"I've come fully armed," she planned to say. "Here's the book you mentioned yesterday, and here's a box lunch so you won't have to choose between eating airplane food or starving. Outside of the fact that we haven't had any real time together ever since Florida, I'm worried about you. You don't have a minute to wind down."

She had thought, and thought now, how lonesome the city became when he was not in it. It was a comfort to feel that he was only a ten-minute taxi ride away. Yet, when waking alone in the silence before dawn, those ten minutes, that fraction of space, extended toward unknown distances and uncounted years.

How long was it going to be? Oh, if one could only rub Aladdin's lamp and make everything come right! Rub the lamp and eliminate the obstacle, the unwanted, stubborn wife, the frigid failure who can't keep her husband's love.

And suddenly there he was. Here was the dear face, here the familiar, rushing steps. Gaily, gladly, she went toward him, calling his name.

She was met with a look of total, startled horror. A woman was with him. In a flash almost subliminal, Nina encompassed the whole woman: smooth, tawny hair; pink face; raincoat; large, pregnant belly.

In another flash Keith's eyes appealed: For God's sake, don't. Don't.

"I brought these papers from the office," she said. "You forgot them."

"Thank you," he answered, taking the package. "Very thoughtful of you." And he repeated, "Thank you."

He expected her to turn and go. But first she had to control her legs. And so there was a pause that had to be filled, a few seconds in which the pink face was raised expectantly toward her husband—for what could this woman be, with that expression and that body language, if not a wife?

"My wife," said Keith. "Miss—Jordan."

The pearly face smiled: *How do you do?* The upper lip was shaped like the top of a heart, and the dark-fringed eyes, perhaps blue, perhaps green, were gentle.

Nina's legs began to manage themselves. She nodded, said, "Well . . ." and backed away. She could not have, and would not have, stayed there more than fifteen seconds, yet this was long enough to hear a full story contained in a sentence or two.

"Keedy, don't worry about a thing. I'll bring your mother home from the hospital tomorrow, and as for me, I'm not due till next week. You'll be home before I have to go."

Muffled in a fog and unsure of her steps as she walked away, she heard the voice continue, "Take care of yourself, darling. I put your cough medicine in your pocket."

Darling. Keedy. The wife had her own name for him, an intimate name. Intimate indeed, with that full belly! At the corner past the newsstand Nina looked back. He had his arms around her and was kissing her good-bye.

She fled. Down the long walkway she went, running like mad, as she had run that night in a foreign city. Out on the street she hailed a taxi and collapsed with her head on the back of the seat.

"You all right, lady?" asked the driver.

"Yes, all right. It's only a headache."

Over! The whole fraudulent affair was over. She had just witnessed its death. And she fought to think clearly: I must pull myself together. I can't afford to collapse. A client's coming to the office. What's her name? Stout woman, thick white hair, about sixty years old, nice woman. Needs wallpaper. Samples. Who? Can't think.

Good Lord, where were the samples? She had had them home overnight, had had them this morning. Good Lord, she had handed them to Keith! The book and the lunch were here on the seat beside her. She wanted to scream, to cry, to be alone, to lie down. But there was no place to go. . . .

"You look as if you'd lost your best friend," Willie said when she entered the shop.

"I think I'm coming down with something. I don't feel well."

"Don't give it to me," said Ernie. "You know what a cold does to me. It flattens me. Maybe you should go home."

"I can't. Mrs. What's-her-name is coming," she wailed. "And I've lost her samples. I spent all afternoon looking at wallpaper for her, and now I've lost the samples!"

Willie said gently, "You really are in a condition, poor girl. Go on home. I'll take care of Mrs. What's-her-name. Go on. Take a couple of aspirins."

The rain had stopped, leaving a dull, sultry day, as if the world were dying. Let it die, she thought, prone on her bed. Let it. She cried and trembled. Her teeth chattered. Awful sobs shook her, subsided, and shook again. Even here in her own place, she dared not scream. Somebody would hear and call the police or an ambulance. Once, as she raised her head and met Keith's gaze framed in antique bronze on a table, she got up and smashed it to the floor, where it broke with a scattering of glass.

After a long time her thoughts began to take shape. Ah, she ought to have known! And the signs had been present, but she had simply not understood how to read them. This man, son of that meticulous mother, with his love of order, his educated tastes—all that history and art in Prague—and his discreet manners, would be the last to make an impetuous, ill-considered mistake in marriage and the last to tear his life apart. Any idiot would realize that such a man would hold on to his lovely wife, his lovely house, and lovely children.

And do you really think, Nina, you poor fool, that he would give up all this pride and pleasantness for you? You were the toy, the champagne cocktail, the icing on his cake.

He lied to me, Nina raged. He promised and he lied. He made a fool of me. And he was getting tired of me. Yes. The signs were there, only I didn't want to read them. I hope he dies out there in Phoenix. I hope he dies.

Late on the next afternoon the doorbell rang. Swollen from crying, full of aspirin and headache, still in her bathrobe, she refused to answer it.

"We know you're in there," Willie called. "Ernie's with me. Let us in."

"I'm sick. I told you when I phoned that I wasn't able to go to work."

"You're not sick. Something's happened. I could hear the tears in your voice."

"No, I'm really sick," she protested.

"If you don't let us in, we'll stand here all night and make a scene."

So she had to let them in and had to tell the whole story. When she finished, Ernie sighed.

"Well, I don't mean to be unkind, Nina, but it was predictable."

"Why?"

"Shall we tell her, Willie?"

"Of course."

"Well, we saw him a few months ago at an antique show. He was with his wife, looking at English furniture in a booth next to ours. He recognized me, but very carefully pretended not to. Afterward we learned from the dealer that they were building a wing on their house, enlarging the library and adding a computer room. Providing for the future, in other words."

"Why didn't you tell me?" Nina wiped her eyes, which had begun to tear again. "Excuse me for blubbering."

"Blubber away. You need to get it out and over with."

"But why didn't you tell me?"

"For the same reason people don't tell a wife. Nobody wants to be the bearer of bad news. You don't want to make trouble, so you mind your own business. Besides, you wouldn't have believed us. You wouldn't have listened."

"You're right."

The three sat still in a bleak silence.

"Why did he do this to me?" Nina implored, shaking her head as if to question the very possibility of such perfidy. "Why did he lead me on?"

"You're an unusually attractive woman, Nina. You're different from the run of the mill."

"Oh, sure, sure," she said bitterly. "That's what he told me too. Different!"

"But you are," Willie said. "There's a freshness about you, an old-time charm you seldom see anymore. And yet, you are also a new, independent woman. In short, you're a find, a discovery."

"In short, a *thing* that he used as long as it was convenient." And as people do when their thoughts stray, she studied her fingers, recalling here and there an endearing word, a walk in the snow, a passionate night, three years' worth of jumbled recollections. "I shall have to start fresh and make myself over," she said.

Both men's faces were very kind, so kind that she was able, with no sense of humbling herself, to make an admission.

"I have been feeling for a while that he might be tiring of me. And yet, whenever I felt that way, I told myself it was ridiculous." She paused, and then jumping up, exclaimed, "Still, if he really was ready to end it, why would he have given me this? Let me show you."

"A very, very pretty piece," Ernie said. "Twenty-five or thirty thousand, I would guess."

"Twenty-seven. I'm returning it, of course."

Willie admonished her. "Absolutely not! Don't be a fool."

"I never wanted it in the first place, Willie. He insisted that I take it. That's why I think he must still love me."

Ernie shook his head, saying, "That's your innocence speaking. Let me be blunt, may I?"

"Go ahead."

"This was the farewell gift, the tidy finish, darling, the phaseout, so you wouldn't make too big a fuss at the end. It was cheap at that. He could at least have given you earrings to match, or better still, a necklace."

A world I never knew, thought Nina. It was false from the start, wasn't it? And Margaret was right.

"A tidy finish," she said. "And what happens now? Is there someone waiting to step into my place?"

"Possibly. Or it could be that he's tired of the chase, temporarily, at least. Or maybe he's really had enough and has decided to be a loving husband, a family man. It happens."

"I feel numb," Nina said, "all cried out, for the time being, anyway."

"You'll cry some more," Willie assured her. "And then you'll get over it."

She gave a short, ironic laugh. "How can you know so much, Willie?"

"Just by keeping my eyes and ears open. Say, when's the last time you ate anything decent?"

"I don't know. Breakfast yesterday morning, I guess."

"You need a good meal. You go take a shower and fix yourself up while we run out and get some dinner for you."

"I'm not hungry."

"You will be. Go fix yourself. You look like hell."

What a nice, funny pair they were with their "tough love!" She did not want to, but she had to obey them. And so an hour later, while the three were having an excellent dinner, she listened to this advice.

"What you need now is to unwind in a quiet place and settle your nerves. Go home to your family. You haven't been there in a year. Oh, we know why, but Mr. Keith's no longer an issue. Just swallow your pride and go. Don't call ahead. It's hard to say all this over the phone. Just walk in and surprise them."

She got off the commuter plane, rented a car, and drove toward Elmsford. At first sight of it across the river, the bridge, the high school, Danforth's Department Store, the whole busy, dowdy, growing, familiar home-place, she felt a lump in her throat. In ten minutes she would be welcomed into the heart of it, on the old street in the old house, free of lies or deception. There they waited: her own people, a simple family, safe and solid.

I hope I won't cry, she thought, laughing a little at herself. But if I do, I do.

Fred Davis's dusty van and Louise's BMW were parked in the driveway, which seemed strange on a weekday afternoon. Otherwise, everything was unchanged. Rufus, lying in the shade, rose to greet her as if she had never been away. She stroked his head, went up the walk, and rang the bell. Louise opened the door.

"Well," she exclaimed, glancing at the suitcase, "I didn't know anyone had gotten in touch with you."

"What's wrong?" Nina cried. "Has there been an accident?"

"You might call it that," Louise said grimly. "Adam has left, that's what."

"Left?"

"Yes. Found himself another woman, and walked out Monday morning. Come on in. Margaret's here."

EIGHTEEN

Except for Margaret, who, at Louise's insistence, had been ordered upstairs for a rest, they were all in the front parlor—how strange that such an outdated term should still come naturally—sitting in stiff, formal postures like people waiting in a hospital for the doctor to emerge from surgery with news. Nina had the impression that they must have been there like that since Monday, speaking out as sudden, disconnected thoughts occurred, and as suddenly falling silent.

"I never did see her with him, anyway," Gil said. "He always was an oddball. You can ask Louise how many times I said so. Thought he was so great! Standing around with that sarcastic little smile on his face because he had a Phi Beta Kappa key and the other people didn't."

To Nina the scene was surreal. That they were talking about Adam—Adam!—was incomprehensible. All she had expected was to go home, to fall into Margaret's arms, blurt out her story, apologize for her own mistake, and be kissed and comforted. All of that had indeed happened within the first few minutes, but then had come this other story, this hammer blow. She sat now, speechless, with her suitcase still on the floor beside her feet.

Louise's full torso was tense with indignation. "He never liked anybody. Anyone could see that. We knew he certainly didn't like us. He was always polite enough, but he hardly spoke to us. I guess he thought we weren't worth his time."

"He was always quiet," Nina said.

"Quiet! He had the personality of a clam."

They were talking of Adam in the past tense. They were talking about a man she did not recognize. And yet, what they were saying had to be true. Adam had left Margaret. He was gone. She felt sick, chilled, even in this stuffy room in midsummer.

Gil inquired, "Fred, have you told Margaret you saw him with the woman?"

"No. Maybe I should have and probably I shouldn't have. Anyway, people don't tell wives. No one wants to be the bearer of bad news."

Nina went from cold to hot. And because there were too many eyes across the room, eyes that she was not ready to meet, she looked down at her shoes.

"Margaret! Three children!" Louise exclaimed, as though she were still trying to comprehend the enormity of what Adam had done. "And when I think of her—why, think of all the years she had his mother here, suffering from Alzheimer's! Most daughters-in-law would have put her in a nursing home long before."

Gil said, addressing Nina, "It's been pitiful to hear her. She keeps asking what she could have done differently, how she failed."

Louise protested, "I've told her a dozen times that she has no cause to blame herself. Blame him and that common slut. That's all right, Gil. It's a dictionary word for a woman with no morals."

"This sort of thing doesn't help," Fred objected quietly. "We have to help Margaret think. The first thing she needs to do now is get a good lawyer."

"Lawyer," Margaret said, coming into the room. "I suppose I'll have to. Mom always advised, 'Stay away from lawyers.'"

"If you can," Fred agreed.

Margaret's sigh was audible. Nina was shaken by the sound of that deep sigh as by the very sight of her. Taking a closer look now than her earlier one at the front door, she saw how striking had been the change since last year. She was older and thinner; her bright, youthful hair contradicted her darkly ringed eyes and sad mouth.

Margaret asked Fred, "Have you any suggestion?"

"Actually, I do. I spent part of this morning making inquiries and came up with the name of Stephen Larkin. His uncle, Bart Larkin, was one of the top divorce lawyers in the state. He died last year, but Stephen's continued the practice. The funny thing is, he's one of my tenants in Shady Hill. I recognized the name. Do you want to talk to him?"

She sighed again. "I suppose I'll have to."

"The next thing is, what about the kids? Julie upset me yesterday. It seems to have hit her especially hard."

"I know. She is—was—especially attached to her father. I'm going to send her for help." Margaret stood up. "Speaking of the children, they'll be back soon. My neighbor took them someplace for the afternoon, but I have to think about dinner."

Nina said quickly, "I'll make something. You sit there."

"Nonsense," Louise objected briskly. "Gil and I will run out and get pizza. They've been well fed all their lives. It won't hurt them to go without a balanced dinner for once."

"You've all been so good to me," Margaret said.

"That's what family and friends are for," Fred told her.

At supper around the kitchen table the talk was subdued and desultory. Yet it was plain to Nina that the girls and Danny were very, very glad to see her. It crossed her mind that she, who had come back to find comfort, would instead need to be giving it. There were four needy people here.

After the short supper the house fell quickly still. Margaret, obviously trying to keep to routine, asked Julie to play, but Julie refused, and so they all dispersed to their rooms. Margaret brought sheets for Nina's bed and hugged her.

"I'm just so thankful that you've come. I've missed you terribly."

"It's funny that I've come because I need you, and—"

"And now I need you."

For some reason Nina laughed, although she was also crying, and although there was nothing to laugh about. "What a pair we are! And all because of a man."

"What else?"

"Do you think we'll get over it?"

"We have no choice but to get over it, have we?"

Brave words when your self-esteem has been shot away, Nina thought. Well, first things first.

"I'm dead tired and you must be too. Let's get some sleep. Tomorrow we'll talk."

It seemed to Nina that the very house was tired and so was the very night outside, in which no leaf was moving. When she had made up the bed, she sat for a while at the window looking out at the yard. The earth was moonlit, so that shapes were distinct, and her moving gaze was able to distinguish among the trees. When it reached the mountain ash, it came abruptly to a stop. This was the tree that Margaret had helped her plant on her seventh birthday.

"It's only a stick," Margaret had said, "but someday it will be as tall as this house. It's your job to make sure it has plenty of water. Take care of it."

Now Nina's mind made an instant association. Keith's wife, for whom she had felt such hatred, had also been helping a child or children to plant a tree. She had expected to stay in that place and see the tree grow. And suddenly Nina saw her again in all her vulnerability, with her tender face and pregnant belly; she imagined her turned abruptly old and frightened, like Margaret sitting in that room downstairs, or lying alone in her bed.

Like Margaret she, too, had planned for the future, a future that Nina had tried to take away from her.

This time when she wept, and she did so for a long, long time, there was shame in her tears.

Across the hall Megan lay staring at the moonlight on the ceiling and whispering to herself.

"Oh, I *knew* that night when you were arguing and Mom said you had someone else. She believed you when you denied it, but I didn't believe you. Then I saw you in that restaurant. I hate that woman, and she knows I do. We looked right into each other's eyes. I'd like to kill her. How can you do a thing like this to Mom? When I think of her in school, how the kids like her! When I think how my friends' parents talk about her with such respect! How can you do this to her? And now she has to sit here and cry because of you. I think men stink. Boys tell you how pretty you are. They tell you they love you, but they really only want to feel you. Next week, they'll have somebody else. You can't trust them."

Her heart was going wild. She got up and sat on the edge of the bed, still whispering. "I loved you so. You were the best father in the world. How could you do this? That morning when you just walked out and drove away! How can I ever trust anybody again? No, you're not my father anymore. And I loved you so. I never want to see you. I suppose you're living with that nasty woman. I suppose you think I'm going to visit you and be nice to her. Well, think again, because I'm not going to."

Julie turned her pillow, which was damp, to the dry side. People said it was silly to think hearts would break, she thought, but since the morning Dad drove away, she had felt hers wearing out. And she put her hand under the little swell of her left breast to feel what her heart was doing; it seemed to her that it was thumping too hard, like an engine that is about to break down. She didn't really care, though. Let it break! Dad would know what he had done, and he would be sorry.

His face had been so cold and angry! He hadn't even looked at them, had just walked away and gotten into his car. Mom must have done something awful to make him that angry.

Still, Mom had been crying. So if she did do something, she was sorry for it, wasn't she, or why would she be crying? Why would he run away with somebody else? Megan saw the person, and she said she's lousy. It doesn't make any sense. I don't understand it. I'm going to ask Dad when I see him. I'm going to tell him to come back. I want him to come back.

As if he knew Danny needed him, Rufus, who always slept in the hall, had come in to lie next to the bed. When Danny let his hand dangle, he could reach the top of Rufus's head.

He was trying to sort out his feelings. There were so many of them, and so mixed up. At the moment, his embarrassed thoughts had strayed where they should not, imagining his father and a slim young woman, blond, no doubt, with long hair to her shoulders, and then breasts, small ones that turned up. . . . He had been thinking about that tonight while he was eating pizza and glancing at his mother when she wasn't looking.

His mother wasn't old, though. Not old-old. He had noticed her hands with the gold band still on her finger. The nails were pink and clean: the hand, the arm, the white collar, the white cheeks, were all clean and helpless and sad.

His throat hurt. Could it be, could the reason why Dad had left this nice woman and this nice house, could it have anything to do with him, Danny? Was it my fault? he cried quickly to himself, and as quickly recalled the article he had seen in a magazine at the dentist's office about how children of divorce believe they are part of the cause. And he remembered that as he glanced through a couple of paragraphs, these children had meant nothing to him but statistics. And now he was a statistic.

He thought maybe he ought to go downstairs and get something to eat, some chocolate-chip cookies or something. They might make me feel better, he said to himself, although he knew they wouldn't.

Margaret pulled down the shade against the moonlight, which disturbed her thoughts. It was absolutely necessary now to have orderly thoughts, to cease all wandering lamentations, to cease the search that came to nothing.

That night in New York when they had met the woman—was that the night, were those the few minutes, when she had bewitched him? Later in that room they had drunk champagne, and—she remembered it clearly—he had kissed her and blessed them both; had he not loved her, Margaret, with that blessing?

Fruitless questions. Think now, she thought sternly, about what you must do.

First above all, you must guard your children. It is essential that you never belittle their father. You must keep yourself calm; they have seen enough tears that you were not able to hold back; there must absolutely be no more of them. Understand that each child will react in his own way. A twelve-year-old boy has different responses from those of a teenaged girl. Make sure that they keep in touch with their friends, and you must keep in touch with their teachers. See the lawyer whom Fred has recommended. If I ever need to lean, although I shall try not to, I shall lean on Fred. He wants me to.

When she had finished her mental list, she turned over and willed herself toward sleep. Yet even as she felt its approach, unanswerable questions still floated in the darkness: What is Adam thinking about all this tonight? And where have they gone, our nineteen years?

"Adultery means nothing anymore," said Stephen Larkin. "You're looking for some sort of penalty for it, but there is none."

He was a young man about Margaret's own age, dark where Adam was blond, but with the same lean bones and rather grave, ascetic look. She was aware that already she had begun to relate other men, even a man seen in passing, to Adam.

"So it comes down to what you've been telling me: who sues whom, on what grounds, how much money I'm to have, how we divide what we own—papers. Everything, all the despair, the heartbreak, everything is reduced to a pile of papers."

"I'm afraid so."

She looked around the room, at the heat-wilted leaves of the maple framed by the window, and at the walls of legal writings in their dreary brown bindings. All was dry and hopeless.

And she who had been so correctly businesslike until now let her emotions explode, crying out to the stranger on the other side of the desk.

"How did this happen to me? No woman ever thinks life will do this to her!"

He replied quietly, "You live in America in 1993. What reason can anyone have to think it will not happen?"

"There was a worldwide flu epidemic in 1918, but my grandmother didn't know of anybody who died in it. You don't live expecting to die in an epidemic, and you don't live expecting to have your family torn apart. He was my whole life. I wanted to be a doctor, but it didn't fit in with his plans, so I gave it up. I did it gladly. Gladly, for him! I never in any way, even in thought, belonged to anyone but him."

And then, in spite of all her sturdy resolutions, she began to cry. Humiliated by her own sobs, yet unable to stop them, she covered her face with her hands.

Considerately, he looked away to leaf through papers. After she had quieted, blown her nose, and wiped her face, he said, so softly now that she strained to hear him, "I hear your pain."

"Maybe I'm a coward," she said. "I don't know."

"I don't think you are. Your friend Fred Davis has an entirely different opinion of you. He gave me a lot of helpful background for this case."

"He spoke well of you too. That's why I'm here."

"You'll be here more than once, you know. The law moves slowly, as you've no doubt heard."

"The next step, you said, was for you to get in touch with Adam?"

"With his lawyer, if he has one yet."

"I don't know whether he has one yet. I haven't talked to him and don't intend to. I let the children answer the phone. Except for Megan, who doesn't speak to him, which worries me so. . . . You'll need his address, anyway, won't you? I'll get it for you. He's staying with—with her."

"No need to. Fred gave it to me first thing."

The meeting was over. At the door Margaret turned back and said sadly, "I don't think this will be a hard case for you. There'll be no custody fight, and there's no fortune to be fought over."

They shook hands. "You'll be all right," Larkin said. "You may not think now that you will be, but you will."

It was deep night when Adam woke up. What had awakened him he did not know, unless it was the inner happiness that had simply burst through his skin. Looking up through the clerestory windows at the vast brilliance of the stars, he felt a compulsion to go outside. Without dis-

turbing Randi he slid from the bed, unbolted the door, and walked in
the silent grove. A night bird twittered and was still. A raccoon sped
across the lawn and rustled through the underbrush. It seemed to him
then that the loudest sound in all that enchanted place was the steady
beat of his own heart.

And he felt a great peace. True, there were many things yet to be
considered, loose ends to be gathered up, but for the moment he would
consider only the end that had finally been accomplished. He was here
with Randi; they were healthy, young, and free.

That morning, just a few days since, he had driven away from
Elmsford with a sense of relief that was almost wild. On a sudden crazy
impulse he had even stopped at a jewelry store in town and bought a
gold bracelet. Having never bought a piece of jewelry before, he was
astonished at the price of it; yet the reckless sensation of taking it out of
his pocket and handing it to Randi had been worth any price. And he
chuckled now, remembering her delight.

He had told the office that he was sick and would be out for the
next few days. Having taken no more than three sick days in all his
years at ADS, he felt no guilt. He felt, as a matter of fact, no guilt about
anything.

"What *are* you doing out here?" said Randi.

"Do you mean to say you heard me get out of bed? I didn't make a
sound."

"No, but I felt your absence." She put her arms around him, murmuring, "I'm so happy that I still can't believe this is true."

"I love it here with you, Randi."

"Of course. This is home. Tomorrow you will even have your kids
here."

"Just two of them. Megan won't come."

"Girls that age are stubborn. Don't worry. She'll change her mind.
And we'll have a great time with Julie and Danny. I hope you told them
to bring their swimsuits."

"I surely did. I notice a box of chocolate-chip cookies in the
kitchen. You remembered that I told you Danny could live on them."

"I remembered. It's important that your kids should feel that this is
their home too."

"You're so good, Randi. The only thing that bothers me is the
holidays. I wish they could have Christmas here with us."

"We'll have it the next day, that's all, a second Christmas. Now let's
go back to sleep so you can get up early in the morning and get them."

* * * *

The day was beautiful, breezy, blue, and not too hot.

"Gee, this is great," Danny said, giving approval to the house, the pool, and probably, Adam thought, to Randi as well.

She looked like a kid herself in her white shorts and red sandals. She said all the right things, admiring Julie's sundress and telling Danny that no one would ever guess by his height that he wasn't at least fourteen.

Having made the tour of the house, the four now stood uncertainly, watching Rufus nose his way around the pool.

"I didn't think you'd mind our bringing him," Adam said.

"Goodness, no. He's a gorgeous dog. His hair must need a lot of brushing."

Danny said promptly, "That's my job. I do it every day. You don't have to worry about allowing him in the house. He never does anything in the house."

Randi smiled at Adam. *Adorable,* the smile said, an adorable boy. Yes, he was. And Julie, thin little thing with shoulder blades like wings and enormous eyes, was a hidden treasure, the kind of wispy adolescent who grows up to be a woman of unusual grace, delicate and piquant. She was unusual already. And Adam was filled with a warm, fatherly pride.

"What do you say to a swim?" Randi proposed. "Danny, you change in the bathroom, and, Julie, come along and I'll show you the guestroom. Let's swim, too, shall we, Adam?"

There was for Adam an awkward moment when he followed Randi into their bedroom. His children, in passing the door, had certainly glimpsed the bed, and he knew as if he had been told what had gone through their minds. The moment passed, however, as the reality of the day returned to him, the lovely reality of being with Randi and his children all at the same time.

When he emerged into the sunlight, Danny was already in the pool, while Julie, immaculate in her blue sundress, sat in the shade.

"Why, Julie, no suit?"

"I don't feel like going in."

"What's the matter, don't you feel well?"

"I'm all right. I just don't want to swim."

"Okay," Adam said cheerfully. "Do you want something to read? A magazine or the paper?"

"No, I'm fine."

Julie was furtively observing Randi's white satin bikini. Danny, too, had taken rather a long look. Poor kids, he thought with a sudden shock of understanding, and was ashamed that he had not before considered how they would actually *feel* on seeing Randi. He had thought only how glad they would be to see *him*.

"Well, let's go. Come on, Danny," he called. "I'll race you for six laps."

After Danny had won by an arm's length, he challenged his father to an underwater race.

"I'm no good at that," Adam said.

"I am. I learned how last year at Scout camp."

"Aren't you going this year?" asked Randi, who was tanning herself.

"No," Danny said, and when Adam, surprised, asked why not, he replied soberly, "We don't want to leave Mom."

The introduction of the word *Mom,* however innocently spoken, was disconcerting and produced a silence that needed to be quickly filled.

It was Randi who filled it by remarking, "Your father tells me you're quite a pianist, Julie."

"Not really," Julie said.

"Well, you're not Rachmaninoff, but you're mighty good," Adam asserted. "Did Mrs. Watts give you another piece yesterday, or are you still on the waltz?"

"I didn't have a lesson yesterday."

The child had no expression on her face or in her voice. Sitting there with her legs crossed neatly at the ankles as she had been taught in dancing school to do, she looked as if all the air had gone out of her. Adam felt slightly irritated, but chiefly worried.

"Well, as long as you don't skip too many lessons," he began, when Julie interrupted.

"I'm never going to take any more lessons."

"What? You can't mean that."

"I do mean it," Julie said in the same flat voice.

This was not how Adam had envisioned the day. He could not, however, let the subject drop, so he tried coaxing.

"You'll be making a big mistake. It's a great joy to be able to make your own music. I wish I could play the way you do, but I've no talent." Starting to say something about Julie's evening performance, he stopped himself just in time.

Danny, who had been throwing a stick to Rufus out under the

trees, came running back to announce that Rufus's tongue was hanging out.

"I think he needs water, Dad."

"I'll get a bowl," Randi said. "I have to go to the kitchen anyhow, to see about lunch."

"Listen to me," Adam said quickly when she was gone. "I know this must be very strange for you both, and we'll have to talk more about it, but for now I want to say one thing. Nobody's angry at anybody. I'm not angry at your mother. She's a very good mother."

There was a pause. The children were scrutinizing his face, expecting more. And since of course he knew what they wanted, he gathered his courage and proceeded.

"That's not why I left. I left because I love Randi."

They said nothing.

"You'll like her when you know her. You really will."

"Do you want to bring Rufus in here?" Randi called. "It's hot out there, and he's got so much hair."

Danny went in with the dog, but Julie, whose eyes shone with tears, held back, taking a tissue out of her purse.

Proper little old lady with a purse, Adam thought, and he put his arm around her shoulders.

"It's not so bad, honey. Everything's going to be all right. You'll see."

"Don't," she said, pulling away. "It's worse when you do that."

"All right, I won't."

They stood there for a minute or two while Julie sniffled, and Adam had his thoughts. Surely this business would straighten itself out soon enough; millions of kids went through it and survived. It was just that Julie was especially tender and always had taken things harder than most kids do.

In all other respects his children's lives would be unchanged, he swore. He would see to that. Tomorrow he had an appointment with a lawyer. They would settle everything decently. He would do his full duty by his family. . . . He wondered what they would say at the office when they heard the news. They were definitely not going to hear it from him; he had never been one of those garrulous types who talked all over the place about their personal affairs.

"Do I look all right?" asked Julie. "I have no mirror."

"You look just fine. Pretty as ever. Go on in and offer to help Randi with lunch."

The rest of the afternoon passed pleasantly. Food always helps,

Adam thought. Randi, the good cook, had made a fine pasta. The salad and dessert were all delicious, and Danny ate enough for two.

"You're really giving them a good time," Adam whispered.

"They're sweet, Adam, and they're yours," Randi replied.

When it was time to go home, his children were gracious with their thanks. And again, he felt pride. Margaret had brought them up well; they were not like so many of the raucous, rude teenagers that one saw these days. And the meeting that could have been difficult, he reflected, had really gone rather well. The next time would be easier still.

Back in Elmsford, Adam sat for a moment in the car watching Danny and Julie go around the side of the house. He felt a curious shock at the realization that he might very well never enter this house, that had been his home, again. Had he been asked whether he was feeling grief because of it, he would have said: No, not grief, but rather the pathos that change brings, even change for the better. It is a kind of lament over the passage of time.

As he was moving away from the curb, he was astonished to see Nina coming down the walk. She had a sheaf of letters in her hand.

"Hey," he called. "Nobody told me you were in town. What's going on?"

She stopped, stood with hand on hip, and gave him a long stare. "Why nothing, nothing at all. What should be going on?" Then she smiled. "Everything is just perfect. Perfect. I'm surprised that you need ask."

This was going to be difficult. . . . "Are you on your way to the post office? I'll drive you. Get in and we'll talk."

"Thank you, Adam, but I don't want to talk. Actually, I know very well what's going on, and I don't care to hear whatever phony explanation you may have to offer for it."

The mockery in her eyes infuriated him. Yet he replied calmly, "It isn't phony, Nina."

"Yes, it is. Nothing you can ever say will justify what you've done here."

"Not so, Nina. One doesn't have to 'justify' love."

"Love! It's a dirty affair, your love, and nothing else, so don't try and wipe it clean. Save your energy."

"You're hardly the one to talk, are you?"

"Yes, I am. What I did was wrong, and I'm finished with it. *I'll* admit it, and *you* won't. When I look at Margaret, I see the other side, and then I really know how wrong I was."

"So you've had a religious conversion, have you? Suddenly you've seen the light."

"You aren't going to knife me with sarcasm, Adam. You've knifed me with disillusionment instead. I thought you were the best of the best, the king of the world, and now you've fallen off your throne. But *me*! What am I doing talking about me? It's Margaret and those children. . . ."

For a moment he had to look away from Nina's outrage. And then, hesitantly, he asked, "How is she?"

"Great. Just fine. How the hell do you think she is?"

"Now it's your turn for sarcasm, is it? I only asked a decent question, Nina."

"I'll tell you what. If you're so interested in her, go inside and find out the answer for yourself."

Watching her go down the street, Adam was keenly hurt. She was his Nina, his young sister, and he had always been there for her. He had always understood. Yet, he supposed, it was only natural that, being a woman, she would condemn him. . . .

With some defiance then, he raised his head, thrusting out his chin. Eventually, she would get over it. They all would. All the hurts would mend, and life would go on. It always did. With this consoling certainty he drove away.

The evening meal was the worst time, Margaret reflected. They were all scattered these summer days, for which she was thankful. Even Nina had been spending some afternoons with people she had scarcely seen since her high school years. And so Margaret was left with long periods alone, which might or might not be good for her. But she welcomed them, nevertheless, because speech came hard now; even response to the kindness of her cousins and Fred, and the very few others who yet knew what had happened to the Crane family, came hard. Sessions with the lawyer, pleasant as he was, required endurance, as did the work on what seemed to be endless questionnaires. Never had she been so physically exhausted. It seemed as if now, in the third week after the disaster, every part of her body was afflicted with some sort of ache or pain. Her teeth hurt, her head throbbed, and sometimes her back felt broken. Nevertheless, she was determined to ignore every complaint. There was work to be done. The house had to be kept up. The vegetables had to be weeded; she couldn't expect the children to do their usual stint and take over Adam's jobs as well. Besides, there was therapy in stooping over the soil; alone there in the back garden one could let one's tears drip unseen.

But the evening meal was difficult. Everyone except Nina and me, she thought, brings his moods to the table.

Danny, contrary to his nature, was sulking. She wasn't just imagining, either, that after those Saturdays with Adam, he was always sulky. Yet he looked forward to the visits.

"You said we could get a puppy this summer," he shouted. "And this was the summer we were going out west to Yosemite. You've broken all your promises."

Margaret's glance met Nina's across the table. *Poor kid,* the glance said.

And Margaret answered kindly, "I'm sorry, Danny. But we've all been having a hard time. I've not been able to think about training a puppy just now. I would have done it if—"

Danny was not about to let her finish. "Well, then, we could still drive out West. There's time. Dad says we could. You're not working now, and we could do it."

Dad said so, did he? I should just merrily set off across the plains and the Rockies, three thousand miles round trip, with three kids in my old car, in my state of mind! And does it perhaps occur to Dad that the money he's been sending is barely enough to get me to the supermarket and back?

"We can't do it now, but there'll be other summers, Danny," she said.

"Aw, I don't believe you. We'll never get to go. Never."

"Why don't you shut up?" Megan said. "You're a big baby."

"Don't you call me a baby, you shithead!"

Oh, God, not tonight again, Margaret prayed, and she gave a calm reprimand, "We don't talk like that in this house, Danny. You and the boys can say what you want when you're out together, I know, but it's not allowed here."

"You should hear what he says to me when you're not around, Mom." Megan, who had never whined, had begun to develop an irritating nasal tone. "He's disgusting lately, ever since he began seeing Dad's girlfriend."

Margaret opened her mouth to say, "Please, Megan," when Danny shouted again, "Don't say things about her! You don't even know her. She's nice, nicer than you are, shithead!"

She's nice. And am I supposed to suffer that, too, Margaret asked herself? There was no doubt this time that the pain in her chest and the pulses in her neck were real. Psychosomatic, of course, but real all the same.

"Listen to that," Megan said. "He thinks that cheap tramp is nice. But what does he know at his age? Do you think she's so nice, Julie?"

Julie's eyes filled. "I don't know. I don't know anything. I hate everything now. You're always fighting. At least they don't fight at Dad's house. Oh," she cried, "oh, Mom, what did you do to make Dad leave us?"

What did you do to make Dad—

Margaret heard Nina's gasp. At that moment the phone rang.

"I'll take it," Margaret said, running.

When she returned, they were all talking at once. In her state of agitation she interrupted more harshly than she ever would have done in the past.

"That was Mrs. Watts, Julie. She says you phoned her to say you don't want any more lessons, ever, and she's naturally concerned. So am I."

Julie looked down at her plate and mumbled something.

"Please look up at me and speak so I can hear you."

"You knew I haven't been going."

"Yes, and I understood why. I even explained to Mrs. Watts that you needed some time off. I told her why, too, and she understood. But this is something else."

"I don't need time off. I'm quitting. I hate music."

From the dining room Margaret could look across the hall to where the piano stood, now silent with the lid closed. I haven't dusted it in weeks, she thought suddenly, and as suddenly the instrument became to her a symbol of the whole house, the family and the life: deserted. She gripped the edge of the table and sat down heavily.

"You don't hate music, darling. You never could. I wish you'd go to Mrs. Watts and try another lesson. Then you'll see how happy it will make you feel, as it always did."

"I don't have to. I told Dad, and first he said I shouldn't quit, but then he said, well, I don't ever have to if that's the way I feel about it. Dad said so," Julie sobbed.

He was brainwashing the children. Naturally. Being the good guy. Go to Yosemite. Sure. Get a puppy. Drop piano lessons. Anything you want. Just ask Dad, the all-American dad.

"Julie's always crying," said Danny, coming into the attack. "Up at Dad's half the time she sits there with a sad face until he makes her smile."

"You shut up and leave me alone," Julie shrieked, "or I'll kill you."

"Oh, nice," said Megan. "Really nice. If I had any brains, I'd stay over at Betsy's house for dinner every night."

Nina got up. "While you're all fighting like a pack of hyenas, I'll get the corn. Your good mother went out in the heat and picked it for you, not that you deserve it."

The three were immediately crestfallen. Nina's rebuke, coming as it did from a beloved person not tremendously older than they, always had had a special effect upon them. And Margaret gave her a look of gratitude.

The air began to settle, and Megan began a conversation.

"Betsy's sister's having a Christmas wedding."

Nina picked up the conversational ball. "That could be beautiful. I see red velvet bridesmaids' dresses and white poinsettias. I love white poinsettias."

We're all a bundle of nerves, Margaret thought, but we have to try, don't we? And she, doing her part, asked whether Megan expected to be invited.

"More than that. Joan even asked me whether I'd like to be a bridesmaid."

"That's so nice," exclaimed Margaret. "After all, you're Betsy's friend, not hers."

"Well, let's face it, her mother probably suggested it because she wants to do something for me. Everybody on the street feels sorry for us."

The air in the room began to roil again.

"Oh, I don't think it's all that bad, Megan. I hope you accepted graciously."

"I was gracious, Mom, but I didn't accept."

"You didn't? Why ever not?"

"Because I don't believe in weddings. I always did think they're an extravagant show, but now I think they're hypocritical."

"Hypocritical?"

"Yes. Why celebrate something with all the permanent vows, so serious, so holy, when the woman's only going to be tossed out whenever the man finds somebody he likes better? I looked at bridal finery in Danforth's window just this week, and it made me want to puke."

Megan's eyes glistened, and she closed them, fighting tears. Grieving, bitter and cynical, at her age; this is what he's done, Margaret thought.

"You mustn't look at it that way," she said. "Every marriage doesn't fail."

"Fifty percent of them do, Mom. What kind of odds are those?"

"I suppose," Margaret said slowly, "I suppose it's a question of one's point of view, whether the glass is half empty or half full."

"And you always find it half full. I know you, Mom."

"Speaking of glasses, how about clearing the table," Nina suggested. "You go sit on the porch, Margaret. The rest of us will clean up the kitchen."

Margaret did not protest. As she left the room, she overheard Nina.

"Your mother's more exhausted than any human being should be. Now listen, everybody. You're all pretty tired, too, whether you know it or not. You're tired inside, in your heads, and you're taking your bad feelings out on each other. Okay, but do it outdoors where Mom doesn't have to hear you. She's had enough, understand? So let's finish the dishes and go together to watch the news or something. We're still a family, no matter what."

God bless Nina, thought Margaret.

"You need to get away," Nina said one afternoon. "You need a rest and a change."

"It's out of the question. I can't afford to. He"—and Nina realized that Margaret almost never called Adam by his name now—"knows I have no income of my own during the summer, and yet he's cut his contribution. My lawyer says that's what usually happens. It will have to be worked out either by settlement or in court. Meanwhile, I must do the best I can, and that's what I'm doing."

"I hope your lawyer knows his business."

"He does. And he's very nice, reserved, doesn't waste words, but lets you see that he understands. I really like him, which makes things easier. Fred did me a good turn."

"Will you let me lend you the money so you can all go away to a lake or someplace for a few days?"

"Thank you, no. Julie sees the psychologist twice a week, and I'm only beginning all the legal business. I have more to do than I've ever had in all my life. People think that planning a wedding is a big job. Let me tell you, it's a breeze compared with a divorce."

So Keith said too. Nina shuddered.

All of a sudden Margaret clasped her hands in a beseeching gesture.

"Tell me honestly, tell me the truth, you grew up here, where did I go wrong?"

"I never saw anything in you that could be called a real fault. But then, I never saw anything bad in Adam either."

"There are two sides to every story. I know that, and so I keep thinking—thinking. Maybe I'm too opinionated. Am I?"

Nina smiled. "No more than Adam is—was."

"Or did I pay too much attention to the children and neglect him?"

"I never saw it if you did."

"I guess as long as I live I'll keep asking myself how I failed, and I'll never really know."

Margaret's rueful little smile did not fool Nina. Eyes did not have to be extra sharp to notice trembling hands and what must be ten pounds of lost weight.

"Margaret, I'm worried about you. Don't you think you ought to see a doctor?"

"I have already. Dr. Farley says my symptoms are typical. They're just nerves. Nerves." Margaret tried to laugh. "I'm thinking up a good name for this disease. How about Falling Apart Syndrome, or better still, Discarded Wives' Syndrome? Your back aches, your skin erupts, and you can pull your hair out into your hands. Look, I'll show you."

"Don't," Nina said.

"When I wake up, I don't at first believe what has happened. I lived half my life with him, really all of my adult life. . . . But what's the use? Other people are dying of cancer while I eat my heart out here. And what about you? You've had an awful time. You don't complain but I know you have. Is it getting any better for you?"

"Yes, yes, much." And what is my hurt compared with hers? Nina asked herself.

Margaret got up and walked to the table on which the family's photographs were arranged. "I forgot this was still here. That was a marvelous wedding dress! Isabella made all the tucks and ruching by hand. You were too young to appreciate it."

"I remember it, though." She gazes at it, Nina thought, like a woman holding the portrait of someone dead. And of course, that trusting bride is dead.

"Well, I'll just pack it up in the attic with the dress in blue tissue paper. Maybe some year, a hundred years from now, one of my great-grandchildren might be curious to see what I looked like." Then, saying quickly, "I don't want the soup to boil over," she sped into the kitchen.

Nina went to the telephone. When in need, you called Fred.

"I took a chance that you might be home," she said. "Tell me truthfully, are you doing anything urgent this afternoon?"

"Going to the club for a swim. In this heat I call that urgent. Actually, I sent everyone home before anyone keeled over."

"Do you think you might take Margaret's kids with you? They're all out on errands now, but they'll be home any minute. And for her sake I'd love to get them out of the house. I never thought I'd hear myself say that, but I'll tell you, I don't recognize in them the nice, easygoing kids they used to be. All they do is bicker and scream at one another."

"I'll be right over. How is she today?"

"Trying hard to live as if nothing has changed. You know her."

"Yes. Yes, I know her. Nina, when you leave again, don't worry. I'm here for Margaret."

"Thank you, Fred."

Now, there's a natural solution for the rest of Margaret's life, she thought. You don't have to be a rocket scientist to see that he adores her.

Margaret was in the kitchen shelling peas for the vegetable soup when Nina went in.

"That was Fred, inviting Danny and the girls to swim at his club. That'll take care of a hot day for them."

"He called? I didn't hear the phone ring."

"No? Here, let me do some of those peas."

"Thanks. I have enough for now."

Margaret stood up, grasped the chair back, and sat down heavily, sighing. "It's my darn back. It acts like this sometimes. I can't get up after I've been sitting for a while. Don't look so alarmed. The body plays tricks when you're tense, that's all."

"You're too controlled. You haven't once let yourself go since this happened. In the first place, you felt ashamed, and in the second, you haven't wanted to alarm your children."

"What do you mean, 'let yourself go'?"

"Scream and cry. Just howl. You're grieving, you're frustrated because you want revenge, but you can't get it because there is none. So go up and howl. Nobody's here but me, and I don't mind. I'll put cotton in my ears if you want me to. I know you think it's a crazy idea, but—"

Margaret struggled up and walked gingerly across the room. "No," she said. "It's rather a good idea. I think I'll go to the attic and try it."

Nina lay down on the sofa, propped on an elbow to read. She was just beginning to drowse in the heat when she heard the sounds of human anguish carried down through the floors and walls, the very bones of the old house. She got up to listen at the foot of the stairs. Once, on a Scout's hike through the woods, she had heard the shrieks and moans of an animal caught in a trap, and had never forgotten the horror. Now in these human sobs was the same intimation of despair. And she remembered, too, that Margaret had once said of Adam: "The thought of his death is enough to stop my heart." If she could only hate him the way I do now, Nina thought, there would be an end to this suffering. Unfortunately, she loves him. . . .

After a while the sounds ceased. Margaret must have fallen asleep.

Sometime later Megan came in flourishing a magazine. "Nina! A lady at the club gave this to me because you're in it. Did you know you were in it?"

There it was, spread out in lustrous color, the Florida pink house, on four pages of "strikingly original rooms designed by Nina Keller of Crozier and Dexter."

"I didn't expect it to be on the stands this soon."

"You never said a word about it!"

Nina smiled. "I had other things to think about."

Indeed, she had them still. Those views of Florida, those vivid pages, brought with them a stream of images: the dinner by candlelight, the Spanish bed, the kisses, the lies, the perfidy. . . .

"Does this mean you're famous?" asked Danny.

"It means that I've worked hard and that I've been lucky. Both."

Julie asked, "Aren't you proud?"

"No, I'm grateful."

"Grateful for what?" inquired Margaret.

In a fresh plaid cotton dress with fresh lipstick and a little black bow at the nape of her neck, she seemed, if not rested, at least as if she *cared*.

"She's famous," Danny declared. "She says she isn't, Mom, but she's got to be. See? Here's her name."

After they all crowded around Nina to read the article over her shoulder, and when the two women were left by themselves, Margaret said softly, "I am just so proud of you. But I'm not surprised."

"Never mind about me. The question is, did it do you any good?"

"Yes, some of the knots have come untwisted. But I worry about you."

"I'm okay, not as much sad anymore as angry. Damned angry."

"I wish I could help you."

"Just being here has helped me."

"The lame and the halt," Margaret said, and they both laughed.

"I have to leave on Thursday. I wish I could stay, but they've already given me two extra weeks, and I can't ask for more."

"Of course not. Go on up and start your packing."

From her window Nina looked out at the familiar place. It would be a long time before she would return here to stay for more than two or three days. And so, with mingled feelings, she stood watching this afternoon play itself out. The girls were washing the car and quarreling over the suds; Danny was pushing the hand mower across a square of dry brown grass. The dog slept in his usual spot under the oak. And over all this homely scene there lay a subtle desolation.

And she thought with sorrow of the upward climb that, for all of Margaret's determined courage, lay ahead of her. The discarded wife, mother of children, and the unencumbered single woman with all her choices, even with her lingering anger, were very different. Both of them knew it, and would feel it as they embraced and parted.

NINETEEN

It was good to be back home in her own apartment. Clearly, Elmsford, for all its warmth, was to be always a place for return and welcome respite, but no longer her home. She had outgrown it.

The answering machine bore so many messages that the tape was filled. After opening the windows to all the street noises that over the years Nina had actually come to find companionable, she sat down to listen to her messages. Most of them were routine. Then, suddenly, Keith's voice jolted her.

"Where are you, Nina? I've been trying to reach you. We need to talk."

"I'll say we do," she answered.

There were five more messages from him on the tape, the last one anxious, almost fearful. Good, she thought. Let him sweat. It was little enough revenge, yet little as it was, it was sweet.

She had never telephoned him at his office, but there was always a first time, so this would be that first time as well as the last one.

"I've been calling you," he said, confirming the anxious note that she had detected. "Where have you been?"

"What difference does it make?" she retorted. "I'm here now, and I suggest you come to see me today on your way home. To your family," she added.

"I'll be there," he said.

He sounded like someone quivering in his boots. He feared trouble, big trouble. And smiling to herself, enjoying her power, she went about the apartment in search of every article that he had ever given her. There was very little besides books; of these there was a fine collec-

tion with which she was sorry to part. Still, wanting no slightest reminder of Keith Anderson, she piled them on a table along with his
photograph, the watercolor bought in Prague, a bottle of perfume, and
the diamond bracelet. Finally, she hauled forth a grocery carton. Let
him pack it and stagger out into the street with it as best he could.

Not half an hour later he was at the door in his tidy suit and
impeccable white shirt. He smiled uncertainly. For a moment she stood
there, staring. Adjectives took shape in her mind: *humbled, terrified,
woebegone.*

He began timidly, "Nina, I know how you must feel. I want to
explain. I—"

She shook her head. "Save your breath. It's my turn to talk. Have
you ever heard of a righteous rage? Well, that's me. A lot of time
wasted on a fraud!"

"Nina, please—"

She put up her hand, palm out. "No, don't interrupt me. You made
a fool of me, and you're going to hear me out. It's not that marriage
ever was the sole object of my life. Maybe I never will be married, or
maybe ten years from now I will be, I don't know.

"But you led me on like a con man selling worthless securities to
an innocent old lady. I'm ashamed of myself for not having seen
through you."

Her heart was thudding. She was so full of what she had to say that
she had to pause for an instant to arrange her words.

Keith started to say, "I understand how you—"

"No, you don't understand! What have I had from you outside of
sex and fake promises? Skulking around this wonderful city, not even
able to go to the museum with you, or a walk in the park, for fear of
being seen. And all the time you knew what you were doing. You made
love to me, you looked into my face and knew you were lying. I wonder
about your business deals. Do you shake hands on a deal while all the
time you know that the contract you signed is the one you're planning
to slip out of, the minute you need to? Are you the used-car salesman
who takes people's money knowing that the car is going to fall apart ten
miles down the road?"

"May I say something? May I sit down and talk to you? Please,
Nina, we don't have to be enemies. If there is anything I can do for you,
I'll—"

Do for her! Buy her off! She was enraged. And it came to her
suddenly that this rage was not directed only at the man who stood
there, but at Adam, too, and all men's broken promises. . . .

"No, you may not sit down and talk to me. Oh, I pity your poor wife! What are you doing to her? I suppose she trusts you. . . . I never thought of her before. . . . But I've learned things as I've gone along."

Keith was silent. And she saw that she had pricked his balloon.

"She must have had the baby by now. What is it?"

Almost whispering, not looking at her, he replied, "A boy." Then, raising his head, still whispering, he asked, "What do you want, Nina? Let's talk sensibly. I—"

She smiled. "Do you really think I can't read your mind by now? You're terrified that I'm going to go to Cynthia. That's why you telephoned so often. That's why you're here. That's why you gave me the bracelet. It was your farewell present, wasn't it? If we hadn't had that meeting at the airport, there would have been a few more fine presents to ease you out with grace." Now Nina laughed. "Look at you! You're ghastly. Well, I don't want any heart attacks in my apartment, so calm yourself. I am not going to go to Cynthia. Ever. Not for your sake, oh, dear, no, not for your sake, but for hers and for the three babies'. But your next woman may not be so decent, Keith, so I advise you to choose her carefully. And now, just get out. And take this stuff with you. It's all yours."

"Really, I don't want—"

It pleased her that she had hardly allowed him to complete a single sentence. And again, she cut him short.

"It's yours, I said. Give the bracelet to your wife. She deserves it. She just gave you another son. Now pack up and go."

She watched him put the bracelet in his pocket and stack the rest of the things in the box. When it was filled, it was heavy enough for two men, and he strained to lift it. No word was spoken. She held the door and closed it behind him. For a few minutes she stood without moving, until the elevator door opened and clanged shut upon the last of Keith. And a sense of grievous loss trembled through her. He had been wonderful, so wonderful! As long as the blinders had covered her eyes. . . .

"Well, that's that," she said to herself.

For a while she sat wondering about the curious contradictions that she was feeling. Filled now with abruptly renewed and youthful energy, she was yet aware of having grown much older. Trusted people betrayed you. Plans came undone. So much that had once seemed unchangeable had changed. And finding it all too painful, Nina got up and began to put her little house in order.

TWENTY

"I hope I've filled everything out properly," Margaret said, indicating the pile of papers that lay between them on Stephen Larkin's desk. "I never dreamed I'd face a questionnaire like that, considering that I'm not the one who wanted the divorce."

"Don't ask me why. It's the law, that's all."

"Excuse me, nothing personal, but Dickens wrote that the law is an ass, and I'm inclined to agree."

Stephen laughed. "I am too. At any rate, I should hate to be responsible for these divorce laws. They used to be different, you know." Then he said seriously, "The way it is now, the man's standard of living rises by over forty percent, and the woman's drops accordingly."

"What if I didn't have a job? What if I were home with a big family of small children?"

"Well, then, he wouldn't be able to count your earnings among your assets, and he'd have to give you more alimony. Assuming, that is, that he was able to."

"I know he told Danny and Julie that he promises to 'take care of us'—whatever that means." She felt the anger thick in her throat, pulsing in her ears. "He knows very well what it should mean. He knows what my salary is and what the expenses are. Why, the property tax on the house has quadrupled since my mother left it to me. That alone is—" She stopped. "But you know all that."

She felt blinded, deafened, with her hands tied; the indignation, the outrage, that was beating within her was like some live, imprisoned thing fighting to get out.

" 'Equitable distribution'!" she cried. "And if whatever some judge decides is equitable turns out not to be enough, what happens then? Welfare?"

"In too many cases, yes. But that won't happen to you."

"I can barely make it now. It's been four months, and I've had to dip into my savings, which don't amount to much, I assure you. I don't want to deplete them. I need to have a bit of a cushion, after all."

"Unless we can reach a settlement, as you already know, we're simply going to have to go to court for more. But that will be expensive, and I hate to do it to you, Mrs. Crane."

"Do please call me Margaret. I don't feel comfortable anymore with his name. I only wish my students would call me by something else." She looked at Larkin, confiding, "Once in a while I find myself thinking, or worse, saying something that's petulant and childish. Do you think it's childish of me to want to discard his name?"

For a moment Larkin looked back at Margaret as if he were studying her. "No," he said, "you have been grossly insulted. I understand."

Insulted. Yes, that's what it is. *He,* living there with *her.* Danny, in his innocence, prattling about "Dad and Randi." "We" had a picnic. "We" had fun. "We" covered the pool for the winter. *Insulted.*

"Living in luxury! He's probably enjoying it all the more for never having had any luxury. Is that where the money is going, Mr. Larkin?"

"I don't know. I'm still waiting for his questionnaire. But again I must warn you that moral obligations won't enter into all this. The law says that he has to live too."

"Yes, of course. Equitable distribution. Randi, sharing what should go to me and my children. *My* children, whom he abandoned, whether he thinks he did or not."

There was a silence. From long habit she had been twisting the place on her finger where her wedding band had been. It annoyed her now that she was still doing it, and that the skin on which the ring had rested was still marked by it. The silence was continued. Larkin was watching her, no doubt expecting her to rise and leave, for everything had been said.

She got up and apologized. "Excuse me for venting my rage, Mr. Larkin. I'm sorry."

"No need to be," he said gently. "Rage is healthier for you, anyway, than grief is, and I'm relieved to see it."

"Thank you. You *are* kind. Fred said you were."

Her appointment later that afternoon was back at school with the psychologist. Audrey Swenson had come to the school not long before

Margaret had begun to teach there. They had, however, never developed a close friendship, which, conversely, made it easier for Margaret to talk to her.

"You're looking well today," Audrey said.

Her manner was cordial and her smile friendly, while her eyes, Margaret observed, were keen and could be stern. The two women were the same age, yet now, for the first time in her life, Margaret had a feeling of inferiority. She was a supplicant, asking for advice and succor; she had been degraded. Adam and his woman had brought her here to this place on this afternoon.

"It must be the pink shirt," she replied lamely. "I don't feel all that well."

"Don't you really agree that you should be seeing a psychiatrist? Most women in your situation do."

Margaret made herself speak firmly. "No. I believe I have the resources to deal with this. Eventually, I'll pull out. Anyway, I have neither the time nor the money. It's my children who worry me, as you know."

"Of course. We'll get to that. But you do realize don't you, that how they are affected by this breach depends so much upon how you are affected?"

"I know. I don't think I need feel much guilt in that respect, though." She sighed. "I've said scarcely a word against their father. Believe me, it's tempting to ask questions whenever Julie and Danny come home from their Sunday visit, which I hate, but I never—"

Audrey interrupted. "Does Megan still refuse to go there?"

"Yes. Sometimes I think she despises Adam more than I do. It worries me that she's so angry."

Audrey nodded. "She has been frightfully wounded, as a daughter and as a woman. Her father is not the man she adored. Now she distrusts all men and doesn't know what her life is going to mean. She has very high principles and sees things in black and white, as adolescents can do. Don't push her. But let's get back to you. Tell me something."

Again Margaret became aware that she was looking down at the finger where the marriage ring had been. And she laid her hand on the arm of her chair. She must remind herself to keep it there.

"Fortunately," she said, "I'm so busy that there isn't a lot of time to give to my feelings. They attack me in spasms, painful spasms. Yesterday after my last class one of my former students came to visit me. I recognized her immediately. She had been one of my best, and now she's in her third year at medical school. She came to thank me for having inspired her."

"And you felt?"

"Quite touched by her gratitude. Happy that my work as a teacher can bear such good fruit." She paused, drew a breath, and continued, "Rage too. Awful rage that I gave all that up for myself, and now this, and now it's too late."

"You're saying all the right things, Margaret. Anger is healthy as long as you keep it under control."

Healthy, said Stephen Larkin an hour ago. Like radiation therapy, perhaps?

"I do control it," Margaret said with sudden pride. "I do plenty of things wrong, I'm sure, but that's not one of them."

"Good. Now about the children."

"No change yet. They're scared, miserable, and trying. I know they're trying, poor babies, to keep themselves under control too."

"I want to make a suggestion. Don't ever think of them, and don't treat them like babies. Especially don't do it to Danny. I know he's the youngest and it's natural to do it. Try calling him 'Dan.'" Audrey smiled. "He's 'Daniel,' I suppose, whenever you're annoyed with him."

"Oh, yes. He never has been a top student, you know, but now I have a hard time getting him to do his homework. He plays ball, watches television—and telephones his father. His all-American father."

Audrey said gently, "Don't be easy on him about the homework. Set penalties. You mustn't let him go downhill simply because his father isn't in the house."

"I understand. And Megan is the opposite. She has six majors and wants me to tutor her in college-level chemistry. She's become a fanatic about work. No telephone, no boys, and no girls either."

"Tell her to come see me. Do you think she will?"

"Megan will do anything I ask her to do. She identifies with me. She has always been so good, maybe too good. It's Danny—Dan—who refuses. He says it's 'sissy'—only that's not the word he uses—and he can take care of himself."

"Perhaps he can." Audrey looked at her watch. "We've only five minutes left to talk about Julie, so let me sum up. It's going to take time. If I see that I'm not making progress at all, I'll tell you to take her to a psychiatrist. For the present I believe I understand her."

"My tender one. She has been that always, probably from the day she was born. Who knows? Is it because she's the middle child, or is it genetic? And anyway, what's the difference? She was getting along quite well, living her little life in her own way, until this—this thing happened." And Margaret heard her own voice tremble. "It's as if she had been hit by a truck." She stood up. "Well, thank you, Audrey. You've got more troubles sitting in your waiting room, so I'll be going."

Megan was doing homework in the den when Margaret came in, apologizing for being late.

"I'm sorry I was delayed. Here are the car keys. You should be able to get there in twenty minutes, though. Tell the dentist it's my fault." Her words rushed as did her hands, rummaging in her pocketbook. "Can you stop and get some fruit on your way back? Whatever you see that's not too expensive. Apples, mostly, this time of year."

On the back steps in the mild October sunshine, Danny sat idly scratching Rufus on the head.

"What's up?" asked Margaret.

"Nothing."

"Have you got much homework?"

"Some."

"It's after five. Don't you think you should start doing it?"

"No," Danny said.

Be firm with him.

"Well, I know you should. First history quiz of the semester last Friday, and you got C-plus. There's no excuse for that."

"Maybe I'm just stupid."

"No, you're not, Daniel. You simply didn't do the reading. Now go on upstairs and get to work while Julie and I put supper together."

"I'll go later, Mom. Will you leave me alone?"

"No, I won't. After supper you've got to take the mower and go over the front lawn. It's a disgrace. And then you can get back to your homework."

"Oh, all right." He got to his feet and climbed the steps, scuffing his new shoes as he went. "All you do is nag me, Mom. Nag, nag."

"That's not true, and you know it, Dan."

The potatoes were on the kitchen table. Julie had not peeled them. I don't recognize these children, Margaret thought; I feel as if I'm swimming against the tide and can't get anywhere. She went to the foot of the stairs to summon Julie.

"Please come down and peel the potatoes," she called. "I asked you this morning to have them ready for me."

"Well, I forgot," Julie called back.

She looked sullen and unkempt. Her tawny hair—Adam's hair—had obviously not been washed all week. A mother was not supposed to nag, but what else could she do when no one paid attention anymore unless she did nag? And deciding to forget the hair for the moment, Margaret spoke pleasantly.

"Well, anyone can forget. So do them for me, will you? I'm going to broil some chicken on the grill and make the salad while you set the table."

It was strange that the absence of just one person had made the dining room feel too large. Yet it seemed important to keep the family's habits as unchanged as possible, to say, in effect: We are not going to weaken simply because he has left us.

At half past six, at seven, at seven-fifteen, Megan had not come home. Margaret paced the front porch to search up and down the street. Behind her, silent and round eyed, stood Danny and Julie.

Margaret talked to herself. "I can't imagine where she is. I phoned the dentist, the office is closed, I can't imagine . . ." Her heart pounded.

It was dark, and she was about to call the police, when Fred Davis, in his van with Megan beside him, drew into the driveway.

"Oh," Megan cried, "where were you? I called and there was no answer. Then I only had a quarter left, so I called Uncle Fred, and he came for me. All of a sudden in the middle of downtown in all the traffic, the car just stopped! It was awful, cars honking at me as if it was my fault! Then the police came and pushed it out of the way, and I didn't know what—where were you, Mom?"

"Come sit down. We must have been outside at the grill, so nobody heard the phone. Listen to me. As long as you weren't hurt, nothing matters. What was the trouble with the car?"

"It had to be towed," Fred explained. "The transmission fell out."

"I don't know what I would have done if Uncle Fred hadn't come," Megan said, almost wailing. "He took care of everything."

A warm sensation of relief flooded through Margaret, and she looked at Fred. "You always do take care of things. Thank you," she said. "Let's all go in and have supper. Will you stay, Fred? The supper's sort of wilted by now, so you will have to excuse it."

At the table Fred, in the seat that had been Adam's, explained the situation.

"A new transmission will cost twelve hundred dollars, they told me. There's a question, though, whether it's worth putting that much into a fairly old car. You'll need to give it some thought."

"Fairly old!" Danny blurted. "It's ancient. Nobody around here keeps a wreck like that. Let's get a new car, Mom."

Poor innocent, thought Margaret. And she said quietly, "I wish it was that easy, Danny."

"I told Dad we needed a car. He took the good one and left us with a—a jalopse."

"You mean 'jalopy,' " Julie said.

"What's the difference? Stop correcting me, smartass."

"Your language, Daniel," Margaret said.

The boy needed a man, a father.

"He's right, though," Megan said. "Dad took care of himself and didn't worry about us."

"I told him!" Danny shouted. "And then *she* said he needs one to go to work, and she said I should remember that if he didn't work, we'd be in real trouble."

This discussion ought to be dropped at once. Yet Margaret could not keep herself from asking, "What did your father say then?"

"Nothing."

Fred asked quickly, "Who wants to go to the football game with me Saturday afternoon?"

Danny's and Julie's hands went up, and Megan declined.

"Thanks so much, Uncle Fred, but I have to work on my English paper."

Margaret objected, "You said it wasn't due till the middle of November. Go to the game, it'll be fun."

"Mom, I can't afford to. I need straight A's if I'm going to get anywhere with my life."

Fred's glance met Margaret's. *Poor kid,* the glances said.

"Okay, another time. Why don't you three clean up the kitchen and then go do your homework?" he suggested. "I can see that as usual your mother has a pile of papers to do. So I'm going to go home and get out of her way."

"You're hardly in my way, Fred," Margaret told him.

At the front door he paused to say, "I didn't want to mention this at the table, but really, Margaret, you need a new car, and I'll be glad to help you out with whatever you need."

His mild eyes seemed to be pleading with her. The genuine goodness of this man brought the start of tears to her own eyes. But there was within her a stubborn independence that forbade her, perhaps against her better judgment, to accept aid. Louise and Gilbert, even

Nina, young and striving as she was, had made loving offers that she had turned down.

"I know you," Fred said, "so if it will make you feel better, let's say it's a loan. You will repay me whenever you can."

She smiled. "I know you, too. You're a dear, and I thank you, but it is Adam's job to take care of us. After nineteen years I think he owes a car to his wife and his three children."

"But if he will not? Have you talked to Larkin?"

"Many times, and the answer is that Adam is giving all he can. He's only paid for half my insurance on this car, so maybe he'll pay half on the transmission. Maybe. In the end I'll have to wait for the final settlement when we go to court."

"Are you satisfied with Larkin? If not, my feelings won't be hurt just because I'm the one who recommended him."

"I'm satisfied. I like him very much."

"Good. Well, chin up, Margaret." He kissed her cheek and went down the walk.

For a moment she watched him go. His erect height, his wide shoulders, his very stride, gave an effect of confidence and rocklike security. But on particular occasions his eyes, with their mild, thoughtful gaze, said something different. And she reflected that, although he had for so long been there on the fringe of her life, she really did not know him very well. She did not even know what his feelings toward her might now be, not that it mattered. Regardless of whatever exterior strength she had mastered, inside she was damaged and suffering; her nightly dreams were of Adam, of bereavement, betrayal, and sorrow.

On the desk in the den her work was waiting, a pile of quiz papers to be graded, the first quiz of the season, given to learn how much the class remembered of what it had studied so far. They were bright kids in this class, nice kids. This year, though, as she stood before them looking at their faces turned toward her, she often considered the possibility of concealed heartache. She had really never thought much about that until this year.

Now, to the left of the desk, she could see through the door into the living room, where Adam's new computer and shelves of software were housed. He hadn't asked for them. And if he does, she thought fiercely, he isn't going to get them. They belong to my children.

Her mind was agitated. There was all this work to be done before midnight, so she must quiet her mind. Tomorrow morning she would order a transmission. It would take a nice chunk out of her savings, even if he should pay half.

Damn him! Damn the laws that made it so hard for a woman to get what was due her!

On the table facing her desk stood the family photographs. There was more space, now that Adam's picture and the bridal photograph had been removed, to see what remained. In front was her father's young face; she had not known him, and yet because of her mother, she could almost believe that she had. Mom had talked about him so much, remembering him with sweetness and laughing often over funny things that had happened to them together. . . .

Death is easier than this, Margaret thought. There is nothing sweet or funny about this. Then, switching on the desk light, she went to work.

TWENTY-ONE

Adam felt his mouth stretching into an artificial smile, his whole manner forcing a bright enthusiasm that he did not feel. In reality he was tense because the children's visit was not going the way it should. It hadn't gone exactly as he had wished the last time either.

"Queen Anne's lace is in the carrot family," he explained. "You wouldn't think so to look at it, would you?"

"It's ugly," Julie said.

"That's because it's dried and dead. You need to see it in August when it's blooming."

He had taken them for a walk into the upland meadow that lay between the river and the woodland patch around the house. Randi, making lunch, liked to get them out of the kitchen.

"I think, but I'm not sure, that it was actually developed by botanists. It might be interesting to look it up."

But they were not interested. Their gaze was fixed instead on Rufus, whose head was barely visible above the tall brown grass through which he appeared to be swimming.

"Well," Adam said, "I guess we should go back. Randi has probably got lunch ready."

"Why can't we eat outside?" Danny demanded, seeing that the picnic table was empty.

"It's too chilly. It's the end of November," Adam answered.

"No, it's not. It's hot in the sun. I could even take my sweater off."

"Call Rufus and come inside. Don't complain, Danny."

The boy had an unbecoming pout, something brand new, Adam thought.

At the lunch table Randi addressed Julie. "I'm sorry you don't like the piano. When I saw it at a house sale, I thought of you. And it fits perfectly in the cellar. Sometime soon we plan to make a gorgeous recreation room down there."

At Julie's failure to respond Adam said quickly, "It was so good of you to think of Julie. I'm sure she'll use it whenever she decides to start playing again. But we won't rush you, Julie."

"I don't know," Randi said, smiling. "I think she just doesn't like the piano. It's not nice enough for her. Am I right, Julie?"

A flush appeared over the girl's cheeks, and raising her eyes toward her father, she murmured, "I just don't want to play."

It was all quietly polite. And yet the atmosphere was unnatural. The small talk that followed this exchange was meaningless, merely a time-filler. And he missed them so! They hadn't had Thanksgiving with him, and they wouldn't have Christmas. Children went with the mother. So his thoughts ran.

When lunch was over, the two children went outside while Adam and Randi had coffee.

"I really did think Julie would be pleased with the piano," Randi began.

If she would only drop the subject! It had been kind of her to buy the thing; obviously, though, she did not realize that it was an ancient, jangling wreck that had never amounted to much when it was new. At home Julie had her mother's baby grand, meticulously kept, a gift from Jean in the prosperous days of her second marriage.

"Don't feel bad," he said patiently. "She's very upset right now."

"Well, it's trying to see a kid sitting there moping. She scarcely says a word."

"It's been awfully hard for her, Randi. I knew there would be some effects, of course, but I didn't expect her to take this so hard."

"For heaven's sake, you haven't died or been put in federal prison, Adam. The fact is, darling, your kids are spoiled."

"No, Randi. They've got their faults, as we all have, but they're not spoiled."

"Tell me why Danny has to lug that dog along everywhere he goes."

"He doesn't take it everywhere. He takes him here so he can have a good run. Besides, the dog is a comfort to him now."

"Comfort! You'd think he was being tortured. Your kids have it pretty good, darling. You're just a sweet soul, Adam Crane, just too darn softhearted for your own good."

He felt hurt. And yet it was true that neither Danny nor Julie had been exactly endearing today. On the other hand, why should they always be on their best behavior? But, back to the other hand, it was true that Randi was always lovely to them. And she hadn't had any experience with teenagers. . . . And no doubt it was an imposition to expect her to entertain them every Sunday. . . . Although there was really no other time for him to see them except on the weekends. . . . And she was so even tempered, so sweet, so rarely the least bit cranky. Surely, she was entitled to have an opinion about the kids. . . .

"Oh, now I've upset you," she murmured. "You're thinking I don't like your children." She got up from her chair and took his face between her hands to kiss him. "Darling, I'm sorry. You know I like them. For heaven's sake, they're yours! But can't I feel free to express myself honestly sometimes? Anything I say is for your good. Please don't misunderstand. I love your kids! Tell me you're not upset. Please?"

"I'm not upset."

"Truly. Smile when you say it. Please?"

He smiled.

They were quiet on the ride home. Danny wanted music on the radio, some singing group with one of those crazy names that Adam could never remember, the Cemetery Bouncers, or something equally crazy. Ordinarily, their racket would lift off the top of his head, but today, full of thoughts, he was almost grateful for them.

The hardest thing about this homeward ride was seeing the two go up the walk to the front door of what had once been his home. At the curb he was about to say as usual, "See you Sunday," when Danny turned back and asked, "Are you ever going to go in with us?"

"Well, we'll see," he replied, knowing that Danny, walking away, had recognized the answer for the fatuous evasion that it was.

The car had begun to roll when he saw Megan approaching from the end of the street. She was carrying books, so that he guessed she had come from the library. His heart leapt. She was lovely in her dark blue skirt and sweater with her long hair, still wheat colored from the summer's sun, lying on her shoulders. He hadn't seen her since the day he left. Sliding over to the passenger's side, he leaned out of the window and called, "Megan! Megan! How are you?"

She stopped. "Wonderful," she said coldly. "How do you think I am?"

"Not very well, I know. I worry terribly about you. But we can't talk here. Won't you please come with Julie and Danny to see me?"

"No, not at that woman's house. You can't be serious."

"Don't say that, Megan. Randi's a good person, kind, warm-hearted."

"Oh, yes, warm like a cobra. And you ask me to be civil to her after what she's done?"

He was tired, so tired. How was he even to begin to explain himself to this young daughter?

"What she—and you—have done to Mom, who is so brave! You threw her away as if she were a used paper towel. You don't care about her at all."

"I do care very much about her, Megan."

The girl's eyes flashed. "Then why don't you come home? We could start again—we could all love each other again—" Her voice broke.

"Megan, I can't. It's not so simple. I can't explain. . . . You don't understand."

"Is that all you can say? 'You don't understand'? You're right. I don't understand how you can turn your back on us and walk away. Sometimes I wake up at night and think I've only been dreaming that you've done it."

Her eyes were fixed upon him; her body was stiff and tense. And he knew that she was waiting for the answer he was unable to give, knew that she was in pain. A few seconds passed, while he watched the hope die on her face.

"You don't even support us decently," she cried then. "That old rattletrap car."

Adam interrupted. "I paid half the cost of the transmission."

"It's still an old rattletrap. And we need winter clothes. And the lawn mower's too heavy for Danny. What's going to happen to us?"

He pleaded. "I'll do more. I'll try. I know you need things, but I'm spending all I can. I have no extra money right now, nothing to spare. Really not."

"You have money enough for *her.*"

"That's not—who told you that?"

"Don't tell me you live there for nothing. And you bought her a gold bracelet and afterward a gold necklace for her birthday. Mom never had things like that."

Randi must have shown them to Julie, he thought. A weight sank inside his chest. It was all so complicated, so difficult.

Megan's bright, frightened eyes were fixed upon him. "The way you've made all of us so sad," she said, "even a thirteen-year-old boy like Danny. He used to be jolly and funny, but not anymore. And it's all your fault! Do you want to know something? I despise you and your dirty woman with you."

She walked away.

That he had lived to hear the vituperation, this outburst, from his beloved child, his Megan! Megan was even tempered, cerebral, prudent. . . . Megan was a gem. . . .

And wondering how he would manage to drive back without having an accident, he shifted gears and moved slowly away. It seemed to him that no matter how he tried, he would never be able to make her or perhaps anyone else ever understand. Even at the office he had caught glances, and even once in the washroom had overheard remarks.

"I hear he's getting a divorce."

"She's probably better off without him, the cold son of a gun."

"I always liked Margaret."

The fools! What did they know about it? It was none of their business. They were, all of them, a superficial, antiintellectual lot of money-grubbers, anyway.

Some of them had real power, nevertheless. Hierarchy gave them the right to humble and humiliate. Even Ramsey, who was generally fair and quiet-spoken, had given him a nasty turn last week. He flinched now as he remembered the Monday morning, when after a late night, he and Randi had both overslept.

"What can you be thinking of, Crane? Half an hour late for an appointment with a man who stands to give us two hundred thousand in business! He flies in from Chicago and you keep him waiting! Punctuality is a matter of common courtesy, no matter who the person is, but here it almost looked as if you were indifferent. . . ." And so on, and so on.

Adam smarted. And he worried. The rumors about a possible takeover had now become too loud and frequent to be ignored any longer. The company was no IBM, to be sure, but it was attractive enough to arouse the interest of any of the country's largest software producers. This possibility had even been mentioned by a couple of stock analysts in their last month's reports. If the stories were accurate, who could tell what the future might hold for him? Possibly something wonderful. Or not.

Expenses were swamping him. Living with Randi, it certainly behooved him to pay half of them, and they were higher than he was used to. Naturally, he had known that she had a big mortgage, but he had not realized how big. She had bought the house on the proverbial shoestring. And the monthly payments rolled around. Still, she never demanded anything much.

But he was always aware of what she wanted. One thing she wanted was to have a baby. And he had promised that they would have one as soon as he was divorced. My God, but lawyers took so long! For them to file a paper was to move a mountain.

Perhaps because she was not yet bound to him, he felt—or he thought he felt and did not want to feel—that he must make sure of her, must satisfy her and keep her happy. She made *him* so happy! She made him feel like a man who was lord of the earth.

"You worry too much," she would tell him when they were in bed together. "You always did. Years ago, it was your marks and your career. Now it's the office and your kids, when the only thing that's really important is the two of us."

When you come down to it, she's right, he thought. The thought was like an arc light flooding his brain. *The only thing that's really important is the two of us.* Yes, yes, he said to himself. In spite of everything, I have never been as happy as I am now. And that's fundamental.

When he reached the house, he saw her waiting for him at the door. Hearing the sound of tires on gravel, she had come, as she always did, to greet him.

TWENTY-TWO

"**T**his makes more sense than having you come back another day to finish all this stuff. We only have twelve more pages to go through," said Larkin.

He collected the residue of the sandwich-and-coffee lunch and put it neatly in the wastebasket. All his motions were economical, as were his balanced sentences. If the subject weren't so nasty, Margaret thought, it would be a pleasure to hear him speak. The thought amused her.

"Mr. Larkin," she said then, "can you tell me what sense it makes that I must answer these ludicrous questions? 'How many rooms are there in the house and to what use is each of them put?' As if, after all these years of living there, he doesn't know."

"As I've told you, don't look for sense. It's the law. Your house is part of your assets, and so it figures in the settlement."

"My assets," she mocked. And aware that she was probably being a nuisance, she apologized. "I'm sorry, Mr. Larkin. I realize that this kind of emotionalism is wasting your time."

"You're entitled to some emotionalism. Don't worry about it, Margaret. And by the way, if you're to be Margaret, then I must be Stephen. Now, page fifty-four. Take your copy and let's get to it."

When they were finished, he slapped his files shut. With the cessation of speech came an awareness of the surroundings, of wind shaking the windows and a torrential rain sluicing the glass. Stephen got up and looked out.

"The streets look like a river. You'd better stay here until this dies down. These downpours don't usually last long."

"I'll sit in the waiting room and read," she said, rising.

"No, stay here and tell me how you're getting along."

Making a small gesture, as if to convey that a clear reply was impossible, Margaret began, "I'm going through all the correct motions, I know I am. I'm holding things together for the children, I know I am. But inside—inside I see my life cut in two: before Adam, and after Adam. It's like a map of Europe before the end of Communism and after, with all the countries having different names and shapes. Now I'm a different shape, and I'll soon have a different name too. One of the things that troubles me is the thought of the other woman's bearing the name that has belonged to me for nineteen years. Silly, isn't it?"

"I don't think so. To you the name is a symbol of everything she's stolen."

"Tell me, I've wondered, with all you've seen, have you had many cases in which the husband sues the wife for adultery?"

"Only a few. Women know that adultery shatters the intimacy and the trust of marriage, that a marriage afterward can never be the same. That's why adultery usually ends in divorce, and that's why women, as compared with men, usually don't try it."

"Do you mean, then, that men don't know all that beforehand?"

"Most of them don't. I should imagine that Adam Crane, when he started this affair, had no intention of ending up in the divorce court."

"You're saying that the affair took on a life of its own."

"A sad life, and saddest of all for the children."

Margaret's next words escaped her. "Your daily work must be sad for you too."

"Very."

She was curiously conscious of the man, of his hand with its immaculate nails, the wristwatch, the dark suit, the dark, glossy hair. . . . But this was absurd.

"I often think," Stephen said, "that I must give it up, that I want to do something that will build instead of tear down."

"Are you really tearing down?" she asked gently. "I've been thinking how much you help me."

"That is another way of looking at it, I suppose."

"I hope you won't give up before you've seen me through."

He smiled. "I promise I'll see you through. Maybe I'm just talking, anyway."

She could not help but wonder about him as she drove home through the slackening storm. It was foolish that you tended to identify a person only through his work, seldom imagining, for instance, what the doctor *was* once he removed his white coat and professional manner; so she had not before today seen Stephen Larkin in any setting other than in that room with the desk and the brown books on the shelves. It was surprising to learn that he was not satisfied with his work, he was so understanding! She wondered whether he was married or whether perhaps he had had a bad marriage. It was, however, no business of hers.

The first thing she saw when she entered the house was a kitchen in total disarray. The rack from which pots had hung was empty, and every cupboard door was open. In panic she ran into the hall, calling her children's names.

"Up here, Mom," came the answer. "We're up in the attic. There's a flood."

It was disaster. Through two great holes where the roof had simply caved in, the rain was pouring as from a faucet. The buckets that they had brought up were about to overflow. And Margaret stood there stricken, ready to weep.

"It's come through my bedroom ceiling," Megan said, "although not badly. Just some pretty big stains." She tried to smile. "One of them's the shape of South America."

Stains. New plaster. No, new ceiling. New roof. The cost of it? Astronomical. New arguments between the lawyers.

Margaret clapped her hand to her head, where, at the temples, the pulses were almost beating, then she swallowed the stupid lump that always gathered in her throat and said only, "We'll need something right away to cover these holes. We can't leave them all night, or all the bedrooms will be ruined. I wonder—"

"There's that blue plastic stuff—I guess it's plastic—sheets they pull on houses when they're building," Megan said. "Uncle Fred's a builder. He must have some."

Of course. Leave it to Megan.

"I'll phone him. Meantime, I'll take two buckets on my way downstairs and empty them. You come, too, Julie, and bring back the empties."

Later that evening Fred sat in the den with Margaret, going over the situation.

"You're okay for a few days unless a tornado comes and whips those sheets off."

"Will it be awfully expensive to patch it?" she inquired hopefully.

"You can't patch it, Margaret. You need a new roof. You've been needing one for a couple of years. Didn't you ever notice how many shingles were missing?"

She sighed. "I did, but it was so expensive, and Adam thought maybe—" She stopped, trying to recall exactly what it was that Adam had thought.

"Well, there can be no question about it now. He'll have to do it."

"What if he won't?" she asked faintly.

"What do you mean 'won't'? I should think he has no choice."

"Fred, you may think so, but it doesn't work that way. It has to be done through lawyers. Everything has to be. And if he didn't want to spend the money last year—" Again she stopped. Naturally he hadn't wanted to; he had had his plans with *her.* "Why would he want to do it now?" she resumed. "Of course, we can take him to court, but the roof can't very well wait for that, can it?"

"No. And I hate to pour salt on your wounds, but the truth is that the whole house needs work. I've gone over it pretty thoroughly. The furnace—didn't you have a problem with it last winter?" When Margaret nodded, he continued, "I'd say you'd be lucky to get through another winter with it. The cellar stairs need fixing, too, before someone trips and breaks his neck. The windows leak on the whole north side of the house whenever the rain drives from the north. I've seen you put towels on the sills—"

Margaret clapped her hands to her ears, crying. "Stop! Don't you think I know I have no right to stay here?"

"Why, what do you mean 'no right'? You have every right. It's your home, your family home, and it's a solid old house. It's simply in need of some repairs. It's not a question of a million dollars, for Pete's sake."

"It might as well be," she said.

They sat still. She thought: It is his expenses with that woman that are ruining me and my children.

Presently Fred spoke. "If you will let me help you. I know you wouldn't let me help with the car, but this is more serious. Please let me. You know I can afford it."

"I will let you send your men to patch the roof temporarily because it's an emergency. I will be so grateful for that, but I can't accept anything more. You are the best man in the world, but don't you see, Fred, that I have to get used to a different way of life? That's simply the way it is. Husband leaves wife, his income goes up and hers goes down. The way it is."

"You're being stubborn," he said gently.

"No, I'm being realistic. The fact is that even if it were in perfect condition, we wouldn't belong here. It's just too big, too hard to maintain by ourselves, and I can't afford help to take Adam's place. The snowstorm last month was a killer. The children are all overburdened. They're good kids and they haven't complained, but they're overburdened."

There. She had finally spoken the dreaded words. And she looked around the room, out to the hall where the clothes rack and the tall clock still stood where they had always been, in the dear house where she had been born.

Fred, following her look, said, gently still, "This hurts you too much, Margaret. Are you sure?"

She nodded, biting her lip. "Yes. It's an old-fashioned concept, anyway, isn't it? How many people in this country still live where they were born?"

"Not many, I suppose. But if a person wants to, why—"

"If a person can. I could have once, but now I can't."

Adam, and Mrs. Randi Bunting, had made the decision.

"So," she said, "I shall call a broker tomorrow. I should get a good price for it, in spite of its needing repairs. You don't find woodwork like this nowadays. And the yard is beautiful."

"If you want to see something unbelievable," Margaret said to Fred a few days later, "look at this broker's appraisal."

When he read it, Fred put it aside, hesitated for a moment, and with obvious reluctance told her that it was indeed believable.

"It's a wonderful old house on a wonderful old street, but unfortunately, there's not a big market for these places. Especially not for one that has no air-conditioning, an antiquated kitchen, and the original claw-foot bathtubs. Plus high urban taxes."

"But the neighborhood! The yard!"

"The neighborhood is gradually changing. People with money are moving to the suburbs, out toward Beachcroft."

"You make it sound awful, Fred. Won't *anybody* buy it?"

"Yes, people who have a big family and a small amount of money. You'd better take what you can get. I'm sorry, Margaret, but that's it."

That's it. And for the thousandth time came the inward cry: How is it possible?

Between shadow and lamplight the two sat silently. Random thoughts went flickering past the eye of Margaret's mind, such as:

Adam knows we're on short rations here, so why doesn't he come home and do what a man ought to do? Yet she knew that if he should return, begging on his knees, she would not—could not—take him. And she wondered, too, whether he ever reckoned up his past, and if he did, how. For he had started out with such enthusiasm, such hope, such pride in himself. And yet, after nineteen years, he had made but a small advance from his starting point. Three children, up to the time he left, had been living on very little more than their newlywed parents had possessed. Now, at this moment, they were living on less. Did he ever ask himself what was wrong? Did I ever ask myself, and if not, why not?

Because I loved him so. Unconsciously, her lips had formed the words, and startled, she looked up to see Fred gazing at her with a look of deep compassion.

"Hold on," he said. "Margaret, you'll be all right. Hold on."

She raised her head and smiled. "Don't worry, I'm holding. I'll give the listing to the broker in the morning."

Then the wait began. People came, trudging through the house, looked—looked askance—and left.

Friends and family had varying advice. In the teachers' lounge a friend said, "Much as it hurts, in the long run the change will be good for you, Margaret. You'll be ridding yourself of a lot of baggage and starting fresh."

Another, much older than Margaret, reminisced. "I have a memory that goes back to the time I was four. My mother took me to visit at that house. Your great-grandparents were there. He had whiskers and she gave me gingerbread."

Stephen counseled, "It's a wise decision. At best, when we go to court, you'll have considerably less to live on. At best. So it's prudent to prepare accordingly."

Nina, on the other hand, was indignant. "He gets himself another woman, he walks out, and now you'll have to leave home. Is this modern justice?" She offered money. "I'm doing really well, I have some nice savings, and I want to help you keep the house. I know I've asked you to let me and you've always said no, but will you let me?" And when Margaret still declined the offer, she demanded, "Where will you go?"

"I'll have to find an apartment someplace."

"With what he gives you now, it will have to be pretty cramped for the four of you. Do you think that's fair to the children?"

"It won't hurt them," Margaret told her. "Millions of people have
to live in cramped places."

Stalwart sentiments, these were, but even as she expressed them,
she did not mean a word.

Louise and Gilbert were shocked. And in a curious way their anger
consoled her.

"Poor sap," Gil said. "Feels like a rooster with two hens to choose
between."

Louise declared that all men were fools. "Remember that typist
you had, Gil? She had her claws out for you, and you didn't even know
it. But I took one look at her and I warned you not to start any monkey
business. Gil was a good-looking young man, Margaret. I wasn't taking
any chances."

Gil looked sheepish and pleased. Margaret thought tenderly that it
was hard to imagine him with a full head of hair and no paunch, hard
also to imagine Louise, with her comfortable print dresses and tight
gray permanent wave, in her twenties. But they were here for her in
their fullness of heart.

"I'd like to make you a loan," Gil offered. "If we didn't have four
grandchildren, family responsibilities, by God, I'd give it to you outright, Margaret. But tell me what you need to borrow, and you'll have it
in the morning."

Margaret shook her head. "I would never be able to repay you,"
she said quietly.

And still she wondered what Adam felt about his children's loss of
their home—his children's loss, not hers. For was she not the enemy,
the impediment that had kept him so long away from the "love of his
life"?

On Sunday, Julie reported, "Daddy would like to talk to you about
the house."

"I don't want to talk to him, Julie. He can talk through his lawyer.
He already has." Then as curiosity overcame her, she asked, "Why?
What does he have to say about the house?"

"I think just that he's sorry he can't help out. Anyway, he says
you'll probably marry Uncle Fred, so you won't be needing this house.
Are you going to marry Uncle Fred, Mom?"

"I'm not going to marry anybody. And you can tell him for me that
nothing I do is any business of his."

She should not have said that. She had broken her own rule against
involving the children. But how dare he! He had no right to discuss her
private affairs with them. No right!

It was true that Fred sometimes gave hints, the most delicate, vague hints.

"Sometimes I think about selling my own house. It's much too large for one man and a little dog. Still, I keep thinking that someday I might need it, so I hold on to it."

He was the finest kind of man. But men and marriage were the farthest thing from Margaret's mind.

One morning the broker showed the house, and in the evening returned with an offer close to his prediction. The buyers were a couple with six children. They were handy people who would be able to make most of the needed repairs themselves. But they wanted possession within six weeks. Margaret agreed.

Six weeks gave little time to clean out three generations' worth of goods and find another place to live in.

"Would you consider moving into my house?" asked Fred. "You understand . . . I didn't mean . . ." He stumbled and flushed.

Margaret, too, stumbled and flushed. "Of course I understand, and thank you, Fred. But we need our own place."

Elmsford was not an apartment city. It soon became evident that there was nothing to be found. And she began to feel panic.

"I would suggest my garden apartments in Beachcroft," said Fred, "except that I don't have anything larger than two bedrooms. You seldom find anything larger in the suburbs."

"I'll look at it, anyway," Margaret told him.

"The rent will be moderate. In fact, if you'll allow me, the rent will be zero."

"Fred, you know better than that. I will not allow you."

He laughed. "I didn't think you would."

The area was beautiful, close to a park with a lake. There were walks and safe places for bicycling. It was a distance from downtown, but as long as the car held out, it was feasible. Feasible and cramped. . . .

"The girls will have a bedroom, Danny will have the other, and I'll sleep on the sofa," she told Fred, who was showing the apartment.

Fred shook his head. "No, no. Let Danny take the sofa."

"He needs a room to himself with a desk and quiet. He's been slumping badly with his studies, and I'm worried."

"I'm not happy about seeing you here," Fred said disconsolately. "And I'm not happy having to tell you something else. No dogs allowed."

"Fred! You can't mean that."

"Listen, it breaks my heart. I know what Rufus means to Dan. But if I allow you to have a dog, I'll have to allow every other tenant the same, and that won't work. You can see why."

As if Danny hadn't been through enough! And this one would be the worst.

"Will you come over one evening and help me explain it to him?" she asked.

"Of course I will."

So they told him, the three of them sitting in the den, while the subject of the discussion lay on the floor, holding a biscuit in his mouth as if he were smoking a pipe.

Danny did not cry. Instead, until they were through explaining, he sat quite still.

"What's going to happen to him?" he asked, looking straight forward into the air.

Margaret's throat quivered with her reply. "I'll find a wonderful home for him. You know I'm good at that."

"It won't be his own home."

"No, it won't. This is something that Rufus, like the rest of us, will have to bear."

Fred, also carefully avoiding anyone's eyes, was staring at the floor. There was a long silence until Danny spoke again.

"It's funny how I was promised another dog last summer, and now you're even taking this one away."

"It's not your mother who's taking it away," Fred said with emphasis. "Not your *mother*."

"I think—I'll go up to my room now," Danny said. And he walked out slowly while Rufus followed.

Things moved rapidly during the next weeks. There was to be a house sale, and Nina was coming to help sort out the worthless from that which was worth storing for the unknown future. Above all, the piano must be kept in storage.

"I'll never be able to afford another one like it," Margaret said, "in case Julie . . ." She did not finish.

Julie moved almost soundlessly through the house on tiptoe, as if she were trying to be unheard and unseen.

"Daddy feels sorry that we have to leave here," she reported once and, with lifted eyebrows, searched her mother's face for a response.

Margaret said only, "I'm sorry too."

In the last week the evening came when Rufus was to be taken to his new home. Herself close to tears, Margaret collected the beloved dog's possessions, ball, leash, basket-bed, and a bag of kibbled food. Danny watched.

"You don't want to go, do you?" she asked as she put on her jacket.

"I have to go," he answered.

Rufus, being too large to make a third in the front seat, rode in the back this night with Danny. No one spoke until they were almost at their destination, when Margaret said, "We have an understanding. They will give him back if we ever have room for him again."

"We never will," said Danny.

Carrying Rufus's possessions, they went slowly up the walk, slowly enough to allow Rufus some sniffing time.

The front door opened, and a woman exclaimed, "Oh, here he is! Isn't he beautiful! Come in."

"No, thank you," Danny said, handing over the leash.

"But do come in," the woman urged.

Margaret said quickly, "I think we'd better not. We have to get home."

Rufus turned with them as they turned to leave.

"No," Danny told him. "No, stay. Good dog, stay. Good-bye, Rufus."

On the way home the silence in the car was fragile; a word would have shattered it into fragments. The merest touch of sympathy would have shattered the boy. When they reached home, he went to his room and closed the door.

Much later, on her way to bed, Margaret heard him crying, stifling his sobs in his pillow. And in her heart there arose a hatred such as she had never yet known, even during these last bad months.

"Adam Crane, you son of a bitch," she whispered, she who despised coarse words, "I hope you burn in hell for what you've done."

They left the house on a splendid day at the end of May. For the last time, when everyone was already sitting in the car, Margaret walked around the yard. They had left the croquet things in the hall closet; perhaps the new kids would play. The grill was there at the kitchen door; perhaps the new family would like to barbecue. She hoped they would keep the birdbath filled during the summer heat. Looking up, she saw that the mountain ash, Nina's tree, was tipped with buds, each a little ruby-colored cone, a gem. Stooping, she saw the green thrust of

tulips breaking through the earth: *Angelique,* they were; in a few weeks
they would be all pink and frilled like roses. So life went on.

Then she raised her head, stiffened her back, and climbed into the
car.

TWENTY-THREE

"I thought you'd need a little time to get settled before you had visitors," Fred said on the third day.

He had brought an arrangement of irises and lilies in a wicker basket which, after he looked around the living room for a flat surface and found none, he placed on the all-purpose table in the "dinette."

Margaret giggled. "Everything seems to end with *ette*," she said. "Dinette. Kitchenette. Why not 'bedette,' or 'bathette'?" She was absolutely drunk with fatigue.

"Seriously, you've done a great job here in no time," Fred said. He looked around at the tasteful arrangement of photographs on the wall behind the double pullout sofa, the scarlet Oriental screen, and the overlong curtains from the old den, now looped back to fit the window.

"Louise and Gil gave us the screen. They bought it in Hong Kong and never used it. It'll come in handy to hide a messy kitchen if there should be unexpected guests, won't it?"

In the fragile state of her emotions a silly giggle could in a moment turn toward the brink of tears. Never in her life had she been on the receiving end of so much generosity. The double sofa-bed, on which she had been sleeping with Nina, had come from Gil and Louise; Nina had brought some lovely clothes from New York for the girls; a friend whose husband was in the moving business had refused to accept payment. All of this generosity had been bestowed with so much tact. . . .

"Everybody's been so kind, and you most of all."

"Why shouldn't they be? You've always done your share. And more than your share. Here, can we move these books and make room for the flowers? Don't tell me you're already back at work."

"I have to be. It's the end of term with finals coming up. Also, I have to prepare for summer school."

"You're not having a vacation, some time off?"

"I can't afford to."

"It's a disgrace. If anyone had told me twenty years ago that Adam Crane could do this, I'd have told him he was crazy."

"And Adam Crane is worse than crazy," said Nina, walking in with an armful of books. "But come, let me show you around. Here's the girls' room. The twin beds don't match, but we'll call that an original style. Style Nina Quatorze. The plaid rug that I adored is from my old room, and the cupboard—when Margaret was a child, she used to think it was a monster in the night—can hold some clothes, since there's only one closet. Now here's Danny's room—I've put that—excuse me—that bastard's computer in here. It's a tight squeeze, but they're all trim enough to squeeze. Kids need a computer, and this one is tops."

"Well, it's nice, mighty nice," declared Fred. "Of course, it's crowded. Actually I've built these apartments for young marrieds, retired couples, and singles. Hey, your lawyer lives here, Margaret! His apartment's in B section over the slope. Come to the window."

In a long curve the low red-brick buildings marched up from the road and scattered themselves among thick stands of trees.

"When we planned this, the idea was to save as many trees as possible. It makes it cool for walking and biking. Then there's the park over there. It's really beautiful. You can't see it from here, but the first chance you get, you should go. It's not far. Take Danny. He'll make friends at the baseball field and get into a game before you know it."

"Fred's always so enthusiastic, so encouraging. He makes you feel optimistic," Nina said after he left.

The two women, in jeans and work shirts, sat resting on the front steps. In reply to Nina's observation Margaret only nodded. Her thoughts were tired and random. Suddenly she remembered Fred's bouquet in its basket. Adam had never sent flowers. . . . And as suddenly, this fact took on a great significance: a man who had never given a flower to his wife! She sat there very still, absorbing the fact.

Nina patted her arm. "This won't be forever," she said.

"I'm only concerned about my children. Danny's not himself at all. He's too quiet, drawn inward."

"Well, for one thing, it's been a terrible blow to part with Rufus."

"No, there's something else. He doesn't talk much about Adam anymore. Until recently, it used to be 'Dad this' and 'Dad that.' I wonder . . . Poor little boy. It's funny, he's thirteen and almost as tall as I am, but I still see him as a little boy."

"There they come," Nina said, pointing down the road where the three were walking from the direction of the park.

And Margaret, gazing at the pair of girls and their younger brother, at these three who were now all she had, said slowly, "It's like a bad dream. Do you know what I mean, Nina? All I ever wanted was to rear a beautiful, intact family. And now the family's tainted and marked. For no matter how much love and care they receive, this will be engraved in their memories as long as they live." Then, raising her voice, she called brightly, "How was it over at the park? Nice?"

"It's a park," Megan said.

"Well, I know that." Better to take no heed of their moods right now, she reminded herself. And she invited them to sit down. "Come, join us. There are plenty of steps to sit on."

"I'm going to my room—our room," Megan said.

"Sure you don't want to stay here? It's Nina's last day tomorrow."

"I know, but I do have homework, Mom. There are still three weeks of school, Mom. Remember?"

"I do remember." Ignoring the sarcasm, Margaret replied dryly, "Go on in, then."

A pleasant little wind moved through the trees. Across the quiet street an old couple were sunning themselves on lounge chairs. This wouldn't be so bad if there were fewer of us, she thought.

Just then, Danny, sitting with dejected shoulders and elbows on knees, gave a loud, attention-getting sigh.

"What is it, Danny? Can I do something?" Margaret asked, and when no answer came, continued gently, "Maybe you want to visit Rufus. Is that it?"

The boy glared and shouted, "No! I never want to see him again. And never *ask* me!"

"All right, I won't. It's just that I heard your sigh." And remembering Audrey's injunctions, she added, "I think, Dan, you'd feel better if you got to your homework."

"I wouldn't feel better. I hate school. What I'd like is to quit and get a job."

"That's silly talk for a boy your age."

"Not really." Megan spoke from the doorway. "It's obvious that we need money pretty badly, and every little bit will help."

Now Julie flared up. "You're always so sarcastic. Dad says we're not that poor at all. Mom got all that money from the sale of the house."

" 'Dad says'! Anything *he* says isn't worth that!" And Megan snapped her fingers.

"You want me to hate him. You all do. You do, too, Mom."

Nina got up from the step and faced the two girls. "Now listen here," she said sternly. "Nobody wants anybody to hate anybody. But truth is truth, and maybe, in spite of all your mother has been advised, it won't hurt for you to know some truths. The small amount—and it's very, very small—that your mother received from the house is all she and you have in the world. It has to be put away for a rainy day—you've heard about rainy days? It can't be touched because nothing very much is ever going to be coming from your father. That's for sure."

"Men!" Megan snorted. "All a woman gets from a man is a raw deal."

"No," Nina said, "you can't put all the blame on men. You have to remember that in raw deals like this one, the third party is a woman."

Nina's honesty brought a sudden silence, since everyone there knew her personal story. Margaret would miss her strength, her loyalty, and the courage that did not blink. Very much moved, she tried to lighten the moment.

"We're going to Uncle Gil's for dinner, a farewell to Nina. Farewell until your next visit." she said, appealing, soft eyed, to Nina. "Now we'd better get dressed."

She would remember that summer, Margaret knew, as a time when only the kindness of friends had gotten them through it. The first few weeks were the worst, with cranky children competing for desk space, for quiet, and for the bathroom. Working on school papers in the middle of confusion was a nightmare. And yet, there were these moments. . . .

The anniversary, the twentieth now, fell on a Sunday. Whether it was Megan or Nina, who telephoned regularly, who had advised Julie and Dan, or whether they themselves had decided not to visit Adam that day, Margaret neither knew nor asked. When she awoke that morning, an instant awareness of the date enveloped her. And she lay there in the cluttered living room wishing that she had not awakened, wishing that she were someone else, anyone but Margaret Crane. The telephone rang, and Fred's voice rang out of it.

"How would you folks like to go to the club and spend the day? Lunch, swim, and dinner too?"

She wanted to answer that she was tired, that she would like most to draw the covers over her head and go back to sleep, but instead she answered, "It's too much for you to take all this crew, Fred. If you want to take Danny—I don't know about Megan and Julie—"

"Excuse me for interrupting, but you certainly know that I know what day this is. I can tell by your voice that I woke you too. Now get dressed, have breakfast, and I'll come around for you all at ten-thirty. No, don't answer me, I'm hanging up."

Of course, she reflected that evening, he had been right. He usually was right. And the day had been good for all of them, especially for herself and her morale. Dressed in a white skirt and a royal-blue top, she had looked smart. This had been the first time in months when, not counting school people, she had confronted a crowd in a social setting, and it had gone well. With Fred beside her she had not felt like a fifth wheel.

And then there was Stephen. He had left a message on the answering machine.

"Looking over some documents of yours, I saw this date. I know it's a hard day for you, so I thought I'd call to offer a little pep talk in case you might need one, although I hope you don't."

"Every little bit helps," she said when she called back to thank him.

"By the way, I just learned that we are practically neighbors. It didn't strike me at first when you gave me your change of address."

"I didn't know, either, until we moved in and Fred told me."

"How are you all liking it?"

"It's a tremendous change," she said frankly, feeling no need for disguise. "It's hard on the children. Danny's lost his ballgame—he's a baseball freak, and there's nobody here for him. Fred took pity on him and had a catch with him yesterday."

"There are always a couple of games in the park. I play myself whenever I have time, which isn't often. I'll be there tomorrow afternoon, in fact. Why don't you bring him down and introduce us?"

"You've been a big help to Dan," Margaret said some weeks later.

Back in his office he was the man she had first met, while on the ball field in his shorts he had looked like an overgrown boy.

"I'm glad. He's a good kid. Well, getting back to business, I'm sorry about all the delay."

"I don't mind the delay so much, Stephen. I'm sure it frustrates my so-called husband and his Randi, which is rather nice. What worries me is having money for college. Megan's starting her senior year."

"Margaret, I don't want to get your hopes up. A man's not obliged to provide college. He's not obliged to provide anything once a child reaches eighteen."

"I can't believe it!" she cried. "She was his pride. I can see them working at the computer, I can hear them talking politics and tennis and—I can't understand it."

"I'm going to argue, of course. But he's away now, his lawyer said. He's gone to California for a couple of weeks."

Margaret was almost speechless. California! How many times had she suggested a vacation, only to be told that it cost too much?

"I am so bitterly resentful, Stephen," she said.

"I know what you're thinking. But the day will come when he will regret everything. By then you won't even care."

"You think so?"

It seemed impossible that she would ever cease to care. Despising Adam as she did, she never yet went through a single day without a thought of him. Passing a bag of popcorn at the market, she recalled the winter evenings when they watched television in the den. Overhearing a stranger say the word *porcupine,* she remembered the time that one of those queer animals had wandered past their picnic table. All the odd moments that kept flashing and flashing!

"I'm certain," Stephen said.

"You sound like the psychologist."

"I've heard so much that sometimes I feel like one." He paused. "Dan told me he's having trouble with French. I thought perhaps I could help him, if you'd like. My mother was French, and I speak it well."

"Why, that would be very kind of you. Thank you," Margaret said.

Very kind, she reflected on the way home. At the same time she knew that there was more than kindness behind Stephen's offer. Certain glances and tones that a woman recognized, however subtle, were unmistakable. Had she perhaps been too cool, too formal, with her thanks? But no, she was not ready to encourage anyone.

And it seemed quite possible to her, so crushed, so burdened, so determined to be self-reliant and courageous, that she never would be ready.

TWENTY-FOUR

A dam's spirit had always responded to the fall, its colors and the return of brisk air. This morning, though, as he drove toward Elmsford on his way to work, he felt no response to the season other than a sickening apprehension, settled somewhere in the region of his stomach. Ever since his return from California—a trip that, while itself enjoyable, had been undertaken only after much persuasion on Randi's part and had cost a very troubling sum—he had been expecting something to happen.

After several years' worth of false, tormenting rumors, of plans altered and delayed, the die had finally been cast. Magnum was taking over ADS. The expanded operation was to be entirely reorganized. Day by day, drop by drop, news of this came filtering down from the top.

Yesterday's latest was Rudy Hudson's return to the main office as head man at triple his present salary. So one of these days there would be news for Adam Crane too. He had an uncanny feeling that this would be the day.

His secretary came in shortly before noon, looking—how? concerned? excited? curious?

"One of those men from Magnum, a Mr. Baldwin, wants to see you."

"When?"

"Now."

His knees went weak when he stood up. And he told himself this was absurd; there was no reason why the news should not be splendid. He had, after all, been with the company for twenty years.

Mr. Baldwin rose to greet Adam. He was a tall man, fit and youth-

ful, with just the right touch of gray in his thick hair. Adam thought
immediately how interesting it was that top executives were so often
men of striking good looks. His next thought was: But I am good looking too.

They sat down, and Mr. Baldwin smiled. "I'm told that you've been
here a long time," he said.

"Yes. It's my first and only job."

Mr. Baldwin nodded. "You don't find much of that these days.
Unfortunately. With all the reorganizations going on."

There were too many pauses in the man's speech. They meant that
he was uncomfortable with what he had to say. There could be no other
interpretation, could there? If he had good news, wouldn't he start out
with something hearty, such as "Congratulations! I know you'll be delighted to hear . . ." But not necessarily. It might just be his manner.
And Adam waited, leaning forward in the chair.

"The downsizing that results from these reorganizations. . . . We
all know that it can be economically healthy. . . . Making the new
company, while larger, nevertheless leaner and stronger. . . . Although
that does sound like a contradiction." Then came the smile again.

The tension of expectation drained out of Adam, and he leaned
back in the chair. He did not need to hear any more. He knew.

"Unfortunately and undeservedly, too many individuals have to
suffer in this process. I'm so sorry, Mr. Crane, that you have to be one
of them."

Adam's mouth went dry and he thought his lip twitched. For an
instant, afraid that his voice would quaver, he was afraid to speak.

"I'm sure you'll have no trouble being placed somewhere else. And
of course, we'll give you the finest possible recommendation. In fact, we
are setting up a service right in this building to assist—"

"No," Adam said. That would be the final humiliation, to crawl
back here and ask for help. "No, thank you. I'll—I'll manage."

What could the man be thinking, with that quiet expression and
that quiet voice, so correctly sympathetic? Was he feeling calm, indifferent, or cruel in his possession of the power to destroy—all so easily—
another human being? No, Adam decided after a few silent, heavy-
laden moments, he's probably just embarrassed and wishing he hadn't
been given this nasty job to do.

"I'm sorry, really sorry," Baldwin said.

The tall clock in the corner of this handsome office went *bong!* The
short interview had fulfilled its purpose. It was time to go. And yet
Adam was not quite ready.

"I've been here twenty years," he said.

"I know. It must be hard. Very hard."

"Will you tell me something? Since there has had to be some selection process, who is to remain and who is to be let go, I would like to know: Why me? I have kept abreast of everything that's happening in the field. I know my job. Why me?"

Baldwin was playing with his pen, rolling it on the desktop with a gesture that did not quite befit his dignity. It was evident that the question troubled him exceedingly.

He began, "Well, I—" When Adam interrupted.

"I know I've asked a question that you're not obliged to answer and probably don't want to answer. Yet, I believe I have a human right to know. And so I'm asking for an answer, confidentially and man to man."

A softness passed across Baldwin's face. He pities me, Adam thought.

Presently, Baldwin said, "Under those conditions I will tell you. I hope I'm not making a mistake. I'm a newcomer here, and I can only repeat what I've been told."

"And that is?"

"That you have not been carrying your weight. I don't know whether it's true or not."

Adam got up and bowed. "It's not true," he said.

"I'm sorry, Mr. Crane, I'm genuinely sorry."

"Thank you." And bowing once more, Adam went out.

He was burning within. He thought his very heart was on fire. Of course they had to let someone go, and of course it had to be he because they had never liked him. And he recalled that day in the washroom when he had overheard them, Jenks and some others, discussing him.

"*—cold bastard, thinks he's too superior to bother with you.*"

"*—he'll never get anywhere.*"

"*—I always liked Margaret, though.*"

In his office he stood in the center of the room and stared without aim. Except for the photograph of his children—the one that included Margaret he had discarded—there was nothing in the room that belonged to him. In a few days someone else would take his place, here at this desk, on this chair. He had simply passed through.

His secretary came in to remind him that he had an appointment right after lunch.

"Cancel it," he said. "I'm going home."

And with that he went out, leaving her to stare after him in aston-ishment. No doubt, before the day was over, she would understand.

He drove home in a state of deadening fatigue, his vision blurred. The landscape was gray with fog, as depressed as he was. Fall was edging into winter, and the air was musty with the smell of wet fallen leaves.

At a stoplight he drew up alongside Gil and Louise in their BMW. For an instant their glances crossed until Louise, with a look of utmost contempt, turned her head away. This brief contact reminded him that it was the night of the party at their house when he had made his final decision to leave Margaret. The contact reminded him, too, of the day not long ago when he had seen Fred Davis getting gas at a service station in Randolph Corner. He had had then an aborted impulse to get out of his car and ask Fred how things were really going at the apart-ment. Fred would know. Julie and Danny—usually Danny, the bigmouth—spoke often enough of Uncle Fred, of treats and movies. Suddenly now he felt a pang of jealousy to think of Fred Davis with his children.

A strange thought occurred to him: If Randi were a *wife,* he would not be so much in dread of bringing this disaster home, for a wife would have to accept it, whereas before Randi he must appear impressive, a worthy, undefeated lover. Aberrant, crazy thoughts!

After a while, though, and very gradually, he began to argue him-self into some semblance of resolve. Wasn't he only one among many who had lost a job? He would certainly find another. And he went into his house—half of it at least was his, considering how much money he had put into it—poured a small drink, and lay down on the sofa, there to plan what his next move could be.

A few minutes later he heard Randi's car. She came crying, "What are you doing home? Are you sick?"

"No, no. But what are you doing home at two o'clock?"

"I had no appointments. No business appointments, that is. But what's the matter? You look queer."

"Don't be alarmed. Take your jacket off, sit down, and I'll tell you."

She looked particularly rosy, he thought, vivid with healthy blood and energy. As if responding to her affect, he sat up straight and, speak-ing almost with bravado, told her what had happened.

"I lost my job this morning. I'm out."

"You what?"

"Yes, it happens. I'm one of the great unemployed. But don't worry, it won't be for long."

"I can't believe it! A job like yours . . . Why, you're one of the big shots!"

Big shots. The irony of it.

"It's not that simple," he said. "Nobody's that big. Nobody's immune."

When she got up from the chair, he thought she was going to come to him and offer comfort. But she only stood there indecisively, with a frown and compressed lips.

"Not for long, you said? How can you be sure of that?"

"I can't be sure, but I believe it because I'm going to do my darnedest."

For a second or two it seemed to him that she looked *angry*. She hadn't asked for any details, how the blow had been dealt, why it had been, or how he felt.

So he filled the gap. "It took five minutes, maybe even less. Oh, he was decent, all right, couldn't have been more so. But after twenty years . . ." He could say no more. Bravado had fled.

She was elsewhere, in her own place, not his. "This is some fine mess. My God, I came home so happy over my news, and this is the news you give me. Do you know where I was just now? At the doctor's. I'm pregnant."

Perhaps it was because he was shaken from the first blow of the day that her words did not at once take effect.

"Well, can't you say something, Adam?"

"You were on the pill," he said and felt, abruptly, a dull thudding in his chest.

"Nothing's a hundred percent. Everybody knows that." She stared at him. "Is that all you have to give me? No smile?"

The thudding went wild in his chest. He could not have said whether the reason for it was anger, despair, or fear. He only knew that all of these were whirling in him. The divorce, the job, his children, his pride, the bills, and the dwindling bank account all went whirling. And now this.

"I wasn't counting on having a baby now," he said inadequately.

"You may not have been, but I was. How long did you expect me to wait? Till I'm sixty? You promised me a baby. You promised!" And she stamped her foot.

Did I actually promise? he wondered. He wasn't sure. Perhaps he had. It was all such a blur, like the fog on the road.

"I just plain got sick and tired of waiting," she said.

With these words of hers all the turmoil and rage in Adam flared abruptly into fire, and he attacked her, shouting, "Then you did it on purpose! You weren't using the pill! Knowing that this isn't the time, that I didn't want a baby yet, that we aren't ready and can't afford one, you tricked me anyway!"

"Why? Are you such a pauper that you can't afford my child—our child?"

The word *pauper* enraged him further. "This pauper has done pretty well by you. He's kept you afloat. Without him this house of yours would have drowned. Do you ever keep touch of the expenses? Do you even know what's in the checking account this minute? Or, I should say, what isn't in the checking account."

"I know damn well. I know why. If it weren't for that blood-sucking wife of yours, sticking her hands in your pockets every week, it would be a different story. Damn bitch! She knows you don't love her, and still she won't let go."

"Don't be a fool. You know I have no choice. Am I to let them starve? They're my children."

"She works, doesn't she? Let her do more for them. They're her children, too, not only yours."

"I wonder where your brains are when you talk like that."

"And I wonder where yours are. You don't even know how to handle your lawyer. Why don't you ask him why this divorce is taking him so damn long?"

"The courts are jammed up with divorces all over America. Haven't you heard?"

She began to cry. "You make me sick. Here I was looking forward to meeting you at the front door with my news, I was thinking how excited you'd be, and we'd start talking about names, and you'd get out the champagne, only I wouldn't have any because I'm not supposed to drink now—and instead we're standing here having a fight."

"Randi, I don't want to fight. I want the two of us to quiet down and see how we can work things out."

"If you mean work things out by having an abortion, you can drop dead, because I want this baby. Hear? I want this baby."

"Randi, I didn't say anything about an abortion. I'm just awfully upset, I'm pretty frantic, and I need to—"

Loudly sobbing, "Oh my God," she ran into the bedroom, slammed the door, and locked it.

Adam knocked. "Let me in. Let's talk. Please, Randi."

"No! Let me alone. I want to be alone with my baby."

In all his distress he was still moved by these last words. *My baby.* It was, after all, normal and laudable for a woman to want a child. If the circumstances were different, he, too, would welcome a child of hers, a love child. But the circumstances were terrifying.

He had had no lunch, yet he was not hungry. He recognized that in his present state he could not possibly concentrate on a book, nor could he fall asleep. Not knowing what to do with himself, he took a disk from the shelf and put it on the player. Beethoven's Ninth might either calm or uplift him toward acceptance and courage. In either case it would not fail. And lying back again on the sofa, he let the miraculous, the almost holy sounds sweep over him. He was still awake and dreaming, watching a ribbon of sunlight move across the ceiling, when Randi's voice broke into the spell.

"Will you for heaven's sake shut off that racket! How you can stand it, I'll never know."

He sat up and, mildly enough, refuted her. "The world has loved this music for almost two hundred years, and you call it a 'racket'?"

"I do, and I hate it."

Occasionally she did surprise him. . . .

"I only put up with it because you like it."

"Well, that's all right," he said reasonably, "since I put up with things for your sake too."

"Really? What do I do that bothers you?"

Actually, he was unable to think of anything much. Oh, perhaps a few small things: her grammar sometimes, although not often, was one. He was a stickler for proper grammar. Also, she could be a trifle flirtatious on occasion. But then, he was jealous of her, too, so it was possible that he imagined that.

Indeed, he was jealous of her! Here she stood, still flashing with anger, her big eyes still wet with tears, breathing so fast that he could see the heaving of her breasts under the cream-colored silk of her blouse. She looked so soft inside the brittle shell of her anger! And she was carrying his child.

Then he, too, went soft. For this was her day of celebration and should be recognized, regardless of all else. So with outstretched arms he went to her, held her while she cried out on his shoulder, and kissed away her tears.

Behind them the music, still playing, had reached that great, climactic, hopeful chorus, the "Ode to Joy," which he loved and knew by heart. But quite perversely, he was chilled by a shiver of sadness.

TWENTY-FIVE

This was the second Christmas without Adam, and the first that in the life of each had not been spent in the familiar house where, year after year, the tree had stood in the living-room bay, and the dining-room mantel had been festooned with greenery and hung with stockings.

"I'd like you to have dinner at my house this year," said Fred.

Margaret objected. "All your friends are at your club's party, and you always go. I know you're thinking of us and it's just like you to invite us, but I don't want you to do it."

"And *I* know you think it's a matter of compassion," he answered firmly, "but you happen to be all wrong. This is for me. I want a family Christmas, and yours is the family closest to me. I've already invited your cousins Louise and Gil. They're not going to their son's in Florida till after the first. So that's that."

It was a kind of comfort to be ordered around in such a nice way, and so she accepted, although with a condition.

"The girls and I will cook the dinner, at least."

"You will not. The dinner's being catered. I want you to get dressed up and be waited on for a change."

All through the day before and through most of the night, it had snowed, and on Christmas morning a great white peace lay over the blizzard-beaten landscape.

"A postcard," Margaret said. "All it needs is a horse-drawn sleigh with fur robes and harness bells. But come look at the drifts. There's no way we can leave here today."

The girls, who had already laid out the extravagant dark red velvet, lace-collared dresses that Nina had sent, were dismayed. Danny insisted that he could shovel the car out.

"You can't, and even if you could, I wouldn't dare venture on those roads with that car."

Fred lived in what he jokingly referred to as "exurbia," meaning a house not exactly in the country, but that, set within its two or three wooded acres, looked as if it were.

Just then the phone rang. "I'm coming for you around noon," said Fred. "That Jeep of mine can go up Mount Everest."

So, carrying gifts and pumpkin pies that Margaret, regardless of caterers, had baked, they climbed into the Jeep and started over the hill. In the dip beyond the crest they came upon Stephen Larkin trying to extricate his half-buried car.

"What the devil do you think you're doing?" Fred called. "Wait till tomorrow and get a tow."

Stephen tramped over to the Jeep. He was laughing. "I can't wait. You're not going to believe it, but I'm all out of food. I was supposed to fly to my sister's over the holiday, but of course there are no flights. So I'm trying to get to a restaurant."

"Climb in here," Fred told him. "I've got dinner enough for an army at my house. And if we get stuck on the way, which we won't, Margaret's got two big pies. Come on."

"I'm not exactly dressed for dinner in these clothes."

Actually, Margaret thought, in those clothes, the jeans, the rough jacket, and the cap pulled down above his reddened cheeks, he looked especially attractive.

Fred ordered, "Get in."

She was unusually observant lately, especially sensitive to trivia, to atmosphere. And so she had been noticing, or had thought she was noticing, small alterations in Fred's manner. Now hearing him, she was abruptly certain there really was a difference, as if in a benevolent way he were taking command. He had always seemed so mild, especially toward her. But she had had a husband then. . . .

No matter. She did not want to think about it. And she settled back to enjoy the ride. It felt good to be dressed up and going someplace. She felt loose, lightened, if only for this day, of all that weighed upon her. She was determined to separate this day both from before and the inevitable after.

Fred's house was large and white with the rambling aspect of a farmhouse. Denise had been a lover of gardens, and even under snow their shape was evident in long, lovely curves and billows. Indoors, the comfortable, spacious rooms remained as she had left them, the soft chintzes, now sun faded, the Christmas roses in the same white china bowl on top of the piano, and the piano with the lid down and probably, by this time, out of tune.

They had made a good home, a good life, together. Now these friendly rooms belonged to a man who, living alone, must scarcely use them; they had that look. Understandably, he wanted most to reestablish the life he had once lived here.

In the long dining room the table was set with Denise's blue-and-white Wedgwood; the silver glowed; there were more crimson roses bedded among sprays of holly. The dinner, the wines, and the service were all perfect. Fundamentally a simple man not given to displays, however tasteful, Fred had nevertheless made a marked display. It embarrassed Margaret to think that it had been done for her. Gil and Louise, though not among Fred's circle of friends nor of his generation, had been invited only for her. Even Nina had been asked; she had been busy in New York, and anyway, the storm would have prevented her from coming, but she, too, had been asked for Margaret's sake.

These thoughts silenced her, and she was careful not to meet Fred's eyes. He was discreet. His own thoughtful eyes told her often, without words, that he respected the uncertainty of her position and her concern for her children; for the present he would ask nothing of her.

Louise said, "You ought to think of marrying Fred when you're free. It would seem so natural."

"He hasn't asked me," Margaret would answer lightly.

"But you know he will. The children need a father, and you go so well together."

Why did people always want to marry you off? She was confused and did not want to feel any man's intrusion on her privacy.

Yet she could not help but glance up at herself in the mirror that faced her above the sideboard. Tilted slightly over Stephen's head, it showed her every motion, every angle: the scoop of vivid dark blue wool, below the white neck; the white smile, and each nervous glance as it met Stephen Larkin's and turned nervously away.

It was enough to listen, holding apart from all the others' conversation. I am like someone who has been starving, she thought, who must not be given too much food at once. And so she sat quietly, wearing a careful, cordial smile.

After the plum pudding and the pies the presents were given out next to the tree in the living room. Each of the young ones had a gift for Fred, paid for with their own earnings from the summer and Saturdays in the fall. Megan had worked at Danforth's in the sweater department, Julie had baby-sat, and Danny had caddied at Fred's club. Gil and Louise gave Margaret a beautifully bound album of old photos that Louise had saved, pictures of Margaret's grandparents taken on their honeymoon before the First World War, of her father, in Marine uniform, dozens of pictures to be cherished. Fred gave her a handsome leather carryall.

"To tote your books and papers to school in style," he said. "You'll also find it handy for travel."

She laughed. "It's beautiful right now, Fred. I'm not likely to be doing any traveling."

"You never know," he replied.

The young ones had been given a quiz game, which they began to play on the floor. Margaret, wanting to look at the album, sought a corner chair and lamp, while the rest watched *A Christmas Carol* on television.

Presently, Stephen left the television and went to her. "I have some information that came late yesterday, Margaret. If you want me to spare you another office visit, since I know how busy you are, I can give it to you now. Or, if it will spoil your day here, tell me. Be frank."

Oh, why couldn't the severance be swift and clean? Adam had left her. Why, then, didn't he move to Timbuktu so that she wouldn't ever have to hear his name? Only a week ago Louise had reported, "We saw them last night at that French restaurant where I took Megan that day. I said to Gil that it's a mighty expensive place for a cheap woman."

She put the album aside and asked Stephen to go ahead.

"Item one is that he's found another job. Didn't Julie and Danny tell you?"

"No. They never even knew he had lost the first one until I told them. I'm sure he was too proud to let them know himself."

Strange that she was still able to comprehend or pity his loss and his pride! And yet, what does he care about us or about me, who was his wife and mothered his children? she asked herself.

"Thank goodness for our sake that he's gotten another one," she said.

"Unfortunately, he's taken a slight cut in salary."

"A cut? At his age he should be getting a raise."

"There's more. The woman is pregnant."

Pregnant! A half-sibling from that woman for my lovely children. . . . From that woman.

"Another child," she cried, trying to curb her outrage. "He can't even do right by the ones he has. It's disgusting." Anger choked her, and she said fiercely now, "I want more money for my children. Megan has applied to Harvard. And her advisor says there's a good chance that she'll be accepted. She deserves to go, and I want her father to pay for it."

"You can't get blood from a stone," Stephen said gently.

"His lawyer claims he has mortgage expenses for that house, doesn't he? So let him sell the house. I had to sell mine."

"Unfortunately, it's not his to sell. It belongs to the woman, and she isn't even his wife."

"Then let him leave her and cut his expenses. Tell me, has he gone completely crazy, or is he just bone evil, or is he both?"

"I can't answer that," Stephen said, still gently.

A Christmas Carol having ended, Fred went over now to Margaret's corner, questioning, "You're looking anxious. Is something wrong?"

"Only the usual. It's a complicated business, getting a divorce."

Fred's reply was a pointed question, directed to Stephen. "How long do you think it will take?"

"That depends. A year, or even two."

"It's an outrage. Does the law think people live forever? Two years while life stops. Everything on hold."

Margaret stood up. Suddenly she was overwhelmed. She wanted to get home, lie down, and pull the blanket around her ears. And she had hoped so much to set this day aside, as if there had never been a catastrophe, as if hers still were an ordinary life.

She was conscious of Stephen, watching her. "It's been a wonderful day, an unexpected treat for me," he said quickly. "But perhaps we should start back. I'm wondering whether my car is permanently frozen in the parking lot."

The streets around the apartments had been plowed so that the going was smooth. Margaret's house was the first stop. Politely, as they alighted from the Jeep, Julie and Megan thanked Uncle Fred. And Danny said, "I wish we lived in your house, Uncle Fred. Did you tell Mom we could?"

Concealing her embarrassment, Margaret reproved him. "You *are* silly."

"No, I'm not. Uncle Fred told me we could if you wanted to. And we could get Rufus back if we lived there."

This was the first time in a long while that he had mentioned the dog. The boy's eyes were round with innocence and candor, with a sweetness almost babylike in spite of the starting down on his upper lip.

Always, always, he had been able, unknowingly, to pull at his mother's heart.

"Don't be stupid," Julie said sharply. "We can't live there and you're old enough to know it."

"Why not? Look at all the empty rooms he has. We could, only Mom won't."

"Louder," Megan said, "I'm sure the neighbors are fascinated. Keep it up."

The two men in the front seat were silent, facing forward. Suddenly Stephen got out, saying, "Don't go out of your way to drop me off, Fred. It's a short walk, and I like the cold air."

The car rolled away, the young ones went indoors, and Margaret, since he did not immediately move toward home, stood with Stephen.

"Danny doesn't understand," she explained. "He was just excited. The day was so exciting, with the presents and the snowstorm and Fred's lovely house. Then he comes back, and reality strikes again."

In the apartment the light went on. There was something forlorn about that small light, when all around lay the spread of white slopes and dark sky, a tingling stillness and enormity.

Stephen smiled. "I'm sure Fred didn't mind. Don't worry about it."

"I'm worried about my children and no one else, including myself."

"Yes," Stephen said, "I've noticed. Are you aware that you don't speak so much about Adam anymore?"

"I wasn't aware. But now that you tell me, I can see how that can be. I'm not mourning for him anymore, Stephen. I really don't care how many women he takes or what else happens to him. I only want his money for my children."

He looked down at her with an expression that she could not fathom, searching her, as he had done at Fred's dinner table.

"They will survive," he said, "because you are a survivor." He smiled again. "I have every confidence in you. Just don't make any final decisions until you're ready."

"Such as?"

"Such as anything. Well, Merry Christmas and good night."

Quite suddenly, he had brought her close to tears, which was strange, considering that she had just said she cared about nothing except her children. Probably, though, it was only because he reminded her of what it was to be young. Although he was her own age and was often grave, there was still a shining about him. She sensed a quality of hidden joy. And it came to her that the only person close to her who had that quality was Nina. Yes, a shining. And she watched him to the bottom of the hill as, lightly, with rapid grace, he moved across the snow.

TWENTY-SIX

As spring came in and the days grew warm enough to sit indoors, Margaret began the habit of taking her work to the park. Sometimes she stopped at the ball field to watch Danny play, but mostly she went straight to the lake, where drifting swans, indifferent and patrician, marked the still water with their wakes. At them and at the windblown trees one could gaze and gaze without thought.

On this particular day, however, she was full of thought. The college letters had arrived. Megan, unable to bear the tension of waiting for the mail, had taken the car and gone on errands, while Margaret, herself tense with expectation, had waited at the window for the mail truck.

"Thick envelopes mean acceptance, Mom. Thin ones are thumbs down. I don't mind if you open them," Megan had said.

If only the advisor and all her teachers had not encouraged the girl to apply to Harvard! If only they had not raised her hopes! In some ways Margaret had almost wished that Harvard would not take her; the disappointment then would not be even close to the heartbreak that would come from having to refuse their acceptance.

Ah, but what a pity! Megan had had the highest grade average of any student in the previous twelve years. She deserved this honor. And Margaret, examining her own heart, knew beyond any doubt that there was not within herself or her daughter the slightest trace of snobbery. It was only that Harvard was so highly selective. It was only that in applying there Megan had been challenging herself to do her best. And she had won.

She's smarter than I ever was, Margaret thought. Her mind is remarkable. She is a remarkable person. A trifle too rigid, she is what you might call a Puritan: stalwart, driven, and uncomplaining. She never asks for anything. You cannot move her when she knows or believes she's right. But she is so decent, honorable, and kind, so thoroughly good. She was never a humorous person, but she did used to laugh. And boys like her. They used to come around and the telephone used to ring. . . .

He did this to her. Her father and Randi, they did this to her. . . . Margaret's hands turned to fists on her lap.

She raised her eyes to the swans, circling, circling, in their dignity, their composure. The sun glittered on the lake. Such a beautiful world it was! And people ruined it.

Then she saw Stephen jogging down the path. When he saw her, he stopped.

"Five times around every Saturday and Sunday. I try to make up for all the hours I spend on a chair. Is Dan playing ball?"

"No, Fred took him to the football game."

"Fred has a fatherly way with Dan."

Whether that was a statement or a question was not quite clear, and so she answered simply, "Yes."

"I'm really fond of Dan, you know."

"Thank you. And as always, many thanks for his improvement in French. His teacher doesn't know what to make of it."

Stephen laughed. "By the way, you shouldn't have done that."

"Done what?" But she knew he meant the six volumes of Proust in French that she had sent him.

"The books. It's a marvelous gift, but you shouldn't have done it."

"People get paid for tutoring, and you wouldn't let me pay. You've spent hours with Dan that you could have used for something else."

He smiled. "I try not to do things that I don't enjoy. I enjoy Dan."

"You speak it like a native. Did you always speak French at home with your mother?"

As quickly as it had come, the smile disappeared. He shrugged. "That's a long story. Too long. Dan said Megan's waiting for college letters."

"They came just now. Four acceptances, including Harvard."

Stephen whistled. "Fantastic! Does she know?"

"Not yet. She'll be home soon, and I dread it. I'll have to tell her she won't be able to go." And Margaret looked into his face as if pleading. "Unless there's a chance that Adam—"

He shook his head. "No. He doesn't have to, and even if he wanted to, he isn't able to."

"Oh," she cried, "if we were together, we would manage it. We never lived extravagantly. We might have to borrow a little against his salary, or Megan might get some financial aid from the college, but we would manage."

"He has two families now. And double expenses. That's what divorce does."

She felt desperation rising in her chest. "I could dig into the money I got from selling the house. But I need the income. And I don't dare touch that money yet."

There were two more coming along. Julie was only two years behind Megan. She was bright, not like Megan, but doing well. And so was Dan.

Abruptly then, becoming conscious of Stephen's jogging suit, she apologized. "Go on. I'm keeping you from your exercise. This is no place to air my worries."

"Margaret, I don't mind," he said. "I wish I had a solution for you."

"No, go jog. I have to get back to see Megan, anyway."

Long after Dan and Julie were asleep, Margaret and Megan were still in the outer room.

"After all, most people don't go to Harvard or Oxford or any of those world-famous places. I myself went to the state university, and I haven't suffered any." Margaret could have added but did not, "And so did your father."

"Mom, I know that," Megan said patiently.

"You can go to Harvard and not fulfill yourself. I'm sure there are plenty who do not."

She was arguing not only, or even mainly, for her daughter's benefit; she was, and she knew she was, rationalizing for her own sake. If there had been any valid, any honorable, reason why the money was not available for Megan, she would have accepted it, just as most of the country's population had to accept things. But the reason was not honorable, the reason was Adam's infatuation.

"Mom, I understand, I really do. And I'm fine, I really am. But I'm tired now, and I want to go to sleep."

"Of course. It's late."

The worst would come on Monday back at school, with all the eager questions, congratulations, comparisons, and explanations. And, indeed, it happened so. Megan came home earlier than usual, briefly mentioned an upset stomach, and went to bed. In the morning her eyes were swollen, but she was cheerful and, as always, went to school on time.

Nina telephoned. "You were out when I called, and Julie gave me Megan's great news."

"What news?"

"About going to Harvard, naturally."

"Nina, she isn't going. She can't."

"Why, what do you mean?"

So came the same explanation that Margaret had had to give to every questioner in the teachers' room.

"I won't hear of it," Nina said. "It's a criminal shame to deprive that girl of what she earned. I'm going to lend her that money."

"Nina, you've no idea what it costs."

"Yes, I have. I've got some savings that will take care of one year at least, and we'll cross the rest of the bridges when we come to them."

This optimism, this confidence, and this generosity were so like Nina!

"Nina, you're a dear, but I wouldn't dream of it. You're a working woman, and all alone."

It took almost half an hour to win the argument with Nina.

From Adam came a letter to Megan with a five-hundred-dollar check enclosed. It was meant to be moving. Perhaps it was moving, thought Margaret, depending upon how you saw the whole situation.

I send this letter, he wrote, *because you will not talk to me, which I understand. When you are older, much older, perhaps you will understand. Maybe you will not, but I hope you will at least try. In the meantime, need I tell you how proud of you I am? If I could do more for you than this, God knows I would.*

"I'm going to tear it up," Megan said with flushed face and eyes filled suddenly with tears.

"What, the check?"

"The whole thing. The check too."

"Don't be foolish. You need clothes," Margaret told her, thinking that here were five hundred dollars that Randi wouldn't get.

The next day at school a message from Fred was delivered to Margaret. *Will you drive to my house this afternoon? I want to talk to you in private, and we can't do it at your place.*

Meeting Megan in the corridor, she told her casually about the message. "I might be late getting home. Fred wants to see me at his house. I have a hunch it's about you. What else could it be?"

"Mom, if it is about college money, I don't want any. I wouldn't feel right about it."

"I wouldn't either. But," Margaret said curiously, "you've always been so fond of him."

"If he were my real uncle, or even a stepfather—" Megan stopped.

"He's neither, honey, so don't worry about it."

She was stepping into the car, the old "jalopy" with the new transmission that was still going strong, when Megan's advisor, Mr. Malley, hailed her. "Is it true that Megan's not going to Harvard?"

An invisible sigh rose and fell as, for what might be the twentieth time, she had to answer that question. And she made the answer very brief.

"Money," she said.

With decent tact he asked no more but murmured only as he moved on, "Too bad. She's a true scholar."

"Why am I going to Fred's?" she asked herself as she drove away. "Unless I'm very much mistaken, it will only be more of the same."

It was unseasonably warm, and he had put up the awnings. Broadly striped in green and white, they overhung the porch, giving to the space, with its white wicker chairs and hanging baskets of ferns, an old-fashioned, friendly aspect that spoke of Sunday afternoons, leisure, and comfortable prosperity. He had put out a pitcher of iced tea, and they sat down.

"Dan told me about Megan," he began.

"Dan should be a town crier," she said.

"Well, maybe you need one. Why didn't you tell me yourself?"

"Fred, I'm not going to run to you with all my troubles."

"The only time you 'ran' to me was when your roof leaked. Have I complained?"

He looked injured. And, as often during this last year, Margaret had the feeling that he was chastising her as one reprimands a beloved child.

"What are you going to do about Megan?" he demanded.

Again there came that invisible sigh, rising and falling. "You know," she replied.

"You cannot do that to her," he said sternly. "You cannot."

"It won't be the end of her world," was all she could say.

"No, certainly not. Nevertheless, she has suffered enough. She has had a dreadful time, even worse, I think, than Julie has. Megan is an adult. She holds it all back."

It surprised Margaret that Fred had made so subtle an observation. One thought of him as being competent, righteous, and strong whenever right had to be enforced. But subtle, never.

"That's true," she admitted. "Still, she must face reality."

"She deserves to have something wonderful happen for a change, particularly since she has earned it for herself."

"Still, that has nothing to do with reality," Margaret said mournfully.

"My reality is this. Life has been good to me, in one respect at least. I have money. I want to use it for Megan, for what she needs."

"Fred, please don't. Don't make it hard for me."

"Then I'll leave you out of it. I'm going to give it directly to Megan. You won't have anything to do with it, and you can't stop me."

The words were gruff; nevertheless, when she looked into his eyes, she saw that his own words had moved him. His hands trembled on his glass, and he set it down. The little dog Jimmy leapt on his lap, and he stroked it.

"Megan will be in heaven when she hears this," she said. "But I don't think I can bear so much kindness."

He stood up. "Come. Let me show you the garden."

Glad to follow into the open afternoon, she went with him. Hundreds of daffodils had been scattered in a copse under the pines. And she stood there quite still with the words in her head: *A host of golden daffodils.* White, too, they were, airy and clean under the dark trees.

"It's a little paradise here, isn't it?" said Fred at her shoulder. "I don't think I'll ever ask for much more."

"Yes, it's perfect."

"Margaret, I know this isn't quite the time yet," he began, when suddenly a rabbit, fooled into boldness because they were not moving, scuttled through the grass near their feet and stopped to chew.

Margaret laughed. "It's not nice, I know, but one of the gym teachers chews like that and somebody nicknamed him 'Rabbit.' "

He did not answer. She had spoiled the moment for him, and she was sorry. But she was not prepared for anything decisive or profound.

"Fred," she said earnestly, "I need to say something. Since you are determined, I must be determined about one thing. I want to sign a note, an IOU. Somehow, someday, either I or Megan, or both of us, will repay you for your unheard-of generosity."

"If you insist," he replied in a flat, courteous tone.

Yes, she had hurt him. And contritely, she reached up to kiss his cheek, declaring, "You are the best man who ever lived."

He put his arms around her. "Oh, Margaret," he murmured.

She understood that he knew she was not ready yet for emotion. And as if to confirm his understanding, he said gently, "I'm not in a rush," and smiled and let her go.

The slight embrace had not displeased her, nor had it activated any feeling other than a very deep affection, the same affection she had always had for him. Or somewhat deeper, maybe?

On the homeward drive she worried, asking, *How shall I ever be able to repay?* And at the same time she seemed to feel a strange conviction that ultimately she would marry Fred, as people told her she ought to have done in the first place. Perhaps she should have. Perhaps, even though marriage was far from her mind, it was inevitable. He was intelligent and manly, clean and kind and good. Quite obviously, he wanted her. Besides, her children loved him. . . .

TWENTY-SEVEN

In the bedroom on Memorial Day, Adam sat staring out of the window at the radiant afternoon. On the bed Randi lay in a defeated sprawl, with arms and legs flung out. The pregnant belly, not much larger than a basketball, was round and tight.

When he made a move as if to rise from the chair, she objected, "No, stay here with me."

"Maybe you'll fall asleep if I leave you alone."

"I can't sleep. I'm miserable. Can't you see? I'm disgusted with everything."

"I'm sorry," he said. He had made this reply so many times that it came automatically.

"Anyway, you only want to be with your kids, as usual. You're thinking they should be outdoors on a day like this, not sitting inside watching television."

How well she knew him! If he believed in mind-reading, he would swear that she could read his mind. But he was too tired to argue. There had been too much arguing, so he sank back into the chair.

And he tried to understand why Randi was so irritable. Her ankles were swollen, and now, in her seventh month, she still had occasional bouts of morning sickness. She wanted him to wait on her, which he tried to do. A woman expected a certain amount of homage given to her pregnancy. But it was difficult for him to live with, probably because he had never experienced it before: Margaret's three pregnancies had been cheerful, even euphoric, for her, and so, quite naturally, for him too. However, people were not all the same, so he could hardly blame Randi for her condition.

Torn between exasperation and sympathy, he gave a sigh of fatigue. He looked at his watch. It was still too early to drive Julie and Dan back home; he wouldn't want them to feel as if they were being shoved out. This had already been a disappointing visit, for Randi had really been cross with them. Somehow, he must make up for it, maybe stop off for ice cream on the way back. No, that was foolish. They weren't babies to be compensated with an ice cream cone for poor treatment. . . .

It had been a terrible year so far. He could only hope that the second half of it would be better. Of course, he was lucky to have found a new job, even with a cut in salary. But the commute, a sixty-mile round trip, was exhausting in bad weather. He had suggested that they sell the house and move to something closer to his work, something, incidentally, less expensive. And she had gone absolutely wild.

"It's not as if you had always lived here and had some loving attachment to the place," he had argued.

And she had gone wilder still. "Oh, you have to live in your great-grandfather's house to feel love for it, is that it? Well, excuse me! Sorry I'm not an aristocrat like some people, but I love my home too."

So he had dropped the subject.

Money worries still gnawed at him, gnawed and clawed in his dreams and when he awoke at night. What if he should lose this job too? Every day the newspapers reported more downsizing, thousands of men in midlife losing the jobs that once seemed so secure, so permanent. Maybe, he thought, it would be prudent to make some friendly, social connections within the new firm. Maybe if he had done so before, had "cottoned up" to Jenks and Ramsey, or to Hudson, he would not have been among those outsiders who were tossed away.

Yet he realized now that it was too late for that sort of thing. These new people, like the ones at ADS, were conservative types, family people who would not look favorably on this household, this separated man—he had written "separated" on his job application—with his pregnant companion.

Then something else came creeping slowly into his thoughts as he sat there by the window. These new people were not like Randi's friends, all those natural, wholesome, unselfconscious folk with whom he had been so comfortable lately. These new people wouldn't care for Randi's casual way of displaying the top half of her breasts as she bent or leaned, nor would they care for her blatantly uninhibited remarks, her four-letter vocabulary.

Surprisingly enough, there had been some recent occasions when he had found himself wincing with discomfort because of the things that she said in company. Had she always done that and had he just not noticed? It was all confusing and dispiriting. He could hardly believe his own treacherous thoughts. He felt—he felt uprooted.

He looked at his watch again and stood up, whispering, "I hate to wake you, but I have to tell you I'm going to leave now to take them home."

"I'm not asleep. I'm just lying here thinking."

"About what?"

"About," she said, rising on her elbows, "how secretive you are. What's the matter? Were you afraid to tell me that you're sending your daughter to Harvard?"

He was dumbfounded. "I?" he said. "I'm sending her—where the hell did you get that idea? I'm not even aware that she is going to Harvard."

"Yeah. Sure. It's funny that your kids know. They told me while we were in the kitchen."

"It can't be. Unless she got some sort of scholarship. And still, that wouldn't be enough. Or unless Margaret borrowed the money somewhere. I can't imagine where. No, it can't be."

"You're not even a good liar. 'Borrowed it "somewhere." ' You're not even a good liar. The somewhere is named Adam Crane."

"You're out of your mind. I only wish I had it to give, let alone lend. Get real, Randi."

"I am real, and I don't believe you. You're a pushover for that family of yours. I didn't marry you, I married you and your three kids."

He could have reminded her that she wasn't married to anyone at present, but he had no heart for hurtful jibes, no will to push a confrontation to the edge. He was a swimmer startled into awareness that the water beneath him is fathoms deep.

"And her too," Randi resumed, "with her paws in your pockets. She's a bloodsucker, that's what. You think I don't remember that insurance policy you told me about?"

"When did I ever tell you about an insurance policy?"

"A couple of years ago. I remember everything, Adam. Everything."

When and why had that ever come up in conversation? He had no idea.

Then he replied, "You must remember that Margaret owns the policy, not I."

"But you pay for it."

"No, I don't. Not anymore. I should, but I haven't been able to afford it."

"I still don't believe you. Anyway, why should you, when you have no insurance for me and this?" She laid her hand upon her belly.

"I told you I intended to take out a policy as soon as I can. Right now I can't afford to."

"You could if you would put your past behind you. They're all fastened onto you like leeches. They're not helpless babies anymore. Are we ever going to get rid of them?"

Adam put his hand to his forehead, groaning. "I don't understand what's wrong, Randi. My nerves are frayed. You've got to stop it."

"They're not frayed because of me. *I'm* not a leech."

"No, but your mortgage is."

"You knew from the beginning that I had a mortgage."

"Yes, but I didn't know how big. And I certainly didn't know that you had a second mortgage on top of it."

"Yes, you knew. I told you."

"No, you didn't, Randi," he said quietly.

"Well, I did. But if I didn't, you've still no complaint. It hasn't been bad, has it, living in an air-conditioned house for a change and taking a swim after a day's work? Not bad."

"I've paid my share and a lot more," he said, still quietly, still keeping control. "Anyway, this is no time to talk about money. You have guests coming tonight and I have to take Julie and Danny home."

"You couldn't possibly stay here and help me, I suppose. You see how I am."

"Everything is ready. It's a buffet. There's nothing else to do. But if you're really sick, you can cancel it."

"I don't want to cancel it."

"Well, then, I'll take them home now, and when I get back I'll help you do whatever needs to be done."

"It's absolutely ridiculous that every single weekend or holiday you have this routine."

"When else can I see my children?" he asked with his hand already on the doorknob. "Besides, I almost never do see them on holidays."

"It's a thirty-mile trip there and back. Why can't they come less often and stay overnight for once and make it easier for us?"

He knew, and was certain Randi knew, that this was something Margaret would fight to the end to prevent.

"It's better this way," he said. "I feel more comfortable this way."

Her laugh was loud and shrill. "Oh, I can see right through you,

Adam. Do you think I don't know that you're squeamish about their seeing us sleeping together? God, I can't believe it! In 1994! Do you think they think this is going to be a virgin birth?"

"Will you pipe down, Randi?" he demanded through clenched teeth. "They can hear you."

"Maybe it's just as well that they do. Let them go back and tell their mother how I feel about her. That we—you and I—are not going to take any more. I'm protecting you, Adam. I'm angry on your behalf. Hard as you work! While they milk you! Threatening to take you to court. For what? So those big, demanding girls can live on the fat of the land? This mopey one here and the stuck-up Harvard lady who treats you like dirt. They should be going to secretarial school and then to work, the same as I did when I left high school. It was good enough for me."

"All right," Adam said, "all right, Randi, take it easy. I'll be back soon."

The two were sitting together on the sofa with the television turned off. It was plain to him that they had heard everything, and he felt sick.

"Come," he said, "it's time."

They rode for a way before anyone spoke. He was trying to think how to begin when Danny said, "We heard everything."

"I thought you did."

"She stinks," Danny said, "I hate her."

It was all so ugly, so degrading. In his misery Adam could only say, aware of the inadequacy of the excuse, "She was sick today. I'm sure she's sorry already. People say things they don't mean."

"She meant it, Dad. Being sick is no excuse. And I do hate her."

"Please try not to, Danny. I know it's hard, but try."

"Why did you do it, Daddy?" Julie asked. "Weren't you happy with Mom and us?"

He felt a shock of surprise, a realization that no one had put that direct question to him until now. And how was he to reply? How to say, yes, I was happy, or thought I was, until I found out that I had to have this woman, wasn't able to stay away from her, and your mother, once she knew, was the impediment?

A man could hardly tell that to his children.

"There are things between people that anyone who hasn't experienced them can't easily understand," he began, and then as this pompous evasion, which he knew to be useless, even stupid, was met with total silence, he suddenly gave way to emotion, crying, "It's been terrible for you. . . . It always is for the children, isn't it? That's what you read. But you don't quite accept it until you see it for yourself." And he turned toward Danny, who was in the front seat beside him. "If I've hurt you too much, will you at least understand that it was nothing I wanted to do—or could help?"

"She—Randi—wants to pretend we don't exist," Julie said. "Don't you see that? She's a horrible person. The way she talked about Mom . . . And you let her."

He struggled for a place between his children and Randi from which, equidistant from either side, he might pull them together again. "What happened today is nothing permanent. You've gotten along so well together until now, and you will again."

"No. It's been an act to please you," Julie said. Her tone was sad. "I didn't see that at the beginning, but I see it now."

Suddenly, with these words, he remembered that she was sixteen. He had for some reason been thinking of her all along as the fourteen-year-old, young for her age, that she was when he left home. And he saw that, as one might expect, she had changed a lot in those two years. Also, she was seeing a psychologist, who had no doubt helped her toward some adult insight.

The sadness that had been in her voice now seemed to permeate the car. He asked himself: What will this lovely daughter, for whom I am supposed to be the measure of manhood, of a future husband, remember of me? And my son, my son whose body as he sits here seems to be shrinking away from me? And my Megan . . .

They came to the development, the monotonous red brick apartments marching up the hill.

"It's pretty here," he said. "They've left the trees. That's nice."

"You live in a better place. You have a beautiful house," Danny objected, with unmistakable emphasis on *you*.

As if he had not heard—for what could his response have been?—Adam said only, "Well, here we are. The usual time next Sunday?"

"One of the guys is having a birthday party," Danny said.

"Well, how about Saturday, then?"

"I might have to go to the dentist," Julie said. "You'd better call up."

"No cavities in your good teeth, I hope?" he questioned, being cheerful, being natural, being, as he well knew, given the circumstances, an idiot.

"Not that I know of."

"Shall we go get some ice cream for your dessert tonight? We just passed a place only a stone's throw from here."

Danny declined. "Mom always keeps ice cream in the freezer," he added, as if to say, *which you ought to know.*

When they alighted from the car, Julie looked at Adam. Her eyes were wet. "Good-bye, Daddy," she said softly.

For a moment he watched the two walk to the door and go in. Neither of them looked around to wave. Then he turned his car and started back to the Grove, where a jolly party would just be getting under way.

"Well, how was it?" Megan asked.

Danny said, "It stank."

"Why, what happened, Julie?"

"I'll tell you later. I don't feel like talking about it now."

"Stink, stank, stunk," Danny said. "Where's Mom?"

"Went to dinner with Uncle Fred. She left a note. I drove to Betsy's on our old street. She had a crowd over, and I just got back."

"How's the old street?" asked Danny. "And what's for dinner?"

"Number one, the street looks the same, except for our house, which looks awful. Number two, Mom left chicken pot pies and she made rice pudding. Your favorite, Julie, without raisins."

"I'm not hungry. I think I'll take a walk."

"Where to?"

"I don't know. Just around."

"It's six o'clock," Megan protested.

"What's the difference? I need to walk."

At half past eight, when Fred's car stopped before the door, Danny and Megan were standing on the step looking up and down the street.

"I don't know what's become of Julie," Megan cried. "She went for a walk at six o'clock."

An instant ripple of cold alarm ran through Margaret. "Did she give you any idea where she was going?"

Megan said anxiously, "She only said she needed to walk."

"Needed to? Why! Did anything happen today?"

"We had a lousy time," Danny reported, "and I think it got to her. You know how Julie is."

Margaret looked at Fred. "It's getting dark," she said.

"Come." He took Margaret by the elbow. "Get in the car. We'll drive around and we'll find her. She might have gone to the mall. It's still open."

"Julie's not a mall person. She never goes unless she needs something."

"Well, maybe she needed something. Come on," he said heartily and added, "We'll keep phoning you in case she should come back before we find her."

In the car Margaret sat twisting her fingers in her lap. "There's nothing here," she said after a while, "but these empty suburban streets and that highway with God knows who out there scouting for young girls with long blond hair. Fred, I'm pretty frantic."

They had been driving and searching without clue or aim for the last hour. Fred reached over and patted her shoulder, saying only, and this time not heartily, "I know."

The party was swinging. It moved from the house to the flagstone terrace, which had been newly ringed by a circle of expensive, half-grown ilex and rhododendron shrubs. Large stone tubs overflowed with white petunias. A second bar had been set up on the redwood table, and a few people were already pleasantly drunk. Some danced to the music that came from the loudspeakers on the wall. Some had come equipped for swimming, and were fooling around in the pool.

Randi, watching this scene with great satisfaction, observed to Adam, "Some party, isn't it? Last fling before the baby comes. For the next year, at least, we'll be too busy."

Incredibly, to him, she had recovered from the afternoon's mood as if it had never existed. Wearing, along with shoulder-length rhine-stone earrings, a white baby dress, tier upon ruffled tier, even in her seventh month, she sparkled. In one way, he reflected, you could admire her spirit, while in another way you could say that she looked absurd.

"Well, can't you answer me? Can't you take that glum face off?"

"Okay," he agreed, wanting least of all to argue here before these people, not that it would have disturbed Randi; public "scenes" did not faze her. "I'm not glum, only tired. I'm going to get something to eat."

Instead he went to the telephone in the bedroom. For a few minutes he sat on the bed before lifting his hand to make the call. Over and over the same thought kept running as if on a track: If I could only explain! Yet it wouldn't be seemly for a father to talk about his passion, his infatuation, his love, or whatever it was. For what, exactly, was it? And even if it were seemly, he wouldn't know how to describe it.

Yet he had to speak to Julie. It seemed to him that he would never forget her face when she said good-bye today. For him it had been like looking at the end of innocence. He—they—had hurt her so! And hurt

Danny, too, although in a different way, according to the person that he was. And Randi had known they would overhear. She had said so.

Danny answered the call. "I need to talk to you, Danny," he said, "about today. And to Julie too. I don't want you to think—"

"She isn't here. We don't know where she is. They've gone to look for her."

"Not there? What happened?"

"I don't know. She went out at six o'clock. I think she felt very bad. And I think it's your fault. Yours and Randi's."

The phone clicked. With the dead phone in his hands he went blank. Then he looked at the time. It was half past nine, and she had been gone since six. Far out on the terrace there came loud whoops of laughter; somebody must have told a joke. But what might have happened to his Julie?

Randi was standing with a group when he came tearing outside, gasping, "I have to leave, I have to go back. Julie's lost. Something's happened."

She whirled upon him. "Leave? In the middle of your party with all these people here?"

"I have to. They can't find her."

"Who is Julie?" someone asked.

"My daughter. You will excuse me. I have to go."

Randi's furious eyes reminded him that most of these people did not know that he had a family. She had wanted him to have no past, no other life but the one he had with her. Well, it was done, he couldn't help it.

And repeating, "Please excuse me," he fled.

There were two cars at the curb when he arrived at the apartment, Fred's and Margaret's. He leapt out, ran to the door, and, having rung the bell, came face to face with Fred.

"I came—I heard—Dan told me Julie—"

"I know. Julie is here. She's quite all right. A friend found her and brought her home."

"Is she—"

"She's fine." Fred spoke not unkindly, but surely without welcome. "She went for a walk and foolishly stayed out too long. There's nothing wrong with her. She made a mistake, that's all."

Behind Fred were lights and voices, a sense of people in a small space, a sense of warmth. For a second only, Adam had a glimpse of Margaret's head; it was the first time in two years that he had seen her.

"May I, I should like to say something to Julie, only a minute—"

"Not here, not now, Adam. This is Margaret's house."

Fred's tone, still not unkind, reproved him as if to say: You should know better, should have some conception of what is fitting and what is not.

He understood. Julie was neither hurt nor ill, so there could be no reason for his intrusion into "Margaret's house." And still he stood there, a supplicant, a beggar, unable to take no for an answer.

"If there is anything I can do—" he began.

"Nothing. We're taking care of things here." Fred moved slightly, the bulk of his shoulders barring the entrance should Adam have tried to go in. "You really needn't have come. But thank you," he added in his gentlemanly way.

The door closed.

"Luckily for you," Margaret said, "it was Mr. Larkin who was jogging around the lake. It might have been someone very different."

"I know," Julie said humbly. "It was stupid of me."

"As it was, I think I scared you, jogging up out of the dark," said Stephen.

"What were you planning to do, what would you have done if he hadn't seen you there?"

"I was coming home."

"We were beside ourselves. What ever possessed you?"

Now that she's safe, Margaret thought, I can afford to be angry—although not too angry. It's plain that she has gone through some sort of an epiphany.

Julie opened her lips to reply and closed them again. Raising her head and looking into space beyond the circle in which they all sat, she reflected. Then she spoke.

"Well, I've told you, and Danny's told you, what happened today there."

Danny interrupted. "She said rotten things about you. You should hear—"

"I don't want to hear, Dan."

"She said you're a blood—"

"Dan. I said I don't want to hear it."

He subsided. "Okay, but I'll tell you one thing. She's tough, but Nina could take care of her."

On Fred's face there appeared a touch of humor and muffled laughter, to which Margaret had to respond. How well they all knew Nina!

"I don't ever want to go there again," Julie cried. "I'll meet Dad some other place, but never with her. I feel so sorry for him! I felt sorry for him just now when he came to the door. And I think he's sorry for himself too."

Softly, Margaret asked how she could know that.

"I can't know it, of course, but I feel it. All the way home in his car, I kept thinking: Poor Mom. Poor Dad. I understand how terrible this has been for you, Mom. Megan and I, but especially Megan because she grew up faster than I did, have worried about you so much. But now I think you're much better, while Dad is beginning to be miserable."

Margaret caught the two men looking at each other. They were moved. The simple sincerity of this naive, or perhaps no longer so naive, young Julie had moved them.

"You don't have to worry," she continued, "that I will ever do anything eccentric, Mom. I'm not crazy or even especially neurotic anymore, if I ever was. Going to Audrey has taught me a lot. I wasn't going to run away or do anything like that."

"None of us ever thought so for a moment," Margaret said. "You were very disturbed, and you wanted to be alone. You needed to think."

"That's right. I did need to think. I started back in the direction of our old house to look at it again. I didn't realize how long it would take to walk there, so I turned around when I was halfway and came back through the park. Then I saw that all the swans weren't gone to their nests. There were two still floating, so I sat down to watch them, the way you do, Mom. They were so peaceful. And while I sat there, I couldn't help thinking how, if he were here, Dad would get a book and find out everything about swans. The way he always did, you know."

"Yes, I know."

"I guess as long as I live I'll remember things like that about him. And I suppose I'll always remember, too, the morning he left us, and I'll never understand how he could have done it."

Suddenly, Stephen spoke. "No, you never will understand, so it's best to give up trying. Put as much behind you as you can. You'll never be able to put all of it behind you, but just try to do your best. Of course, I'm speaking to you, too, Megan and Dan."

The room was very quiet. Now everyone watched Stephen. When he spoke again, he looked at no one. His eyes were downcast, and he seemed to be reciting the contents of a dream.

"My father was in the contingent that invaded France on D day in 1944. He fought through Normandy. And while he was there, he met a girl, a beautiful girl, my mother, and he married her. She had a good home with parents who cherished her. Understandably, they didn't want to lose their daughter to America, so they fought against the marriage. But she was determined and insisted against all their arguments that she would be happy.

"Well, she and he seemed to be happy as far as I, up to the age of twelve, was able to judge. At least, she always told me afterward that she had been. Then one day he informed her that he had fallen in love with a girl who worked in his office. I don't have to relate the details; the plots are all alike. He left. There wasn't enough money for two families. There seldom is. There were four children. I was the youngest. We all worked. Before I was old enough to get working papers, I shoveled snow for the neighbors, I ran errands for old people after school, I even did some baby-sitting. It didn't hurt me. More likely it did me some good. What did hurt me was the knowledge of my mother's pain. Thrown away in a foreign country after eighteen years and four children! She never informed her parents. She was too proud. Till the day she died, they thought she was having a wonderful life in America." Abruptly, Stephen turned to Margaret. "So you see, I do know something about these things," he said.

"Gee, you never told me all this stuff," Danny said.

"No. I never told anybody until just now."

"I guess that's because it makes you feel too sick to talk about it."

"Danny," said Margaret.

"No, Margaret, let him be."

"That's why you know so much French," Danny said.

Stephen smiled toward him. "That's right. And that's why you're getting A's. Funny, isn't it?"

"Yeah," Danny said. "But not really funny."

Now Fred asked Stephen how he had made his way into the law.

"My father had a relative, a responsible, religious man who was shocked at the whole affair. He lent me some money for law school, not all of it because I earned some myself. But he's the reason I'm here." Then, with a brief, cautionary gesture, Stephen raised his hand to address the three youngest, who were sitting in a row.

"Why have I told you all this? Because I wanted to show you that no bad thing, barring an incurable disease, is forever. I know it's a cliché to compare life to a river, but, believe me, it really is a river. You have to dive in and swim. Now Megan's about to swim to Harvard. She's the first, and the rest of you will dive in too."

With this tale, so clearly wrung out of painful memory, Stephen had miraculously altered the spirit of the room. Everyone sat up

straighter. Megan turned on another lamp. Margaret brought out a
bowl of fruit and a cake. And they all sat down around the table to this
little feast. It was almost midnight before they arose and the two men
left.

"Well, it was quite a night," Fred remarked.

"All's well that ends well. That's Shakespeare," Danny said impor-
tantly, so that the door closed on the men's laughter.

"What would we do without these good friends?" Margaret murmured to herself as they cleared the table. When Megan asked what she
had just said, she repeated it.

Danny scoffed. "They're not 'friends.' They've got a thing for you."

"For a bright boy," said Margaret, "your brother can say the
dumbest things."

"Not always." The two girls spoke together. "Not this time, Mom."

TWENTY-EIGHT

Adam drove in just as Randi, standing in the doorway, was waving the last carful of guests good-bye. As soon as it disappeared around the bend, her enthusiastic hostess's smile also disappeared, and he saw by her very posture that she was furious.

"Well," she said, "you surely did your best to ruin the evening, didn't you? I was never so embarrassed, with you running out like that."

He was overwrought, so much so that he scarcely had energy enough for ordinary speech, let alone the altercation that was coming. His reply was very quiet.

"I was frightened, Randi. I had to find out about Julie."

"I know. If it isn't your Julie, it's your Danny. Or your Megan, Miss Intellectual. Well, don't just stand there! Come into the house and sit down or go to bed. You look like something the cat dragged in."

He had never felt the need for liquor; a drink was what you took to be hospitable or sociable. It was a social custom. But at the moment he had a need for it. Randi, spread out on the sofa, observed him as he walked to the cabinet and poured brandy.

"So what was the big emergency?" she inquired.

"They thought—Danny told me on the phone—that something had happened to Julie. They couldn't find her. But she had only gone out for a long walk."

"So she's all right."

"Yes, thank God."

"So for a trick like that you ruined my party."

He wished she would stop beginning every sentence with *so*. Had she always done it? And it seemed to him again that he had lately been too irritated by little things like that, things he had never remarked before.

"It wasn't a trick, and your party wasn't ruined. People understand."

"And I understand a lot more than you think I do. It was a trick to bring you back. That woman will never let go of you, Adam. Even after the divorce comes through, if it ever does, she'll keep you tied because of those children."

"You knew I had children, Randi."

"I didn't know you were tied to them hand and foot. She ought to manage them herself like a grown-up woman, but she doesn't want to, and that's the whole story."

The lamplight glittered on the glass in Adam's hand and the golden liquid swayed. Ancient magicians might read portents of glory in its depths, but he was seeing only time, flowing, flowing, through the liquid and the light. Days that never would return, days when his children had been growing older and he not there to see.

Randi whined, "She only wants to get you back. That's what this was all about. It's all one thing. Margaret and money, they're the same. And now that you've had a salary cut, it's going to be worse. Frankly, I don't know how we're possibly going to manage on what's left after she gets hers."

"People manage on less," he said.

"Well, I sure wasn't planning on it at this stage in my life. I thought you had a big job and we were all set."

"I hate it when you use that expression 'big job.' Besides, I never told you anything of the kind."

"You most certainly did."

"Randi, I did not."

Anger began to fill him with strength, or perhaps it was the brandy, which he had drunk too fast, that was pouring through his veins.

"And what if I had?" he demanded. "What was this all for? Was it for money? I thought," he said, aware of his own sneer, "I really thought it was about love."

"Try living on love without money."

Years ago, he thought, she left me for a swimming pool surrounded by palm trees. . . .

"What if I should lose this job, too? Would you be through with me?"

"Darling, of course not. We would simply move out of the state, and you'd surely find another job somewhere."

"When I suggested moving nearer to Elmsford, you said you'd never give up this house."

"I've thought it over, and I've decided it's worth doing. We'd be rid of the noose around your neck. She'd get sick of hiring expensive lawyers to track you down in another state. She'd give up, and high time too. In fact, it might not be a bad idea to do it right now."

"It's a very bad idea because I'm not leaving my children," he said.

"We always get back to that, don't we? God, if I'd known, if I'd known . . ."

The brandy was boiling in his gut. I'm not drunk, he thought, but my heart is pounding, my head is pounding, and this has been one hellish day from the time we got up.

Sprawled as Randi was, one shoulder ruffle had been pulled down to expose her breast. For some reason the sight offended him, and he said irritably, "Fix your dress."

"What's the matter? All of a sudden you don't like to look at me? Here." And laughing, she pulled the other side down. "I don't know why I'm laughing. I'm disgusted with everything. Seriously, we need to get away from here, Adam."

"I told you," he said, almost shouting now, "I am not going to leave my children!"

"You've already left them. What do you get out of them except bills?"

He did not reply because it was true. He had left them.

"I'm with you a hundred percent. I'm still your father," he had told them. But a weekly lunch together—was that being a father? Megan knew otherwise. . . .

"You're afraid. You're a weakling, Adam, that's your trouble. You should have married me at the start, but you were afraid of your mother and of what people would say. Look how long it took before you got up courage enough to tell Margaret you wanted a divorce."

The taunt stung: weakling! To be thrown at him who had so cherished her! Weakling, indeed. And at the same time, with some irony, he was aware that this was one insult that the male ego would not endure. Call him an adulterer and betrayer, and he would have to accept it, but never this.

"Look at yourself!" he cried, enraged. "Who are you to criticize me?" Bare breasted as she was in her crumpled dress and with tousled hair, she repelled him. Plainly, even though she was pregnant, she had had much to drink. "You're disgusting, Randi. Go in and lie down. Cool off."

"And just who do you think you are? Yes, you think you're better than everybody else. You and your high-toned music and your fancy talk. You with your prissy Harvard kids. If I'd known what I was getting into, and how different it would be, I would never have come to Elmsford."

He was astonished. "You mean you came here purposely to find me?"

"Don't look so surprised. You ought to be flattered. Yes," she said, thick tongued, now, "I came to find you. First I went to New York, but the place is crawling with women looking for a man, so when I saw I wasn't getting anywhere, I went back to California. I could always get somebody there, but the good ones only want to sleep with you, and the ones who'll marry you are all old guys on their last legs."

He was hearing every word she spoke, and yet through it all there was an undercurrent in his consciousness: For her, I traded in my children.

"Then, gradually I thought about our running into each other that day in New York, and I remembered how crazy you once were about me, so I decided I would make it happen again. You were still young, good looking, and doing well. At least, I thought you were."

Too appalled to speak, Adam stood leaning against the wall for support, just staring at her. Then, as the full import of her words struck him, he murmured, "You came on purpose to destroy a family."

"Adam, please, don't be holy. That was her lookout. When I saw her in the hotel that night, I knew she didn't have any street smarts, not enough sense to come in out of the rain. You deserved better."

"You wrecked a family," he repeated in a daze.

"I didn't have to try very hard. You were a pushover. You almost tore my clothes off that afternoon when your gang was in Canada. You couldn't wait."

It was true. *But the woman tempted me.* The ancient excuse went ringing through his head.

She lay back on the sofa, supine, with the silly dress bunched around her middle. Her spread position was meant to be enticing, but he could not look at her. She had ruined him, and he had allowed himself to be ruined. And why had he endured these miserable months since the day when he lost his job? Maybe she was right about his weakness.

In any case he was trapped. And feeling a frantic claustrophobia, he opened the outside door.

A soft rain, sweet summer rain, was falling. He stood there listening to its drip upon the leaves. He thought of the toil and trouble of mistakes that could never be undone. He thought of the passions that blaze and die without any explanation. You look for reason in yourself and find none. You go along with blinders on, until one day they fall off and you realize how many things there are that you were not seeing.

All right, he hadn't had before, whatever the fault or cause, the fiery sex he had had with Randi. Fire was simply one of those things that sometimes blazed, or they didn't. So now he had had it, and now it was gone. As it had come, so it had left.

"Come here," Randi said. She sat up, straightened her dress, and beckoned to him. "Come here, I said."

He looked back outdoors. The moon was in the third quarter, far from the hovering rain cloud. The air was cool. There on the hilltop, in all that glimmer of moonlight and rain, he had a sense of space without end. And he imagined, as he stood there, some sort of flying seat, a kind of bicycle with wings, on which he might soar, just leave now without baggage and go anywhere, over continents and oceans, clouds, moors, anywhere under the calm stars, leaving every weight, sorrow, guilt, and memory behind him.

"What in blazes are you doing there with the door open in the middle of the night? It's cold."

"I was thinking of getting away."

"You were?" she responded, misunderstanding. "Will we really go?"

"I don't mean what you mean," he said.

"Ah, don't look at me like that! So we've had our spat and it's over. Come on," she coaxed, opening her arms. "Come on, I'll make it nice for you."

"No," he said. "I don't want it."

Then suddenly the truth of what she was beholding on his face came clear, and she was frightened. "You don't really want to get away from me. You're only angry because you think I tricked you. Well, suppose I did. I wouldn't have done it if I didn't love you, Adam. Doesn't that make sense?"

"Nothing makes sense to me anymore."

"Don't look so grim," she cried. "I had a few drinks—and I haven't had any since I've known I was pregnant. They got to me, that's all. You take everything too seriously. I always tell you that."

"It's when people have a few too many that the truth comes out."

She got up and tried to put her arms around him.

"No, Randi," he told her, disengaging himself. "No, Randi." And he pushed her, not roughly, but unmistakably, away.

"You son of a bitch," she said. "You make me sick."

They stood there staring into each other's eyes.

"You hate me," she said. "I see it in your eyes."

"You're wrong. What you see isn't hatred. It's contempt, and it's as much for myself as it is for you."

"Contempt!" she cried. "I think you're crazy. Listen. It's two o'clock. We've talked enough. Come to bed."

"I'm not going to bed with you, Randi. Not ever."

She ran to him, flailing him with her fists and shrieking. "Bastard! Crazy bastard! Drop dead."

Trying to calm her, Adam led her toward the bedroom and said, "Randi, we're both exhausted. Lie down and rest. We'll talk later, in the morning. Go rest."

For an answer she slammed the door and turned the key in the lock.

She was still sleeping when he left for the office not long after dawn. He had a long day's work ahead and he had hardly slept. Even so, a day at the office would be less wearing than yet another in the series of his troubled days at home with Randi. By nightfall, he hoped, she would have calmed herself enough for them to talk reasonably. He had no idea at the moment what he wanted to say to her. She had in his mind become a horror, and he knew only that he had to be free of her. A future with her was unthinkable. And still he wanted in no way to hurt her. Perhaps by nightfall his thoughts would clarify themselves.

At a diner where he stopped for coffee and a bun, he lingered in a kind of dreamy state, observing people. There were truckers, a pair of motorcycle cops, and some nurses on their way to the morning shift at the hospital. He wondered, as people do when they are beset, whether any of them was as beset as he was. A couple came and sat at a booth with their two small boys, one of them a clown like Danny, talkative and bright eyed. Once the young father reached across the table and squeezed the wife's arm.

Adam asked for a second cup of coffee and sat holding it between his hands, staring at the wall. After a while he went out and got into the car. At the next intersection came the turnoff so familiar to him, the way to the old street. On impulse he made the turn and drove slowly past the house. Already neglect had overcome it; two shutters were loose. A diagonal glimpse of the vegetable garden showed a scrubby patch of weeds. Too lazy to care for it, he thought, and sped the car away. How it must hurt Margaret to see her cherished family home falling into decay!

He drove on through downtown, past Danforth's, where he had bought Danny's first grown-up suit with a white shirt and regimental tie, past Magnum ADS, and on toward the bluff along the river where rose the gray roof of the high school. A thousand years ago, beneath that roof, he had fallen in love with a red-haired, gray-eyed girl.

The teachers were filling their segregated parking lot. Margaret had always tried to find a certain spot near the side door and now, for no reason he could explain even to himself, he drove in toward it. Really, he did not think he wanted to see her or be seen. Yet he cruised slowly in a wide circle and found the car with Margaret just getting out of it.

When she saw him, she looked fearfully startled, and stopped. They were only a few feet apart, so close that he was able to see the scattered, pinhead freckles on her forearms and to note that her face and neck were still purely unmarred by any. Her hair was damp; she must have showered late and in a hurry.

"Hello," he said. "You're wearing your favorite color."

She looked down at the periwinkle blouse as if she had forgotten what she was wearing, or as if she had not understood.

Around her neck there hung a thin gold chain with three hearts dangling from it.

"That's pretty," he said, pointing to it. "Is it from Fred?"

"Does it matter?" she replied.

Her arms clasped books to her chest, thus revealing her hands, and he saw that she had taken off her wedding ring. Well, naturally she had.

"Why have you come?" she asked, not unkindly.

"I don't know. I guess I just wanted to see you."

For a long moment she looked at him, and then gently, very gently, replied, "Well, now that you have, I have to go. I'm late this morning."

He nodded. "Take care of yourself," he said.

But she had not heard him. He watched her rapid steps up to and through the door. Then he swerved into the exit and drove away, eastward, toward the sun.

We were married twenty-one years ago this month, he thought.

There before him lay the river with the arch of the bridge making its leap across to the low bluffs on the other side. There it rested on its huge cement legs, and they on their concrete elephants' feet. The tires whistled on the pavement as the car accelerated down the hill.

Twenty-one years, they whistled and sang. Twenty-one years.

It was all green, a dazzle of gold and green, as spring turned into summer. Bands of shade like rippling water, cooled and dark, crossed the road beneath the trees. All the beauty, all the peace! he thought while the blood went thundering through his head.

Twenty-one years!

The car sped faster and faster down the hill, flying over the road, under the sky, aimed toward the huge gray elephant feet.

Let it end, he thought, for God's sake, let it end. And he pressed with all his strength upon the pedal.

Crushed metal, crumpled like a flimsy can, lay glistening in the sunlight until the tow truck had collected the last torn pieces and carted them away. The crowd that had waited through it all began to disperse.

"Ambulance," remarked one. "What for? There was hardly enough left to—"

"They take them to the morgue, I guess," another said.

"The speedometer stopped at ninety-five miles an hour."

"Was he drunk?"

"What, at eight-thirty in the morning? No, he just wanted to die."

"God help him," said a truck driver, a man with a beer belly and a friendly face. "God help the poor bastard."

TWENTY-NINE

I t seemed to Margaret that everyone she had ever known was at the funeral. Neighbors from the old street, the old couple from the apartment across the new street, half the faculty at school, Tony the barber who had given Danny his first haircut, all were there. Even Jenks, the erstwhile enemy, came in and grasped Margaret by both hands.

"You realize that they've come because of you, don't you?" asked Nina.

She did not answer. Inevitably, while seeming not to, she was focusing attention on the other side of the aisle, sliding her eyes without turning her head too far. Among people strange to Margaret sat Randi Bunting, visibly pregnant and wearing heavy black. The women had merely passed each other, glanced, and looked away.

A tremendous floral spray from Randi lay on the coffin, while the children's baskets stood almost hidden among other people's tributes. Well, no matter, Margaret thought, it is only another battle, the battle of the flowers. And there he lay, the center of it all. For obvious reasons the coffin was closed, yet even if he had lain in it undamaged, with his hands folded and his thick hair combed, she knew she could not have borne to look. Then she thought of his hair and his habit, when he was reading or concentrating, of twisting a small strand that fell over his forehead.

Randi began to make loud noises, cries and sobs, attracting all the more attention for being concealed behind a large black-bordered handkerchief. People were staring. What are they really thinking of all this? Margaret wondered. No doubt there were some who had come here mainly out of curiosity, but who could blame them? It was a curious situation.

And she, too, stared at the face that emerged from behind the handkerchief, at eyes blurred and smudged with black mascara, at dimples, then at the prominent breasts, all the weapons of allure that had dazzled a good man, a weak, foolish man who had been happy; yes, he had been so in spite of his weaknesses, which we all have in one way or another. God knew what it was in his childhood or in his genes that had made him unsure of his own worth, hence envious, and hence often disliked. But he was a good man nevertheless, until you came, Mrs. Randi, and he lost his sense of decency and moral worth. We were content until you came, Mrs. Randi, knowing well what you were doing and able to do it because he was susceptible. If you have any conscience, Mrs. Randi, look at that coffin, look at your work.

From somewhere, piped into the funeral parlor, came lugubrious music intended to be sacred. An equally lugubrious man appeared, to intone and spoil the majestic poetry of the psalms.

Megan wept. Perhaps she had all along known a deeper disillusionment than either of the other two had, thought Margaret. For her, who was more mature than they, it would have been possible to feel at the very start a stronger bitterness and outrage.

"You're not crying, Mom?" Megan whispered.

"Darling, I'm crying inside."

Crying . . . For the day we bought my wedding ring, the times we went to the opera in New York, for your compassion when I had the miscarriage, for the days we pushed the strollers down our street.

You wretched woman, you thief. You came out of nowhere and you destroyed a family. But you would be surprised to know that his thoughts on that last morning were not at all of you, no, not at all of you.

And she thought, as the man droned on, I wonder what he would have said to me there in the parking lot if I had stayed to listen? Had he perhaps come to tell me that he wanted to die? Or had he been asking me to take him back? I doubt it, what with that other child on the way. But even if he had, I would have told him it is far, far too late.

How strange it is to remember, after you have stopped caring, how terribly you can care when you are young. It is everything to you, everything, more than life. I think of that day—it is so long since I thought of it—when Isabella came to fit my wedding dress, and I was afraid I might be losing Adam. I'm only thankful that she's not here to see this now.

Everyone stood as they moved to take the coffin out. Behind

walked Randi. And this time Margaret looked fully, without avoidance, into her face. For you, she said to herself, I feel nothing but contempt. For the poor life growing in you, though, I feel a pity that you probably wouldn't even understand. Poor, unknowing little creature, ready soon to be born, another American child who, for whatever the reason, will have no father. It seems to be the story of our country in this crazy time.

Out of dimness they emerged into noon glare, where stood the hearse like an ominous black beetle about to crawl. At sight of it tears rose to clog Margaret's throat and stand burning in her eyes.

"Come," Nina said gently, pulling at her arm.

"No, wait."

They were not going to the cemetery. Friends and cousins, Nina, Fred, and Stephen, every one were all agreed that in the circumstances it would be unwise. For Randi had bought a grave somewhere and had taken charge.

So they waited, Margaret and her children, with an awful solemnity upon them, until the coffin was placed and the small cortege moved away. Margaret's head was swimming. And raising her hand in the semblance of a little wave, she whispered, "Good-bye, Adam."

THIRTY

A few months later, in Stephen Larkin's office, the desk was clear of the paper that usually awaited Margaret's visits, the questionnaires and replies, the proposals and denials, the whole paraphernalia of divorce. Now all that was finished, and the only paper that lay there was the receipt for Adam Crane's insurance.

"I've been thinking about that baby," Margaret said. "Do you think I should—"

"No," said Stephen, so decidedly that she was surprised. "The money belongs to your children. Her behavior was irresponsible, and there's no reason why you should take responsibility for it."

"It's a nice sum, but a dreadful way to receive it."

"Life insurance money is never what you might call happy money."

"Well, it does mean that I can pay off my debts. The rest will be safely put away."

"I remember that at one time you wanted to go to medical school."

"Ah, yes," she said ruefully, "that was a long, long time ago."

"Not so long. You're still a young woman."

"Stephen, I'm forty-one."

He smiled. "Where've you been? Your calendar is out of date. That's young these days."

It was odd that this remark should occur on the first day when, after so long, she actually did feel rested, clearheaded, and younger. She was aware, too, that she looked it. Her dress was black linen, a gift from Nina along with a pair of "typically Nina" emerald-colored sandals. She had worn it for the first time today.

"So dressed up to go to a lawyer's office?" Julie remarked, to which Margaret, not making much sense, had answered vaguely, "It's in town."

What actually had she been thinking of when she pinned the black velvet bow at the back of her head? Incredibly, she had been regretting the fact that this was to be her last visit to this office. Poignantly, she remembered her first one two years ago when, mortally wounded and unable to control herself, she had sat there weeping with her head in her hands. She had been such a mess. And he had been so patient. She wondered whether he ever thought about that or, for that matter, ever thought much about her at all. At Fred's Christmas party there had been that subtle appraisal from across the table. And then, too, whenever they met in the park or at the baseball diamond . . .

But a man's glance could, and usually did, mean nothing more than a moment's worth of approval. Anyway, what difference did it make? She was still in recovery, in limbo, an almost-divorcée, and for the last three months a widow.

Stephen got up and crossed the room. "I was in a bookstore the other day," he said, handing Margaret a heavy package, "and I saw something you might like."

A large illustrated volume contained a history of medicine. And flipping through the pages, from Nefertiti holding a mandrake root, to the Black Death and then the first X-ray photographs, Margaret was instantly delighted.

"It's gorgeous! What a gorgeous book!"

"I thought at first that it might be only another coffee-table gift, but when I looked at the text I was impressed."

"How nice of you!" she exclaimed. "I really, really love it."

Stephen was pleased. "I can tell that you do. I hope it will inspire you. If you really love medicine, Margaret, you should go for it," he said, adding quickly, "Unless you have other plans?"

"My children," she replied at once. "They're doing better now, much better, as you know. But their father's death was terrible, on top of everything else, and the wounds are far from healed."

"They never will be, entirely. They'll stop aching, though. That much I know for sure."

"I still think of what you told us that night about your mother. I knew then why you had been able to read my mind when I first came to you. Oh, I needed help so badly! I was drowning. Maybe I would have drowned if so many wonderful people hadn't helped me, teachers and friends, my cousins and Fred. And you, Stephen. I'll never forget what I owe to people."

There was a pause, as though she were about to say more, or as though he were, or as if each were waiting for the other. But the seconds passed. And so she stood up, gave him her hand, and said, "It's an unusual ending to the case, isn't it? All those papers, all those documents you drew up, just to be thrown away. And now we've come to the end."

"We're not going to say good-bye, you know. We're still neighbors."

They shook hands. Faintly disturbed, she went outside and got into the car. Their relationship puzzled her. It had progressed beyond the lawyer-client one to a kind of pleasant friendship, half professional and half not. In a queer way she was embarrassed by it; she felt self-conscious in his presence, and yet she looked forward to his presence. Confused by her own thoughts, she drove past the bank where she was to deposit the insurance check and had to drive around the block again.

Some days later Margaret went to see Fred. It was Saturday, and she had told him to expect her. In her purse was her repayment of his loan, and the pleasure of being free of debt was something she did not want to postpone.

"I would like to insist that you take this check back," he told her. "You know I want to make a gift to Megan. After all, I knew her before she was born."

"I understand. But we've been through all that before, haven't we?"

"You're as stubborn as a mule." He laughed. "That's why I'm not even trying."

They sat down under the trees, which now, in late August, were still in lush leafage. The air thrummed with the drowsy, continuous chirp of cicadas. Yet the earth had begun its tilt away from the sun, and there was in the angle of light a presage of fall.

This awareness of season, of time, of some imminent change—but what change?—increased the uneasiness that she had lately, and for an unknown reason, been feeling.

Fred studied her. "You're looking like your old self again, dressing up, fancy green shoes—that's great. No more divorce papers, all that behind you."

"Yes, everything's over. No more lawyers."

Fred was still studying her. She expected him to say something, but he did not. And feeling that queer awkwardness, that disturbance almost ominous, that sense of some unknown, pending change, she continued, "Stephen handled the case very well, as far as it went. You made a good choice for me."

"I hoped so."

Then suddenly she realized that Fred was nervous. He stood up, set Jimmy, who had been on the bench beside him, onto the ground, and walked over to pull a weed out of the rosebed.

"Yes," he repeated. "I hoped so. He's an attractive man. Sensitive. I was very touched by his story about his family."

"I was too."

"He's moving, you know."

She felt a small shock. "I didn't know. Where to?"

"I haven't spoken to him. The agent told me he hasn't renewed his lease."

"Oh. Perhaps he only wants a larger place, unless—" And now she made her tone very light, very casual, remarking, "Do you suppose he's going to be married?"

"I've no idea. Why? Does it matter to you?"

She raised her eyebrows as if in surprise at the question. "Why on earth should it matter to me?"

"Don't be annoyed," he said. "It matters awfully to me. You know I have always loved you, Margaret."

Extremely agitated, she wasn't ready for anything more urgent than packing Megan off to college, for going back to work, for wiping Adam and their disaster out of her mind.

"Please," she said brokenly as she stood up, "please."

There he waited, flushed and trembling before her. And looking into his broad, healthy, not unhandsome face, a benign, familiar face now at this moment filled with an anxious pleading, she, too, was overcome with love—though of a different kind.

He put his arms around her. Her head went to his shoulder, he was kissing her hair and her neck, kissing and holding her.

"I can make you so happy, Margaret. We know each other so well. And your children will be happy. That should matter to you too."

"Yes, yes," she murmured, crying.

He raised her head, asking gently, "Why are you crying?"

"It's just that you're so good, and I can't . . ."

"Can't what?"

"Can't answer, or even think." She tried to smile. "Maybe it's only that I'm not back to normal yet. Maybe I'm crying because I'm starting to relax. They say people do when they're finally past the worst. I really have hardly cried, Fred, in all this time. Hardly ever."

"Don't apologize." He kissed her lips, softly.

"I'm not ready." She faltered. "I have to get Megan off to school."

"I won't press you. But when you are ready? Will you care?"

"I care now, Fred. I do."

Whether he was satisfied with that or not, he let her go, and in a state of some distress, she drove home.

"Stephen phoned," announced Danny. "He wants to take you to dinner."

"Oh, all of us?"

"No, only you. I asked him whether I could come, and he said no."

"Dan, you didn't ask him!"

"Why not? He's my friend. He wants you to call him back. He said something about the Hotel Bradley."

A few hours later she was sitting with Stephen in the dining room that she had not entered since the night of the office party years before. Am I always to be reminded of these things, she wondered, or will time eventually fade them?

"This was a last-minute invitation, and I apologize," said Stephen. "I usually do have better manners. I really do."

Their small table was in an alcove near the window. The sky had clouded over so that the view was dismal, and in contrast the room, with its ruby-colored hangings, and the table, with its pot of cornflowers, was snug. She felt a little thrill of pleasure. It was as if she were expecting a surprise. This was her first time at a table with him except for the time at Fred's house, and then there had been a crowd.

"Dan told me you were at Fred's today," he said.

"I repaid his loan. It was a good feeling."

"He's a very fine man, Fred is."

"Yes, I've known him forever."

"A family friend."

"Or practically a cousin, like Gil. You remember Gil."

She was prattling. What difference was it whether or not he remembered Gil? Yet she knew why she was prattling: It was to emphasize that Fred was no more than a cousin, a family connection. Nothing more.

"I remember Gil. I have one of those memories that photograph people, a politician's memory, and no credit to me. He is a simple man, I thought, without airs. I liked him."

"Adam despised him," Margaret said.

The waiter came and the menu was discussed. When he left, Stephen was looking out of the window at the starting drizzle. Their dialogue had suddenly gone flat, and she wondered why.

Then he said, "I wanted you to be the first to know I'm going away. I'm quitting, closing the office."

"Fred told me you hadn't renewed your lease." And she remembered her little shock and mental denial at being told. Her surge of happy expectation died away, and she knew that she had become too accustomed to his presence in the red brick building on the corner of Elm and Main.

"I've had enough and more than enough of divorce law. It's all about disrupting and tearing down. I've been thinking about environmental work, of saving what we have. Here in the heartland there's so much to save, land overplanted and ruined, rivers dammed and flooding. So much."

As he spoke, he moved his hands. They were quick and graceful; all his motions, whether he was running or simply turning pages, were quick and easy.

"Where are you going?" she asked.

"To the State U. The law school has a graduate course. After that I can either work in government or in some conservation movement. It'll be a fresh start for me, doing something useful. I can't wait."

"Still," she said, "you can't think your work has been useless. I know you've helped me build myself up again, and there must be many more like me."

"No, Margaret. You've been building yourself up. It's women like you who make me feel that the world can be a hopeful place."

The intimacy of this comment, this serious compliment, confused her, and she made no reply.

"There's so much strength in you," he continued. "Even after what's been done to you, you're still not cynical. I believe you even have trust in faithful love."

"Oh, I do," she said. "Because what will we be if no one tries anymore to make marriage work?"

"I'll tell you what we'll be. Look around you. We're halfway there already."

There was something she had for a long time wanted to ask him and had hesitated to do.

"Excuse me for being inquisitive, Stephen. I know it's none of my business," she said, "but were you ever married?"

He smiled. "I notice you don't ask whether I am now married."

Margaret shook her head. "I don't because I know this much about you. You wouldn't be here with me if you were."

"That's true. No, I'm not, and I never was. I've had my share of women, but I long ago promised myself that I'd never make a commitment, a promise, that I wasn't certain I could keep."

As he spoke, he looked with such intensity into her eyes, that she had to turn from him. And she sat there looking instead at her fingernails. A sensation as acute as pain or some celestial, imcomparable joy was shooting through her flesh.

There was silence.

"I want to know you better," Stephen said.

She looked up, seeing in a wavering blur dark shoulders, white collar, dark hair . . . She was in love with him.

"But you're going away," she said.

"That doesn't matter. I'm not going far."

The cheerful boom of Fred Davis's voice crossed the table. "Hey! This is a surprise. What are you doing, moving your office to the Hotel Bradley?" He bent to kiss Margaret's cheek.

"Stephen is telling me about his move," she said, feeling embarrassment, feeling resentment, and wishing Fred would move on.

But Fred was interested. "Buying a house?" he inquired.

"No, leaving Elmsford."

"Really? Tell me about it. Mind if I draw up a chair?"

"Go ahead," Stephen said politely.

"I've had my dinner. A couple of investors from downstate are staying in the hotel here. The food's not bad. So where are you going?"

Frustration, like a fire, was hot in Margaret. She sat there watching the rain on the windowpane, going through the motions of eating while listening first to Stephen's responses to Fred's questions, and then gradually just to men's talk, which was mostly about Fred's business and the economy of Elmsford. After a while the fire cooled, leaving her with the dull, defeated feeling people have when they have lost something valuable or missed a flight.

"And so you're going," Fred said at last. "When's the move?"

"Friday. I start my first class Monday."

"Well, you leave a fine reputation behind you, Stephen. I can certainly vouch for you, and this lady of mine can do the same." He laid his hand over Margaret's, continuing with emphasis, "She's told me many times how helpful you've been, and that's made me feel pretty pleased with myself, because I'm the man who got you together. Right, Margaret?"

"Yes," she said flatly.

He was making a statement, being proprietary, with his hand still resting warmly on hers. Lest there be some misunderstanding, she thought miserably, unable to retrieve her hand.

And she tried in some way to catch Stephen's attention so as to convey a message, but he was busy paying the check, and besides, what message did she want to convey?

In the underground garage both men's cars were in the same row.

"If you've finished with your legal business and if you don't mind, I'll drive Margaret home," Fred said.

"Of course," replied Stephen, and they parted.

In Fred's car Margaret sat silently staring out at the rain. She thought that her face must look like stone. Fred had disposed of her as if she were a bundle to be delivered, a bundle that could have no preferences about who was to do the delivering. And who had ever given him permission to speak of "this lady of mine"? Yet, since he was Fred Davis, she could hardly turn upon him with her anger.

The lights were on in the apartment, for which she was thankful because it meant that the children were home. Otherwise, Fred would want to come in.

"I hope I didn't interrupt any business tonight," he said. "I didn't mean to be rude."

"It's all right. My business with lawyers is finished."

"When shall I see you again?"

"It will be a busy week, Fred. School starts, Megan leaves, and we've hardly begun to pack."

"I understand. But I have important things to say to you."

Yes, she knew. Only last week Louise, with the best intentions in the world, had given her another motherly piece of counsel.

"You really ought to settle things with Fred. He told Gil that he's ready anytime you are. You've been through so much, Margaret. You should think of yourself, now. You'd have a peaceful home with a trustworthy man, and your children would have a father."

"A woman doesn't have to be married to have a peaceful home."

"True. But you need more than peace, Margaret. You're too young to have no one to love you."

He had shut off the engine. They were enclosed in a sudden stillness, the dark, and the pattering rain. He would reach over, draw her to him, and kiss her. She had never minded his gentle, swift kiss, but the thought of anything more dismayed her. Now he was about to pin her down, and somehow—somehow—she would have to say no to him, to kind, good Fred, who had made her so angry.

"Important things," he repeated. There was a pause. "You don't want me," he blurted.

"You don't under—"

"Understand? I never really tried to, and that's been my whole trouble. I should have seen. It was perfectly clear."

"Fred, no!" Her dread for herself turned quickly to pity for his humiliation. "I would never hurt you! Not you! How could I, ever?"

He said quietly, "Surely I know that. But without admitting it to myself I've felt your unwillingness. And I know you were angry tonight. I can't blame you. I made a fool of myself."

"No, no, you didn't. Forget it. It wasn't important."

"Yes, it was. We need to see everything very plainly, Margaret. Neither one of us needs to make any more mistakes. To have you take me out of old friendship or, God forbid, a sense of gratitude—no, no!"

"You deserve better," she said, very low.

"Don't cry, Margaret."

"I'm not."

"But you're about to. And I don't want you to. I don't want to see you cry. Things happen, or they don't. That's all there is to it." He started the engine. "The rain's let up. Go in before it comes back hard."

"Fred, I don't know what to say. I can usually find something." She gave a small, sad laugh. "But right now, I just don't know what to say."

"Say nothing. I'm flying to see the folks in Canada next week. You'll be going back to work. And that's it."

Emotional storms besieged her every night. All that week they raged.

There was the ache of saying good-bye to her first baby, a Megan grown now, going away, and never—if you looked squarely into the blunt eye of truth—never really coming back.

There had been no word from Stephen since their parting in the hotel's garage, where apparently he had made his final farewell. What more had he been about to say when Fred interrupted? Well, whatever it might have been, Fred's message had been clear enough: Keep away.

She lay there wondering what she might do about it, tossing out one thought after the other because each was impossible. Each, whatever careful phrasing she might use, was only a way of offering herself, and he would see that. Very likely she had read into their brief encounter far more than he meant, anyway. So she would be making a humble fool of herself and embarrassing him.

Yet she knew that she was in love with him.

On the day before Megan was to fly east, a moving van came down the street and turned at the end toward where he lived. They were all at breakfast, but Margaret got up, saying that she would be right back, and walked down the slope to see where the van had stopped.

At the top of the rise from behind a thicket of evergreens, she could see the men going inside and the first possessions coming out: a bookcase and a desk. Something in her wanted to run down there, but inhibition stopped her again, and so she stood watching with an ache of helplessness in a heavy heart. Then after a while she walked away, and, not yet ready to go back to the bustle of home, took the path to the park.

The pond was dozing in the morning's heat, and the swans were making their endless, circular voyages. She sat down on her familiar bench as if there were some sort of healing to be had in this quiet place. I don't understand it, she thought. I would never have believed that this could happen to me again. There was such a terrible sense of loss in her. Yet how could one feel the loss of something one had never had? He had simply left, as he had every right to do.

Back in New York after Thanksgiving at Gil and Louise's, Nina was still trying to piece together some odds and ends of information.

After dinner Louise had taken her aside to lament the fact that Margaret had turned Fred Davis down.

"It would have been a wonderful match," she mourned. "Everybody says so. The only reason can be that she has somebody else. But who?"

At breakfast Megan asked about Stephen. "I always thought he was the true Renaissance man," she said in her new adult importance. "He was a scholar, a lawyer for Mom, and a baseball nut for Dan. Remember the night he told us about his father's leaving? It's funny that nobody ever hears from him. He seemed to like us all so much."

"Oh, he was sweet on Mom," Dan said.

"That's a stupid remark, and I've asked you not to make it," Margaret said sharply.

Naturally, everyone looked at her, who almost never talked that way. Her face had gone quite unmistakably bright red.

Later that day Nina and Margaret had gone for a walk. After a desultory conversation, chiefly about her own life, Nina had posed a bold question. "Why were you so upset this morning when Dan said that about Stephen Larkin?"

"I wasn't upset. It's just that Dan's too old now to be so silly."

"Oh. They really do seem to be missing Stephen, though."

"Yes."

They had walked on over crackling leaves.

"Of course, I only met him once, but he sounds to me like a very special person."

"Yes."

They had walked on into the wind. And suddenly Margaret stopped, saying, "Why not get to the point? You want to know whether there was anything between him and me."

"Well, yes, frankly I do. Not that it's any of my business, I admit. So, was there?"

"No, there wasn't. I thought there might have been, but nothing happened. He went away, and that's the whole story."

Nina sat now in the apartment, reflecting over a cozy cup of tea. *That's the whole story.* But there had to be something deeper, more complex, than that. There had been tears in Margaret's eyes. The picture was vivid to Nina: Margaret in the November wind with her brilliant hair blowing, beautiful in her calm dignity, while one large, slippery tear slid down her cheek.

"Shall I be a meddlesome fool?" she asked herself. "Will I be doing any harm?"

After a while she decided that there would be no harm in a try, and as to being thought of as a meddlesome idiot, it didn't really matter. So, after inquiring from long distance information, she telephoned Stephen Larkin and told him what she knew.

"I just thought you might be interested," she concluded.

"Then she really didn't—she isn't with—Fred Davis anymore?"

"She never really was."

"But I thought—it seemed—and so I—"

"I hope you don't think I'm an idiot with a hell of a nerve besides, but I decided it was worth taking a chance to tell you. And if you ever let Margaret know I did this, I swear I'll murder you."

He began to laugh. "You won't have to murder me, I promise. I'm going to love you forever. And now, will you please hang up so I can make my call?"

EPILOGUE, 1995

William and Ernie's East Side house was alight from bottom to top. The Christmas setting was still there in the window of the shop on the ground floor; the wing chair at the fireplace, the golden candles on the antique mantel, and the dried flowers in a great brass bowl came straight out of a hearty nineteenth-century novel.

This was the last night of 1995. On three floors above there was a lively celebration. Up and down the white marble stairs and through the private quarters—which their owners were only too happy to display—the guests paraded in their clothes and jewels, greeted friends, were introduced, examined paintings, stopped at the buffet table, and drank champagne. Over all, was the sound of music.

"Quite a spectacle," remarked Stephen, enjoying it.

"Can you believe it?" said Margaret. "All this white marble, even the walls, and yet, somehow, it's not too much."

"I suppose that's why they're famous. Did you go into the small red library on the second floor? I can see myself some cold night, stretched out on the sofa under the Winslow Homer with a book or a brandy."

"I wish I could stay and talk to you," Nina said, "but since I've been promoted and given a raise, I feel terribly responsible. Willie and Ernie have some customers here tonight, or possible customers, who positively need to be stroked. But it has been a wonderful vacation week for me, just having you here. It's been a vacation and a celebration. I wish I could be at your big day next month."

"It's going to be a very simple big day," Margaret said. "No wedding finery. We'll be too busy moving into the house."

"No more grabbing a night at a hotel midway between us anymore," Stephen said.

"I'll come out and decorate your house for you," Nina offered.

"No marble walls, please. But a Winslow Homer would be nice," Stephen said.

"I'll do my best."

"Seriously, it's a nice house, not far either from my work or from the university for Margaret. We're almost all moved in. Julie's piano arrived last week, all tuned and ready to work again."

"Yes," Margaret added, "and it's so wonderful, Nina, we've got Rufus back. A neighbor is dog-sitting for him right now."

"Oh, I'm glad. My heart was broken for Dan's sake. Listen, I have to go downstairs. Save a place for me at supper."

In the long hallway a young man was standing alone examining a cabinet filled with antique silver. Having a feeling that he might be a customer, Nina stopped to introduce herself.

"I'm Willie and Ernie's woman Friday. If you have any questions about the silver, maybe I can help."

"Thanks, but I was just looking. Actually, I am interested in silver, but mostly in nineteenth-century stuff, old Tiffany pieces. I like more decoration than you find in the Georgian period."

He was immediately interesting, an obviously cultured man who knew something besides finance and sports.

"The shop will be open after the holiday. If you're a collector—"

"Not really. I only pick up a piece now and then if I happen to fall over one."

He had a nice smile and looked as though he laughed easily. His direct manner, his quiet, pleasing voice, appealed to Nina, too, so that when he asked her to have a drink with him, she accepted.

"I'm here alone," he explained. "I came with a friend, but he left for another party, and I was about to leave soon myself, just lingering and looking around when you came over. Now I am definitely not going to leave."

For a while they stood holding their drinks, and then, finding an unoccupied love seat, sat down.

"So you work here, Nina?"

"Yes, and I love it. I love being around all these beautiful objects."

"You're a rather beautiful object yourself."

There was nothing bold or cheap about the compliment, because there was nothing bold or cheap about the man. They talked for quite a while; she learned that he was a coffee importer and knew South America with its art, its crime, and its politics very well.

"How about dinner some night this week?" he asked. "You name the night."

"Any night, really?" she responded. "Wednesday, maybe?"

"That's the one night I can't. We have theater tickets. My wife—"

She took a long breath. Hold on, she said silently to herself, and aloud, "Your wife? I think I may know her."

"Oh, I don't believe so. She's really"—he gave a slight, deprecating frown—"she's really not your—"

"Not my type? Of course not. She's old as God and homely too. And you haven't had sex with her in years. I know all about her."

He stared as if he couldn't believe his ears. Then, believing, he was outraged. "Well, excuse *me*! You really are something, you are, you little—"

But she was already ten steps away. "Yes," she called back. "I'm something, all right. But one thing I'm not is a married man's little pickup."

She was angry, but she was also laughing when she went back upstairs. They were all sitting at the table waiting for her.

"I went looking for you," Margaret said, "but you seemed to be involved, so I didn't interfere. Was he nice?"

"Very nice. And his nice wife is probably very nice too."

"Oh," said Margaret.

The two women's glances met, and both smiled. Memories, Margaret thought. We have them, Nina and I.

And she looked around the table, as had always been her habit when the family was assembled at a table.

There was Megan, already a sophomore and a scholar, but a recluse no longer; she had a serious boy who also wanted to be a doctor, but Margaret must not worry, she had no plans to promise anything, not yet, not nearly so soon. She knew better.

There was Julie in her vivacious blue dress, telling Nina now about her music teacher, "My new one, where we're moving soon. She said I haven't lost much time. I might even go to a conservatory after college."

Dan had a heaping plate and a mouthful of food. "What's this stuff?" he demanded.

"Caviar," Stephen told him.

"I never had it before. It's great stuff."

"You're a gourmet," Stephen said. "This is the best ever."

"I thought it was gourmand."

"No, a gourmand is somebody who eats too much."

"I fall into that category too," Danny said, laughing at himself.

Then all at once, laughter left him, and he said soberly, "Dad was a gourmet, wasn't he, Mom?"

"Yes," Margaret answered, meeting Stephen's eyes.

"Dad knew a lot of things."

"Yes, he did."

This was hardly an appropriate subject for the occasion. But what could you expect? The boy was only fifteen, and the hurt was still with him.

I suppose, she thought, it really is like a wound. People say that for the rest of your life, in certain weathers or simply from time to time, it will come back, and you will feel it.

Under the table Stephen seized her hand and clasped it. His eyes were smiling. Don't be afraid of anything, they said. I love you and I will be with you always.